"Good morning," he drawled.

Caroline watched him approach, taking in the tilt of his head, the play of his thigh muscles beneath his snug buckskin trousers. Zachary Griffin was magnificent.

"Good morning," she returned, attributing the sudden tightness low in her stomach and the heat running beneath her skin to the desire to begin sketching him again at once.

"It definitely is now." Lord Zachary touched her cheek with his fingers. Leaning down, he took her mouth in a slow, soft kiss.

For a dozen heartbeats Caroline froze, every ounce of her being focused on the warm touch of his lips against hers. Then, gasping, she pushed backward. "What— what are you doing?"

His fine brow furrowed. "Kissing you."

"Are you mad?" Caroline was still trying to remember how to breathe, and her voice squeaked.

"You invited me up here for a private rendezvous. I don't—"

"I invited you to my studio so I could sketch you."

"When you said you wanted to sketch me, you actually wanted to *sketch* me?"

"Yes. What did you think . . . ? Oh! I am not some . . . lightskirt, sir!"

"Bloody hell."

By Suzanne Enoch

AN INVITATION TO SIN
FLIRTING WITH DANGER
SIN AND SENSIBILITY
ENGLAND'S PERFECT HERO
LONDON'S PERFECT SCOUNDREL
THE RAKE
A MATTER OF SCANDAL
MEET ME AT MIDNIGHT
REFORMING A RAKE
TAMING RAFE
BY LOVE UNDONE
STOLEN KISSES
LADY ROGUE

Coming in January 2006
The Exciting Contemporary Romance

DON'T LOOK DOWN

SUZANNE ENOCH

AN INVITATION TO SIN

AVON BOOKS
An Imprint of HarperCollinsPublishers

AVON BOOKS
An Imprint of HarperCollins*Publishers*
10 East 53rd Street
New York, New York 10022-5299

For Meredith Foster,
my best friend through fair and foul,
and one of the few people
who understands my obsession
with Star Wars *action figures.*

Chapter 1

Lord Zachary Griffin lifted a glass of claret from a passing footman. "For God's sake, hurry it up," he muttered, gazing at the pair of dancers twirling halfway across the room.

Thirty other couples swished about the Tamberlake ballroom, but he scarcely noted them. Likewise the half dozen single young ladies edging toward him along the wall—they occupied him only insofar as they kept him on the move to stay ahead of the silk and lace-draped gaggle.

Under normal circumstances he had no objection to waltzing with pretty young chits; he enjoyed it, in fact. However, the first order of business tonight was, well, business. He could dance later.

Across the room, his older brothers, Sebastian, the Duke of Melbourne, and Charlemagne, had also declined to waltz. The pair of them were in deep conversation with Lord Harvey and were no doubt finalizing negotiations to buy out the viscount's shares in their shipping business. He wished them well, but just the thought of all the damned numbers and percentages flying back and forth over there made his head ache.

The waltz finally swirled to an end. Most of the dancers headed back to their companions or toward the refreshment table. The pair Zachary was after separated in front of the chocolate cremes. With a last glance at his brothers, he moved in.

"Glad to see you still in London, Major," he said, putting a hand on the gentleman's red-clad shoulder.

John Tracey faced him. "Zachary," he returned with a smile, offering his hand.

Zachary shook it. "You look well."

"Is there a reason I shouldn't? Other than your sister deciding she didn't want to marry me, that is."

"None of us expected that," Zachary conceded, his own smile tightening. Damn Nell. He didn't need any complications tonight. "Except perhaps for Melbourne, of course. He tends to know everything."

"He might have informed me then, that Lady Eleanor meant to marry the Marquis of Deverill before he asked if *I* wished to join the family."

Zachary shrugged, not certain how genuinely perturbed Major Lord John Tracey was by recent events. As much of a handful as his sister Nell had turned out to be, *he* wouldn't have wanted to be leg-shackled to her. "She eloped with Deverill. We even caught up to them once, and they still got away from us. After that, there wasn't much we could do. Valentine and Eleanor together are rather unstoppable."

"So I gathered. What can I do for you, then? It can't be marriage again. You don't have any other female siblings to send in my direction, and Melbourne's daughter is what, eight?"

"Peep is six," Zachary returned. "Actually, I have a favor to ask of you."

"Ask away."

With a deep breath Zachary stepped off the cliff. "I intend to join a regiment and head for the Peninsula with Wellington."

The major laughed. "Oh, that's . . ." He trailed off. "You're serious."

"Of course I'm serious." Damn it all, nobody believed him. Hence this secret conversation out of the Duke of Melbourne's hearing. The laughter and teasing from his family members was becoming bloody tiresome.

"My apologies, then," Tracey said. "But Zachary, you do realize that once you join the army you can't simply change your mind. Not without some dire consequences."

"I'm aware of that," he returned, ignoring the insult to his resolve. "I'm not asking whether you think I should join the army. I'm asking which regiment would give me the best opportunity to see action. I don't intend to end up in charge of lugging whiskey barrels somewhere twenty miles behind the front lines."

"You want my regiment, then. The Forty-fifth Foot," the major answered promptly. "And if you're serious, I'd be happy to put in a word with Major General Picton. Not that you need much of a recommendation, with your family's name and reputation."

"I would appreciate if you would speak with the general," Zachary said, otherwise ignoring the familiar compliment to his family. As far as he was concerned, he had the important qualities—skill with a weapon and the desire to excel. But if money qualified someone to be a competent soldier, well, he had that, too. "If you could arrange an introduction, I would be in your debt."

"If you promise never to mention my name and marriage in the same sentence again, I would consider us even," Tracey said, smiling again.

Out of the corner of his eye Zachary noticed the meeting breaking up across the room. He shook Tracey's hand again. "That's a promise. And my thanks."

"I'll send word when I can arrange a meeting. The general and I are both returning to Spain in another fortnight, so it'll be soon."

"I'll be waiting."

As the two of them parted, Zachary caught Melbourne gazing at him. Favoring the duke with a lifted eyebrow, Zachary went to find a dance partner. Whether his family in general, and his oldest brother in particular, had decided to take him seriously or not, he was going to decide his own future. And tonight he'd taken a large step in that direction—which meant that now he could find a chit and enjoy himself.

The next morning Zachary sat at the breakfast table to read the missive Major Tracey had sent over. It seemed that Major General Thomas Picton would be *very* interested in adding a Griffin to his staff, and that both men would be dining at White's for luncheon. Folding the note and sliding it into his pocket, he turned his attention to the slightly wrinkled copy of *The London Times* that waited for him. From its condition, he surmised that either Shay or Melbourne had had a tea mishap earlier. He would wager it had been Charlemagne.

According to the latest printed reports, Eleanor and Valentine were enjoying their honeymoon in Venice. Nell's latest letter said the same thing, but he always found it interesting to hear about the Griffin clan's exploits from an outside perspective.

"Good morning, Uncle Zachary," six-year-old Penelope said as she pranced into the breakfast room.

"Hello, Peep." He leaned sideways to plant a kiss on her cheek. "Nell and Valentine went for a gondola ride last week."

With the butler's assistance Peep selected her breakfast from the sideboard and plunked herself down at the table beside him. "I'm going to go to Venice. You may come with me if you want to."

"I'm meeting someone for luncheon at White's today," he countered, hiding a grin, "but I'm available tomorrow."

"Not now," she protested, rolling her pretty gray eyes at him. "When I grow up."

"Oh. I'll be available then, of course."

"Good." She bit into a peach. "Because I think Papa and Uncle Shay might be too strict."

"And I won't be?"

"Uncle Zachary, you let me taste your glass of scotch."

Wonderful. "We aren't ever going to mention that again, remember?"

"I forgot." She smiled, carefree and fearless as only six-year-olds could be. "Papa's taking me riding this morning on Buttercup. You may join us, if you'd like."

Before he could decline, Peep's father strolled into the room. Sebastian, the Duke of Melbourne, looked like precisely what he was—at age thirty-four one of the most powerful, influential men in England, and the head of a famously distinguished family. What he didn't look like was a man dressed for riding.

"I was beginning to wonder whether either of you was going to appear at all today," Melbourne drawled, moving around the table to kiss his daughter.

"Late night," Zachary said, declining to mention in whose company it had ended. The waltz was only one of Lady Amelia Bradley's talents.

"I had to dress Mrs. Hooligan." Peep looked up at her father. "She wants to go riding, too."

The duke tugged one of her dark, curling ringlets. "My apologies, Peep, but I've been called to Carlton House."

Penelope bounced in her seat. "Are you going to see Prinny?"

"I imagine so." Melbourne straightened. "Perhaps Uncle Zachary will take you and your doll out riding."

Zachary stifled a scowl. "What about Uncle Shay?"

The duke's gaze slid over to him. "Shay would suffice, I'm sure," he continued in the same easy tone. "Did you have something else planned?"

"He's going to luncheon at White's," Peep supplied, starting on her honey and toast.

"Really." Melbourne nodded, turning for the hall door. "That reminds me. Do you have a moment, Zachary?"

Zachary nodded and rose, reminding himself that while Eleanor swore their eldest brother could read minds, it had never been proven. "Leave my strawberries be, Peep," he warned his niece, hearing her responding giggle as he left the breakfast room.

Melbourne led the way into his office. *Hm.* An office chat was never a good thing. Zachary headed for the window; he wasn't going to sit in one of the "victim chairs" as he and his siblings called them, whatever the duke had in mind.

The door clicked shut behind him. "I have a task for you," Melbourne said.

"I'll take Peep riding tomorrow," Zachary countered. "As I told her, I have a few obligations today."

The duke took a seat behind his massive mahogany desk. Zachary kept his gaze out the window at the Griffin House garden, reminding himself that however much power Melbourne had over the rest of the world, he was still just an older brother.

"I don't care about your luncheon," his brother returned dismissively. "Shay can escort Peep. I wanted to discuss a family matter."

That didn't sound too ominous. Nobody had strayed from the well-delineated Griffin boundaries lately—not since Nell and Valentine had made their much-reported run to Scotland. And Melbourne had somehow managed to turn even that into a preapproved romantic escapade by the time the newspapers got hold of it. Zachary turned around, leaning a haunch against the deep windowsill. "Discuss away, then."

"Aunt Tremaine has asked me to provide an escort for her."

"She wants to go to the races at Derby again, doesn't she?" Zachary cracked a grin. "The last time she attended, th—"

"Her gout is acting up," Melbourne cut in. "She wants to take the waters at Bath, probably for the remainder of the Season. I told her that you would be happy to accompany her."

Zachary took a moment to absorb that, though his mouth had already formed an answer. "No."

"I beg your—"

"Send Charlemagne. I have plans."

"I need Shay in Brighton to finalize the purchase of another half dozen cargo ships. And you never have plans."

"I do now."

Melbourne sat back in his chair. "Care to enlighten me about them?"

"I did enlighten you," Zachary retorted, trying to keep his voice level. He didn't need to fight about it; he'd already made his decision. "You just chose not to take me seriously."

For a long moment the room remained so quiet that Zachary could hear Peep chatting with the butler down the hall. The duke didn't move, but Zachary knew Sebastian was running past conversations through his mind, calculating responses, deciding how to enter the discussion at an angle that would give him the greatest advantage. There was a reason Zachary never played chess with Melbourne; he never won. Ever. But this wasn't chess. This was his future. And as long as he remained resolved, he couldn't lose.

"Tell me then," the duke finally said, "why you have the sudden urge to join the army."

So he had been paying attention. "It's not sudden. I've been thinking about it for some time. I tried to discuss it with you a month ago, and you weren't interested."

"I'm interested now."

"I thought you had a meeting at Carlton House."

"Zachary, I don't want you to join the army."

Resisting the urge to shoot to his feet, Zachary settled deeper into the window. "What do you want me to do then? Chaperone Nell at parties? Wait, she's married now. I'm not needed for that any longer. Which leaves me with escorting Peep to her tea parties, I suppose, and Aunt Tremaine on made-up journeys."

"It's not made up. And there are always—"

"Business concerns? That's you and Shay. Buying and selling things for no discernable reason makes me want to lock myself up in Bedlam, anyway."

"I'm certain there's something you'd enj—"

"*You* enjoy doing that," Zachary interrupted again, willing his oldest brother to understand his frustration. "You and Shay. I don't. I want something else. I want some damned responsibility, Sebastian. And if some excitement and some glory come with it, so much the better."

The butler scratched at the door. "Your Grace?"

"What is it, Stanton?" Melbourne called, irritation edging his voice.

"The coach is ready, Your Grace."

"I'll be there in a moment."

Zachary straightened, pushing away from the window. "I believe we'll have to finish this conversation later, then," he said, taking Melbourne's usual parting line. And after luncheon with Ma-

jor General Picton, he'd have considerably more ammunition—
and perhaps even a commission.

"We'll finish it now."

"But you—"

"No, now it's my turn," Melbourne countered sharply. "What
about when you were going to take your orders?"

Zachary frowned. "I never really wanted to join the priesthood.
That—"

"That's why that scheme only lasted a week. And then there
was training racehorses."

"That is not fair, S—"

"You sold off your interest in that after two months," his
brother cut in again. "What about taking up land management?"

Straightening, Zachary aimed a finger at his brother. "That was
your fault. Bromley Hall is the least significant property you own.
It was dull as damned door knockers there, Seb."

"The irrigation channel was a good idea—or it would have
been, if you'd finished it."

"So I'm useless. Is that what you're saying?"

"I'm saying you have no patience for anything. If it immediately satisfies your requirements, then you're done with it. If it's
something that takes work, you lose interest. So if you want responsibility, get a dog. If you're bored, take up painting. You
don't need to parade about the Peninsula in a bright red uniform
so some bloody Frenchman can blow a hole in you."

"Thank you very much for your faith in my stupidity and utter
incompetence."

"It's not stupidity by any means, but you know how you are,"
Melbourne countered. "And a lack of patience wouldn't serve you
in the army, either. You aren't going to buy a commission,
Zachary. I won't permit it, and you know I can prevent it."

Zachary glared at him, his jaw clenched so tightly that the
muscles trembled. "I'm a third-born son in a noble family, Seb.
My opportunities—"

"Are more than sufficient, if you would make a choice and
abide by it."

"I have made a choice. Thank you for the advice." Turning on his heel, he strode for the office door.

"Zachary, you—"

"I what, Sebastian? We're at an impasse. And while you might have the ability to prevent a Griffin from joining the military, I can pretend to be someone else." He stopped, taking a breath and hoping he hadn't just foiled his own plans. He really needed to learn when to stay silent and just leave the room. "I know what you're afraid of," he continued anyway. "And I'm sorry Charlotte died. I know how much you loved her. But you—"

Melbourne shoved to his feet with enough force that his chair went over backwards. *"Enough!"* he roared. "My wife has nothing to do with this."

"She has everyth—"

"You will escort Aunt Tremaine to Bath," Melbourne snapped, his gray eyes glinting with barely suppressed anger. "When you return and *if* you have proven to me in the meantime that you can show some patience and restraint and a reasonable level of responsibility, and *if* you're still determined to join the army, we will continue this discussion."

Zachary took a deep breath. As usual, he'd gotten angry and said the wrong thing, and now that Melbourne had handed down his proclamation, he couldn't take it back. "I apologize, Sebastian," he said.

"Don't." His oldest brother strode to the door and back, obviously in an attempt to regain his usually even temper. That in itself was unusual; Melbourne rarely let anyone see him out of countenance.

"All I meant to say was that you can't keep all of us safe in glass cabinets and expect us not to try to get out," Zachary said more quietly.

"I suggest you go pack a trunk," Melbourne returned in the cool voice his siblings dreaded hearing. "You're leaving in an hour."

"Very well. One day though, Melbourne, you're going to give

one order too many, and you'll find that all of your troops have deserted."

Damn it all. They both knew that the threat was empty, but at least his brother didn't laugh at him. Zachary had his own generous monthly income, but it had all been set up by Melbourne. If he pushed too hard, the duke could simply cut the purse strings—which would ensure that his next career choice would be the one he stayed with.

Chapter 2

Caroline Witfeld pressed her pencil so hard against the sketch pad that the lead snapped. "Grace, will you please stop fidgeting?"

Her sister scratched her left ear. "It's not my fault. This hat itches."

"It's not a hat. It's a turban. And please sit still. I only need two more minutes."

"That's what you said five minutes ago, Caro. And it still itches."

For the space of a breath Caroline closed her eyes. Trying to focus on a subject who squirmed every which way was giving her nothing but an aching head. That didn't mean, however, that she had any intention of giving up. Patience might be a virtue, but in this instance it was also a necessity. "It's taking longer because you keep moving. And you're the one who wanted to be a Persian princess."

High-pitched voices echoed up from the foyer two stories below. "Grace! We're going! Hurry up!"

Damnation. Caroline grabbed another pencil and began sketching madly, concentrating on the wisps of her sister's blonde hair where it curled from beneath the silk turban. She could sketch the turban sans occupant later. "Wait, Grace," she muttered as she drew. "You promised."

The wisps of hair began edging for the door, along with the rest of her sister. "They'll leave without me," she protested, "and I need a new bonnet."

"Grace—"

The turban hit the hardwood floor. "Sorry, Caro," Grace called over her shoulder as she hurried down the hall toward the stairs. "I'll be back after luncheon!"

"But the shadows will be diff . . . ," Caroline started, then trailed off. With a grimace she set down her pencil and stood to stretch her back. Grace didn't care about light or shadows; she cared about a new bonnet.

She could recruit another sister, she supposed, but as she went to the window and looked down at the drive, she counted six bonnets wedging themselves into the Witfeld barouche. Apparently all of her siblings needed new bonnets.

Of course the urgency they felt to visit Trowbridge might have had something to do with the fact that it was Tuesday—and that Mrs. Williams's son Martin, recently returned from the Crimean, helped restock her linen shop on Tuesdays. Caroline smiled. Poor Martin. After three months of Tuesday torture, she would have changed restocking day, or at least done it after hours. Of course the shop sold more on Tuesdays than any other day of the week, so perhaps Martin's appearance in the middle of the morning wasn't a coincidence at all.

Caroline retrieved the turban and set it on a stack of books at the appropriate height, then returned her attention to the sketch pad. By now she could probably draw any of her sisters from memory, but the slant of the head, the light in their expression— she'd never been able to capture any of that without the subject in front of her. She could finish the hat, however.

"Caro?"

She started, blinking. "Up here, Papa. In the conservatory."

"What do you think of this?" her father asked as he walked into the room. In his arms he hefted a wooden box filled with a tumbled chaos of miniature papier-mâché columns and blocks of faux stone. "It's not to scale, of course."

Edmund Witfeld looked how she imagined any father of seven

daughters would—fingertips stained black from doing the accounts and trying to come up with a way to provide seven dowries, hair silver and beginning to thin now that five of those daughters were of a marrying age, jacket a little loose across the shoulders and a little snug around the waist from worry and frustration and the inability to do anything about it. He was, after all, badly outnumbered.

Caroline looked over the meticulously arranged diorama. "Those are new," she said, indicating the pair of broken columns resting beside the miniature painted streambed.

He smiled. "Yes. I thought adding a sixth and seventh column on the north side would balance the quarter-wall on the south."

"It's beginning to look like the Parthenon in ruins—or what I imagine it would look like, anyway. Antique and romantical."

"Ah ha! That's what I was attempting to evoke." He kissed her cheek. "I'm going to order the additional columns for the meadow tomorrow." Muttering figures to himself, he toted the box into the hallway. "Oh, I nearly forgot." He reentered the conservatory. "The post just came. You have a letter."

Her body turned to ice. "Is it a reply?" she asked.

He fumbled in his pocket with his free hand. "I think so. Here. Hold this a minute."

She took possession of the miniature ruins. "Papa."

"I'm not trying to torture you, but I knew I'd never get an opinion from you about the ruins after I told you about the letter. Ah. Here it is." He pulled a letter from his inside jacket pocket.

Caroline took it, nearly dumping his diorama as she handed it back. Her fingers shaking, she turned the missive over to view the address. "It's from Vienna. The Tannberg artists' studio."

"Open it, Caro."

Sending up a quick prayer, she slid a finger under the wax seal and unfolded the letter. Her heart hammering, she read through it—and the breath froze in her throat. "Oh, my goodness. Oh my, oh my."

"Well?" her father prompted, carefully setting the diorama on the floor. "Do they accept you? It's past time somebody showed some damned sense."

She cleared her throat to read it to him. " 'M. Witfeld, Thank you for the series of portraits you sent with your application. I see no reason you should not be admitted into our apprenticeship program. For final consideration,' " she continued, her voice shaking with a sudden wave of breathless excitement, " 'please submit a portrait of an aristocrat, along with a signed affidavit from said aristocrat attesting to his or her satisfaction with your work. Yours in anticipation, Raoul Tannberg, director, Tannberg Studio.' "

"That seems a reasonable request," her father said, nodding. "All the money in portrait painting likely comes from commissions from wealthy citizens. They probably want proof that you can bring the studio income and clients."

She didn't know how he could be so calm. Caroline could scarcely breathe. It wasn't an unconditional acceptance, but it wasn't one of the twenty-seven rejections she'd received previously, either. One more step, and she would be able to grasp her dream. No more fighting to make her sisters sit still while she tried to shape them into something a studio would find artistic. No more having to ask Cook if she could borrow dinner for half an hour in order to perfect the sketches of chicken or quail beaks. It would be real. It would be heavenly.

"I suppose you'll be calling on Lord and Lady Eades, then."

The excited bubble of her dream popped.

She'd painted the earl and countess before, actually, and the portraits hung in Eades Hall. But this was the most important work of her life, and the local aristocrats were two of the most eccentric people in Wiltshire. She wasn't about to submit *Lord and Lady Eades as Egyptian Pharaohs* to Vienna. Raoul Tannberg, director, would laugh her off the Continent.

"You need to secure their agreement for this," Edmund Witfeld pursued, his voice solemn.

"Yes, I'll manage something." Perhaps she could switch paintings. Lord and Lady Eades would never know. All she needed was a letter expressing approval—it didn't have to describe the painting.

"This is good news, Caro," her father said, taking the missive from her to read it again himself. "I hadn't wanted to say anything, but now that you have a letter, you need to know."

She frowned, her chest tightening. "What's wrong, Papa?"

"Nothing. But you're three and twenty. And as your mama keeps reminding me, you have six younger sisters all eager to marry. For their sakes we can't keep doing this."

"Doing what? I'm not hurting anything. This is my dream, Papa. It has been forever."

"I know that. And that's why I've been encouraging and supporting your efforts. Lord knows I understand what it's like to have a dream. But you *are* hurting something—your sisters' chances at finding husbands. This is a small estate with a limited income and a desperate need to find dowries for seven dau—"

"Six," she interrupted, tears trying to push to the front of her eyes. She felt what she wanted so clearly that she tended to forget that her sisters wanted different things. So now she was a roadblock to what they all considered to be their path to happiness. Marriage. "I've asked you to pass me by."

"I accept that, my dear. But you are still a part of a household with limited resources. Paints and canvases and—"

"I pay for most of the supplies myself," she broke in.

"Don't get upset now that you have good news," he returned, handing back the letter. "But I wanted you to know. This is the last year we can allow this."

"So what happens if I'm rejected by Monsieur Tannberg?"

"You won't be, of course."

"But if I am, what happens?"

He drew a heavy breath. "Then at the end of the summer you will either marry, or you will accept the governess position generously offered to you by Lord and Lady Eades. They would love you to teach their children how to paint."

"Their chil . . ." She trailed off. *Horror*. No other word could describe the ice that gripped her heart at the thought of teaching wealthy, spoiled children how to paint posies.

"But you don't have to worry about that now, do you?"

From his mouth to God's ear. "No, I suppose not."

"That's the spirit." He lifted his box again. "I'm going to pace off the new columns," her father said, leaving the room again, "and to tell your mother that you've been all but accepted at the Vienna studio. We're all relieved."

She watched him go down the hall, then sat again. The situation was worse than she'd realized. The frustration and the humiliation of being repeatedly rejected because she was a female, or because the studio had too many applicants, or because she couldn't afford the attendance fees, was nothing compared to being a governess. She'd have to put away her brushes, and would never have an opportunity to pick them up again. No more painting, no more feeling that . . . lift inside her when she captured part of someone's life on canvas. It would be like cutting out her own heart.

Thank God her father had told her the consequences of failure this time. She *would* convince Lord and Lady Eades to dress in their present-day finery, and she *would* be accepted as an apprentice at the Tannberg Studio.

There was no other choice.

"Zachary, if that blasted thing bites my toe one more time, I am going to have someone serve it up for dinner."

With a sigh Zachary leaned down and grabbed the dog by the scruff of the neck, returning it to the carriage seat beside him. "Apologies, Aunt."

Gladys, Aunt Tremaine, looked at his new companion. "What is it, anyway?"

"I believe it's half foxhound and half Irish setter," he returned, absently wriggling his fingers so the pup would consume him rather than his aunt.

"And you've acquired it for what reason?"

"Melbourne said I should get a dog. Apparently to him it

demonstrates patience and responsibility." He winced as a sharp tooth grazed one finger. "I named it Harold."

"That's your brother's middle name."

"It is? What a coincidence."

His aunt turned over her embroidery hoop and lifted it to bite off the blue thread she'd knotted. Without pause she pulled a spool of green thread from her sewing basket.

"I have a knife, you know," Zachary said, watching from the opposite seat as she measured a length of thread and bit that off, as well. "And a sharp-toothed attack beast."

"This is faster," his aunt returned, deftly threading her needle and going back to work. "You never know when it might be handy to be able to embroider in an emergency."

"Yes, one never knows when one might need one's initials put onto a handkerchief," he said dryly, the sight of the intricate stitches making his eyes want to cross in sympathy.

"Make fun now, but I have thirty more years of wisdom than you, my boy."

"But you'll be blind by the time we get to Bath, trying to embroider in a moving carriage, and toothless from chewing off the threads."

She chuckled. "I've been doing this since before you were born, Zachary. It passes the time better in a moving carriage than attempting to read, or than sitting about while a wild dog attempts to chew off my foot."

He had to agree with part of the statement, anyway. Zachary eyed the book his brother Charlemagne had foisted on him yesterday morning when they'd left, as if two dozen Byron poems would compensate him for being exiled to Bath. Harold obviously felt the same; he'd already torn the cover off. And in addition to the feeble quality of the bribe, he was certain it was worse than that. No, he didn't doubt at all that Aunt Tremaine had instructions for her gout not to subside until she received word from Melbourne that he'd found a way once and for all to prevent his brother from joining the army.

Yes, Melbourne's delaying strategy annoyed Zachary, but

whether it took a week or a month, it wouldn't stop him. He needed a change. And unless the almighty Griffin clan came up with some miraculous plan before then, he was going to join Wellington on the Peninsula. At least there he could be more than the extraneous third brother, the spare's spare, the token escort for the family's females, famed more for his healthy appetite and popularity with chits than for any other attribute or interest he might have.

"I was actually going to recommend napping," he put in when he realized his aunt was eyeing him.

"You could ride," she suggested. "You did go to all the trouble of bringing your horse along. And I'm perfectly happy to embroider in solitude."

His first response was to ask why his presence was necessary at all, then. Everyone knew, however, that he wasn't journeying to Bath for Aunt Tremaine's health but for his own. Zachary pulled out his pocket watch and glanced down at it. "We only have another hour to the inn. Harold and I will just stay and doze, if you don't mind."

Aunt Tremaine shifted her large frame. "Actually, I arranged for Phipps to take us on a short detour."

"What sort of short detour?" he returned suspiciously, straightening again. They'd better not be trying to lock him into a monastery somewhere.

"I thought we might spend a night or two at Witfeld Manor so I might visit with my friend Sally Witfeld."

Zachary looked at her for a moment. "This isn't a Melbourne-devised detour, is it?"

"Heavens, no. Sally and I went to finishing school together. It's only an hour out of our way, and I have a standing invitation to visit. I haven't seen her for nearly six years."

He held up his hands in surrender, then had to block Harold with his elbow when the pup tried to leap onto his chest. "Bath or Witfeld Manor—it's all the same to me. Far be it for me to stand in the way of finishing school friendships."

"You are a wise young man."

With a grin Zachary settled back into the leather cushions again, wrapped his fingers into Harold's collar, and closed his eyes. Inconvenient though the entire journey might be, he did like his aunt. And under the circumstances, if napping the afternoon away in a warm, well-sprung carriage had any drawbacks, he couldn't see them.

In another twenty minutes the coach turned off the main road and onto the deeply rutted and pockmarked route that turned off to the south. Zachary opened his eyes again as he nearly jolted off the seat. Napping was obviously finished with. In fact, he anticipated having a black-and-blue backside by the time they arrived at Witfeld Manor. He grabbed one of the coach's hanging straps and held on, while the dog bounced to the floor and dove between his Hessian boots to cower. Good God, who lived at the other end of this road—wild, blue-faced Celts? Aunt Tremaine, of course, continued her needlework, though he wouldn't care to wager on how straight her lines would be.

Finally the coach bumped onto a smoother, better-maintained stretch of road, a hopeful sign that they'd entered a private drive. Zachary released the strap and flexed his fingers. "There's supposed to be some good fishing in this part of Wiltshire," he said, deciding to make the best of the situation. "Is there a Mr. Witfeld?"

"There is." As Aunt Tremaine packed her embroidery back into the basket, she gave him a sideways look. "I don't imagine you'll have much difficulty keeping yourself occupied for a few days."

A tiny spark of uneasy suspicion tickled at the back of his brain. "Sally Witfeld doesn't have a young, marriageable daughter, does she?" he asked as the coach stopped.

"No."

"Good."

Huffing and puffing, a rotund butler appeared to pull open the coach door. With Zachary and Harold's assistance from behind and heavy reliance on her cane and the butler's proffered arm, Aunt Tremaine crabbed awkwardly to the ground. She looked up at him again, grinning.

"She has seven, actually."

"Seven what?" Zachary bit out, despite the sinking realization that he had a very good idea what she was talking about.

A high-pitched tittering began from the window that apparently opened onto a downstairs sitting room. A moment later, females began streaming out the double front doors in a flouncing rainbow of sprig muslin.

Harold lowered his head and barked. It was too late to duck back into the coach and escape, though Zachary couldn't help thinking about it for a bare second. Watching over Aunt Tremaine was supposedly a test of his ability to be responsible and patient, and he wasn't going to give up that easily. Seven daughters, though. *Good God.*

Deciding he would voice his annoyance with his aunt later and in less crowded company, he pasted a smile on his face and finished his descent from the coach to the ground. The puppy followed, beginning a mad tear around the drive in pursuit of a trio of hens.

The chits seemed to know Aunt Tremaine; deafening shrieks and trills of "Lady Gladys" filled the air, nearly drowning out Harold and the chickens.

"Girls, girls, hello!" Aunt Tremaine returned, beaming as she took a dozen kisses to her round cheeks. "This is my nephew, Lord Zachary Griffin."

The feminine army curtsied in an undulating wave. "Lord Zachary."

Zachary sketched a return bow. Just as he was being surrounded, two more females emerged from the house. *What was this, a bloody finishing school?*

"Gladys!" the older one, nearly as broad as she was tall, shrieked, grabbing his aunt for a sound hug. "Oh, my dear! I'm so pleased to see you!"

The mother of the brood, obviously. He could see where the daughters learned their reserve. When his aunt beckoned at him, Zachary deepened his smile and waded through the crowd to her side. "You must be Mrs. Witfeld," he said to his aunt's companion, taking the woman's plump hand and bowing over it. "My aunt Tremaine speaks very fondly of you."

"Oh, heavens, what a charmer," Sally clucked, blushing. "You were right about him, Gladys."

They'd been discussing him? That didn't bode well. "You have lovely daughters," he continued, thankful that he came from a large, boisterous family himself. Otherwise the onslaught would likely have been overwhelming. And if he fainted here, there was no telling where he would wake up.

"Tut tut," Mrs. Witfeld chided. "Let me introduce you. Come on, girls, stop gawking, you silly things." With that she began towing the chits into a long line that wasn't dissimilar to a regiment at attention, except for the gowns and bonnets, and the giggling and whispering. Apparently sensing the lessening of chaos, Harold bounded back over and began attacking Zachary's left boot. Thankfully he'd worn his old, comfortable ones and packed the better pair.

As they organized themselves, one of them—the chit who had emerged last from the house—caught his attention. It wasn't that she was particularly striking, though she did have soft copper hair a few shades darker than her next sister, clear green eyes, and a trim, tall figure. No, it was the way she kept eyeing him from head to toe, even edging around to view his profile, as if he were some sort of insect and she an entomologist.

"Lord Zachary," Mrs. Witfeld said, hauling the copper-haired girl to the head of the line, "this is my eldest girl, Caroline."

He bowed. "Miss Witfeld. Pleased to meet you."

Caroline Witfeld nodded back at him. "I advise you to save the bowing till the introductions are finished, or you'll end up dizzy," she returned in a low, amused voice. Since her mother had moved on to the next daughter, he was probably the only one who'd heard it.

"Susan," the matriarch was saying as she traveled down the line, "then the twins, Joanna and Julia. Grace is just eighteen. The youngest are Anne and then Violet."

Zachary shook Harold off his foot, waited a moment to be certain Mrs. Witfeld was finished with the introductions, then bowed again. "It's good to meet all of you," he said, glancing again at the oldest girl, who seemed to have forgotten her wit of a moment ago and was now staring at his left hand. He experimentally wiggled his fingers, and she blinked.

"You've all grown so much," Aunt Tremaine commented to the brood. "And into such lovely young ladies. My niece married a month ago, and I'm afraid I've been a bit starved for a good chat and a look at the fashion plates."

One of the twins rushed her, clasping her hand. "Then you must stay! Mama, tell Lady Gladys she and Lord Zachary must stay!"

"Of course they'll stay. I wouldn't have it otherwise, and I'm certain Mr. Witfeld would agree."

Aunt Tremaine smiled. "If it's not imposing, we would love to visit for a few days."

Caroline hung back a little as her sisters swarmed around Lord Zachary, each vying to be the one to show him to a guest bedchamber. She watched as he smiled again, diplomatically offering his arm to Violet, the youngest, and gestured the rest to lead the way.

With deep brown, almost black hair that glinted a slight bronze in the afternoon sunlight, eyes that seemed to vary between a dusky charcoal and cloudy gray, and a pleasing figure both tall and athletic, Lord Zachary was an exceptionally handsome gentleman. In addition, his face, with its high cheekbones and aristocratic brow, had some very nice angles to it. Caroline would have smiled, but it wouldn't do to announce victory until she'd made a few preliminary sketches and discovered whether she could do him justice on canvas.

At this moment, though, it seemed as though her prayers had been answered. She'd asked for an aristocrat, and Lord Zachary Griffin had practically sprung to life on her doorstep. And with him, her way out of Wiltshire.

Chapter 3

Her sisters joined the parade of people and luggage as Witfeld Manor's unexpected house guests were shown to private rooms, but Caroline climbed the back stairs to the third floor and her conservatory.

The large turret-shaped room with its half circle of bow windows had previously been Edmund Witfeld's study, his refuge from the female horde. She'd been the only one allowed to join him there, and as her interest and skill in painting had increased and her mother had seen a possibility for her unexpected talent to snare attention and income for the family and perhaps even an art-appreciating husband, Caroline had moved her studio into a corner of the room. Gradually she'd taken over more and more of it until two years ago her father had voluntarily and completely evacuated in favor of his smaller, if equally isolated, office on the ground floor behind the kitchen.

She made straight for an unused sketch pad and carried it to one of the deep seats that circled half around the room beneath the windows. The conservatory gave her a good degree of light all day long, with perfect morning sun for painting and sketching subjects until just after noon.

At the moment, she didn't want to paint. She wanted to sketch. Under normal circumstances she liked to have her subjects pose for the preliminary sketches, and at the very least she needed to observe them for more than five minutes. Today, though, she scarcely remembered to breathe as her pencil scratched across the pad.

This subject was different—not just because it was for the most important portrait she would ever paint but because not many men had ever sat for her. Her father, of course, and Lord Eades dressed as King Arthur and various other historical figures, and Mr. Anderton, the village solicitor, who'd wanted a confidence-inspiring portrait of himself for his office. All older men, and men with whom she had been acquainted all her life.

Her hands, however, didn't share any of her mind's hesitation. With quick, short strokes she formed the overall shape of Lord Zachary's head, then feathered in the dark, wavy hair. She generally didn't attempt the eyes without her subject being in front of her, but when she closed her own eyes she could see his clearly, light gray and amused despite the straight, sensual line of his mouth. They were remarkable eyes. Unforgettable.

The conservatory door rattled and opened. Sisters began bouncing and skipping into the room, all of them chattering so fast and so loudly that they couldn't possibly be listening to anyone but themselves.

She tucked her pencil behind her ear, quickly stifling her abrupt annoyance as she closed her sketch pad. "Will you please be quiet? You're going to shatter the windows."

Julia sat beside her. "But didn't you see him?"

Susan dragged over the painting stool and joined them. "He's the most handsome man I've ever set eyes on," she breathed.

Grace plunked down on her other side. "Don't tell me you didn't notice him, Caro."

"Of course I noticed him. I'd like to sketch him, I think. The letter from Monsieur Tannberg requested the portrait of an aristocrat. And he is definitely an aristocrat." She would have known that, she thought, even without hearing anyone calling him "my lord." His bearing, his confidence, the light in his eyes—she would have known.

"I'd like to sketch him, too," Joanna said, giggling.

"Or make a model out of clay," Julia suggested, her fair cheeks darkening.

"Oh, yes, clay," Joanna seconded with a breathy sigh. "I could shape him with my hands."

Violet made a face. "*You* make a model. *I* want to marry him."

"You're barely fifteen, silly girl. He'll never marry you with the rest of us here." Julia gave a condescending laugh.

"He won't marry you, either," Violet grumbled. "Caro's the oldest. She has to get married first."

A low, uneasy flutter ran through Caroline's stomach. "I'm not marrying anyone," she stated, keeping her gaze on her closed sketch pad. He was in there, and she wanted to go back to working on him. "And you all know it. I'm going to the Tannberg Studio and paint portraits and travel the world."

"Well, if he stays until after you go to Vienna, then *I* can marry him," Susan put in.

"He has to ask you first, Susan." Julia shrugged. "Besides, he's probably betrothed to someone else already. How could he not be, handsome as he is? And wealthy, too, from the look of that carriage and his fine clothes. And another carriage with their luggage and servants is following."

"Mama said he's not married." Violet still looked annoyed that her marriage plans had been so swiftly thwarted. "And he *is* wealthy. And he has two older brothers. They're not married, either."

"He has two brothers?" Clapping, Grace shot to her feet. "That's husbands for three of us. I'm going to talk to Mama."

"You don't even know him," Caroline protested. "Or his brothers. How do you know you want to marry any of them?"

"You don't know anything, Caro, unless it's on canvas," Susan returned. "So don't criticize us."

Well, that was hardly fair. "I—"

"Yes, *you* can be an old spinster. *I* want to get married." Joanna bounded to her feet again. "Come on, let's ask Mama."

In a flash of muslin skirts, the conservatory emptied. Caroline shook her head, removed the pencil from behind her ear, and flipped open her sketch pad again.

"So you're not interested at all?"

Caroline jumped. "Anne," she exclaimed. "I thought you were going down to hear the Griffin family history."

"I already know it." The pretty seventeen-year-old, her honey-colored hair piled atop her head, crossed the room to sit beside her. "Unlike certain other members of the household, I read the news and Society pages instead of just looking at the fashion plates. The oldest Griffin brother is the Duke of Melbourne."

Caroline's heart stopped, then began hammering again. "Oh, goodness. He's one of *those* Griffins?"

"Yes, he is."

"But they're . . . famous."

"And extremely wealthy. Mama was correct about that. So I repeat: You're not interested at all?"

"In him? Of course I am. If I can secure a Griffin on canvas, Monsieur Tannberg will have to take me on. It's only a shame the Duke of Melbourne didn't come instead. I'd get into Thomas Lawrence's studio if I painted him."

"Lawrence's studio rejected you."

"The Duke of Melbourne's portrait would make them reconsider."

Anne shook her head indulgently. "You are very single-minded."

"Honestly, Anne, do you think it matters whether I might be interested in Lord Zachary or not? For heaven's sake, with his family's pedigree he could marry Prinny's daughter if he wanted. I doubt that with a choice of hundreds of eligible young Society ladies he would choose a Witfeld girl." She chuckled. "Even Susan."

"Don't tell her that." Anne looked at the sketch. "I can see who it is you're drawing, already. And he *is* very handsome."

"And thank goodness for that. But pleasant or frog-faced, painting him is more important than marrying him."

Anne kissed her on the cheek and stood. "To you, yes. I, however, don't paint."

"Does that mean you're joining the fox hunt, as well?" Caroline asked, a little disappointed in her usually pragmatic younger sister, if not all that surprised.

"Well, someone has to catch the fox. I'll run with the other hounds for a bit, so at least I'll have a good view of the proceedings."

"Mm hm. Best of luck, then."

Caroline watched her sister out the door. It didn't bode well for family harmony if even sensible Anne was mooning after Lord Zachary. Of course he *was* undeniably attractive, but she had no intention of marrying anyone—much less a lord. Marriage meant gossiping, doing embroidery, buying clothes, anything to fill up the waste of useless, endless days. That might be what the rest of her sisters wanted for themselves, but she would rather die.

However handsome he was, she needed—wanted—him for one thing only: His likeness on a canvas that was going to arrive in Vienna by the twentieth of the month.

Caroline Witfeld was staring at him again. Zachary tried to ignore it, a feat that should have been easy amid the cacophony of questions being thrown in his direction, but every time he looked around the table to avoid excluding any members of the huge family from the conversation, her gaze was on him.

If she'd conversed it would have been less noticeable, but all she seemed interested in was staring. In truth, perhaps he looked at her more frequently than he did at the others, but Caroline Witfeld was the only chit he didn't have to keep at bay with a pitchfork. And the flecks of brown in her green eyes . . . Zachary shook himself. Losing concentration here could lead to some very sticky entanglements, multiplied by seven.

"Lord Zachary, is it true that you have two older brothers?" one of the twin Witfeld girls asked.

He finished his bite of roasted chicken and nodded. "Yes. Charlemagne and Mel—"

"And all of you are unmarried?"

No wonder just about everyone at the table had finished their dinner except for him. He didn't have time to get words out or food in. "Melbourne is a widower, but yes, technically we're all—"

"Mama said that your sister recently married the Marquis of Deverill. Is that true?"

Zachary sighed. "Yes, last month in Scot—"

"How do you like your chicken, Lord Zachary?"

The two bites he'd managed had been cold by the time he'd gotten to them. "It's quite delicious. Thank y—"

"Chicken is my favorite, as well, isn't it, Anne? Do you like to waltz?"

And the oldest girl kept staring at him. This was beginning to be annoying. "I enjoy dan—"

"We had a private tutor teach us all the latest dances. The assembly rooms at Trowbridge are fabulous for balls and soirees. They put up silver ribbons and balloons."

Zachary was beginning an internal debate—not something he generally wasted time on—over whether it was more rude to stare or to interrupt. He enjoyed a good conversation, and definitely a good meal, but though he'd been gazed at admiringly before, he couldn't remember so . . . intense or extended a look before now.

"Lord Zachary, do—"

"Lord Zachary, how—"

"My lord, did—"

He set down his fork with a clatter and turned to face her. "Miss Witfeld, is something troubling you?"

The corners of her eyes crinkled as she gazed back at him. "No, my lord."

He noted that the rest of the horde stopped peppering the air with questions. They stopped talking altogether, as a matter of fact. Even Mr. Witfeld, who'd been ignoring the female cacophony in favor of his roasted potatoes, stopped a forkful halfway to his mouth. "Oh. Good, then," Zachary muttered, disconcerted at the abrupt silence, and went back to his meal.

The chaos resumed before he could begin chewing. "Lord Zachary, what is your horse's name?"

"Sagramore."

"Like the knight in the King Arthur legend?" another of them asked.

"Yes."

"And your dog?"

"Harold."

And the eldest sister still looked at him and still didn't participate in the general roar of conversation.

"Lord Zach—"

"What are you staring at, then, Miss Witfeld?" he interrupted again. So he wasn't working on being patient tonight; no one would tell Melbourne.

"Your ears, my lord," she returned promptly, her voice perfectly serious.

"My—" He hadn't expected that. "My ears?"

"Yes, my lord."

Surreptitiously he angled his knife to take a look at them in the reflection. He hadn't cut either of them off while shaving before dinner, at any rate. "What's so interesting about my ears, if I might ask?"

"The shape of them."

He thought her mouth twitched, but he couldn't be certain. Now the rest of the Witfelds were staring at his ears, as well. *Bloody wonderful.* "Aren't everyone's ears nearly the same as mine?"

This time he was certain he saw amusement touch her eyes, and the crinkles at their corners deepened once again. "Oh, no, my lord. Your ears are quite unique."

"That's probably from having his oldest brother yank on them so frequently to get Zachary to behave," Aunt Tremaine put in.

"There's nothing wrong with my ears," he stated.

"I think you have lovely ears," the youngest Witfeld offered.

"No, they're handsome, not lovely," another one argued.

The next argument was over whether a man's ears could be

termed "pretty" or "lovely" or if more masculine compliments were appropriate. Zachary took the moment to lean across the corner of the table toward the oldest girl. "What's wrong with my ears?" he murmured.

Soft color touched her cheeks for the first time since their odd conversation had begun. "Nothing. You only asked me what I was looking at, and I answered. If I've been too direct, I apologize."

"Not necessary. Why my ears, though?"

She lowered her lashes. "I'm studying them. I wish to draw you."

"Draw me," he repeated in a low drawl. "Do you often tell men with whom you are barely acquainted that you wish to draw them?"

Her color deepened, her eyes lifting to meet his again. "No, my lord. You are the first."

Well, it was certainly a unique approach to a flirtation. And exceptionally bold, considering the fact that her parents were seated just a few feet away. Hm. Whether she called it drawing or kissing, he had no objection to playing along. At least she didn't babble like the rest of the brood. Technically they were family friends, but all that meant was that *he* couldn't initiate anything scandalous. *She,* on the other hand . . .

"Then draw me," he said with a smile. "But you have to let me view the results."

"Of course, my lord."

Perhaps staying a few days at Witfeld Manor wouldn't be as dull as he'd thought, then. "Where shall we meet for you to . . . draw me, then?" he went on, adopting her rather obvious innuendo.

"How about in the conservatory tomorrow morning?" she suggested. "About eight? I don't think the family will disturb us before nine o'clock."

"I'll bring my ears," he returned. And the rest of him.

"Did you see her letter?" Mrs. Witfeld was tittering to his aunt as he straightened.

"Yes, it was very promising."

"Monsieur Tannberg writes in a very gentlemanly manner, don't you think?" the brood's matron continued. "And he's not even English."

Zachary drew his brows together. He'd missed something, obviously. "Who's—"

He didn't get to finish the question, since abruptly the conversation turned to Beau Brummell and his gentlemanly manner. The man was a fop, but obviously the Witfeld girls didn't want to hear that. Zachary therefore kept his opinion to himself and commented only on the handful of actual encounters he'd had with Brummell.

His attention, though—wherever he happened to be directing his conversation—was on Caroline. Before he embarked on a flirtation, and whether he'd instigated it or not, he needed to get a few answers from Aunt Tremaine. Though she was their small brood's closest living relation, she had what Melbourne considered an alarming tendency to plan and follow her own agenda.

This scheme, though, might even be Melbourne-sanctioned. Sebastian had only suggested he get a dog, however, and Zachary didn't think he'd meant even *that* seriously. As soon as dinner ended he made his way around the table to his aunt. "Allow me to help you to the drawing room," he said, offering his arm.

"Oh, we can manage that," Mrs. Witfeld countered before his aunt could respond. "You'll be wanting to smoke a cigar and have a glass of port with Mr. Witfeld. I know how you refined gentlemen like your port."

Zachary glanced up at the family patriarch, the only other family member besides Caroline who'd barely spoken a word at dinner. "I don't wish to disturb Mr. Witfeld's routine," he said, reluctantly relinquishing Aunt Tremaine's arm.

"With seven daughters I don't actually have a routine to be disturbed," Witfeld said unexpectedly, rising and gesturing for Zachary to follow him.

The two of them made their way to the hall and past the kitchen to a small corner room on the bottom floor. As Mr. Witfeld lit the two lamps inside, Zachary stopped. Wooden spheres, planks with wheels attached to the top and the bottom, clay pots with dried hay stalks sticking out the bottom, miniature Greek columns made of what looked like papier-mâché: Odd objects filled the room practically to the rafters.

"Have a seat, my lord," Mr. Witfeld said, clearing a chair by setting a large circular mesh of wood onto the floor.

"Thank you," Zachary returned, gingerly making his way through the clutter. The sheer magnitude of . . . things amazed him. "Might I ask you a question?"

"I have no control over the girls, if you're asking for an explanation. I wanted two children. My wife decided they must be boys, and she wasn't going to stop having them until she succeeded in that."

Zachary cleared his throat. "So you're still . . ."

"Good God, no. A man can only suffer so much in the world without resorting to suicide. One more infant of either sex, and I'd put a pistol to my skull."

"I have two brothers and a sister, myself," Zachary commented. "At times I wish there were more of us." Though lately the idea of being an only child also had its appeal.

"More siblings? You are either mad, or very lucky."

"A little of both, I think."

"Ha, ha. Well said, my lord. Port or brandy?"

"Brandy, if you please."

Mr. Witfeld poured two snifters of brandy. "I do prefer this to port."

With a smile Zachary took one of the snifters. "As do I."

The Witfeld patriarch took a long swallow of the amber liquid. "I hope Caro didn't offend you with her ear comments. She can be rather . . . direct. Gets that from me, I suppose."

Zachary blinked. Apparently she had either used the sketching ruse before, or she had a known ear fetish. With what he'd seen of this family, he didn't care to lay odds over which it might be. "I wasn't offended at all," he returned belatedly.

"Thank you for that. She's one of only two girls in the house who have any sense. The other ones are so silly I'm not certain what to make of them."

"If I might ask, why are none of them married?"

Witfeld laughed. "Didn't you notice how they practically tore you to shreds when they caught sight of you? Imagine being a fellow coming to court one of them. All bachelors run for the hills in under a minute."

He could understand that. If not for Aunt Tremaine, he would have invented an excuse to be out of the house by sunrise tomorrow. And he wouldn't have looked back. "They were friendly," he said, remembering that he was a Griffin and that Griffins were unfailingly polite. "After the artifice of London, it's actually rather refreshing."

"If you say so." Witfeld took another drink. "For me, I'm glad to have this tiny sanctuary."

Taking what was probably the best opening he was likely to get, Zachary leaned over to touch the sphere that had occupied his chair. "Speaking of your sanctuary, you have a very . . . eclectic collection. What's this?"

"It's not a collection. They're my inventions." Mr. Witfeld gave the room a fond glance.

"Your inventions."

"Yes, indeed. That one, for example, is an egg transporter."

Zachary looked at it dubiously. "I see."

"I know it doesn't look like much, but with some tinkering it could be very useful." Witfeld stood and picked it up, lifting a small hatch in the mesh wood top. "You see, there's a second, suspended sphere in the middle. A bit of a gyroscope, I suppose. The idea is to place the sphere beneath a chicken's nest, which has a hole in the bottom. When an egg is laid it drops inside, and then the weight causes the sphere to roll down a ramp to a basket below."

"I see," Zachary repeated, not certain whether to be amused, impressed, or worried. "Does it work?"

"Actually, yes. The problem is that unless you only have one chicken or unless they all lay their eggs in the correct order, the first-filled sphere knocks all the other waiting ones down the ramp, which is then peppered with broken eggs." Sighing, Witfeld set the sphere down again and nudged it with the toe of his Wellington boot.

"One egg a day wouldn't be very profitable," Zachary ventured.

"Exactly. Ah, well. I'm still working on a solution."

"Are all of these works in progress?"

"Some of them are prototypes. A few of the actual pieces are in use about the estate. I'll take you on a tour tomorrow, if you'd like."

Well, that would be different, at any rate. "Certainly." Zachary looked down at the egg-catching sphere again. "Have you considered a line of short ramps all connecting to a main one? Then it wouldn't matter which chicken produced an egg first."

Witfeld looked at him for a moment. Usually when one of Zachary's brothers eyed him like that, it was followed by one of them calling him an idiot or a blockhead. He automatically braced his shoulders for the insult.

"And the short ramps could be angled slightly to enable the spheres to make the turn onto the main ramp," Witfeld said slowly, pulling a piece of paper out from a stack and beginning to scribble on it. "I'm a fool."

"Nonsense," Zachary returned, beginning to warm to the discussion. "You'd still have a problem if two spheres collided and blocked the main ramp."

"That's still less of a problem than I had a moment ago."

"So you think it might work?"

"I think it might." Witfeld stood. "If you'll excuse me, I need to pull out my blueprints."

Zachary rose as well. "Of course. I should see how my aunt is faring."

They shook hands. "Good night, my lord. And I've found it's best to go along with the tidal wave of femininity, then escape as soon as their backs are turned."

With a chuckle Zachary nodded. "Thank you for the advice."

As he headed back toward the second floor and the drawing room, Zachary wasn't all that certain the advice was necessary. Yes, there were seven daughters, but two of them weren't yet of age, and God knew he'd had his share of females in pursuit. The only difference here was that all the chits were related.

Outside the drawing room doorway, though, he stopped. It sounded like a henhouse in there, with all the female voices tittering and giggling. And he could swear that in the space of thirty seconds he heard his name mentioned at least nine times and by a half dozen different voices.

Well, if there was one thing he'd learned, it was to admit when he was wrong. Five marriageable females plus two younger ones and their mother *and* his aunt—he'd never been that badly outnumbered before. And they expected him to walk straight into the spiders' web.

"Devil take that," he muttered and turned on his heel, retreating to his bedchamber. He might not yet be an expert in army tactics, but he did know about strategic retreats and living to fight another day. He would deal with the assault after he got a good night's sleep.

Actually, the next assault came immediately. As he opened the bedchamber door, a thigh-high brown tangle of legs and ears leapt up to hit him in the chest. Reflexively he caught the beast in his arms. "Did you miss me, Harold?" he muttered, setting the dog down again.

"Thank goodness you've come, my lord," his valet yelped, dropping a frayed blanket to the floor.

"What's amiss, Reed?" Zachary closed the door behind him just before Harold could reach the opening.

"That . . . that animal, my lord," the valet sputtered. "I've been trying to fend him off, but he nearly ate me alive." The servant stuck out one foot, showing off a shredded pants leg and stocking. The man's shoe was nowhere to be seen.

"He's still a pup, Reed; we have to make allowances for high spirits."

"If you say so, my lord. Will there be anything else?"

Hm. Whatever Miss Witfeld had in mind for the morning, he needed to be prepared for it. "Lay out my gray day jacket, if you please," he said, patting his thigh to get Harold's attention, "and be up here by seven o'clock. I have an early engagement." That should do; elegant but conservative would seem to be a match for a country miss's expectations.

"Very good, my lord, except—"

"Except what, Reed? Come here, Harold. Here."

"Except that your . . . Harold . . . ate your gray day jacket."

Zachary looked from the dog to the valet. "Beg pardon?"

"Well, not the entire garment. The right sleeve, actually. I had taken it from the wardrobe to press it, my lord, and evidently he thought I was playing or—"

"That's fine," Zachary interrupted, swallowing his annoyance. "The rust-colored one will suffice."

"Of course, my lord. And I'll see that the other gets to a tailor. Perhaps it can be repaired."

Nodding, Zachary retrieved Shay's poetry book and sank into the reading chair beneath the window. Once Reed had gone, he sent Harold a glare. "Stop eating my things," he ordered.

The dog wagged its tail at him. For the moment Zachary would take that as agreement.

He was nodding off over the Byron poetry when someone scratched at his door. For a fleeting moment he hoped it might be Caroline, but she'd already set their rendezvous for early in the morning.

"Come in," he called, settling upright in his chair.

Aunt Tremaine limped heavily into the room. "Coward," she said, closing the door behind her.

"Beg pardon?"

"You left more than half a dozen very disappointed young ladies waiting for you downstairs."

"I was tired," he returned, snapping his book open again. "And I had to discipline Harold."

She lifted an eyebrow, taking in the dog snoring in the middle of the bed. "You've never disciplined anything in your life." Moving closer to Zachary, she rapped the back of the book with the tip of her cane. "At least it gave me a chance to answer all their questions in depth."

He looked up again. "What questions?"

His aunt smiled. "The questions about you. Your favorite food, favorite color, favorite flower, fav—"

"I don't have a favorite flower."

"You do now. White lilies."

"So I'm maudlin and sentimental."

"Apparently," she returned, unfazed.

"And what are you?" he asked, tugging at the end of the cane until she lowered it. He'd been thwacked across the ankle or knee with it enough to know how much it could sting. In fact he thought his aunt sometimes faked gout so she would have an excuse to carry the weapon.

"What do you mean?"

"Had you planned all along to make this detour?"

"I knew Sally lived close along the road to Bath."

Zachary stood. "And you knew she had seven unmarried daughters."

"Yes."

"None of which was information you chose to share with me until we'd stopped on the front drive."

"Don't accuse me of any matchmaking nonsense, young man," she said as they headed back to the hallway. "Sebastian was the one who assigned you to be my escort. I could easily have traveled here or to Bath with Charlemagne or even Melbourne himself. I was under the impression that they were both occupied elsewhere."

And so was he supposed to be. "Mm hm." Zachary continued to eye his wily aunt as he escorted her to her own bedchamber. "So you have no ulterior motives for anything."

"You're entirely too suspicious. Now lend me your book so I'll have something to read in bed."

"Fine." He handed it over. "It's Shay's, so don't be surprised by the notes in the margins. And Harold ate the cover."

Aunt Tremaine took his arm and pulled him down so she could kiss his cheek. "You'll enjoy a few days here. It's different than what you're accustomed to. Just remember, my boy, Sally is a dear friend, and her daughters are terribly naive. You are not."

"Never fear, Aunt. I won't lead any young things astray."

"I know you won't."

After he returned to his own room, he undressed and shoved the snoring hound to one side of the bed. He *wouldn't* lead anyone astray. If one of them wanted to lead him somewhere, though, that was a different matter entirely. And he had an appointment to be sketched—or whatever she chose to call it—in the morning. Yes, the damned trip to Bath was beginning to look up a little.

Chapter 4

Caroline set out four pencils with various thicknesses of lead. She didn't want to look foolish and run out of drawing implements in front of Lord Zachary—not when impressing him with her professionalism and competence would be as important as her skill at painting him.

She frowned. Considering the way she'd stared at him all through dinner, she could probably stand to do a bit of work on her professionalism. For heaven's sake, he was a Griffin. One of *the* Griffins. He'd probably had his portrait painted by Lawrence or Reynolds. Or both.

But in her defense, he'd arrived in Wiltshire with better timing than a white knight. And aside from desperately wanting to memorize the angle of his jaw and the curve of his brow in case he should vanish again, all but the excited core of her couldn't believe he was there in the first place. Since he *was* there, however, from this moment on she needed to be absolutely, unquestionably professional about sketching and painting him. No more mooneyed staring, whatever her reasons for it. This was her one blasted chance.

She'd barely slept, and not just because Susan had kept her up half the night chatting about how princely and royal and handsome and wealthy their houseguest was. Her fingers had practically itched—and still did—with the desire to pick up a pencil and sketch him. Even after just half a day she felt as though she knew every bit of him. Considering the importance of the portrait, however, she wanted him seated in front of her. Only her best work would get her to Vienna—and away from Wiltshire and the Eades family and their governess position.

The door clicked shut behind her. With a start Caroline turned around. Lord Zachary stood just inside the conservatory, gazing at her. "Good morning," he drawled.

For a moment she simply looked back at him. Susan had been correct. He wasn't heavy or hairy or overly muscled, but masculine in the best sense of the word. And no man had ever before looked at her with that expression on his face. She swallowed as he moved forward, closing the distance between them, his lovely gray eyes focusing on her mouth.

Caroline watched him approach, taking in the tilt of his head, the play of his thigh muscles beneath his snug buckskin trousers, and storing the memories for future recall on canvas. She didn't care how many epithets her sisters piled on his head—physically, he was magnificent. "Good morning," she returned, attributing the sudden tightness low in her stomach and the heat running beneath her skin to the desire to begin sketching him again at once.

"It definitely is now." Lord Zachary touched her cheek with his fingers. Leaning down, he took her mouth in a slow, soft kiss.

For a dozen heartbeats Caroline froze, every ounce of her being focused on the warm touch of his lips against hers. Then with a start daylight broke through the mist. Gasping, she pushed backward. "What—what are you doing?"

His fine brow furrowed. "Kissing you."

"Well, stop it at once!"

"I did." He lowered his hand, his expression darkening at the same time. "You don't have someone hiding in here as a witness, do you? Because this was your—"

"Are you mad?" Caroline was still trying to remember how to breathe, and her voice squeaked. "What are you talking about?"

"You invited me up here for a private rendezvous. I don't—"

"I invited you to my studio so I could sketch you." She'd never heard that insanity or soft-headedness ran in the Griffin family, but then they wouldn't make any such thing public. Certainly none of her subjects had ever kissed her before. "And open the door at once, before my maid comes to investigate and catches us in here alone!"

His gaze left her face, traveling toward the sketch pad and the carefully laid out pencils, then moving on to the walls at the back of the conservatory. She didn't need to turn around to know what he was looking at; for heaven's sake, she'd painted all of them. Finally his gaze returned to her again.

"When you said you wanted to sketch me, you actually wanted to sketch me."

"Yes. What did you think . . ." Abruptly, the kiss and the expression in those gray eyes made sense. "Oh! I am not some . . . lightskirt, sir!"

"Bloody hell," he muttered, stalking back to pull open the door again. "I'm a damned blockhead. Apologies, Miss Witfeld." Lord Zachary stood in the doorway for a moment, then looked at the back wall again. Finally, almost as though it was against his better judgment, he strolled over to look at her artwork.

She turned around to keep him in sight, mortification and anger pulling her in opposite directions. How could he have thought such a . . . scandalous thing? And about her? "So you often have ladies offer to sketch you and then—"

"No," he cut in, his face darkening as he faced her again. "It was a mistake. A stupid mistake. This"—he gestured at the wall of paintings—"well, you have to admit, it's a bit unusual."

Caroline drew her shoulders straighter. "Not to me, my lord."

With a slow breath, he nodded. "Of course not. My apologies once again." Giving her another tight look, he turned for the door.

Blast it all. Uttering a dismayed curse as her hopes strode for the exit, Caroline scrambled to beat him to the door. "I . . . Don't go, my lord," she squeaked.

He stopped. "What?"

If you leave, I have to become a governess. "This was obviously just a silly misunderstanding," she offered, forcing a chuckle. "We're both adults. Let's begin again, shall we?"

One curved eyebrow lifted. "You're not serious?"

Caroline made herself smile. "Unless you'd rather we had a duel out in the meadow over a kiss."

A deep chuckle rumbled from his chest. "No. I'm actually fairly good with weapons, and I'd hate for you to win and humiliate me."

She snorted. At the sound she blushed and covered her mouth and nose, but Lord Zachary laughed again. Caroline took a deep breath. Back to professionalism, before it was entirely too late. "Then we're agreed. We'll begin again."

"Agreed." He returned to the back wall of the conservatory. "How long have you been painting?" he asked, following the sequence of work.

"Since I can remember. Some of those aren't very good." She felt her cheeks, already heated from his kiss and his near escape, warm even further. She didn't normally feel the need to defend her work, but since she was scrambling to regain her professional standing with him, it seemed important that he knew she wasn't just a dabbler in paints. "My earliest ones have all the emotion and depth of a tree stump," she continued.

"Then why do you keep them about?"

Her sisters repeatedly asked her the same question. Coming from him, though, it sounded different—not that he couldn't believe she would keep her failures in view but that he was genuinely curious as to why she did so. "They remind me that I've improved, that it's a process, and that I learn from experience—and from my failures."

"You *have* improved," he noted, gesturing at one of her most recent portraits, one she'd done of her father. "This is quite good, in fact."

"Thank you." She'd heard that before, too, though the compliment was usually followed by something conditional, like she painted well for a female. He'd already called her hobby odd. "You've studied art, then?" she couldn't help asking.

"Some. More than my family probably realizes, anyway." With

a slight grin he turned around, facing her again. "There aren't any paintings of you."

"There's actually one, in the hall behind the drawing room." She scowled. "I don't like it very much, but Papa insisted that there be one of each member of the family or he wouldn't hang any of them."

"So you capture all of your guests and ask to sketch them?"

He stepped closer again, and that same tightness in her chest started once more, constricting her breathing. "Yes. To sketch them," she emphasized. "Nothing more."

"Then sketch me," he said, gazing down at her. This time she saw humor in his gray eyes. "Where do you want me?"

Caroline blinked. So far, so good, despite the fact that she'd been half ready for him to kiss her again. "Um, by the window, I think, to begin with. This is just preliminary, so I can try different poses."

"I am at your disposal. Standing, or sitting?"

"Standing is good." Renewed excitement and anticipation flooding through her, she collected her pad and pencils, then pulled her stool toward the middle of the floor to get a better angle. "Perhaps you could gaze out over the field."

"Should I put a hand to my eyes, as though I'm overseeing my vast domain?" he suggested, demonstrating.

She snorted again before she could stop herself. *Stop it, Caroline. Act like a blasted professional before it's too late.* "Whatever you feel comfortable with, my lord."

He cocked his head at her. "All I need is a portrait that would land me in Bedlam," he commented, grinning. "My brothers could throw darts at me in absentia."

Caroline began to sketch, starting this time with his eyes. "You and your brothers don't deal well, then?"

"We generally deal excessively well. They are my dearest friends."

"Then why in the world would they throw darts at you?"

Lord Zachary laughed. "They would only throw them at my

likeness. The only barbs they actually throw at *me* are verbal ones."

"And you retaliate in kind, I suppose?"

"One-sided barb throwing is never any fun." Holding his head rigid, he managed to look at her from the corner of his eye. "Could you paint me in a military uniform?"

Drat. He was just as peculiar as the Earl and Countess Eades. Still, at least it wasn't a monkey suit or a Greek god's toga he'd asked to be sketched in. "I could, yes."

"Excellent. I'll send it off to Melbourne. He'll have an apopl—"

"No!"

Lord Zachary looked full at her, so that she had to stop sketching his ear. "Why not?" he asked.

She drew a breath. "*I* need the portrait."

"To add to your wall? I'll pay you for it, of course, Miss Witfeld."

"No. It's . . . I'm applying to a painters' studio. The application is the portrait." Caroline gestured at him, trying to calm herself down. Of course he couldn't have the portrait when she finished it. "I can paint a second portrait for you later if you'd like, after this one is finished. Please turn your head again."

He complied. "Which studio?"

For a bare moment Caroline closed her eyes. If she told him, he'd undoubtedly ask why she hadn't applied to the best-known British painters and studios, and she'd have to explain that she had, but each and every one of them had turned her down. "I'm sure you've never heard of it. Lady Gladys said your sister recently married."

"Yes, she did. To my eldest brother's closest friend—which, I suppose, is a good thing, because otherwise we would have had to kill him."

"Good heavens, why?"

Lord Zachary cleared his throat. "It's a long story."

She smiled. "I doubt we have any of the same acquaintances, even if I made a habit of gossiping—which I don't."

His head shifted for a brief moment as he glanced in her direction. "They eloped."

"They did?"

"Twice, actually." His sensuous lips curved upward. "We caught up to them once, and they slipped away from us again. Set our damned horses loose. It took me twenty minutes to track down Sag—Sagramore. By then Melbourne had decided to let them go."

"I appreciate your trust, my lord. I won't tell anyone."

"Call me Zachary," he returned. "And I'm trusting you with my image on canvas, so I suppose Nell and Valentine's reputations are fairly safe with you."

Despite the easy tone, she understood the steel beneath the words. If she *did* tell anyone, he would know about it. And then she could bid farewell to his image on canvas. "Exceedingly safe," she said, noting that his smile deepened and his expression grew more attractive. If she could capture that look, she might have a chance with one of the painting masters after all.

Zachary smiled at the enthusiasm in her voice. Caroline Witfeld liked him. And that was despite his ham-fisted misinterpretation of her invitation. She also had a temper, and that interested him, as well. " 'Exceedingly safe, Zachary,' " he prompted.

He heard her blow out her breath. "Zachary, then. Thank you for doing this for me."

"My pleasure."

The whole strangeness of the situation rather appealed to him. In most circles he knew, if he'd made the error in judgment he'd made with her, their morning chat would have concluded several minutes ago with a slap across his face. And yet there he sat, posing for some sort of art project and telling her about his family's one scandal. Melbourne would be having an apoplexy at his unfounded decision to trust her. Melbourne, however, wasn't there, and his own presence was his brother's fault, anyway.

Even with their decision to forget the kiss, in London they would have been pushing the limits of propriety. Open door or not, here in the country, in a house filled with seven sisters, her parents, his aunt, and two dozen servants, it could still be trouble. Her father at the least, however, knew about her interest in sketching him, and no one had even looked at the idea askance. Witfeld Manor didn't seem quite as balanced as most other households of his acquaintance. It was refreshing.

At the same time, he wasn't going to be tricked into a compromising situation and a marriage if he didn't even get another kiss first. "Shouldn't we have a chaperone or something in here?"

"My maid is in the hallway by now, if that makes you feel safer," she said absently, obviously concentrating on her sketching. "She generally stays out of the room because she either snores or fidgets. It's very distracting."

It began to dawn on him that she truly had forgotten the kiss, put it completely behind her. Hm. Chits didn't do that where he was concerned. And it had been a pleasant kiss, damn it all. "It actually wasn't my safety I was considering," he returned.

"Your virtue, then." With a self-amused smile she continued scratching the pencil along the paper.

So now she felt comfortable enough with him to make jokes. Next she'd be laughing to all her sisters about how he'd kissed her and had had to apologize for it. "Mm hm." Before he could change his mind about the wisdom of his actions, Zachary pushed away from the window. He could always just apologize again.

"You're moving. Stop moving."

He ignored her admonishment, not stopping until he stood directly in front of her, perched on her prim little stool. "Miss Witfeld," he said, tilting her chin up again with his fingers, "I don't think you know me quite well enough yet to comment about my virtue—or lack thereof." Slowly he leaned down toward her.

"Oh," she breathed.

He meant to stop an inch away from her, meant only to point out that he wasn't merely a clay model waiting to be drawn onto paper, or a jester because he liked to jest. Instead her soft mouth, the startled but unafraid expression in her deep green eyes, beckoned him. Closing his own eyes, he touched his mouth to hers for the second time that morning. A moment later the pencil hit the hardwood floor and her hand slid around the back of his neck.

"You know Caro must be sketching him," a female voice came faintly from the bottom of the stairs, and he broke the kiss.

Her eyes were still closed, her face upturned. "Miss Witfeld," he murmured, "we're about to have company."

"I'm going to take up painting, if it means I get to spend time with Lord Zachary," another voice said from closer by.

Caroline's eyes flew open. "Get back over there," she hissed urgently, grabbing up her pencil and jabbing it toward the window.

"I am," he returned in the same low voice, backing to the row of windows and returning to his pose.

So she truly wasn't interested in trapping him into marriage, then. If she had been, wrapping her arms around his shoulders or falling on him would have taken care of that. The first time, he could claim an honest, if witless, mistake on his part. But now Zachary was sweating. Good God, that had been a stupid, reckless thing to do. And as before, it left him not precisely reeling, but tingling all the way down his spine.

"Caro?" The first girl scurried into the room, one, two, five others on her heels. All six dipped into a wave of curtsies in his direction, so many skirts waving he could practically feel the breeze. "Lord Zachary."

"Good morning, ladies," he returned, smiling.

"We looked everywhere for you," the youngest, Violet or Viola or something, said. "Breakfast is ready, Lord Zachary."

He looked over their heads at Caroline. Her color was high; if the sisters' attention hadn't all been concentrated on him, she and he might still have been in trouble. "May I move now, Miss Witfeld?"

She shook herself. "Yes, of course. I'd like to sketch your hands later, though. Perhaps out in the garden?"

"Certainly." Caroline Witfeld was a single-minded chit, and more composed than he would have expected, if she was still thinking about the portrait after two damned kisses.

"You can't monopolize him, Caro," one of the twin girls

protested, grabbing his arm and towing him toward the door. In the flurry of activity he couldn't even tell which of the sisters had hold of his other arm. "We want to show him Trowbridge."

"And the garden and the pond," another said.

"The wildflowers on the hillsides are lovely this time of year."

"We could take one of the riding trails, Lord Zachary. You could ride Sagramore."

"I'd be pleased to go," he commented. "But of course I am at my aunt's disposal."

"Oh, you *must* come visit with us!"

Well, at least here he seemed to be more than an extraneous sibling. Zachary nodded. "I'll do my best."

Halfway through breakfast Mrs. Witfeld appeared, arm in arm with Aunt Tremaine. "Girls, what do you think?" their mother said, her voice quavering with excitement. "I've been talking with Gladys, and she's agreed to stay for at least the next fortnight."

"Hurray!"

"And so, even with the monthly soiree at the assembly rooms already set for Thursday, I thought this would be a wonderful occasion to hold a ball of our own!" Her pale green eyes swept around and caught Zachary.

He'd seen that look before. Aunt Tremaine might not have matchmaking in mind, but someone did. Amid the general cheers and cacophony that followed Mrs. Witfeld's pronouncement, he did some surveying of his own. All the girls were making plans for buying new gowns and deciding on a theme for the party—all but one.

Caroline finished her buttered toast, her gaze on her plate and her focus on something private and personal. He wondered whether she'd even heard the announcement of the ball. Her father had said that two of his daughters had common sense; she was obviously one of them.

"Caro, are you going into Trowbridge with us?"

She blinked, looking up. "Hm? No. I have some work to do."

"You always have work to do." The one with the lightest-colored hair, Susan, he thought, leaned over to touch his arm. "You're coming with us, aren't you, Lord Zachary? We promised we'd show you the town."

He knew where he'd rather stay, but Griffins weren't rude. "I'd be delighted—if Aunt Tremaine has no objection."

"Heavens, no. Sally and I have planning to do."

"I can't wait to see the look on Mary Gorman's face," another Witfeld chit whispered. "She'll die when she sees who's staying with us."

"Are you certain you won't come, Caro?"

Zachary glanced at her again. She wasn't daydreaming now. In fact, she was looking straight at him—and unless he was greatly mistaken, she didn't look very happy. Apparently he'd done something to provoke her again. Good. "I'm afraid I can't leave my ears behind," he said, to the laughter of the others. "But they'll return."

Her jaw twitched. "Don't mind me. I'm certain I can make do without your ears for the morning."

One of the other girls stood and moved behind Caroline, placing her hands on her sister's shoulders. "Do come with us. If anyone's going to help me choose colors and material for a new gown, I want it to be you." She leaned over and kissed Caroline's cheek. "Please?"

Ah, the other one who had some common sense. Zachary couldn't remember her name, but he felt unexpectedly grateful to her. Honey-colored curls framed her oval face as she glanced at him from beneath long eyelashes. Very nice, but uncharacteristically for him, it was still the Witfeld chit with the quick mouth and the unladylike snort who kept his attention. "Allow me to add in my request for your company, as well, Miss Witfeld," he drawled. "The more the merrier."

Caroline sighed. "Oh, very well. *If* you'll still allow me to sketch you in the garden this afternoon."

"Caroline," her mother admonished. "You shouldn't make ultimatums to our guests. And you shouldn't monopolize his company, especially when you have unmar—"

"I always keep my word," Zachary cut in, unwilling to hear that particular sentence completed. "My hands will be in the garden this afternoon, alongside my ears." Until he could figure out why he preferred the one Witfeld girl who didn't seem interested in pursuing anything more than his image on canvas, he would continue to make an effort to keep her close by.

Chapter 5

Caroline sat back in the barouche and tried to ignore Joanna jabbing at her ribs and whispering silly nonsense in her ear. At the moment she would have given a great deal of money to have a sketch pad in her hands and the elbow room to draw.

Lord Zachary rode beside them, chatting amiably with Violet and Grace about the state of the roads in Wiltshire, and looking like the very model of a proper English nobleman. His gray gelding was at least three-quarters Arabian, though she wouldn't have been the least bit surprised to discover that Sagramore was a Thoroughbred.

Zachary was even more obviously a thoroughbred, sitting easily in the saddle, with one hand loosely holding the reins and the other gesturing at a stand of elm trees as though they were a novelty he'd never viewed before—simply because Violet had pointed them out to him. The breeze caught his dark hair, lifting it from his collar and blowing strands across one gray eye as he laughed at some silly comment of Grace's.

As far as she knew, he hadn't kissed any of her sisters—at least not yet. He'd only been there for twenty-four hours, though. If he wanted to, he could probably ruin every female in the county within a week, especially with the way they all fawned over him. Caroline sniffed, turning to view the creek on her side of the barouche. So what if he'd chosen to kiss her, and so what if he did

it well? Her sisters could have him—once she'd finished sketching and painting him, that was.

Sagramore swung around to her side of the carriage. She lifted
her gaze as Zachary doffed his blue beaver hat at her. "I didn't
mean to take you away from your sketching," he said, smiling.

"Of course you did. What I don't see is why. You have six attractive young ladies here all trying to chat with you. Did you
really need one more?"

His grin deepened. "Yes."

"And why is that?" she returned, annoyed at his presumption.
He undoubtedly thought she would be flattered. She only had
three weeks, however, to submit the most perfect portrait she'd
ever done. And she would need every minute of that time—
especially if her sisters kept trying to drag her subject into town,
and even if she felt as though she could draw him with her eyes
closed.

At the same time she wondered why his presence felt like a
warm afternoon breeze, fresh and alive and a little wild. And she
wondered why she liked that, when in general she had no time
for such silliness, and when now in particular she had more important things with which to occupy herself.

"It's very complicated," he returned. "I think that perhaps I'm
your muse, your inspiration. I'd hate to deny you my presence."

She snorted. "Oh, good heavens." Very well, perhaps taking
the time to visit Trowbridge wasn't annoying as much as it was
distracting.

"I feel inspired," Joanna muttered, jabbing her again.

Caroline had to admit, she hadn't expected one of the Griffin
men to be so good-humored—or so witty. The way the Duke of
Melbourne helped set government policy and bought and sold
property and goods, she'd expected hard, dry, old, cigar-smoking
curmudgeons. Perhaps that was it. She was merely surprised by
Zachary, and thus set a little off balance. Though why that mattered when she only needed his outsides for a painting, she had
no idea.

"If you were my muse, you would be in the garden sitting for me right now while I sketched your hands," she noted, since he continued to gaze at her.

He put an elegant hand to his chest. "One would almost think you're trying to lead me down the garden path, Miss Witfeld."

"Caro?" Susan exclaimed from the facing seat, giving a shout of laughter. "She'd never even look at you if she didn't need your face for her painting. She's never going to get married."

"Really?" Zachary lifted an eyebrow, his eyes dancing with amusement.

"Susan, be quiet!" Caroline snapped, her face heating. "That is neither Lord Zachary's concern, nor his affair."

"I was only teasing."

"It wasn't amusing," Caroline continued, her pride still stinging, though she wasn't certain why. Susan hadn't told anything but the truth. "What if I'd said that your one object in life was *to* marry?"

"Caroline!"

Probably anticipating Susan's mortification, Zachary managed to make himself scarce, trotting up in front of the barouche, where he could pretend he hadn't heard any of the exchange.

"Stop it, Caro," Susan bit out, pitching her voice lower. "Just because you don't want him doesn't mean you have to ruin any chance for the rest of us."

"Maybe if you would all stop assaulting him, one of you might have a chance," Caroline returned. "You frighten me, and I know you. I'm surprised Lord Zachary hasn't fled back to London already."

"Nonsense." This time it was Julia protesting. "I daresay the attention flatters him. And he's bound to choose one of us."

"Oh, yes, I'm certain he's remained single solely in anticipation of his visit with the Witfeld girls. Be serious, Julia. He could marry any female he wanted. Why would he choose one of you?"

"Why not? When you consider it, the odds of him marrying one of six of us are greater than him marrying one of one from some other family."

Caroline eyed Susan. "That's the worst math I've ever heard, even from you."

"Well, I know one thing," Anne finally put in. "If we sit here arguing with one another, he won't want to have anything to do with any of us. And don't forget, it's in our best interest to help Caro get her portrait done."

"So she can move to Vienna, and Papa and Mama can concentrate on marrying off the rest of us." Violet smoothed at her skirt.

"Yes, I'll miss you, too," Caroline noted, pretending her sisters' easy dismissal of her didn't hurt.

"I say that we take turns," Anne suggested. "Then we won't be overwhelming him with numbers, and we'll each get a chance." She reached over and patted Caroline's knee. "And we only want you to go to Vienna so we'll be able to visit you there."

Caroline smiled, hoping Anne could sense her gratitude. "Just please don't divide his time up so much that I don't have the opportunity to paint him."

"I'll give you one of my times," Violet said unexpectedly, scowling. "I didn't mean to sound so awful, Caro."

"Don't worry; I understand," she returned, even though she wasn't entirely certain she did. The life her sisters seemed to crave so desperately didn't seem like much of a life to her. Even if it entailed marriage to a man with warm gray eyes and a very nice seat in the saddle.

"But Violet, you're only fifteen. I don't think you should have any time with him. Or Anne, either."

"I'll be eighteen in nine weeks, Grace," Anne returned succinctly. "I get time. In fact, I'll make out a chart tonight. Everyone think of an excursion or something you'd like to do, and I'll give us each an appointed time."

"Why you?" Julia demanded.

"Because you couldn't make a chart if your life depended on it," Joanna told her twin. "We all get to approve it, though, Anne."

"Of course."

They crossed the ancient stone bridge that spanned Eldridge Creek and turned onto the main street of Trowbridge. Heads immediately began to turn, but they weren't looking at the Witfeld girls; they were all gazing at the Witfelds' houseguest. And Caroline could hardly blame them for their interest as he dismounted and strolled back to the barouche to offer his assistance as they disembarked. She wondered what he would say if he knew the seven girls had just decided to divide him up like a pie.

One by one her sisters grabbed onto him to climb to the ground, though they'd never needed assistance before that she could remember. Caroline waited until last, both because she didn't want to be trampled, and because it seemed the most dignified thing to do.

"All teasing aside, I am glad you decided to join us," Zachary said, curling his fingers around hers as he helped her to the ground.

"I did so because my sisters asked me to," she returned, deciding she needed to make one thing perfectly clear to him. "Not because you kissed me."

He nodded. "But you didn't stay away because I kissed you, either."

Caroline looked up at him; she had to, since tall as she was, the top of her head still came only to his chin. "That would have been foolish on my part," she noted, trying to ignore the warmth of his sleeve as he wrapped her hand around his arm, "since I've already told you that I need to paint your portrait."

"So you're saying that I took unfair advantage of your need," he drawled, following the flock toward a milliner's shop.

"I'm beginning to think you're baiting me, Lo . . . Zachary."

"It's about time you realized. I'd begun to fear for your sensibility, until I heard the way you laugh."

She blushed. "I can't help the way I laugh." She'd tried, endlessly, even to the point of pinching her nose closed when she chuckled. That, though, had only made her choke. "You shouldn't make fun."

"I wasn't making fun," he said, his expression growing more solemn. "I like the way you laugh. Why do you think I've been baiting you?"

Julia swept in to take his free arm before she could conjure a response to that, and Joanna managed to maneuver between him and Caroline. She shook her head at her siblings as she fell to the back of the crowd. For heaven's sake, they hadn't given Zachary a moment to breathe since he'd arrived.

Caroline hung back a moment, watching. Perhaps that was why he seemed to focus on her—because she wasn't trying to smother him.

She shook herself. Of course she wasn't trying to smother him. The handsome features helped, but he could have been a three-eyed serpent as long as he was a nobleman and agreed to be painted. So he had kissed her. If it ensured that he would sit for her, she would tolerate it. And actually, it hadn't been at all unpleasant.

"Caro, what did he say to you?" Anne said from beside her.

"What? Nothing. Why do you ask?"

"You're blushing."

"No, I'm not," she stammered. "It's warm. That's all."

"If you say so."

Violet came bouncing out of the milliner's. "He's going to take us fishing!" she announced.

"How did that come about?" Caroline asked, ushering her sister back into the shop before everyone in town heard her announcement.

"Grace asked him what he liked to do in the country, and he said fishing," Violet returned. "And then Susan said she'd never been fishing, and he said he would take us all. He said everyone should experience fishing at least once."

"I'm still making a chart," Anne grumbled.

"I think he likes us very much," their youngest sister crowed. "And I changed my mind; I'm not giving up any of my time with him. Mama said if I could find a husband, I could get married."

As she stepped inside the small, crowded shop, Caroline began to wonder whether Lord Zachary Griffin might be insane. She could think of no other reason a man would volunteer to take a half dozen young women fishing. As she caught sight of him, he had a bonnet over each hand and was giving his opinion of a third, which Grace was wearing.

Amazing. Amiable and easygoing as he seemed to be, it was no wonder that all of her sisters were half in love with him—though she wasn't certain their enthusiasm had as much to do with marrying him as it did with marrying his wealth and family name.

I must be insane, Zachary thought, sighing as he held two bonnets aloft. One of the Witfeld girls spun and twirled in front of a mirror, though it was fairly obvious that the preening was solely for his benefit. He wondered what she would do if he said he liked the gaudy purple hat in the corner.

For a moment he considered it, but there seemed to be enough mischief brewing already. Instead he indicated the pretty pale blue bonnet and then had to duck backward when three of the sisters reached for it at the same time.

"I was looking at them first," the one with the lightest hair said, holding it over her head.

One of the twin girls sniffed. "Fine. I'm here for silk to make a gown, anyway." She faced him. "Lady Gladys said your favorite color is green. Is that true?"

He had no idea. "Yes, I suppose it is," he said, then watched the stampede to the green-colored silks and muslin.

"Fishing?" a soft voice said to his left.

The smile he couldn't seem to suppress touched his mouth again as he faced Caroline Witfeld. She was so obviously trying to be serious about her painting that he couldn't resist teasing her away from it. If she hadn't been skilled at her drawing he wouldn't have done it, so thank God she was. A sense of humor amid the swarm of high-pitched nonsense at least gave him a little space for what remained of his sanity. "I don't suppose you'd like to go fishing as well? I'd let you sketch my trout."

Her lips twitched. "I have better things to do, thank you very much."

"You'd be surprised, Miss Witfeld, how relaxing a day of fishing can be. It might do you some good."

One fine eyebrow arched. "Are you suggesting I need to relax?"

He took a slow step closer, very aware of the glances they were getting from the rest of the store's occupants. "You're the one who apparently never comes into town, doesn't need any new ball gowns, doesn't wish to get married, and hides in her conservatory all day."

"I do not hide," she stated, putting her hands on her slender hips and now obviously annoyed. "Make fun if you like, but at least I have a purpose in life."

He and his siblings had made annoying one another into an art. Not the same kind of art that she dabbled in, but he had a fair amount of expertise in the other. "Painting things other than fish?"

"Very amusing. You wouldn't understand." She flipped a hand at him. "You should go help Susan and Julia choose their gloves."

"If you don't like me at all," he whispered, leaning in to smell the lemon scent of her copper-colored hair, "then you probably shouldn't keep making excuses to talk to me."

"If I—" She took a deep breath. "If you'll excuse me, I need to go purchase some modeling clay for my father." Caroline turned on her heel and vanished out the front door.

Damn. With a glance at the girls crowded around the mounds of fabric bolts, Zachary edged out the door to follow her.

"Miss Witfeld," he called, trotting to catch up.

She stopped, facing him. "Now who's going out of their way to speak with whom?"

He sighed. The chit obviously had no idea how to flirt. None of them did. Their strategy, if that even described it, seemed closer to a cattle stampede than a seduction. It was a miracle he'd managed a pair of kisses with her. "I wanted to apologize if I said something to offend you."

"Ah. You're being gentlemanly. I thought perhaps you've been paying attention to me simply because I'm the one sister whose name you can remember," she said smartly.

"It would be easier if all of you wore your names on your

sleeves," he admitted with a grin. After all, it was the truth. "I thought portraitists were quiet and refined."

She flushed scarlet. "I—you—I *am*," she stated. "You are very trying."

"And you are quite unique," he returned, realizing he'd stumbled on the perfect word to describe this talented, odd, outspoken chit.

" 'Unique,' " she repeated.

"Yes. And where I come from, uniqueness is—"

"Unique?"

Zachary chuckled. "I was going to say 'unusual,' which isn't much better. I hope my interest doesn't offend you, but I truly would like to know which artists' studio you've applied to. If you won't tell me which one, might you at least give me a clue about where it's located? I've been a great many places. Perhaps I could recommend a nice inn, or a park nearby."

He was certain he heard a faint snort. "Vienna," she said after a moment, and continued toward the mercantile store.

"Vienna," he said, masking his surprise. "Lovely town. Cold in the winter."

"I could have told you that, and I've never been there."

No, he wouldn't have described her as reserved, though she did seem to be trying—which made interfering practically irresistible. "To be honest, I never have, either. I was hoping you'd say London, or Venice."

Her feet hesitated. "You've been to Venice?"

"On my Grand Tour. Rome, Paris, Athens, and everywhere in between. I stayed to the south, where it was warmer."

"So you saw David?" her quiet voice asked.

"I assume you mean the statue?" he returned, sensing that he'd found another weak spot in her armor. Humor and statuary. *Hm.* "Yes, I did. And the Sistine Chapel. The—"

She turned around again, seizing his sleeve. "Was it marvelous?"

He hesitated. This was generally the moment when his brothers began asking him about the selection of wines and the quality of women he'd encountered during his travels across Europe. In fact, when he'd returned to England he'd swiftly come to the conclusion that he'd erred in spending so much of his time viewing antiquities and famous works of art, despite the fact that he couldn't remember ever having enjoyed himself so greatly.

The favorite joke at his expense from both Shay and Sebastian, and even Eleanor, had been his interest in the quality and quantity of the food more than anything else. After a few days of annoyance and frustration he'd shrugged and given in, deciding it was easier to accept the teasing than to keep protesting it—especially when he couldn't really explain why he'd been so captivated by what he'd seen. It had been damned out of character for him, though at the moment he was glad for it.

At least he had more in common with the unique Miss Witfeld than a sense of humor. Of course she would want to know about the artworks he'd seen. She expected that he would have an opinion about what he'd seen, and she actually wanted to hear it— which meant he had to be honest about it for once. And that made him surprisingly uncomfortable.

"When I visited the Louvre," he admitted slowly, "I stood for nearly an hour looking at Michelangelo's painting, the *Mona Lisa*. Have you heard of it?"

Caroline drew a sharp breath. "Of course I have. I've seen sketches and copies, but to see the actual . . . Would you please tell me your impression of it?"

Pretending not to notice the way she'd twined her hand around his arm, Zachary pulled open the door to the mercantile store with his free hand. "I don't know how much my impressions are worth, but I would be pleased to."

She nearly stumbled in the doorway, and he pulled her closer against his side to keep her upright. He couldn't remember ever meeting a woman as focused as she was—and his sister, Eleanor, was famous for her single-mindedness.

Zachary hid the smile that wanted to touch his mouth. "What was it that your father wanted you to get for him again?"

"What?" Caroline blinked, as if suddenly realizing where they were. "Oh. Hello, Mr. Mullen," she greeted the burly man behind the counter. "Did Papa's modeling clay come in?"

The shopkeeper nodded. "It did indeed, Miss Witfeld. And so did those sketch pads you ordered from London."

She grinned, the expression lighting her green eyes. "Oh, that's splendid. How much do I owe you?"

"Thirty shillings."

Putting the money on the counter, she accepted the flat bundle which must have been the sketch pads, and then reached for the damp, burlap-wrapped brick of clay. Zachary stepped in and intercepted it. "Allow me."

"Thank you, my lord."

He caught the straightening of the shopkeeper's shoulders as Miss Witfeld addressed him. If the village was as company-starved as Caroline and his aunt had indicated, the news of his presence would make for an interesting afternoon.

Unfortunately for Mr. Mullen, though, probably half of Trowbridge already knew Zachary was in the area by the time he and Caroline emerged from the shop. The sisters ranged up and down the street calling for him and for Caroline, though he heard his name uttered much more frequently.

"For heaven's sake," she muttered. "Silly geese." She waved her free arm. "Grace, Susan, we're right here."

In a second they were surrounded again, all of them noisily blaming Caroline for stealing him away. "Ladies," he broke in, "I'm merely here to tote purchases." With a glance at Caroline's dubious expression, he relieved her of the sketch pads. "Allow me to put these and your packages in the barouche, and then you can show me the next sight."

The mound of cloth bolts and bonnets, in addition to the heavy clay and paper, nearly broke him, but he managed to make it to the carriage and the waiting driver. Together they stowed the purchases in the back compartment and fastened them down. That done, he turned around to find all the girls watching his backside. He could include Caroline in their number, though her interest was probably purely artistic.

"Shall we?" he suggested as he rejoined the group.

"Oh, the bakery!"

"No, the sweet shop!"

"I still need a new brooch for my shawl!"

So this was how he was supposed to prove he could be patient and responsible, though where the young ladies were concerned, it was definitely his patience being tested more than any sense of responsibility. Shay and Melbourne would be laughing to split their sides if they knew what he was up to. Still, at least the Witfeld household was more lively than the community he was likely to find in Bath.

Offering an arm to each of the twins and finding that he still preferred the company of the sister who only seemed to want to hear about art, he inclined his head. "Lead away, ladies."

Chapter 6

If she hadn't feared how far it would push even Zachary Grif-
fin's definition of professional behavior, Caroline would have
banged her head against the sketch pad. "Joanna, please don't
stand right in front of Lord Zachary," she said, hoping no one
could hear her teeth grinding.

Joanna glared over her shoulder. "We're chatting. I can't very
well stand behind him to talk. It wouldn't be polite."

Blowing out her breath, Caroline stood and, for the fourth time,
dragged her stool through the grass to a new location. Usually she
practically had to resort to bribery to get any of her sisters to sit
for her while she sketched; today, none of them would leave.

Zachary Griffin sat on a stone bench in the midst of the Witfeld
sisters and held court. Of course it probably didn't look all that
regal and haughty to him—he was no doubt used to being fawned
over, the focus of absolutely everyone's attention.

"Which profile do you prefer?" he asked, putting his fingers to
his chin and turning his face to the left and then to the right.

"If you're speaking to me, I'm trying to sketch your hands,"
she said succinctly. "I don't need your head."

"Caro!" Julia chastised. "Don't listen to her, Lord Zachary. I
think both profiles are very handsome."

The duke's brother, though, gazed at Caroline as he chuckled.
He'd done a great deal of looking at her, first this morning in
town, then during luncheon, and so far during the entire time

they'd been out in the garden. She didn't know how he managed it without appearing to ignore her sisters, but every time she caught him looking at her, all she could think about was how he'd kissed her, and how it still made her face warm. And he liked her laugh, of all things.

"So tell me, ladies," he drawled, "does Miss Witfeld speak to all her portrait subjects in such a . . . direct manner?"

"No," Violet offered, shaking her head. "She's usually very professional."

Wonderful. He and her own sisters had her so frazzled that she'd landed on the verge of ruining her own future. After all, she needed Zachary's letter of approval as much as she needed his likeness on canvas. If they would all just . . . cooperate a little.

"I apologize, then," she said stiffly. "But Grace, will you please—"

"Excuse me, Miss Witfeld," the butler said, appearing at the head of the path, "but your mother has visitors. She has requested all of you to join her in the drawing room. You as well, my lord."

Susan swept to her feet. "Who is visiting us, Barling?"

When Barling's eye twitched in response to the question, Caroline knew immediately who it must be. "Mrs. Gorman," she supplied, tucking her pencil behind her ear. Blast it all, by the time Portia Gorman left the house, she would have lost every iota of sunlight.

"And Miss Mary Gorman," Barling added, nodding.

Julia and Joanna began giggling. "It didn't even take them a full day to come calling," Julia chortled.

"Oh, hurry, I want a good seat to get a look at Mary's face when she sees our new houseguest." Joanna led the stampede around the house and toward the front door.

Caroline stood, tucking the sketch pad under her arm. A moment later, though, someone pulled it free from behind her.

"Anything I should know?" Zachary asked conversationally, lifting the pad to look at it. Whether he was impressed or repulsed she couldn't tell, but he did gaze at the various sketches of his hands for several hard beats of her heart.

"Drink as many fluids as you can manage," she said, forcing her voice to sound light and uncaring, as though she didn't give a hang what his opinion of her work might be. "That may prove to be your only means of escape."

He laughed. "Thank you for the advice." Zachary handed back her sketch pad as they reached the front door. "I suppose you'll be hiding in your tower?"

"I don't hide," she retorted. "I'm working." In a house full of noise and silliness and distraction, how else was she supposed to accomplish anything except by putting a door or a floor between it and her?

"I thought you needed me for your work," he commented, allowing her mother to snatch his arm as they entered the house. A second later he was gone into the cacophony of the drawing room.

Caroline stood for a moment gazing at the half-open door. Even though it was Portia and Mary Gorman who'd caused the delay this time, the result was the same. She'd lost another few hours of the limited time remaining for her to complete her Vienna application. And amusing as he was, she would have appreciated it if Lord Zachary had given her requests a little more weight than he had Grace's plea for assistance in holding her hats.

Well, if he allowed himself to be pulled this way and that, it was his business, she supposed. Her life wasn't that aimless, thank God. She headed upstairs. She had a rough model of a man to assemble on paper.

As Sally Witfeld dragged him into the drawing room to show him off to the neighbors, Zachary glimpsed Caroline outside the door. He couldn't hear it over the din of female voices surrounding him, but he imagined she was pacing, angry that her family could be so frivolous as to want to spend an afternoon gossiping.

The rest of the Witfeld sisters didn't seem to have any problem with that pastime. It was becoming painfully obvious to him that what Caroline Witfeld truly needed was a hot, sweaty romp in the bedsheets. That should satisfy her unusual need for being occupied.

He shook himself. Christ. She was a friend of the family. Untouchable. And aside from that, it hadn't even occurred to her that he was a man until he'd bumbled in and kissed her.

"Is it true, my lord, that your sister just married the Marquis of Deverill?"

Before Zachary could answer the shy squeak of Mary Gorman, a half dozen Witfeld chits jumped in to do it for him. Sighing, he managed a smile he didn't feel. The Witfeld girls thought they knew him well enough to carry on his conversation for him. Perhaps they did. As far as he knew he didn't have any hidden depths. No one else thought he did, anyway. Caroline was no doubt finishing his likeness as he sat there. She probably didn't even require his presence. He glanced at Aunt Tremaine, to find her eyeing him over the rim of her teacup. "What?" he mouthed.

She lifted both eyebrows and returned to the conversation. Whatever she was up to, he didn't know, and likely didn't want to know.

What he did know was that these chits' lives must all have been astoundingly dull if they could find him so incredibly interesting.

Zachary seized on the thought. If it was true for the rest of the Witfeld girls, it was probably true for Caroline. She was bored, and being a slightly more discerning . . . breed than her sisters, she'd turned to art rather than clothes and gossip for something with which to occupy herself. He could certainly help her stay occupied.

A smile curved his mouth, and he hurriedly quashed it. *Stop it, Zach.* A bit of teasing and flirting was one thing, but he wouldn't stray beyond that.

What was it about her, anyway? Any of the other girls would literally bend over forwards or backwards to please him. Of course they would expect something in return—and that thing would be marriage. Perhaps that was the attraction of Caroline. She didn't want to marry. No traps, no entanglements. And her soft lips tasted like warm summer strawberries.

If *she* asked *him* to engage in a flirtation, hell, it would be un-gentlemanly to refuse a lady's request. So all he needed to do was to get her to view him as more than hands and ears and a painting on canvas. Taking another swallow of watery Madeira, Zachary surveyed the crowded room. According to his brother, by the time he returned to London he needed to have demonstrated that he could show some responsibility and patience. And simply escort-ing his aunt didn't seem likely to qualify. He was certain that was how Melbourne would see it.

There was, however, another possibility for him to prove him-self. Caroline wasn't the only one who could benefit from his presence. If any of the Witfeld girls wanted to marry—which they obviously did—someone was going to have to whip the household into shape.

He wondered what Wellington would make of seeing the Wit-feld house reform project on a Griffin resumé. This time Zachary couldn't help his grin. Hell, if he could organize the Witfelds, Bonaparte would be easy.

How to go about it, though?

At this point, the hows and wherefores really didn't even mat-ter. A Griffin had decided on a course of action; Griffins always succeeded in their endeavors, no matter how large or small. And this Griffin had a great deal to prove, both to his family and to himself. He was training a dog; this couldn't be any more diffi-cult.

A walking cane thwacked him on the knee, and Aunt Tremaine sank onto the couch beside him. "Ouch," he yelped, stifling the sound as best he could.

"I'm writing your brother tomorrow to tell him we'll be delay-ing here for a fortnight or so."

"That's fine," he returned in a low voice, nodding at something one of the twins was saying, though he didn't have a clue what she was jabbering about. "I don't actually think he cares where we are, as long as I don't have access to the Horse Guards in London."

"I'm not holding you prisoner," she returned, her voice tighter.

"You have a horse; ride back to London if that's where you want to be."

That would only demonstrate that Melbourne was right; he couldn't see any task through to its conclusion. And like a child he had to prove he could do one thing before he was allowed to try another. But none of that was his aunt's fault. With a deep breath Zachary reached over to cover her plump hand. "Melbourne assigned me a task. I'll see it through. Besides, I enjoy your company."

She smiled. "I am glad. I certainly enjoy yours."

Aside from that, if Zachary couldn't manage something as simple as tagging after Aunt Tremaine, Sebastian would move heaven and earth to prevent him from getting near a military uniform. "Then we leave together."

"I thought you'd be in raptures with so many young ladies fawning over you, anyway," Aunt Tremaine said, humor returning to her tone. "Are you certain they're not the reason you're so amenable to staying on?"

He eyed her. They were exactly why, but not for the reason she thought. Still . . . "Firstly, you told me to leave them be, and secondly, you said you weren't matchmaking."

"I'm not. I'm merely pointing out the merits of the local scenery. Scenery. For looking at."

"Yes, well, the scenery's lovely—and rather chatty. I can scarcely get a word in edgewise."

She laughed. "A rare phenomenon for you."

"Don't worry, Auntie. I have a plan."

It was her turn to become suspicious. "What sort of plan?"

"Never you mind. By the end of your visit, all of the Witfeld sisters will be thanking me."

"Zachary, that doesn't sound terribly promising."

One thing had swiftly become clear; Aunt Tremaine was genuinely fond of the Witfeld family. Good. She could report his success to Melbourne. "No worries. But you know how I enjoy a challenge."

"Oh, dear," she muttered.

Now that he had the beginnings of a plan, he wanted to get started with it. Dividing and conquering made the most sense—if he could manage to hold off the other half dozen or so long enough to accomplish anything with each of them individually.

"Zachary."

He started as the cane met his ankle. "What, damn it all?"

"Are you going to pose for Caroline's portrait?"

"I said I would," he returned, surreptitiously bending to rub his ankle. "She's already sketching my ears and my hands. She can't do my legs now, though, because you've broken them."

"Then pay attention when I'm talking to you, you silly boy."

"I can't if you kill me, you mad old woman." He kissed her on the cheek, then stood. Caroline had been correct about the benefits of at least pretending to drink a large amount of liquid. "Excuse me for a moment, ladies," he said to no one in particular, trying not to limp as he made his way to the door.

He'd barely exited into the hallway when a hand grabbed his arm and yanked him sideways.

Startled, he pulled free. "Caro—" he began, then snapped his mouth closed when he realized it wasn't her.

"Shh, lad," Mr. Witfeld whispered. "This way."

"But I—"

The family's patriarch gestured him toward the front door. "Come quickly, or they'll hunt you down."

Although he was fairly certain Mr. Witfeld was joking, Zachary couldn't help glancing over his shoulder as, with a slight grin, Barling the butler opened the door for them and they fled the house. Zachary had felt rather like a fox to the hounds since he'd arrived, after all.

"Thank you for the rescue."

"My pleasure. I promised you a tour of my inventions, anyway."

Ah, so this wasn't a rescue as much as it was a redirection. At least it was a little quieter, and it gave him time to begin thinking of a plan to help the Witfeld sisters. They crossed the front drive, and he looked up at the row of conservatory windows. Caroline wouldn't be gazing out at him, though; all of her attention would be on her sketch pad, on the flat, mono-colored pencil marks she'd spent the afternoon working on. Yes, she definitely needed his intervention, his mouth on hers and his hard cock inside her. *Jesus.* He shivered. *Concentrate, Zach. You're with the girl's damned father. And she has to ask.*

After an hour of viewing original Edmund Witfeld inventions, Zachary felt ready for someone to intervene on *his* behalf.

"It's a cow," Zachary stated, looking across the field.

"Yes, it is." Witfeld crossed his hands over the pommel of his saddle, pride in the straight line of his shoulders.

"Why are we looking at it?" Zachary asked.

"I bred her. She's half Guernsey and half South Devon, with some odd ancestry thrown in on her dam's side. She's my third try. I kept getting bulls. Excellent beef there, anyway." Edmund looked at the cow fondly for a moment, then visibly shook himself. "It's the milk. She gives twice as much as either of her parent breeds."

Thank God. Zachary had begun to think Edmund Witfeld was insane, and that they were going to spend the scant remaining daylight admiring a cow for no good reason. She did have nice tits, he supposed, but he preferred two rather than four, and that they not be covered with white fur or be hanging down into the grass.

He realized Witfeld was looking at him, and that he was supposed to say something admiring about the damned cow. "She looks very healthy," he ventured.

From the farmer's grin and nod, he'd said the right thing. "Yes, she is. I bred her with one of the half-and-half bulls. She gave me a heifer, thank Christ—ha, listen to me, hoping for more females— but it'll be more than a year before I can breed the offspring."

As they watched, a calf trotted out of the grass and began suckling. "Does your cow have a name?" Zachary queried, mostly because he thought the man would be disappointed if he didn't show some interest.

"Dimidius. It's Latin for 'half.' "

"Was that your eldest daughter's suggestion, by any chance?"

Witfeld chuckled. "Yes, it was, as a matter of fact. How did you know?"

"Just a lucky guess."

They sat on horseback for another few minutes gazing at Dimidius and the rest of the herd. Zachary did his best to feign interest in the red-and-white beast, but in truth he would rather have been sitting through one of Melbourne's dissertations on life and Society.

So far this afternoon he'd viewed a horse-drawn field seeder, a goat-powered winnower, the old failed egg ramps and the framework for the new ones, and a cow with excess milk and apparently good beef. He was an expert at pretending interest, but after sitting through the Witfeld-Gorman chit barrage and now this, he was hard-pressed not to yawn.

"We appreciate your helping Caroline," Witfeld said into the silence. "It's a lucky chance, you being here now."

"You can thank my aunt for my presence," Zachary returned. "But surely there are other volunteers or possible recruits for Miss Witfeld's work. She seems quite talented."

"Oh, aye, but that studio requires an aristocrat's portrait. And this part of Wiltshire suffers from an extreme drought of aristocracy, especially during the Season." He chuckled. "I wouldn't have her going into Bath, where the nobles there don't know her from Adam. And I know what they'd say, a young unmarried female soliciting a subject for a portrait."

Zachary cleared his throat. He'd made the same assumption himself. "But—"

"If it weren't for you, she'd be sketching Eades," her father continued, "and he favors dressing up as King Arthur."

"Fortunately I prefer to emulate the Egyptian gods," Zachary drawled.

Witfeld eyed him. "You're joking, aren't you?"

"Good God, yes."

"Thank goodness." The patriarch laughed.

"If I might ask, though, if an aristocrat is so integral, why *not* send her to Bath despite the snobbery, or to London, where they might be more open to sitting for a female artist? A sister could accompany her and lend some propriety."

Edmund's jaw twitched. "I wanted to, but the agreement between Mrs. Witfeld and myself was that unless we could send all of the girls to London for their Season and all that silliness, we couldn't send any of them. And whatever I might privately think, I don't want a half dozen girls at my throat."

Apparently a gentleman farmer, even a viscount's grandson like Witfeld, couldn't afford to give each of seven daughters her own debut in Society. Afraid that he'd offended Witfeld, Zachary prepared an apology for his thick-headed question. His host, though, was already beginning an explanation of the benefits of water over wind power in grinding grain.

When his own sister, Eleanor, had turned eighteen, her debut had rivaled that of royalty. The Griffins *were* royalty, as far as Society was concerned. Since he knew quite well that none of the Witfeld girls had ever been to London, Zachary had simply concluded that their odd parents had kept them away on purpose. Money and the lack thereof had never entered his mind. No wonder all of his siblings railed at him so often for being an idiot.

Of all the sisters, though, he would have tried to send Caroline. She so obviously wanted to be elsewhere, and so clearly craved a more metropolitan existence than the one available to her in Trowbridge. It rather forcefully made Zachary consider the difference between them, since over the course of his life he'd never been denied anything—except for a purpose. She had her purpose, and he seemed to be the only route for her to achieve it.

"We should probably be heading back to the house," Witfeld noted. "If I deny the girls a chance to charm you again over dinner, I'll never hear the end of it."

They rounded a wooded hill, coming out onto an open glade crossed by a picturesque creek. Squarely in the center of the meadow, a tumble of old broken marble arches and pillars, and a half-decayed wall of stone and granite and twisted ivy, caught the last of the sunlight. For an unsettled moment Zachary thought he'd somehow been whisked back to Greece in front of the Parthenon. "What—"

"Oh, those are my ruins," Witfeld said, pride edging his voice again. "What do you think? They're still a work in progress, of course."

"They're . . . ancient-looking," Zachary offered, blinking. Now that he looked more closely, he could make out the artful arrangement of the broken structure, the carefully placed vines and clusters of ferns. Apparently Witfeld had succumbed to the current fad of creating antiquity.

"Thank you. Would you call them Roman, or Greek?"

Zachary mentally flipped a coin. "Greek," he decided.

"Excellent. You have a good eye, my lord."

"Zachary, please." After all, he'd been contemplating seducing the man's eldest daughter—or rather, convincing her to ask him to seduce her.

"Edmund, then."

"So, Edmund, do you think Mrs. Gorman and Miss Mary will be staying on for dinner?"

"Good Lord, I hope not," the Witfeld patriarch said vehemently.

During the course of this odd afternoon, one thing had become obvious. Edmund Witfeld had elevated the chore of avoiding his hen-filled household to an eccentric, all-consuming art. Zachary sent him a sideways glance as they returned to the manor house. Of all the members of the Witfeld family, Edmund might very well prove to be the most grateful for his little plan to teach the Witfeld sisters the art of being marriageable.

Chapter 7

Caroline softened the line of Lord Zachary's jaw with the tip of one finger. She'd begun today's session with more practice draw-ings of his hands, but she knew how to draw fingers and thumbs; other than length and breadth, they didn't vary much between one subject and the next. Faces, though, and eyes, especially—those were unique. And uniquely . . . interesting where her latest sub-ject was concerned.

She feathered in a line of hair obscuring one half-drawn eye. Immediately the drawing became more like Zachary. "There you are," she murmured.

It was him, but at the same time it wasn't. She had the shape of his face, a vague placement of his mouth and nose and eyes, but as she gazed at the flat paper she realized that at the same time the drawing was nothing like him. There was a . . . a light missing, not just in his eyes, but in the whole expression of his face. Hm. She'd never felt that before; when she'd drawn a good likeness, she'd captured the person. This was different. It felt different, even in the light, lifting sensation that came over her when she drew. This time, as always, it was anticipation to see what would appear, but she also felt a large measure of excitement. Arousal. Something—

The conservatory door burst open. Caroline nearly jumped out of her skin as her mother hurried inside. "Mama! What's wrong?"

"He's not in here," Sally Witfeld announced, then vanished again, banging the door closed behind her.

For a moment Caroline stared at the door. "What . . ." Scowling, she set her sketch pad aside and stood. "What's going on?" she called, pulling open the door again and stepping into the hallway.

Anne hurried past her. "Mama thinks someone's kidnaped Lord Zachary."

"Kidnaped?" Caroline repeated, her heart stopping for a panicked second. Who would she paint? How would she find the elusive bit of him that she needed to make the portrait work? Then logic flooded back in, along with the realization that she was perhaps being a bit self-centered. "Why in the world would Mama think that?"

"He vanished out of the drawing room three hours ago, and no one's seen him since."

"He better not have returned to London," Caroline said grimly. If that were the case, she *would* wish him kidnaped. "Is his horse still here?"

Anne's lips twitched. "Oh, dear. You don't think they kidnaped poor Sagramore, too, do you?"

Caroline eyed her, immediately suspicious. "You know something. What is it, darling?"

"Well, since Papa's vanished as well, I think the two of them are out in a field somewhere, looking at cows. Or *a* cow, rather."

"Did you tell Mama your theory?" Caroline asked, falling into step beside her younger sister.

"Mama doesn't want to hear my opinion. She wants to panic and let everyone know that she'll simply die if something's happened to Lord Zachary. Lady Gladys is doing embroidery."

Ah. "Well, panicking isn't very helpful, but it is one of Mama's favorite things to do." Sally Witfeld had seven unmarried daughters; she not only thrived on chaos, but she also tended to encourage it. "Shall we go out to the stable and see whether Papa's horse has been kidnaped, as well? Surely Nelson wouldn't go without a fight."

"And there is of course Harold, who is apparently in the garden eating Mama's geraniums."

"Hm. Perhaps we should save the duke's brother first, and then send *him* to rescue the flowers."

"A splendid idea." Anne grinned outright. "You realize we might become heroines for locating the lost prince."

With a snort Caroline gestured her down the stairs. "I'll risk being worshiped, if it means we can avoid having to carry Mama upstairs to her bed."

While the rest of their siblings and half the household staff ran about like headless chickens, she and Anne slipped out the front door and ran, laughing, for the stables. Caroline reached the wide double doors first and looked back to announce her victory in the race—then slammed straight into a broad, hard chest.

"Oh!" She would have fallen on her backside, but Lord Zachary grabbed her by the shoulders. "I'm so sorry!"

She tried to ignore the way his palms brushed along her arms as he set her upright again. His interest in her was so . . . disconcerting; and it was something she couldn't ignore, considering the close proximity in which her own request had put them. But his interest didn't explain hers.

"No worries," he returned, his eyes dancing as though he knew precisely the effect he had on her. Of course he did, blast him.

"We were looking for you, Lord Zachary," Anne panted, giving Caroline the moment she needed to recover her composure and her balance.

Their father emerged from the stable behind the duke's brother. "Zachary asked to see some of my inventions."

More likely her father had suggested that they go on a tour, and their guest had exhibited more of his annoying tendency to be easygoing and had agreed. *Wonderful.* Now Caroline had all six of her sisters *and* her father vying for her portrait subject's attention.

Zachary's expression didn't even twitch at her father's statement. "Edmund has done some remarkable work."

"Well, thank you, lad."

"Mama thought Lord Zachary had been kidnaped," Anne put in, not trying to hide her amusement.

"Bloody hell," Edmund grumbled. "We'd best return you, then, or I'll never hear the damned end of it."

No, he wouldn't. And he'd probably actually done Lord Zachary a favor by aiding his escape from the Witfeld-Gorman assault. Caroline thought quickly. "Perhaps Lord Zachary could explain that his journey from London left him more fatigued than he realized, and he required a breath of fresh air."

Zachary eyed her. " 'Fatigued,' " he repeated dubiously.

"Oh, yes, horribly so. And perhaps fighting an aching head that would have left him bedridden for weeks, completely unable to attend any social events."

His jaw twitched. "I was nearly dead, obviously." Zachary drew a breath. "Thank goodness the Wiltshire air is so . . ."

"Restoring," Caroline suggested, grinning. Good. He understood how much more harmonious the evening would be if he took the blame for his absence.

"As I knew it would be," Edmund added, sending both her and Zachary a grateful look.

"You're a genius," Anne whispered, hugging Caroline around the shoulders as they returned to the house.

"Just practical." She sighed. "You'd best include Papa on your chart."

"Don't worry, Caro. I'll try to give you time in the mornings so you'll have the light."

"Thank you." She returned her attention to the man walking directly in front of her. "By the by, Lord Zachary, your dog is eating our garden."

"Is he? Damnation. I told Reed to keep an eye on him."

"Oh. I was under the impression that Harold was *your* dog."

He sent her a sharp look over his shoulder as she stifled an abrupt frown. She really needed to learn to quell her retorts before they reached her tongue.

"He *is* my dog. I'll train him away from flowers this afternoon."

"In one afternoon?" she returned, trying to sound curious and admiring rather than skeptical.

"I've trained horses," he said, sounding the slightest bit defensive. "A pup should be easier."

She had her doubts about that, but obviously she'd already said enough. After all, Zachary was doing both her and her father a favor. "Much easier, I'm certain," she agreed, carefully keeping her expression innocent as he glanced at her again.

"Precisely."

As Barling opened the front door to welcome them into the house, Sally Witfeld was descending the main staircase. Her shriek made Caroline wince; she could only imagine what Zachary must be thinking.

"Lord Zachary! Thank the dear heavens! We all thought you must have been murdered!" With a gasp, Mrs. Witfeld sank onto the bottom step in a swoon.

"Oh, good God. I'll be in my office," her husband muttered, grasping Caroline's elbow, then releasing her again as he vanished.

For a brief moment it looked as though Zachary meant to follow, but with a visible squaring of his shoulders he stepped forward and brushed the gathering sisters out of the way. "Ladies, allow me."

"But Lord Zach—"

Amid the protests and statements of admiration he hauled Sally Witfeld into his arms and carried her up the stairs. As he reached the second floor, Caroline realized she was staring—staring at the muscles playing beneath his tight buckskin trousers, at the obvious strength in his broad shoulders.

She swallowed. Obviously she needed to know a little more about the male form beneath the layers of jacket and cravat before she could do the portrait justice. This wasn't just any painting. And it wasn't about the surface, after all; it was about showing the man, and who he was. And this man was strong enough to carry her substantial mother up a flight of stairs.

Shaking herself, Caroline hurried to join the procession heading for her mother's bedchamber. No one chose to inform Lord Zachary that his actions were probably unnecessary; Sally Witfeld saw the need to faint on a fairly regular basis. But if he'd known that, they wouldn't have been treated to that impressive display.

As Caroline topped the stairs, a hand grasped her arm. "Caro," Lady Gladys said, slinging her cane over her free arm and leaning on her new assistant.

"I hope Mama hasn't alarmed you, Lady Gladys. This isn't an uncommon occurrence."

Lady Gladys chuckled. "At finishing school some of the other girls and I made your mother a pillow and awarded it to her for being the best fainter in residence."

Caroline smiled despite herself. "You didn't."

"Oh, yes we did. Do you think we should inform my nephew?"

"He does seem rather proud of himself."

"I suppose you're right. It won't do to discourage him from heroic acts." A shadow crossed the older woman's face. "Though maybe we should," she said more quietly.

Intrigued, Caroline slowed their pace. "What do you mean?"

Gladys drew a breath. "Oh, he has it in his head that he wants to join Wellington on the Peninsula."

That explained his desire for a portrait of himself in military uniform. "He is the third brother, is he not?"

"Yes, he is. But—" Lady Gladys broke off. "It's a very long story, and not one meant for today. We should probably fetch the smelling salts."

With those intriguing words echoing about in her mind, Caroline led the way to one of the servants' closets and found the right bottle. So Zachary wanted to join the army, and at least one member of his family didn't want him to. From his comments about his brothers' reactions to seeing him in a military uniform, several members of his family were against his decision.

Well, she could certainly sympathize with him wanting to do something his family didn't understand or appreciate. But that didn't make them alike. After all, she was taking steps to follow her dreams. Lord Zachary didn't appear to be doing anything but escorting his aunt on holiday and raising the level of chaos in her already unruly home.

What was it about him, then, that intrigued her so much? Yes, he had beautiful eyes and a handsome face and a lean, athletic frame. And yes, he seemed to have the ability to make her laugh when she meant to be serious, and banter when she knew she should be quiet. Caroline closed her eyes for a moment as her mother's maid appeared to administer the smelling salts. She had no control over what he did or who he was or what he wanted. All she knew was what she wanted—and that was to paint his portrait and submit it to Vienna before the deadline. Nothing else mattered. Not even his kisses.

Zachary stepped out of the way as the herd of females rushed in to administer aid to their mama. Personally he thought they were overreacting; on the way up to her bedchamber Mrs. Witfeld had adjusted the drape of her skirt twice.

Aunt Tremaine was obviously fond of Sally Witfeld, but from Zachary's perspective the Witfeld matriarch wasn't doing her daughters any favors. Some gentlemen of his acquaintance preferred delicate, fainting females, but he couldn't think of one soul who would voluntarily ally himself in marriage with a chit prone to scenes and hysterics.

He took another step backward, toward the edge of the room. All the daughters had gathered and were busily expressing varying degrees of concern over their apparently unconscious mother. The twins, Joanna and Julia, both waved fans over her face. Violet, the youngest, held her limp hand, while Susan and Grace argued over whether Mary Gorman should be permitted to dance with him at the ball. Closest to the door and furthest from the chaos Anne looked amused, while beside her Caroline's expression was more difficult to read.

As he watched, she turned her head and caught his gaze. At first he thought she must be embarrassed, but that was wrong, he realized. It was resignation he saw in her eyes. She'd probably lived through this same scene a hundred times, and she knew all the lines and had played all the parts. Yes, he enjoyed chaos, but obviously she at least on occasion found it troublesome. And that bothered him, despite her skepticism over his ability to train Harold.

Moving quietly so he wouldn't attract any of the female attention, he made his way over beside her. "So I looked at the *Mona Lisa* for nearly an hour," he said in a low tone, "and I finally realized what it was that kept my attention."

"And what was that?" she whispered, edging closer.

The hair on his arms lifted. "She knew something," he made himself continue in the same easy tone. "Some sort of secret. I could see it in her eyes, and I just had this feeling that if I looked for long enough I would be able to figure it out."

"Did you figure it out, then?"

"No. And that's the thing; no one will ever figure it out. But we'll all keep looking and wondering."

For a moment Caroline looked at *him*. "That's what I've always thought great works of art should do. It's not the painting or the sculpture itself that matters; it's what the work encourages the viewer to feel."

If he'd tried to have this conversation with any of his siblings—even Eleanor—they would have laughed or come to the conclusion that the *Mona Lisa* must have reminded him of some chit he'd pursued. Not only did Caroline Witfeld listen, though, but she also understood. And at the moment, he very much wanted to kiss her.

"Oh, oh!" Sally Witfeld struggled to sit upright while her daughters piled a mountain of pillows behind her. "I saw . . . I had a vision that Lord Zachary was safe."

"He *is* safe, Mama," Violet said, patting her mother's hand. "He carried you upstairs."

"Such gallantry! Girls, isn't he gallant? And so strong!"

And he'd nearly broken his damned back. Zachary stepped forward. Time to do his part for Witfeld family harmony. "I'm pleased to see you're recovering, and I apologize if I distressed you." He glanced sideways at Caroline. "The trip from London tired me more than I realized, and I badly needed some fresh air."

"Poor lad," Aunt Tremaine said succinctly behind him, but he ignored her. Except for Caroline and Anne, no one could hear his aunt anyway with all the commiseration going on, and they knew the real story.

He sketched a quick bow. "And now if you'll excuse me, I have a dog to see to."

That was only one of his tasks this afternoon. He also had to come up with a campaign to render seven—no, six—rather silly sisters marriageable.

Harold still pranced about the garden. He was easy to track; small piles of uprooted flowers followed a rough line around the entire perimeter. In the south corner, his valet tugged on one end of a branch while the dog yanked at the other.

"Reed!" Zachary called, and the valet straightened.

"My lord! This . . . I'm sorry, my lord, but if you insist that I continue to watch over this animal, I must regretfully tender you my resignation."

"What? Nonsense. You've dealt with me for years. A dog is—"

"My lord, with all due respect, I do not think that is a dog. It is a demon. And I—"

Awkwardly Zachary put a hand on his valet's bony shoulder. "No worries, Reed. Go inside and have a cup of tea; I'll see to Harold."

"I will understand, sir, if you don't want me to continue in your employ."

"I don't intend to speak of this again. Harold is in need of some instruction. I will give it to him, and until then any and all nonsense from the dog is my fault; not yours. Is that clear?"

"Y-yes, my lord. Thank you."

Once the valet had gone, Zachary looked down at Harold. "You nearly cost me a fine valet," he said.

Harold wagged his tail and woofed.

"Yes, that's all well and good, but we are going to get some things straight. Come along."

He patted his thigh, leading the way across the garden. When he turned around, though, Harold's face was buried in a loose pile of daisies.

"Harold, no!"

The dog looked up at him, wagging again. This was going to be interesting. He'd trained horses to race, but they'd already been broken to the saddle and knew right from left and how to trot and gallop on command. Harold obviously knew nothing about being a proper dog.

"Come here, Harold. Come." He patted his thigh again.

This time he wasn't even surprised when Harold rolled onto his back and kicked his feet in the air. Damnation. When Melbourne had told him to get a dog, he'd been so angry and frustrated that he'd gone to the first source he'd thought of: Lord Rothary and his hunting bitch, who'd apparently gone off with a neighbor's mutt. It hadn't even occurred to him that the unwanted pup would be completely untrained. So now he had two problems—an untrained dog, and a growing suspicion that his brother knew him far better than he would have liked.

"Let's go in, Harold. We'll try this again tomorrow, when I've had time to develop a training strategy." And in the meantime he would hope that the Witfeld sisters would be easier to manage than a half-breed hunting dog.

Chapter 8

Caroline came downstairs in the morning to a tumult of activity. For a brief, startled moment it looked as though Witfeld Manor was being gutted and evacuated. Well, that figured—the sisters had been up until midnight deciding their schedule with Lord Zachary. She had won two hours with him this morning, and now more chaos had erupted to rob her of that scant time. Just as she drew a breath to call for Barling and request an explanation for the eruption, her mother came into view. Apparently recovered from her fainting spell, Sally Witfeld stood at the entrance to the morning room in deep discussion with Mr. Henneker, the local florist.

"What's this?" a deep, masculine voice drawled from a few stairs above her.

A shiver ran down her spine. "Preparations for your soiree, I would imagine," she answered.

"Isn't that eight days away?" His white cravat starched and tied to perfection and beautifully contrasting his dark brown jacket and deep yellow waistcoat, Zachary looked like he had just strolled out of one of the finest drawing rooms in London. Perfect, perfect, perfect. Perhaps they could skip breakfast, and she would have an extra thirty minutes to work with him. She scarcely remembered to eat when she became engrossed in her work, anyway. With an easy grin he leaned a hip along the balustrade above her.

"Yes, but it's only four days after the soiree at the Trowbridge assembly rooms. Mama has to surpass every other event in Wiltshire this Season."

"This really isn't necessary, you know. I could say something."

"You'd only be insulting her." Fond as she was of her family, she found the entire thing maddening. She'd been handed an ultimatum, told that after this summer her family could and would no longer support her. And then she had to watch while the household spent a cartload of money honoring Lord Zachary and impressing the neighboring gentry even as they monopolized their guest to the point of preventing her from achieving her goal.

Of course her mother thought one of her daughters was bound to make a match with Lord Zachary Griffin, which would, of course, be worth the most extravagant effort and expense. And Caroline knew just as surely that Sally Witfeld was wrong. Ladies with much deeper pockets, more noble blood, and much more devious and practiced charms had undoubtedly been attempting the same thing for years—and obviously without success.

"Miss Witfeld?"

She blinked. "Apologies, my lord. I was lost in thought."

He descended another step to lounge beside her. "About anything in particular?"

About dreams in danger of being dashed upon the rocks. "About your portrait, of course."

Zachary grinned. "Of course. Your focus is admirable."

Though normally she would have considered that a compliment, she was fairly certain he didn't mean it that way. "I think I'll do you in full figure, rather than just your head and shoulders."

"I was hoping you hadn't been studying my hands for nothing."

His hands, his shoulders, his mouth . . . Caroline blinked. "Would you sit for me this morning?"

"Certainly. Your sisters won't mind?"

Oh, they minded, but they wouldn't defy the schedule on the first day. "Not at all, I'm certain."

"Then after breakfast I'm all yours."

Drat. "*After* break—"

"Good morning, Lord Zachary, Caro," Sally Witfeld broke in, waving a hand at them. "What do you think? Mr. Henneker has yellow lilies."

As her mother approached, Zachary straightened, sketching his polite bow. "Yellow lilies sound splendid."

"Yes, I thought so. Now we'll need yellow ribbons to match. Or do you think white ribbons would be more elegant?"

White ribbons would look like a wedding. "Yellow, definitely, Mama."

"I was asking Lord Zachary, dear."

He cleared his throat. "Yellow would be more festive, I think."

"Good, good. Mr. Henneker is—"

"I think he's leaving, Mama." If her mother pulled Zachary into a conversation about soiree decorations, Caroline would lose all the morning light before she managed to get him into the conservatory. Moving quickly, she wrapped her fingers around his sleeve of brown superfine. "We were just going in to breakfast."

She gave a tug, and Zachary immediately fell into step beside her as Sally Witfeld went chasing after the florist. At least Caroline's subject seemed to be quick to catch onto things—though she'd begun to think that he simply enjoyed eating.

He slowed as they entered the breakfast room. "Has everyone gone to find decorations?" he asked, gesturing at the empty room. Not even a footman remained to restock the sideboard.

"Mama hasn't informed them of her color choice yet," she returned. From the quantity of food remaining on the sideboard, though, it appeared that most of her sisters had already eaten. Good. No one to make a request that might pull Lord Zachary away from sitting for her. "I'm sure they're on their way to town to purchase invitations or more bonnets or something." It sounded more tart than she intended, but she knew for certain that each sister was somewhere plotting how best to spend her allotted time with Zachary in order to net him as a husband. And the poor fellow hadn't a clue.

"All of them needed bonnets? Again?"

Caroline set an orange on her plate to accompany a slice of toast and cheese. "I expect you miss all the attention they pay you," she said as she took a seat.

Zachary stopped midway to dumping a half dozen slices of ham on his already heaping plate. "Well, that's a comment I can't respond to, isn't it?"

"What do you mean?"

He sat beside her despite the plethora of empty chairs in the room. "If I agree that I miss the attention, then I'm a conceited lout. If I protest that I'm pleased your sisters are elsewhere, then I'm an ungrateful lout." He took a drink of his tea. "Damn, I forgot the sugar."

"I'll fetch it."

Pressing her arm to keep her in her chair, Lord Zachary rose. "Nonsense. So which am I?"

"Beg pardon?"

"Conceited or ungrateful? Which am I?"

Caroline snorted, belatedly covering her mouth. "A question *I* can't answer, I'm afraid."

"You are correct. Not if you want my image to grace your painting." He crossed behind her, putting the sugar bowl between them. "Sugar?"

She'd already added a lump but found herself nodding anyway. "One, please."

He complied, hardly splashing any tea over the rim of her cup. He would never be successful as a hostess. Neither, though, would she; the ability to gracefully arrange biscuits seemed the height of absurdity. She watched as he dumped one, two, three lumps of sugar into his own brew, tasted it, and added another.

"May I ask you a question?" he said, setting the sugar bowl away from his elbow.

"Of course." Caroline made a show of buttering her toast, but in truth she felt terribly distracted this morning. She could blame it on the two coming soirees, or the fine weather, or worry over the looming deadline in Vienna, but she wasn't a believer in fooling herself. She was distracted by the tall, dark-haired man beside her who was currently shoveling bites of ham into his mouth as if he expected never to see food again. How could she draw his hunger for life?

He swallowed a mouthful. "Your interest in painting. Is it something you realized recently, or have you always known you wanted to be a portraitist?"

She listened for the usual condescension or snide humor, but it seemed completely lacking. Zachary Griffin's interest was apparently sincere. "I've always loved to draw and paint. Papa arranged for me to have a tutor, but that was after I took it up on my own. I'm afraid the old nursery room walls will never be the same."

He chuckled. "When did you decide that painting would be your profession, rather than something you did for personal enjoyment?"

For a moment Caroline glanced at her hands. "Are you of the school which believes a woman's sole duty is to marry and have children?"

"Did I say anything of the kind? You're very testy for someone who supposedly needs to show patience and meticulous attention to detail in order to be successful."

Despite the intentional baiting, she doubted he would appreciate hearing her undiluted opinion. She'd seen him attempting to train his dog yesterday. He had no patience at all. "You are very trying."

"So I am." He cleared his throat. "I admit, what I'd really like to know is if you'd had your Season in London, would you still wish to be a painter?"

"Would you ask the same question of a barrister or a barrel-maker?"

"If I was curious about the answer, I might."

"Hm. Let's just say, then, that this is another question I can't answer, since I wish to put your image on canvas."

He laughed, the sound surprising in its easy merriment. "That's clear enough. I've seen that look in my sister's eyes, though usually it's followed by her attempting to box my ears."

For the first time Caroline thought it might not have been so terrible to have a brother in the household—though at the same time she was forced to admit to herself that she did not look at Zachary Griffin in a brotherly manner. Not in the least.

According to Zachary's brother Charlemagne, Miss Witfeld would be a bluestocking—or, rather, a *damned* bluestocking. Shay liked educated women, but Caroline's intense focus probably would have disconcerted even him.

Zachary eyed her as she bent her head over her sketch pad and drew some part or other of him. A strand of her auburn hair fell forward into her eyes, and she absently blew it out of her way. He wanted to curl it back behind her ear with his fingers. No, she didn't look like a bluestocking, or at least not what he would expect one to look like; she had a tall, slim figure and lively green eyes, and a wit that definitely kept him, a master of quips, on his toes.

But in other ways, her species was unmistakable. She spurned the idea of marriage and seemed to view the idea of having a London Season with nothing less than contempt. Most telling of all, Caroline Witfeld wished to have a career that would render her financially independent.

She glanced up, catching his gaze. Swiftly she returned to her sketch, but not before he glimpsed the amusement in her eyes. "There's no reason you can't move again today," she said, erasing a line with the tip of one finger. "You're going to strain your eyes, trying to look about like that."

"Fine." With a breath he sank back against the window seat. "I'm only trying to help."

"Haven't you been painted before? Beechey or Lawrence?"

"Apparently I sat for Joshua Reynolds when I was two years old. Sebastian says I piss—" He cleared his throat. "According to the tale I didn't behave myself very well."

"I see. Well, now you're a bit older, and you may move about. I want to get a sense of movement from you, anyway. Muscle and bone."

He flexed an arm beneath his jacket. "All I see is my clothes wrinkling."

"I can also see the places where your clothes don't wrinkle."

Zachary began a quip, then closed his mouth. Still, he could push things a little—no one could be that oblivious to attraction. "You've seen your own bare arms, I assume. Does that help you in your paintings of women?"

"Yes, of course, but—"

Standing, he slid the snug-fitting jacket from his shoulders and dropped it onto the window seat.

"You can't—I—put that back on!"

Keeping a solemn expression on his face, Zachary unbuttoned his shirt cuffs and began rolling up his sleeves. He couldn't resist baiting her; with her serious mask and serious goals, she made it so damned easy. "Don't worry; I won't strip." He grinned. "Unless you ask me to, of course."

She stood, backing away. "I must insist, Lord Zachary. This is not appro . . ."

He pretended to ignore her protest, though he heard every syllable of it—and the changing tone of her voice. And he abruptly realized that he'd opened a very complicated basket of oranges. As he rolled his sleeves to his elbows and sat again, she set aside her sketch pad and approached.

By stripping his arms bare he was inviting her to view him as the model for male perfection. He didn't consider himself a slouch by any means, and he'd never had any complaints from female acquaintances, but Caroline Witfeld was an artist. A talented one, from what he'd seen. She studied the human form more critically than the average chit.

And aside from that, he'd developed an odd and uncharacteristic attraction toward her, and he'd promised his aunt he would behave himself—which in his mind meant that Caroline would have to make the approach. He lowered his lashes and looked up at her.

"I've always wondered," Caroline said, stopping in front of him, her gaze on his arms rather than his face, "why females are encouraged to show their arms and their throats, and men are expected to cover nearly every inch of themselves with cloth."

"Honestly?" he returned, studying the open, interested expression in her pretty eyes. "Women are on display; men are doing the shopping and purchasing."

Slowly she reached out to run a finger along the outside of his hand, past his wrist and up to his elbow. "I suppose you're right," she said, "but I'm discovering that there is something to be said for a revealed mystery over an overly exposed stretch of skin."

He wasn't so certain of that, but he wasn't going to argue. Not when her light fingers across his skin sent his blood racing along the same course. For a brief moment he wondered who might be seducing whom, but one look at the absorbed expression on her face answered that. At the moment he was an arm: sinew and bone, as she'd said.

"So what do you think?" he finally asked.

Caroline blinked. "It's . . . you . . . you have a nice arm," she finally stammered, backing away.

Working to regain his ease, he lifted the appendage in question. " 'Nice'?" he repeated, twisting his arm this way and that. "Why not 'handsome' or 'fit' or 'muscular'?"

She snorted. It was a small, absurdly delicate sound of ill-concealed humor that over the past few days he'd become extremely attuned to. "It is a handsome arm," she amended. "And I suppose it's muscular, though too many muscles in your forearm would just look silly. Muscles are supposed to be in a man's shoulders, are they not? And the thighs, for riding?"

Zachary lifted an eyebrow. "So in your opinion my forearm is spindly."

"No! I—"

"I can't have you disparaging the rest of me," he interrupted, going to work unbuttoning his waistcoat. Aside from amusement, this was beyond embarking on a seduction. This was about defending his manhood and virility.

"Good heavens! Don't—"

"Don't you wish to know if your assumptions are correct?

What if my shoulders are in worse condition than my arms? No doubt you'd wish to find someone else to paint."

"You're teasing me, Zachary," she stated, her color high. "Now sit still and let me sketch you."

"But you told me I didn't need to sit still. I'm only trying to help." He dropped his waistcoat on his jacket and tugged at the intricate knot of his cravat.

Caroline glanced at the mantel clock. "Very well. In the name of art."

He stopped, deeply surprised. "Really?"

"Unless you believe your shoulders won't pass muster."

Oh, that was enough of that. He was supposed to be doing the teasing. And whatever this was about now, he wasn't backing down. "I've been told I'm quite fit, thank you very much. I box, and fence. And ride, of course." He tugged on the knot at his throat again. Damn Reed. The man could find employment securing executioners' nooses.

"Do you need help?" she asked, folding her arms.

Obviously he'd made some poor assumptions where Caroline Witfeld was concerned. She wasn't a fainting violet, and if she *was* a bluestocking, she was not any sort he'd ever heard of. Most of those chits couldn't converse with a man without arguing, and the idea of one stripping in front of them would have caused them to drop dead. Caroline didn't look dead; not even close. Rather, she picked up her pencil and pad again and began sketching him as he yanked at his cravat.

A door closed down the hall, and he froze. "We're not going to be interrupted, are we?" All he needed was for one of the household to barge in while he stood in the bow window with his shirt off. He'd be married by sunset.

Her glance took in the clock again. "No. Not for twenty minutes."

"And how do you know that?"

Caroline cocked her head at him. "Are you nervous? This was your suggestion, my lord. Zachary."

So now she was enjoying herself. And he was annoyed. With a

last pull he freed himself from the cravat and tossed it onto the growing pile of his clothes. Then he tugged his shirttail free of his trousers and yanked it off over his head. "No, I'm not nervous," he said, belatedly unrolling the tight left sleeve so he could get it off his arm. *Dammit.* "Are you?"

"No."

For a long moment, Caroline simply looked at him. *Oh, my goodness,* she thought. She'd seen drawings of famous statues, of David and some of the Greek nudes. In theory she knew how a man was constructed, but seeing one literally in the flesh—the play of his shoulder muscles as he pulled the last bit of sleeve off his wrist, the definition of muscle down his abdomen and disappearing into his trousers—made her forget to breathe.

Dark gray eyes watched her, a mix of humor and even a dare in his gaze. Was he wondering whether she would faint? She had no intention of doing so. As much trouble as this could be, she was, after all, an artist. And she wasn't going to miss the opportunity— probably her best opportunity—to view the male form.

"Spindly?" he asked.

"No. You're beautiful. Or handsome, rather—as my sisters would insist."

"As long as it's a compliment, I'm not going to be missish about it," he returned, chuckling.

Taking a breath, Caroline did a few quick pencil strokes of shoulder and chest, of lean, hard muscle. Her fingers shook a little—not with nerves but because she wanted to touch him. "Would you turn a circle?"

The smile touching his mouth deepened. Arms held away from his sides, he did a slow turn in the reflected sunlight. She flexed her fingers, clutching the pencil and trying to concentrate on form and movement rather than the man. *Draw, Caroline, draw.*

Propriety said that she should have run from the room the moment he shed his jacket. It also said they would be forced to marry if anyone happened into the room. She swallowed, nervous, and . . . and aroused. Alive. Tingling.

"What?" he asked, facing her again.

"What do you mean, 'what?' " she asked, setting her pad on the window seat beside his shirt and jacket.

"You were frowning. I saw you reflected in the window glass."

Wonderful. The only thing worse than forgetting oneself was being caught at it. "Oh. I was thinking of something else," she managed.

" 'Something else'? *Now?* What, pray tell?"

Caroline cleared her throat. "Never mind. May I?"

"I told you I was at your disposal."

Willing her fingers to stop trembling, she touched his left shoulder. Broad and muscled—velvet with iron beneath, she decided, stroking her palm along his shoulder blade. She'd thought he must wear padding to accent his shoulders, since that was very much the fashion, but obviously his form was all his own.

He stood very still and thankfully seemed to have decided not to comment on the situation. It was difficult enough to convince her mind to stay on the task at hand, and not swirl and dive toward the conclusion that if the bared portions of his body were so fine, the rest of him must be equally handsome.

Slowly she moved around him, feeling the solid warmth of his skin, the curve of the pectoral muscles across his breast. *Magnificent.* She ran a finger down his sternum, and he jumped a little. Abruptly he grabbed her hand and took a step backward.

"What is it?" she asked, looking at his face and trying to blink away the unexpectedly dazed sensation clouding her mind.

His breathing seemed a little harsh. "I thought I heard the stairs squeak."

Caroline looked at the clock again. According to Anne's schedule she still had nine minutes. And she wasn't finished with touching him. "No, I think you're mistaken, Zachary. Would you flex your arm?"

"No. I mean—That is, I truly think I heard something."

He turned around, facing the windows and fumbling sideways to grab his shirt and yank it over his head. She watched him for a moment, trying to attribute the keen disappointment running through her to being denied a thorough look at her model rather than to the fact that she wasn't finished running her fingers along his skin.

But if he'd actually heard someone approaching—of course he didn't want to be trapped into marrying a country chit just because he'd been teased into doing her a favor. And neither did she wish to end up married to him—not under those circumstances. She shook herself as she retrieved her pad and paper. Not under *any* circumstances, because a wife, a Griffin wife, would never be allowed to have employment—especially employment where she would be taking orders from someone else and perhaps spending extended periods with gentlemen not her husband.

Then she heard the familiar creak at the top of the landing. "Oh, no," she whispered. He was right, and his next appointment was early. She snatched up his jacket and tossed it at the back of his head. "Hurry up!"

"Stop trying to smother me," he muttered, sending a glare over his shoulder at her. He put the jacket down again as he buttoned his waistcoat. "I'm going as quickly as I can."

He managed to shrug on his coat just as the conservatory door burst open. "Your time is up, Caro," Susan announced, otherwise ignoring her sister. She pranced up to Zachary and made a curtsy. "Would you care to take a turn about the garden with me, Lord Zachary?"

With barely a glance at Caroline, he offered his arm to Susan. "A bit of fresh air would be most welcome," he said grandly.

Caroline watched them out the conservatory door, then plunked herself down on her stool again. Goodness. That had been perhaps the most unique and memorable sitting in her life. And while she'd been interested, she hadn't expected to feel so . . . flushed. Hot. Flustered.

She took a deep breath, shaking herself. She hadn't done much sketching, either. Damnation. If she didn't stop this nonsense of being distracted, she would have no one to blame for her failure but herself.

With his form, his gaze, fresh in her mind, she began to draw feverishly. It was a picture she'd never share with anyone, but she needed to do it or she'd never be able to paint Zachary Griffin with his clothes on.

Zachary glanced up at the conservatory window as he and Susan passed beneath it, but he couldn't tell if Caroline might be looking out at them or not. Probably not, since gazing outside at the world would take time away from her painting. But whether she was aware of more than paints or not, he certainly was. Good God. He'd nearly popped the fastenings of his trousers with her running her hands across him.

"I quite think this is the loveliest weather we've had all summer," Susan said into the quiet of birdsong and distant cattle lowing.

He tried to pull his thoughts back to his current companion. "It's very nice," he agreed. "Might I ask, what did you mean a few moments ago when you told Miss Witfeld that her time was up?"

She waved a hand at him. "Oh, Caro only had until nine o'clock, and she knew it. But if I hadn't gone to fetch you, she would have kept you up there with her silly sketching all morning."

After another five minutes of muscle feeling, the sketching would have been finished with and they both would have been naked. "So you wanted to go walking with me at nine o'clock?"

"No, I wanted the time at noon so that we could have a picnic, but stupid Anne took that. It's only because she made up the schedule and took the best times. And of course she gave almost every morning to Caro."

This was beginning to make sense. "Who's my next sister, then?"

Susan made a face. "Julia, at half past ten. She'll probably want to go into town with you to purchase more hats. She's mad for hats."

They'd decided to divide him up, then. He should have been angry that Witfeld Manor's entire female population viewed him as a game bird to be captured, sliced into equally apportioned pieces, and devoured. Today, though, it was handy. He'd been wondering how in the world he would be able to separate the sisters long enough to get a word in edgewise. Best get started with Susan, then, if he only had ninety minutes with her this morning. "With all of you here at Witfeld," he began, "I imagine your father has to beat your beaux off with a stick."

"We do always dance at the assemblies," she said, feathering a strand of butter-colored hair between her fingers, "but there aren't so very many single gentlemen in this part of Wiltshire. There's a regiment stationed just north of here, but Papa doesn't like the idea of one of us marrying a soldier. Not even an officer."

It sounded odd for a man with seven daughters to object to so broad a category of eligible bachelors—particularly officers. "But you're permitted to dance with them?"

"If we didn't, we'd never get to dance. The single men who *do* live here are so . . . dull. All the oldest sons don't do anything but complain that their fathers won't die, and the younger ones all want to be farmers or vicars or officers. And those—"

"Aren't acceptable," he finished, wondering what Mr. Witfeld's private opinion of *him* must be. Face-to-face he'd been nothing but polite and interested. On the other hand, Zachary hadn't yet purchased a commission, so perhaps he was still to be tolerated. But Mrs. Witfeld definitely and obviously had marriage between a Griffin and one of her daughters in mind. It didn't make much sense, unless Edmund was so distracted by his inventions that he didn't know what his wife might be plotting.

"Exactly," Susan was agreeing. "And who wants to marry a farmer or a vicar?"

Zachary abruptly wanted to go somewhere very quiet and think. With Melbourne insisting that he stay away from the army, Susan had just described the choices left to him. As a duke's son and a duke's brother he certainly wasn't going to become a street vendor or a shopkeeper or a butcher. That would wound his family's standing at least as much as it would be intolerable to him.

Of course he was far from being the only youngest son who sought a military career—though he was probably the only one being prevented by his own family from doing so. And so what if

Edmund Witfeld thought that somehow disqualified him from pursuing any of his daughters? He wasn't going to marry a Witfeld. On the other hand, if a Griffin, even one who happened to be a captain or a major or a colonel, wanted to marry any chit, most fathers would have no objection at all.

"Lord Zachary?"

He blinked. As consuming as he found it, at the moment this wasn't about his situation, other than to see whether he could whip the Witfeld girls into proper shape. Patience and responsibility. "So there isn't anyone in particular who's engaged your interest in Wiltshire?"

She giggled. "Well, there is one, perhaps."

Damn. He'd heard that laugh before, and he knew precisely to whom it applied. "Considering that after my visit here I'll be taking my colors, I sincerely hope you're speaking of someone more worthy of you than I am," he offered, hoping it sounded less insulting than it felt.

"You— Oh, blast!" Susan gave a great sniff, then burst into tears. "You're joining the army? That can't be so!"

If Zachary needed anything to prove to himself that he wasn't a hardened rakehell, it was the occasion of a female bursting into tears in front of him. A seasoned rake would undoubtedly have a *bon mot* or swift kiss or something to at least distract the chit. He, however, had no idea what to do. Awkwardly he patted her on the back. "There, there, Miss Susan. Surely my aunt told you I meant to join a regiment."

"No! She never did!" She stomped her foot. "This is very unfair."

A muscle beneath his eye twitched. "I've been here less than a week, Miss Susan. You can't tell me that before my arrival not one gentleman caught your eye."

She shrugged heavily, nearly poking him in the ear with her parasol. "What do I care about other men?"

"Ah, but *I* care," he said smoothly, tucking her free hand around his arm. "Come now, who are my rivals?"

Her sniffling subsided. "Well, if you put it that way, Mrs.

Williams's son, Martin, is just returned from the Crimean. He sold out his commission to help his mama, and I believe they've purchased a second shop over in Tellisford."

"Two shops? They must be well off."

"Martin works very hard. His father was a barrister, but Martin says he has no tolerance for intricate legalities."

Well, that sounded promising. Susan didn't seem to have much tolerance for intricacies of any kind. "So the two of you have chatted?"

"New articles arrive at the shop every Tuesday." She glanced up at him, her color high. "Last week some new silks arrived all the way from Paris. He promised to hold the blue bolt for me, and let no one else have any of it until I'd made my purchase."

"Then you should wear blue to the assembly rooms, I think. Will Mr. Williams be attending?"

"Oh, yes, because I don't think Mama would invite him to our own soir—"

"I would like to see him at both parties," he interrupted. "I'll mention that to Mrs. Witfeld."

She clutched his arm. "You will?"

He shrugged. "I certainly don't expect to be the only unmarried man in attendance. That would hardly be fair to anyone."

"You are very good, Lord Zachary. Are you certain you intend to join the army?"

"Unfortunately, yes. I'm certain."

One down, six—five—to go. That had been easier than he'd expected. Zachary smiled at Susan. At this rate he'd have all the marriage-mad sisters paired off by sunset, and without having to do anything but invite the correct gentlemen to a party. As for the eldest Witfeld daughter, that remained a much more complex proposition, and one he didn't mind becoming entangled with at all.

Chapter 9

Caroline stepped back from the window. For better than an hour Susan and Zachary had been strolling along the pond in a rather aimless manner. Susan's plans weren't aimless, of course— her hand seemed permanently attached to his sleeve. In her mind she was probably already deciding on her wedding guest list.

No, Caroline didn't need to see that. Nor did she want to see Zachary fleeing for the hills once he realized he'd been divvied up like a Christmas pie. And she'd taken a large share of slices.

What the devil did it matter, though? His coming to Wiltshire was a godsend. For her not to take advantage of his presence was unthinkable. And yet when he'd kissed her, and when he talked with her, he'd been warm and alive and . . . nice. She looked down at her half-completed and very private sketch. She'd drawn him and touched him, and now she was suddenly wondering what he might be thinking and feeling and doing. And what her sisters were thinking about and doing to him.

Did that really matter, either? Once she'd finished her painting, she didn't care what he did or where he went. It was just that he kissed so well.

"Damnation," she swore, flinging her pencil across the room.

Anne slipped in through the conservatory door.

"This is madness," Caroline said aloud.

"What's madness?" Her younger sister bent down and picked up her errant pencil.

Hurriedly Caroline closed her sketch pad. "All of this fawning over Lord Zachary. Nothing good can come of it."

"I'm a bit confused, Caro." Anne handed the pencil back. "Did Lord Zachary say something ill to you? Did you not get your two hours with him this morning?"

"No, he didn't, and yes, I did." She drew a breath. The influx of air didn't help her confusion any. "You mark my words, Anne. If the lot of you continue encouraging his attentions, he is going to break your heart, and Susan's, and Julia's, and Joanna's, and Grace's, and Violet's."

Anne sat beneath the bow windows. "What about *your* heart?"

"Mine? My heart has nothing to do with him. I'm only . . . frustrated. I have under three weeks to submit a finished portrait to Vienna, and my subject is outside wandering about for no good reason."

"We have as much right to try to realize a dream as you do, Caro."

Caroline rolled her shoulders. "Yes, yes, you're right. But I'd like to think—I mean, I have to believe—that my dream is attainable. Yours—"

"Are a foolish waste of your time?" Anne finished with a skeptical look. "You've had several hours to sketch him. Have you decided on a pose for the portrait yet?"

Not one she could display in public. "Not yet. I'm still feeling him—the angles and shading, I mean—out."

Anne looked at her for a long moment while she did her best not to blush. "Don't worry, Caro," her sister finally said. "I've given you three more mornings this week, and two hours on Friday afternoon. By then you should be ready to have him sit for paint, don't you think? And we'll all have a fair amount of time with Lord Zachary."

She wouldn't be ready to paint him if she couldn't get his bare chest out of her thoughts. "I suppose so. I didn't mean to be selfish."

"I know. You're not. You're just dedicated." Anne smiled. "And that will give you five days to finish and still have time to post the portrait to Monsieur Tannberg." Her younger sister grinned. "And I daresay you'll even have time to attend both the assembly rooms *and* Lord Zachary's ball."

Caroline took another steadying breath. As dire as she considered her circumstances, Anne had a point. Every sister would have a chance at her own dream, however poor Caroline considered their chances. And she did have nine days to complete her work, which would still give the portrait twelve days to arrive in Vienna.

"Yes, you're right," she said slowly, forcing a smile. "Perhaps I'll even dance a waltz."

Zachary held Sagramore to a walk, mindful of the wobbling Julia Witfeld was doing on her own mount, Daisy. In fact, it appeared that Julia had never ridden before in her life—at least not without a groom holding the reins for her or without her being tied or glued into the saddle. "You're doing splendidly," he complimented, edging Sag close enough that he could catch her if she should fall.

"I do love to ride," Julia said, then nearly lost her balance and pulled the reins tightly enough that Daisy backed up. "Drat. Ill-behaved horse."

"Perhaps Sagramore is making her nervous. Shall I lead her a little to set her at ease?"

"Oh, that would be very thoughtful."

He leaned sideways and took the reins over Daisy's head, leading the mare and the chit along the wooded path. A groom hung back several yards, close enough for propriety and far enough away that hopefully Zachary only imagined he could hear the man chuckling.

"You were telling me about the dearth of eligible young men around Trowbridge," he prompted, giving a glance back to see her clinging to the pommel of the saddle with both hands.

"It's true; everyone here is so dull. Well, not everyone. Not any longer."

Ah. Well, he'd learned his strategy during the course of this conversation with Susan. "I'm only sorry that as a future soldier I am ineligible to pay my attentions to any of you."

"But—"

"I would never defy your father, of course."

Her mouth gaped a moment, then snapped closed. "Of course," she grumbled.

"So tell me who your favorite suitor is. I know a girl as pretty as you must have one."

Julia giggled. "There is one, perhaps. But are you certain you must join the military? Papa would never give an inch about soldiers."

"I'm certain. I am a third son, after all. Come, now. Give me a name."

"No. You must guess."

"I don't know anyone in Trowbridge. Can't you give me a clue?"

"Hm. Well, he owns a business in town."

"A business." Considering the way the Witfeld sisters seemed to select a male target and then swarm over him, he abruptly had a good idea who the business owner must be. "Could it be Martin Williams?"

"Oh, you've guessed! He's so handsome, and he had a good inheritance from his father."

Devil take it. "You can't tell me that no other gentleman has pursued you, Miss Julia."

"I suppose so. Peter Redford always asks a dance of me at the assemblies. He's handsome enough, but the vicar's son. I should never want to be a vicar's daughter-in-law, or a future vicar's wife."

With seven girls, someone was going to have to marry a future vicar. And she obviously liked this Mr. Redford. "Do these gentlemen know of your interest?"

"Heavens, I don't know. I always try to dance every dance at the assemblies; if a lady isn't diligent, men may be left wanting a partner."

Zachary covered his smile. "So you are permitted to dance with officers?"

"Well, Papa could hardly prevent that. It would be rude, don't you think?"

"Most likely." And the poor man would probably be overwhelmed, anyway, trying to keep seven—six—daughters from dancing. He wondered whether Caroline danced. Hopefully she did; however odd their relationship, he found that he liked touching her. And he liked her touching him.

Julia shifted in the sidesaddle, then had to grab Daisy's mane to keep from pitching to the ground. Once she'd righted herself, Zachary pretended not to notice. He'd catch her in a true emergency, but he certainly didn't want her feigning an accident simply so she could fall into his arms.

"I hope *you* dance, Lord Zachary," she prompted.

"Never fear, Miss Julia. Nothing will prevent me from dancing with you. And call me Zachary, please."

"Oh, yes. Zachary. I think since the ball at our house will have to be even grander than the one at the assembly rooms, we can have as many as four waltzes. You'll save one of them for me, won't you?"

"I will." Surreptitiously he glanced at his pocket watch. Julia had another ten minutes until her hour was finished, and then, according to Susan, he was scheduled for a picnic with Anne. He had no idea what they'd planned for his afternoon, but he imagined it would include Joanna, Grace, and Violet. It would be nice if one of them were to choose fishing, but if they were as proficient at that sport as Julia was at riding, the outing would be more bother than it was worth.

"What time do you have, Zachary?"

He pretended to look again. "Ten before eleven."

"Blast it. I should get more time, since I had to wait for Steadman to saddle the horses."

Zachary nearly suggested that next time she plan ahead how best to use her allotted hour, but Julia didn't have Caroline's wit where he could tease or chastise. At the same time he remembered that only Susan had confessed about his schedule. For this excursion he wasn't supposed to know that he was being sectioned and divided. "We have all day, don't we? Your father said there were some spectacular riding and jumping trails just south of the grazing pasture." He couldn't resist a small tease.

"Jumping?" she repeated with a squeak. "You know, I think Anne was planning a surprise for you. Perhaps we should return home, after all."

Considering they'd only traveled about a mile, and a slow one at that, returning wouldn't be too difficult. "As you wish, of course." Turning Sag and Daisy in a wide circle so he wouldn't dump his companion, he headed them back toward Witfeld Manor, the amused Steadman still following along behind.

At the gap of the stone wall that divided the house, garden, and stables from the rest of the property, the first thing Zachary spotted was a picnic basket. Then the brim of a pink bonnet followed by Anne's oval face peered around the opening.

"Oh, and there she is," Julia muttered under her breath behind him. "She might have given me five minutes at the stables."

He cleared his throat. "Good day, Miss Anne," he said with a smile, tipping his hat.

Being pursued with this degree of undivided attention by a handful of attractive chits wasn't so bad, now that he considered it—especially now that they weren't attempting to overwhelm him in a group attack. If they weren't so hopelessly obvious about their intentions, and if they hadn't been sisters he didn't want turning against one another, he would have enjoyed the situation enormously. As it was, working on making them acceptable to other gentlemen definitely made things more interesting.

"Lord Zachary," the seventeen-year-old returned, curtsying. "Since it's nearly eleven, I thought you might enjoy a walk and a picnic by the pond."

"That sounds charming. Allow me to see Miss Julia back to the stables, and—"

"Oh, go on," Julia grumbled. "Steadman, take my reins."

The groom urged his mount forward, and Zachary handed over

custody of Daisy and her rider. Rather than risk Julia changing her mind, he swung to the ground and flipped Sag's reins over to Steadman, as well. He sketched Julia a bow. "Thank you for a refreshing outing, Miss Julia."

"No, thank *you,* Zachary. On, Steadman." Sending Zachary a beatific smile, Julia waved a hand at the groom, then had to grab the pommel with both hands when Daisy lurched forward.

"Good heavens," Anne breathed as the three horses vanished around the corner. "I hope she doesn't break her head."

"She was doing tolerably well," Zachary put in, surreptitiously toeing the basket. It felt full; always a good thing.

"You should feel honored, my lord. I don't think she's ridden a horse in twelve years."

"Then why—"

"Because *you* ride." She picked up the basket. "Shall we?"

"Here." He took the wicker from her and offered his free arm. "Do we have a chaperone?"

"You and Caro didn't have one."

Wonderful. "Her maid was stationed directly outside the door." He smiled. "My aunt expressly told me to behave. I'm attempting to do so."

"Very well. I was only checking." Anne faced the house. "Sally!"

A maid trotted into view around the vine-covered wall. "I'm here, Miss Anne."

With the servant safely following them, Zachary allowed Anne to point out the path to the pond. In just a few seconds of conversation, one thing became extremely clear; Anne was going to require more care than the two previous sisters. As Edmund Witfeld had said, two of his daughters had sense. She was one of them. The other one was probably still ensconced in her tower with her pencils.

"How has your morning been?" Anne asked, brushing her free hand along the top of the low, bordering hedge.

"Interesting. Posing and walking and riding, and now eating.

All ending and beginning at either the top or the bottom of the hour."

"Hm. Really?"

"Yes. In fact, I was worried that if I should throw a shoe or need a glass of water, I would send the whole house into chaos." He looked sideways at her.

She was eyeing him, her lips pursed. "So you know. We only made up the schedule so we could all be assured of having time with you."

"Very efficient. I understand that you were the architect."

"I'm not going to admit it if you're only going to make fun."

"I'm not," he protested. "I wanted to tell you that as much as I enjoy yours and your sisters' company, it's easier to have a conversation with one at a time rather than half a dozen at once."

"No doubt." She chuckled. "At times I retire for the night with my ears ringing, and I grew up with them."

"I have three siblings myself, and a six-year-old niece. Until a month ago, we all lived under the same roof."

"Until your sister married."

"Yes."

"But why do you all share a household? Surely the Griffins have several houses in London."

"Shay—Charlemagne—and I actually do have our own apartments in Mayfair. Melbourne bribed us, though, to move back into Griffin House. I think he feels better with more people to order about." He shrugged, unwilling to go into the details of his eldest brother's struggle to move past his wife's death. That was Griffin business; Griffins didn't gossip, and certainly not about one another. "The house is large enough to accommodate all of us."

"I can imagine. I've always longed to go to London."

"You aren't yet eighteen; perhaps you could convince your parents."

She shook her head. "I doubt that. They declared Grace and Violet and me all out at the same time. With no presentations to be made at court, I think my mother simply decided it would be easier that way. So I won't have a Season." Anne looked up at him. "But I don't mind. In a sense, my Season has come here to me, hasn't it?"

"What do y—"

"Mama and Papa certainly would never have agreed to hold a ball if you and Lady Gladys hadn't come, and I'm sure once everyone in the shire attends our soiree they'll all wish to hold their own to avoid looking shabby and cheap-minded. So *you've* given me my Season."

"I'm pleased to offer my presence, then."

"The purpose of a Season for a young lady, though, is to find a husband, is it not?"

Zachary's cravat began to feel too tight, and he sternly resisted the urge to loosen it. He'd made a shambles of re-tying it earlier, anyway. "So I hear."

"How is it that you are four-and-twenty and from such a family as the Griffins, and still unmarried, my lord?"

"I'm not in any hurry to don leg shackles. Before I do that I still have things I wish to do. I'm going to join the army as soon as I return to London, and from there journey to the Peninsula."

"The regiment stationed outside Trowbridge has been expecting their orders for six months now," she returned smoothly. "Apparently Wellington feels he has things well in hand without them."

What a difference between her reaction and that of her sisters. Either she'd already heard his plans, or she subscribed to the theory that his family name would overcome any resistance on her father's part. Either way, it didn't bode well for him.

"I don't want to wait to be called," he said. "I intend to take action."

"That's very admirable, Lord Zachary. I'm not one to sit about and wait for someone else to take action, myself."

Well, that was easy to interpret. And it was time to get off the defensive and attack before she guided him to some parson she had hidden in the undergrowth. "So who here in Trowbridge have you been considering for this action? It doesn't sound like a plan you only devised when I appeared."

"No, it isn't. But plans change."

He lifted an eyebrow, thankful that he had a fair amount of experience with ambitious young ladies. "You're direct, aren't you?"

She smiled, gesturing west. "This way. You aren't accustomed to direct women?"

Actually he wasn't accustomed to personal conversations with strangers, simply because most strangers didn't dare. And as for his family, by this point in the conversation he would have been called a blockhead or a halfwit a dozen times already. That was the difference with Caroline and now with Anne, he realized. They assumed he had intelligence and the ability to express himself, and their only preconceived notions were about wealthy gentlemen in general. It was refreshing. "I suppose not. Shall I be direct also?"

"Please."

"I didn't come here to find a wife, Miss Anne. I came here to fulfill an obligation to my aunt, and to do a favor for my brother."

"And yet here you are, having a picnic with me."

"Are you certain you're only seventeen? I have this disturbing sensation that I'm being lured into a trap."

She laughed. "I beg your pardon, then. I'm not attempting to trap you. Just the opposite. I'm making my intentions very clear."

And somehow that was even more off-putting. Christ. He'd been set to take on a handful of silly, tittering chits, not a forthright mankiller. Lord knew he'd met his share of those in London— women who wouldn't blink at intentionally compromising themselves in order to net a husband. He avoided them with a passion. Perhaps, though, that was where he could help Anne Witfeld.

"Do you fish?" he asked, pulling a blanket from the top of the basket when she indicated that they should stop.

"Fish? No, though I've seen it done."

"You know the basics of the sport, then." Offering a hand, he helped her sit and then set the basket and himself down beside her. Mindful of her forceful philosophy, he sent a glance at the maid to make certain she was well within sight and hearing.

"Yes, I suppose."

Zachary accepted a sandwich. "So if you were to go fishing, you wouldn't charge into the water brandishing a club and begin thwacking at the water."

"That would be counterproductive. Peach?"

"Yes, thank you. And that's my point."

"Peaches?"

"No. That you'd catch more fish with a hook and a worm than you would with a club."

She looked at him for a long moment, chewing with a thoughtful expression on her face. "I have a good deal of competition, even here under my own roof."

"It's only competition if you're all pursuing the same man." He drew a breath. "For instance, I couldn't marry all seven of you even if I wished to."

"So we should draw straws?"

If that happened he would have to put a bullet in his head, because his family would never let him live it down. "So you should focus on landing a trout who firstly wants to be caught, and secondly who wants to be caught by you."

Anne smiled a little. "You're not what I expected."

"I hope that's a compliment."

"It is. I read the Society pages, and they're forever filled with tales about your family, and about you. Wagers and horse races and boxing matches. But Caro said you enjoy and are knowledgeable about art. And you seem to have a great deal of common sense."

Knowledgeable? Caroline had said he was knowledgeable about art? It was quite possibly the most . . . pleasing compliment he'd ever received. He shook himself. "The newspapers report things that will sell more newspapers. I don't think my softer side, as it were, is terribly exciting."

With the timing of an actor Harold surged out of the bushes and pounced.

"What the devil—"

Zachary managed to toss his sandwich back into the basket before the dog got hold of it. Grabbing Harold's collar to keep the pup from going after Anne's luncheon, he rolled to his feet.

"Reed!"

The valet crashed toward them through the shrubbery. "I'm so sorry, my lord!" he panted as he emerged. "I was only trying to rescue one of your boots, and the fiend dashed between my legs and out the door."

Zachary looked down at the wagging, wriggling dog. "By God, he *is* half foxhound, if he tracked me here."

"You or our sandwiches," Anne put in with a chuckle. "Caro did say you're an abysmal trainer."

For a bare second Zachary froze, then handed the dog back to his weed-covered valet. "Take him back to the house. I'll let him out for some exercise this afternoon."

"Very good, my lord."

So Caroline had seen him working with Harold yesterday. She hadn't mentioned it this morning, though she'd obviously told Anne her opinion of the proceedings. He took a breath, seating himself again. What did he care what she thought? Simply because with one breath she complimented his knowledge of art and with the next insulted his ability to work with an animal, he didn't—

"Zachary?" Anne said, interrupting his thoughts, "you've given me a great deal to consider." For the first time she sounded like a young lady who wouldn't even have been out if the Witfelds had lived in London.

He shook himself. "So tell me who I should expect to meet at the soiree."

They spent the next hour in very pleasant and unexpectedly witty conversation. As he'd suspected, the Witfeld girls had a great deal of enthusiasm and some odd theories about men, with no chance or opportunity to put them into practice. According to the Zachary Howard Griffin plan of battle, all of this would change by the end of the last dance at the Witfeld soiree. These girls wanted men, and he was going to whip them into the shape necessary to get them.

His mood over the structuring of his schedule, though, soured a little. So he hadn't trained Harold in one day. That didn't mean he'd given up. It just hadn't been quite as simple as he'd expected. And the next session was going to take place somewhere out of sight of the conservatory windows. Finding the time for training, though, was another matter entirely.

Directly after luncheon with Anne, he went for yet another walk around the estate, this one with Joanna, then picked flowers for an hour with Grace. Thankfully for his sore feet Violet wanted to play cards.

In response to his questions, all of the girls had admitted to him that some local gentleman or other had caught their eye. Anne, Joanna, and Grace had declined to name their potential beaux, but he didn't doubt he'd discover their identities at the assembly. His largest task would be convincing Mrs. Witfeld to invite half the single males in the community to compete with him at the Witfeld Manor soiree. If she had any sense, though, she wouldn't object to having more men about. As he'd told Anne, he couldn't marry all of the sisters even if he wanted to.

At half past three he was finished. He found Harold upstairs ripping apart a pillow. "You need a companion, I think," he told the dog. "Marriage is definitely an obsession for my other pupils."

"Zachary, my boy," he heard floating up to him from down below.

Moving out to the landing, Zachary looked down to find Mr. Witfeld standing by the bottommost step. "Edmund. Good afternoon."

"Might I trouble you to come out to the chicken coop? I've put in a prototype of the egg ramp, and I wanted your opinion."

"Of course." As he reached the ground floor, Zachary looked from Edmund to Harold. Obviously he couldn't take the dog out to the chicken coop, or the chickens would end up so frightened that they'd never lay again. After a hesitation he handed Harold's leash over to the butler. "I'll be back shortly," he informed Barling and tried unsuccessfully to convince Harold to sit.

As he left the house, he caught a glimpse of yellow skirts at the top of the stairs. Zachary frowned, then quickly wiped the expression from his face. What the devil did he care what Caroline thought of him and his ill-mannered dog? All he was to her was muscle and skin, anyway. All the same, though, Harold was going to learn some manners, as soon as he could find the time to teach the pup.

Chapter 10

*Considering the fact that she could barely sleep or even concen-*trate unless she had her head down drawing Zachary—to the point where she'd gone through a half dozen pencils in three days—Caroline couldn't believe that she hadn't found a look, a pose that pleased her. She could only imagine how frustrated her subject felt. And the tickle that had begun in the back of her mind—the one telling her she was delaying making a decision because she enjoyed looking at him and talking with him—didn't help matters, either.

"How am I looking?" he asked from his seat halfway across the room.

"I don't know," she muttered, half to herself. "Something's wrong."

"With me, or with the sketch?"

A small laugh escaped her lips. "I'm sure I couldn't say."

"Well, that's enough of that." He stood and strolled over to her. "Let's take a look."

Her first instinct once again was to cover up her work, but she'd drawn him fully clothed. She tilted the pad a little toward him. "Well?"

Zachary leaned close over her shoulder. "I think it looks like me. I like the cravat." He indicated the pencilled knot with one finger.

"Thank you." Trying to ignore his close, large warmth and his breath on her cheek, Caroline darkened and blurred a crease in one of his sleeves. "I think it's the expression on your face. I'm not sure what it's telling me."

"What's it supposed to tell you?"

"Something. I drew it, after all."

"But it's my face. According to my brothers, most of what it would say would be nonsense. I could manage to glare more broodily, if you like, but I still don't see anything wrong."

"Your brothers can't possibly think as poorly of you as you maintain."

"And why not?"

She glanced up at his handsome face. "You are difficult to dislike."

His sensuous mouth curved into a smile. "Perhaps my charm is a natural outgrowth of my propensity for uselessness."

Caroline stood, having to step sideways to avoid smacking his cheek with her shoulder. Having him that close made her uncomfortable, mostly because, despite what she'd seen of his lack of either skill or resolve in training Harold and the way he claimed to be mad to join the army and yet sat chatting with his aunt in Wiltshire, she wanted him to kiss her again. "Please go sit down. I don't have much time left with you this morning."

"Hm." With a sideways look at her, he returned to the seat beneath the windows. "I notice you didn't disagree with me."

"I'm treating you as a client," she said breezily, "so I'm not being contradictory."

"But I like when you're contradictory."

Yes, he did, and that made finding the balance she needed to keep between them exceedingly difficult. "Can't we just chat instead? I've always found that to be a good way to relax a subject I'm sketching or painting."

"I'm not nervous, but please proceed." He gestured expansively at her.

"Very well." She erased the line of his left shoulder, lowering it a little. That wasn't it, though; his body was fine, exceptional. The problem was somewhere in his face. "Tell me about your family. Where do you live?"

"The family lives at Melbourne Park in Devonshire, or at Griffin House when we're in London."

"Anne said you have your own house in London," she returned, gesturing him to lower his head a little. That made him look more . . . dangerous, but it didn't have the missing quality she was seeking.

"Both Shay and I have our own apartments in Town, but when Sebastian asked us to return to Griffin House, we did."

"You just abandoned your own home?"

"No. I stay there from time to time, and I keep a handful of servants on staff, but my main residence is at Griffin House."

"So you . . ." She stopped herself, realizing that she'd been about to question how he'd been able to abandon a chance to be independent and make a life for himself just because he was amiable and unfocused and drifted whichever way the wind blew. *Be quiet and concentrate, Caroline.*

"So I what?" he asked after a moment.

"Nothing."

"I see."

Caroline looked at him again. His expression had hardened, grown cooler. In fact, he looked like she had imagined a Griffin would look before she'd ever met one: aloof, a little arrogant, and practically daring anyone to contradict them. So much for making her subject relax. "Zachary, I didn't say any—"

"Sebastian's wife, Charlotte, died. None of us expected it; she was fine, then just began getting tired and thin. A month later, she went to bed and didn't wake up." He cleared his throat. "We . . . Sebastian was devastated. If he hadn't had little Peep—Penelope—to look after, I don't know what he would have done. So when he asked us to come home, we did."

"I'm sorry," she said quietly, keeping her gaze on the sketch rather than the man himself. It was easier that way. "I had no idea."

"No one but the family knows the details, and I would appreciate it if you kept it that way. But I didn't want you thinking that I had just wandered away from my house and forgotten where it was or something."

His humor did have a purpose. He used it to set the people around him at ease. "I won't speak a word about it to anyone."

Silently she eased the straight line of his mouth, curving it at the corner. There. That wasn't quite it, but it was closer to what she wanted.

He stood again, moving back to stand beside her chair. "I know you won't. Now tell me, what's wrong with my image?"

She blew out her breath, wishing she could explain it, even to herself. The pose was fine and the sketch accurate, but every bone in her body complained that she had gotten something wrong. Something was . . . lacking. He'd told her something intimate about himself, but she didn't see that depth in what she'd drawn. Caroline tilted her head at the drawing. "Would you look at it in the same way you studied the *Mona Lisa?*"

"The *Mona*— Well, I've seen myself in the mirror a thousand times. This looks very like the image I've seen of myself." He checked his pocket watch. "And my apologies, but I'm to go fishing with the twins in twenty minutes. If you'll excuse me, I need to go change my clothes. I have a suspicion I may end up soaked."

She looked up from the sketch. "Then why go?"

"Because they asked me. I have no intention of mucking about with the Witfeld schedule of events."

So he did know about Anne's schedule. She'd suspected for the past day or so, but in his favor he hadn't said anything about it until now. "That's very diplomatic of you."

"It wasn't my idea, Caroline."

But he hadn't fought against it, either. Even knowing that other people valued his time more than he did didn't seem to trouble him. "I only complimented your diplomacy. I know how much you enjoy fishing," she replied.

"Whether I'll enjoy being pitched into the stream or not, though, is another matter entirely." He stopped in the doorway. "Are you attending the ball tonight?"

Caroline shook from her mind the unexpected vision of a soaking wet Zachary Griffin, shirt and trousers clinging to his lean, well-muscled form. "I've been ordered to do so."

A sensuous smile curved his mouth once more. "I had to bribe the head violinist for a list of the dances to be played." Zachary pulled a piece of paper from his pocket. "This is the first time I've had to make myself a dance card."

Trying to remain focused, she erased a strand of hair that strayed across his forehead, then put it back. It looked good there, as it did on him in person. "Yes," she said, her gaze on the drawing. "I'm certain that even without my sisters you will be very much in demand."

He reached behind him for the door and slowly closed it again. "Are you jealous, Caroline?"

"Don't be ridiculous. And I have not given you leave to use my Christian name."

"Then do so."

"No." Pretending to return to her work and hoping her cheeks weren't flushed, she waved a hand at him. "Go fishing."

Silence answered her. When she looked up, he was directly in front of her, close enough to touch.

"If I hadn't felt your mouth on mine," he murmured, tilting her chin up, "or your fingers on my skin, I might believe you didn't care."

"I *don't* care. I told you, I need to paint your portrait. *You* kissed *me*, and as for the rest, I was viewing your musculature solely in order to aid me in becoming a better artist."

Deep gray eyes held her gaze. "Really," he finally said, otherwise unmoving. "So to you I'm not a man but an object."

He had begun that way, at least. She refused to look away. "Yes."

Zachary leaned in until she could feel his breath on her lips. Her body screamed at her to close the space, to drink in the warm masculinity she'd so briefly tasted before. Her mind, though, was shouting with equal strength the word *Vienna*. If she gave in to her senses, to her body, she would love it for a moment and regret it for a lifetime. Caroline lifted her hand and brushed his fingers from her face.

"I believe you have an appointment to go fishing," she said, hoping he couldn't hear the tremor in her voice.

He nodded, backing away. "So I do. But next time, Caroline, *you're* going to have to kiss *me*. I won't pursue where I'm not wanted."

"You're not wanted by me."

Zachary smiled darkly, the expression alone doing some odd things to her insides. "Liar."

Before she could conjure a reply, he slipped out the door and closed it quietly behind him. Caroline dropped her pad to her lap and concentrated on taking deep breaths. When that didn't banish either his image or his scent from her mind, she stood to pace. How could he do that, make her feel as if her feet were hovering an inch or two off the ground? Make her feel like she did when she was in the midst of painting—not quite part of the world, but at the same time touching every bit of it?

"Men," she snarled. He only claimed interest because he thought she must be playing hard to get or some such thing. It wasn't a game, though. How could she make him realize that?

Devil take it. If she'd been one of her overeager sisters, he would be running in the opposite direction as fast as his fit, fine legs would carry him. Caroline slowed her strides. Perhaps that was it. For as long as she needed him she would be . . . herself, telling him truthfully that she didn't want his attentions. That would certainly keep him nearby and interested.

Once she'd finished her work, however, all she needed to do was pretend to be Susan or Joanna or Julia for a half dozen minutes. He would think, as he did with her siblings, that he was being trapped—and then he would flee, thereby leaving her in peace until she heard from Vienna and had been accepted into Monsieur Tannberg's studio.

"Perfect." The only remaining problem—*problems*—was how to resist her attraction to him and figure out what was wrong with her sketch before she began painting. And if she could persuade him to strip out of his shirt again, well, she would consider it as a pleasant bonus to her artistic education.

Aunt Tremaine gave her coach over to the Witfelds. Even two vehicles, though, weren't enough to accommodate the entire household and their guests in all of their evening finery. Despite his best efforts, Zachary found himself in the lead coach with Mrs. Witfeld, Susan, and Grace.

"Oh, this is going to be so delightful," Sally Witfeld exclaimed, clasping one of Susan's hands and squeezing. "I only wish our own soiree might have come first. But no matter, we'll make such an impression tonight that everyone will be clamoring to attend the Witfeld ball."

Zachary tried to crane a glance out the window to see who was piling into the second vehicle, but their own coach lurched into motion before he could see more than a swirl of silks. "I'm sure you're right. The assembly will serve to whet your neighbors' appetites."

"Just so, my lord. And don't my girls look lovely? I told Susan to wear her new blue silk. Doesn't it bring out her eyes?"

"Yes, it does. All of your daughters are so lovely I can scarcely believe my own good fortune at being here."

Mrs. Witfeld batted her fan against his knee. "You are such a gentleman."

"My thanks, madame. Are you certain the second coach doesn't require an escort?"

"Oh, no. Joanna and Julia and Violet are seeing to your aunt."

He hid his frown. "What of the rest of your family?" *And Caroline in particular?*

"We have it all planned out, Zachary," Susan said, batting her eyes at him. "This carriage will return for Papa, Caro, and Anne. It doesn't signify if they're late, because Caro and Papa hardly ever dance, anyway."

Even so, he meant to save a dance for the eldest Witfeld daughter, just on principle. In the meantime, the look in Susan's eyes worried him, despite the subtle instruction he'd given over the past few days. He had no intention of letting either the girls or himself become a spectacle or a laughingstock. "You do look very fine, Miss Susan. You'll have all the young gentlemen falling over themselves to gain a spot on your dance card."

"Well, that's very nice, but what about me?" Grace smoothed the wrist of her white, elbow-length gloves.

"All of you will be setting the Trowbridge assembly on its ear."

They arrived at the assembly rooms in the midst of a dozen other carriages. It took some effort for the family matriarch to keep the Witfelds together, especially as the second coach rolled to a stop behind them.

"Girls, girls!" she called over the general chaos, "stay together and watch your slippers. The horses have been here."

Susan grabbed Zachary's arm, nearly pulling him to the ground. "Stay with me, Zachary. I want Martin Williams to see us enter together."

It seemed a little far-fetched to think that Mr. Williams would even be able to spot Susan in the crush of guests, let alone be jealous to see her in the company of her houseguest. Zachary acquiesced without protest, however, since he had no idea where they were going, and Susan obviously did.

"Let's proceed," Mrs. Witfeld announced, straightening her large green matron's bonnet and ushering the twins before her.

Zachary took Aunt Tremaine's arm with his free hand. "You look very fetching tonight, my dear," he drawled.

"I could wear a sack and no one would notice," she returned promptly, lifting her cane to lean more heavily on him, "as long as you are present."

He grinned. "I've always wanted to be the belle of the ball," he murmured back at her.

"Ah." His aunt glanced ahead of them at the doorway. "Be careful what you wish for, my love."

Zachary followed her gaze. "Damn. So that's what it looks like."

"What what looks like?"

"The road to hell," he answered. "I believe it's supposed to be paved with good intentions or some such thing."

The throng of females gathered around the assembly room entrance terrified him. All sizes, all ages, and all looking at him with that same off-putting light of hope in their eyes. Now he knew what a grouse felt like on the opening day of bird hunting season. Sweet Lucifer. And he'd thought the Witfeld ladies had been overwhelming.

"I've never seen so many people at an assembly," Susan whispered, giggling. "Everyone in eastern Wiltshire must be here."

Everyone except Caroline Witfeld. He pasted a smile on his face, bobbing like a chicken as he was introduced to a hundred people whose names he would never remember after tonight. The Griffins were notoriously charming, however, and he wasn't about to impune the family reputation while he was in the midst of trying to impress Melbourne.

"I've checked with Mrs. Howard," Joanna said, prancing back up to the group, "and the orchestra is only to play two waltzes. She says they're too scandalous."

"Mama, we'll have more than two waltzes at our soiree, won't we?" Julia demanded plaintively.

"Of course, dear. Oh, look, it's Mr. Anderton." She leaned into Zachary, her rose-scented perfume thick and overwhelming. "He's a solicitor, and quite a fan of Caroline's work. She's done his portrait, you know."

Zachary looked at him as he approached. Tall, about fifteen or so years older than himself, with brown hair beginning to thin a little on the crown, he looked like what he was—a solicitor for the land-owning folk of eastern Wiltshire. Normally Zachary wouldn't have given him a second look, but Mrs. Witfeld had made a point of singling him out, and of mentioning Caroline's connection with him.

"Mr. Anderton," Sally said, beaming, "may I present Lord Zachary Griffin? Lord Zachary, Mr. Anderton."

They shook hands. As Zachary sized up the solicitor, he couldn't help wondering whether Mr. Anderton's portrait sitting

had gone anything like his own. For all he knew, Caroline somehow seduced all of her male subjects into kissing her and stripping half naked for her. Zachary didn't like that idea very much,
particularly after she'd rebuffed his last attempt at inviting her to
sin. But damnation, a man could stand only so much temptation.

"You've livened up our dull summer, my lord," Anderton said.
"We've never had so many citizens attend an assembly."

"Glad I could be of assistance." Zachary smiled. "The Misses
Witfeld have all been promising me some fine dancing."

The solicitor chuckled. "Having partnered with all of them, I
can assure you that they're not exaggerating."

So he'd danced with Caroline, who, according to her sisters,
didn't take the dance floor very often. That settled that. He and
Caroline were going to dance tonight.

"Oh, it's Lord and Lady Eades," Mrs. Witfeld exclaimed. "Excuse us, Mr. Anderton. Come, my lord, I have to introduce you.
Caroline is a particular favorite of theirs. They've offered her a
governess position for their children."

A governess position? That didn't make any sense. The family
seemed convinced that the eldest Witfeld daughter would be in
Vienna by the end of the summer. A governess position hardly
seemed worth mentioning, compared to that. Unless he was missing some part of the equation, of course, which, according to his
family, happened to him fairly frequently.

Mrs. Witfeld clasped his arm, keeping him attached to her am-
ple side. "Lord and Lady Eades," she said, sinking into an overel-
egant curtsy that nearly overbalanced the two of them, "may I
present Lord Zachary Griffin? Lord Zachary is youngest brother
to the Duke of Melbourne."

Zachary gave a shallow bow. "Pleased to meet you."

He knew most of England's noblemen; power tended to gravi-
tate toward power, and no one had more of that than his brother.
Somehow, though, his lack of acquaintance with Lord Eades
didn't surprise him. Both the earl and his wife wore powdered
wigs—high style among the aristocracy ten years earlier. The pair
of them probably hadn't been to London in at least that long.

"Likewise, my lord," Eades returned in a nasal voice. "Do come and call on us; our hospitality is much admired, I believe."

"Oh, of course it is," Mrs. Witfeld said enthusiastically.

"I'll do that, then." *When hell froze over.*

"We look forward to it. If you'll excuse us?"

"How old is the earl?" Zachary asked Mrs. Witfeld as soon as they were out of hearing.

"Five and forty, I believe."

"And why are they so . . . formally attired?"

"They do look horribly elegant, don't they? We all aspire to their standards."

He wouldn't have been caught dead aspiring to those standards. As the crowd and the din continued to increase, though, he settled for nodding politely. The assembly room was so jam-packed he didn't see how anyone could move, but as the orchestra began to play, the dance floor miraculously cleared.

"This is our dance, I believe, Zachary," Julia said, deftly separating him from her mother.

They lined up for the country dance. All the other Witfeld girls in attendance joined them with their own partners; evidently Susan had been correct, and her father's edict against officers didn't extend to dancing with them at the assemblies. The sea of red uniforms was rather impressive. Zachary could imagine himself among them in a month or two. Except he wouldn't be dancing in Wiltshire. He would be fighting in Belgium or Spain against Bonaparte.

With the number of dancers on the floor, he assumed they would be split into two groups, but apparently he was the only one with a grasp of logic. Each female, it seemed, meant to take a turn with him. By the time he and Julia progressed down the entire line, the dance had already been going on for twenty minutes.

He'd begun to wonder if Caroline had managed to avoid attending when he finished a turn and saw her. She'd donned a deep gold silk gown with a low neckline, a film of lace across her bosom and frothing at her sleeves. Her auburn hair was piled artistically on her head, and strategic strands escaped to frame her fair-skinned, fresh face.

Zachary nearly lost his place and had to hurry a step to keep from upsetting the flow of the dance. Damn. Just because she didn't look her usual disheveled, preoccupied self didn't mean he had to lose his head.

Finally the dance ended, and he led Julia back to her mother and the rest of the brood. "That wasn't fair!" Violet said, joining them. "We'll only have time for three dances if they all take that long!"

"At least you got to take a turn with him," Anne said, charming in a light lavender silk. "I wasn't even here."

"Oh, never mind that," Susan countered. "Look at all the young gentlemen in attendance tonight."

For a brief second Zachary met Caroline's gaze. He wanted to talk to her, to ask her about Eades and the governess position. For the moment, though, he settled for offering her a smile. "You look lovely tonight," he murmured beneath the female cacophony.

"So do you. Perhaps I should paint you in that jacket. The blue deepens the gray color of your eyes."

That sounded like a compliment he would hand out to a chit he was after. "Are you trying to seduce me, Caroline?"

"You're the one who keeps taking your shirt off," she returned calmly.

"I only took it off once," he retorted, "after you practically dared me to."

She blushed but lifted her chin. "I'm an artist. We don't live by convention."

For a warm moment he wished and hoped that was true. "Then leave your conventional self behind tonight and dance a waltz with me."

The smooth skin of her cheek jumped. "That would cause a riot."

"I'll risk it. Besides, I've given you hours of my time this week. All I ask in return is a waltz."

Her shoulders lifted and lowered. "You've given everyone hours of your time this week, but very well."

A commotion by the refreshment table caught his attention. "What the—"

"Oh, dear," Caroline muttered. "Poor Mr. Williams."

Zachary turned to view the fit-looking young man with the almond-colored hair. So that was Martin Williams. He wasn't easy to make out, because at the moment he was surrounded by six ladies all trying to talk to him at the same time. "Blast it, I thought they all had their own beaux. Not the same bloody one."

"You thought what?" Bright green eyes looked at him suspiciously.

"Nothing."

Caroline tilted her head at him. "You sent them all after Martin Williams, didn't you?"

"I—"

"Why? Just so you wouldn't have to put up with their company?"

"No. Of course n—"

"Or was it so you wouldn't be embarrassed by the Witfeld girls fawning all over you in front of the citizens of Trowbridge?"

"Caroline, have I done anything but be polite and friendly to your sisters?"

"No, but—"

"And do you think it is in their best interest to do nothing but bring me glasses of Madeira and lemonade and complain about the number of dances all evening?"

"So you sent them to pursue Mr. Williams instead?"

He shook his head, unable to hide a frustrated grimace. "I suggested to each of them that there must be a local gentleman they admire, and that perhaps he might find them charming, as well."

She gave her delicate, amused snort. "And they all decided on the same man."

"I didn't mean to set the hounds on him."

Her pretty eyes narrowed. "My sisters might be naive and

somewhat misguided, but I would hardly accuse them of being hounds setting upon anyone."

"I didn't mean it that way, Caroline."

"Miss Witfeld," she corrected sharply. "For the last time, I have not given you leave to use my Christian name."

His vision of the evening flying madly out of control, Zachary took her hand. "I apologize. I didn't mean to insult you."

"It's not me you've insulted." She tugged her hand free. "If you'll excuse me, Lord Zachary. I wouldn't want to monopolize your time this evening after I've taken so much of it this week already."

He stood back and watched her walk away, trying to ignore the soft sway of her hips and the lemon scent of her hair. Devil a bit. Yes, he could be ham-fisted, but generally not with a lady. And Caroline had to know the truth about her own siblings—hell, she'd lived with their chaos her entire life.

Caroline strolled away, not to try to talk some sense into her sisters—that would only make things worse—but to pretend for a moment that she didn't know them. Luckily she came upon Frank Anderton. "Good evening," she said, forcing a smile and pretending she wasn't mightily annoyed.

"Caroline. I've met your houseguest," the solicitor said. "He seems very gentlemanlike."

She couldn't very well say anything disparaging about Zachary until she'd sent off his portrait, and she'd pressed her luck with retaining his cooperation far enough this evening, anyway. She nodded. "And my mother has been quite happy to see Lady Gladys Tremaine again."

"I hope you'll save a dance for me, Caroline."

"Certainly I will. With pleasure."

Unable to help herself, she glanced over her shoulder at Zachary. He was surrounded by guests and regaling his rapt audience with some undoubtedly amusing tale or other. Oh, he was very good at entertaining people, at lighting up a room with his mere presence, but it wasn't his good humor or his warmth she questioned as much as it was his resolve and patience and his sense of responsibility. After all, he seemed to regard taking a walk about the grounds in her sisters' company with the same general interest and easy nonchalance he devoted to posing for her, and from what she'd seen of Harold, the animal was more fit for the zoo than for a gentleman's companion—not that she blamed Harold for that.

Obviously Zachary didn't understand anything—not her, not her sisters, and certainly not the importance of this portrait. Caroline clenched her fist. If he didn't occasionally share those personal confidences with her or show more insight into art than anyone else she knew, then for all she cared, as soon as the portrait was finished, Zachary Griffin could fall into the pond and drown.

Well, perhaps not drown, but at least go away. Or he could stay and marry any one of her sisters, because she would be in Vienna living her dream. And she certainly knew that her dreams—her waking ones, anyway—didn't include him.

Chapter 11

Caroline managed to avoid Zachary for the next two hours, which wasn't easy because everyone she wished to chat with had joined his ever-growing circle of admirers. Of course as a professional portraitist she should have been diplomatic and polite and bland with him from the beginning, but it was obviously too late for that. Thankfully for her portrait application, he seemed to like her uncharacteristically sharp tongue, but she wished he would stop encouraging her to use it.

"Caroline!"

She jumped, hurrying through the crowd to her mother's side. "Yes, Mama? Are you tired? Do you wish to return home?"

"Nonsense, girl. Lord Zachary was just saying he's danced with all of the Witfeld sisters except for you."

At the same moment a warm hand ran down her bare arm to clasp her fingers. "I was only pointing out a sad fact," his easy drawl came, "though I'm hopeful we can remedy my misfortune."

"Of course you can, my lord," Mrs. Witfeld said. "Go dance with him, Caroline."

"But—"

"There," her mother countered as the orchestra began playing. "The last waltz of the evening is beginning. Don't keep Lord Zachary waiting."

Clenching her jaw, Caroline acquiesced to Zachary's gentle tug on her hand. She'd plainly been outmaneuvered. Together they wound their way to the dance floor.

"It was hardly necessary to involve my mother," she said, pretending not to notice his warm hand sliding around her waist as he drew her around to face him. "I agreed to dance with you."

"This is the last waltz of the evening," he returned with an easy smile, "and you seemed very determined to be half the room away from me."

So he *had* noticed her avoidance. They stepped into the waltz. She'd seen him dancing all evening and knew he was skilled and graceful, but being in his arms as they swept about the room was a different experience entirely. "You exaggerate," she said, exhilaration turning the ends of her sentences up. *Feet on the floor, Caroline,* she reminded herself. *Don't forget why you're here.* "I wasn't avoiding you; I was chatting with my friends."

"Well, now you'll just have to chat with me for a few minutes."

"Certainly," she ventured, making herself smile, hoping she could conceal how deeply . . . frustrated he made her feel. It was very like her problem with his painting; she kept seeking, wanting something she couldn't quite grasp. "I only thought you'd appreciate spending time with someone other than a Witfeld, since we've practically kept you hostage for the past week."

He gazed down at her for several turns. "Stop doing that."

"Doing what?"

"Being nice when you're annoyed."

"Beg pardon? I'm being polite, just as any young lady would be expected to do."

"What happened to your 'lack of convention' tack? I liked that better."

"I don't want you to get angry and refuse to pose for me."

He chuckled, a thoughtful expression crossing his face. "With the exception of my family, people of my acquaintance have made an art of telling me what they think I want to hear. I've been feted and flattered nearly into oblivion since I attended my first social gathering. I gave my permission for you to paint me. I'm not going to take it away because you choose to speak your mind. I'll be thankful if you speak your mind, Caro—Miss Witfeld."

In a way that made sense: With the way he waltzed through life, other people's criticisms probably never even touched him. Or if they did, he would more than likely simply adapt his dance to please them once more. Well, now her challenge would be to be direct and diplomatic at the same time. She could tell him what she thought, as long as it wasn't *everything* she thought— particularly about him, both good and bad. "In that case," she began, mentally crossing her fingers, "why did you really encourage my sisters to pursue Martin Williams?"

He nodded, apparently expecting the question. "Because they seem to want to marry."

"And you're removing yourself from consideration."

A smile curved his mouth. "Could I court one of them without causing a bloodbath?"

Despite the violence of his words, his smile had her thinking of his kiss again. "Would you court *any* of them?"

"I'm about to join the army. I'm not marrying anyone."

He'd managed to avoid insulting the rather diluted aristocratic blood of the Witfelds, anyway. At times she wondered if he had a mean bone in his body. He certainly seemed to have passion— and compassion—but where was his drive, his strength of character? Did he ever get angry, want anything enough to fight for it? She doubted he'd ever faced those questions, or had any sort of answer for them.

"You mentioned your plans before," she said, noting how many of the assembly guests were watching her—or rather, him. "Why the delay?"

"My brother asked me to escort Aunt Tremaine to Bath."

She declined to note that Trowbridge definitely wasn't Bath. "But you have another brother, do you not?" she asked instead.

Zachary lifted an eyebrow. "Melbourne asked *me* to do it. Besides, you wouldn't have wanted to paint Charlemagne."

"Why not?"

"Because I'm prettier and less stubborn." He grinned. "And

since we're asking questions, why did your mother introduce Lord and Lady Eades to me by saying they had offered you a governess position?"

Wonderful. So he knew about her darkest nightmare. "Because they offered me one."

"I thought all of Wiltshire knew you were going to Vienna."

Caroline cleared her throat. "Lord and Lady Eades are somewhat eccentric."

"Yes, I noticed."

"We try to humor them." Honest as he claimed to want her to be, she had no intention of letting him know just how vital his cooperation was to her. He had enough power over her as it was. And she had enough trouble concentrating when he was close without giving him even more influence.

"Caroline?"

She blinked. "Apologies. I was just thinking I'd like to start painting you tomorrow."

"About that. If you wanted to paint a nobleman, I was just wondering why you didn't select Lord Eades."

Caroline made a face. "I have done his portrait. Both of theirs, actually. I would rather not have a studio decide whether to accept me or not based on a portrait of Earl and Countess Eades as Antony and Cleopatra."

Zachary laughed. "I'd like to see the paintings you've done of them."

"I imagine they'd be happy to invite you to dine with them."

"They already have. Are you free tomorrow evening? I imagine they could manage that."

"Me?" she yelped. "I didn't mean *I* should accompany—"

He pulled her a breath closer. "Is your objection to visiting the Eades, or to accompanying me to visit them?"

"Neither. I only have eight days to paint and package you off to Vienna. I don't have time for visiting, or for dancing."

It seemed a good exclamation point to their conversation. She tried to pull away, but in response he tightened his grip a little.

"Since you're already here," he murmured, "we might as well finish our waltz, Caroline."

"Oh, very well."

As he gazed at her she sensed it again, that very sexy interior beneath the veneer of easy compatibility. Zachary Griffin generally got what he wanted. And uncertain as his focus was, at the moment he was looking directly at her. Warmth spiraled down her spine.

How could he have that effect on her, when she viewed him strictly as a means to an end? She needed his face, and that was only to get her to Vienna. As for the rest of him, yes, he had very nice musculature and no, she wouldn't have objected to seeing more of it, but she refused to be interested in someone whose companionship would preclude her from attaining what she wanted for herself.

That conclusion did nothing to explain the rapid beat of her heart or why tonight she already knew she would dream of his mouth on hers. It was warm and crowded in the assembly rooms, however, so perhaps she was just a little overset.

"Miss Witfeld," he drawled softly.

She shook herself again. For heaven's sake, she was never this distracted unless she was painting. Caroline met his gray gaze. "What is it?"

"The waltz is finished."

And there the two of them stood in the middle of the dance floor, hand in hand and his arm close around her waist. Her cheeks heated. "Of course the waltz is finished," she blurted. "You're the one who insisted that we dance. Are you satisfied now?"

"That's a very complicated question." As he spoke he shifted her hand to his sleeve and started toward the refreshment table and her mother. Even with all the attention he drew, the end of the crowded dance was so chaotic that she doubted anyone had noticed them standing there in frozen silence. "And by the by," he continued quietly, "you're not packing *me* off to Vienna. *I'm* staying right here. My painting is going. Could you keep the difference in mind?"

Her back stiffened. "Yes, I believe so."

As soon as he could do so without appearing to be rude, Zachary left Caroline with her mother and went to get a drink. He liked Caroline; he liked her directness and her focus. Their conversation during the waltz, though, had made something clear—something he'd suspected but was now certain about. Caroline Witfeld saw him as a collection of parts—his profile, his head, his hands—but she either didn't realize that he was an actual flesh-and-blood man, or she didn't want to see him that way. And whether he pointed the reality out or not, he remained unconvinced that she grasped the difference.

He frowned as he downed a glass of claret. Women liked him; the rest of the Witfeld girls certainly liked him. And he'd kissed Caroline and taken his shirt off to demonstrate that he wasn't just a cravat and jacket that lay in a closet until she wanted to sketch him. She'd noticed something about him; she was the one who'd approached *him* about the portrait, after all. He'd just been polite and agreed. Of course he'd also begun to have the sneaking suspicion that his only necessary qualification where she was concerned was that he didn't insist on being painted in historical costume.

"There you are, lad." Edmund Witfeld clapped him on the shoulder. "You've been busy this evening, haven't you?"

Zachary smiled. "You have a great many daughters who all enjoy dancing."

"Yes, I do." Witfeld gestured at the man beside him, and Mr. Anderton stepped forward. "You've met Frank, haven't you?"

"Yes, I have. Good evening again."

"My lord."

"Anderton and I thought you might like a bit of a change after a week in the henhouse, so to speak," Witfeld continued. "Perhaps a day of sport fishing?"

"There's a perfect spot about five miles north," the solicitor added. "Largest trout in the county."

A day without having to dispense lessons—which the girls obviously needed more of, considering the scene with the near dismemberment of Martin Williams—sounded like just what he needed. In addition, Caroline needed a lesson herself in the difference between a portrait and what lay beneath the paint, and taking a day to demonstrate that was too good an opportunity to pass up. "I'd love a little sport fishing. My thanks."

"We'll set out at daybreak."

"I'll be ready." Zachary finished off his claret. Finally he had something to look forward to without the accompanying frustration and exasperation that marked all his sessions with Caroline. Yes, tomorrow would be a nice little holiday.

Caroline set her canvas out on its tripod stand and clamped it down. She would have preferred not to begin painting the morning after being out so late, but she was running out of time. Lady Eades had even approached her last evening to say what an aptitude her son Theodore seemed to have for art, and how generous they would be toward the right teacher.

That in and of itself would have been enough incentive for her to stop her preliminary sketching to pull out the paints, but however resolved she was, she still had the distinct impression that Zachary regarded her portrait painting as a hobby. It shouldn't do so, but it annoyed her. He certainly treated their time together with the same lack of seriousness he showed his other appointments.

Well, this would be her best work ever, and even he would have to acknowledge that. She went over to the window and adjusted the curtain a little. The light this morning was perfect. A low tremor of excitement and anticipation ran through her. True, she hadn't found the exact perfect pose or angle or expression, but she fully meant to be inspired the moment she seated herself to begin work.

She checked the clock, then sat down to flip through her sketch pad. Zachary was late, but then that wasn't anything new. According to the schedule, Violet had him next, and she could probably bribe her youngest sister for a little extra time. At least Anne had had enough foresight to grant her a full three hours today—despite a strenuous objection from Susan.

His smile, his shoulder, the line of his jaw, the muscles of his thighs when he sat on horseback—any of his parts separately or together would make a fine painting. But setting spoke as loudly as facial expression, and her constant, nagging artist's eye kept saying that perhaps her conservatory wasn't the right setting for him. Out in the garden, though, she would never get a moment's peace. The same applied to anywhere else they might go on the property. Her sisters would always find a vital reason to speak to him if they had the slightest opportunity to do so.

The door opened, and she shook herself. "There you—"

"I wanted to ask Zachary a question," Joanna said, slipping inside the conservatory. "I'll only take a sec—Where is he?"

"He's not here yet. And aren't you having luncheon with him? Ask him then, Joanna."

"You're very selfish. You have three entire hours this morning. I only have one."

Actually her three hours had shrunk to two hours and forty-three minutes with no sign of her subject. "I didn't make the schedule," she returned. "And you all agreed to it, anyway."

"That was before he set all of us to chase after Martin Williams. Do you know that Martin claimed a headache and left after only three dances? Now none of us will have him."

"None of you had him, anyway. You always approach him like a mob of Catholic cardinals after a Jacobin."

"Well, perhaps so, but I'm not the one whose man hasn't even made an appearance."

Caroline frowned. "He's not my man, and if you'll excuse me, I'm going to go find him." She rose, setting the sketch pad on the stool and wondering whether she had stepped too far in speaking her mind last night. It was a fine line she had to tread, after all.

Joanna hurried for the door behind her. "I'll go with you."

From what Joanna had said, none of the Witfeld sisters was very pleased with Zachary this morning. Good. Perhaps his shiny veneer was beginning to wear off. It was about time. Too much more praise of his fine manners and handsome features, and she was going to vomit.

"Barling," she called, seeing the butler manning the front door, "where might I find Lord Zachary this morning?"

"He is out, Miss Witfeld."

"Out? Out where?"

"He and Mr. Witfeld and Mr. Anderton were to go sport fishing today, miss. They promised the cook a full basket of trout for dinner. Mrs. Landis is already making the butter sauce."

He wasn't there. The morning she'd scheduled to begin the painting, he'd decided to go fishing. *Fishing.*

"Did Papa say when they'd be back?" Joanna asked, her expression annoyed.

Annoyed, though, didn't begin to describe Caroline's mood as she stood there trying not to gape at the butler. Damn Zachary.

"I believe they were heading toward Shaverton, so I don't expect them back until late this afternoon."

Joanna stomped her slippered foot. "But we were to have a picnic today."

Not trusting herself to say anything at all, Caroline turned on her heel. She hurried upstairs to the conservatory and slammed the door closed behind her.

"Damnation," she sputtered. "Damn, damn, damn."

And then she saw the dog.

Harold scrambled around in the corner, ripping apart several pieces of paper. Automatically her gaze went to her sketching stool. Her pad was gone.

"No!" she shrieked, storming forward to grab the shredded papers away from the dog.

With a whimper he backed away, his tail tucked between his legs.

Trembling, Caroline looked through the mangled pages. Bits of Zachary were now obscured by tooth marks and dog slobber, while other pieces were missing entirely. Her favorite sketch, the one of a bare-chested Zachary, was in six pieces, though she could only find four of them. With a heavy, shaking breath, Caroline sank to the floor.

"Oh no, oh no," she muttered, tears spilling from her eyes and onto what remained of the sketch pad.

Harold padded hesitantly up to her. Angry as she was, she'd seen the poor, scant level of the puppy's instruction, and she wasn't about to blame him for the disaster. No, she knew precisely who to blame for this.

Not only had Zachary thrown her painting schedule into disarray simply because someone had invited him somewhere and he'd been too polite and amiable to decline, but now, because of his lack of attention toward his dog, better than a week's worth of sketches were rendered unusable. She'd spent days on what amounted to nothing. Days she couldn't spare and couldn't ever get back.

This was too much. She was finished with only telling half her thoughts to Zachary Griffin. He was going to hear precisely what she thought of him—and if he didn't like it, he could go to the devil. He could go there, anyway. With her sisters' stupid schedule she would never have enough time to begin again.

With a half sob, she crawled over to her thankfully untouched stack of other sketches. At this point she would have to be happy with painting Lord and Lady Eades as Adam and Eve, if they would agree to sit for her. They probably wouldn't, but devastated as she was, she still couldn't make herself give up hope yet. Hope was all she had left now.

Zachary jumped down from the wagon as a groom appeared to take the horses. The two servants who'd accompanied them pulled the baskets of caught trout down from the wagon bed and hurried them into the kitchen.

"As I said before, you are a fine fisherman, Zachary."

"Second to you, Edmund," Zachary returned with a grin, stepping back as Mr. Witfeld climbed to the ground. "That reeling-in device of yours is remarkable."

"Ha, ha. A compensation for a severe lack of patience, and in consideration of the fact that I have well over two dozen mouths to feed."

Even with the basket of trout they'd left off with Frank Anderton in the village, the three of them had caught enough fish to feed two families the size of the Witfeld brood, servants included. Even if he hadn't caught a single fish, though, Zachary would have considered the outing worthwhile. No chits, no questions about his matrimonial inclinations or intentions—what a relief.

"If you'll excuse me, I'd best look in on my aunt. Thank you again for inviting me along."

"My pleasure, Zachary."

After his aunt, he would have a chat with Caroline, too, where he intended to make his point about flat portraits versus fully realized flesh-and-blood men. In addition he probably needed to cancel whatever appointment with a Witfeld girl he might have remaining for the day. He badly needed a bath.

The house, though, seemed eerily quiet and empty as he entered. Not even the ever-lurking Barling was about. Making his way upstairs, he knocked on his aunt's bedchamber door. "Aunt Tremaine?"

"Come in," she called, and he opened the door.

"Where is everyone?" he asked, taking in the cup of tea at his aunt's elbow and the borrowed poetry book across her knees as she sat in the overstuffed chair beneath the window.

"Sally's closeted with Barling the butler going over plans for the ball, and six of the girls went into Trowbridge."

Six. "I'd best see to Miss Witfeld, then. I believe we were moving up to using paint today."

"Caro's not here, either. I believe she went for a walk."

Zachary lifted an eyebrow. "Really?" Focused on his portrait as she was, he couldn't imagine her leaving the house voluntarily. "Good. I'm going to change and have a bath, then, I think." He offered her a smile. "And I hope you're hungry for trout."

She lifted the book again. "And I hope you're still hungry by the time dinner has been prepared."

Halfway to the door, he stopped. "What's that supposed to mean?"

"I suppose you'll find out. Or not."

"That's helpful."

Aunt Tremaine turned a page. "It's not meant to be."

Females. He would have been better off if he'd stayed out fishing. At least and despite his aunt he apparently had another hour or two until the horde returned.

Once the footmen had brought the bathtub to his bedchamber and filled it, Zachary shed his mud-and-fish-covered clothes and sank into the hot water. He sighed, closing his eyes and sinking all the way under, then slowly rose again just far enough that he could breathe. This was bliss.

"Comfortable?"

His eyes flew open. "Christ," he growled, grabbing for a towel and pulling it into the water to cover his hips. "What the devil are you doing in here?"

Caroline's gaze was steady on his face, but her color was high enough that a moment ago she'd been looking elsewhere. "We had an appointment this morning," she said, her voice steady, whatever she'd been staring at.

"Your father invited me to go fishing," he returned, refusing to feel at a disadvantage just because he was sitting naked in a bathtub.

"You might have told him that you had a prior engagement." She folded her arms across her pert bosom.

"You seemed only to require my parts, and you had them in your sketchbook. The rest of me wanted to go fishing."

"My sketchbook. I see. Unfortunately, today I required your parts all attached together."

Obviously she still didn't understand the point he was attempting to make. "You indicated that you had a week to box *me* up and send *me* to Vienna. As I said, *I'm* not going anywhere, Miss Witfeld. Have you—"

"I understood your meaning," she interrupted. "And I apologize if I've offended your sensibilities or affected your sense of self-worth."

Now she was making him sound like some kind of spoiled brat. Zachary stood, wrapping the wet towel around his hips. "That's not what my objection was about."

"Nevertheless, I would like you to hear *my* objections."

"If you can't wait until I dress, then please proceed."

Caroline took a step backward as he emerged, dripping, from the bathtub. "Stay where you are, sir!" she ordered, not sounding the least bit tantalized by his near naked self. "I understand you wanting a holiday away from us. I wish you'd waited another few days before you took it, but I understand. And I understand that once anyone suggests something interesting or amusing to you, you're incapable of resisting the temptation."

"I am not some half-wit infant, Caro—"

"Then why do you behave like one, Zachary? I needed your help. I asked for your help. I want to paint. I want to make it my livelihood. Lord and Lady Eades want me to be their governess and teach their children to paint. I would slice my own throat before I succumbed to a lifetime of that drudgery."

"Then allow me to dress, and I'll sit for you right now," he returned, the depth of her anger taking him by surprise. He'd only been gone a few hours, after all.

"I can't paint now, because I've lost the light. And I couldn't do it anyway, because your . . . dog destroyed every sketch I made of you."

His heart stopped. "He what?"

A tear ran down one smooth cheek. "I went looking for you, since you didn't bother to inform me that you'd made other plans. When I went back upstairs, he was ripping . . . ripping my sketch pad to shreds."

Zachary took another step toward her, but she backed away again. "I'm so sorry, Caroline. I'll send Harold back to Lon—"

"I don't blame Harold!" she exclaimed. "I blame you! You acquire a dog for God knows what reason, then decide you have better things to do than school it in proper behavior!" She flung a handful of crumpled, torn paper at him. "What did you expect?"

What remained of his good humor vanished. "I apologized, Miss Witfeld. If there's more I can do, let me know, and I'll do it."

"That's very nice, now that it's too late. If you'd shown the least sense of responsibility, we wouldn't be having this conversation."

That was enough of that. "I'm not the one who decided to divide up my time and section me like an orange. How do you expect me to accomplish anything with Harold when all my time is accounted for by your family?"

"If it wasn't the Witfelds, it would be someone else. It's never you, is it? You claim to have a goal to join the army, and yet here you sit on your backside doing what everybody else wishes. You can't blame us for that."

"Your point being?" he bit out.

"If you want to do something, then do it. Don't claim to have a desire just so you sound like more than the waste of fresh air that you are."

"That is enough, Miss Witfeld."

"Caroline!" Edmund Witfeld skidded into the room, his wife, a handful of sisters, and the butler on his heels. The Trowbridge party had returned. "Remove yourself at once!"

She kept her gaze steady on Zachary. "Go join the army, Lord Zachary. Do it now. At least then if you get killed, you'll provide some useful fertilizer."

"Caroline!"

With a last sniff she turned on her heel and stomped out of the room. Zachary stared after her, scarcely noticing the herd of stammering, apologetic Witfelds as they backed out of the doorway and left him in private. Once the door closed, he ripped off his towel and slammed the wet thing as hard as he could back into the bathtub. The resulting splash soaked the floor for ten feet around, but it did nothing to cool his temper.

"Fertilizer?" *Fertilizer?* She had no idea what he wanted from life; how dare she criticize the way he went about achieving his goals. He hadn't abandoned his army idea by any stretch. Doing a favor for Melbourne and for Aunt Tremaine didn't mean he was some sort of mental butterfly. It only meant he was being polite and responsible. And as for Harold, they'd barely given him a second with the damned dog. What did she expect?

He was not a waste of space, he was not without goals, and he was most definitely not fertilizer waiting to be put under the ground to grow cabbage or something. What he was, however, was leaving.

Chapter 12

Aunt Tremaine stood just outside the bedchamber door as Zachary slammed it open. "Good," he snapped. "You're here. Pack your things."

"I will not. You and Caroline apologize to one another, and we'll all sit down to dinner like civilized p—"

"Fine," he interrupted, gesturing for his valet to hand over a saddlebag. "I'll ride on ahead. I'll meet you in Bath—or in London, if this trip was just a damned ruse."

"It was not a r—"

"Then I'll see you in Bath. Reed, follow with my things."

"Yes, my lord."

"Harold!"

The dog crawled out from under the bed and scrambled into the hallway. Zachary brushed past his aunt and thundered down the stairs, Harold at his heels and for once minding his master. The foyer was lined with Witfeld females, but he barely spared them a glance. Barling apparently realized he was about to have his front door broken down, because the butler pulled the heavy oak open as Zachary reached it.

"Saddle my horse," he ordered as he reached the stable.

"Mine, as well."

Zachary turned around to see Edmund Witfeld behind him. "That is not necessary, sir," he said, anger clipping his words. "I thank you and Mrs. Witfeld for your hospitality. Now, if you'll excuse me, I'm riding on to Bath."

"I'll ride as far as Trowbridge with you."

Zachary gave a curt nod. "As you wish, then."

He paced, unwilling to stand still long enough for Witfeld to begin a conversation with him. He would rather it was Caroline standing there; he certainly had a few choice words for her. On the other hand, he was a Griffin, and Griffins were unfailingly polite—even when he'd been insulted in such a manner that it would have prompted pistols at dawn if it had been a male confronting him.

Harold sat by the stable door and looked at him. Caroline had been right about one thing—the incident with the sketch pad hadn't been the dog's fault. It had been his.

Finally a groom brought Sagramore up. Zachary slung his bag over the back of the saddle and tied it down, then swung up himself. If Witfeld was joining him, he could damned well hurry it up.

Edmund caught up to him at the end of the drive, slowing from a gallop to a canter to match Sagramore's brisk pace while Harold padded behind the two of them. "I know you don't want to listen to anything I say, lad," he began, "but there are things you don't under—"

"I understand quite well, thank you."

"I can't afford to keep Caroline here past the end of the summer."

Zachary opened his mouth to retort, then closed it again. He couldn't imagine not having enough money to keep his family intact, but then the Griffins were supremely fortunate by anyone's standards. "I'm sorry to hear that," he said stiffly. "But I hardly think it's any of my affair."

"She's applied to twenty-seven academies and studios over the past three years. Tannberg is the only one to offer her a place—and that's only if she passes the application process."

The application process he was supposed to have been helping her with. "It's not as though I refused my assistance."

"She overreacted, I know, and I apologize on her be—"

"Don't," Zachary cut in sharply.

Witfeld drew a deep breath. "Very well, lad. If you don't want to hear about her dilemmas, then let's discuss yours."

"Mine?" Zachary glanced at him. "I don't have a dilemma. I'm going to Bath, and if Aunt Tremaine doesn't appear within the week I'm returning to London and purchasing my colors." The hows and whys of that would have to be left to some time when he was thinking more clearly.

"I did that, you know."

Zachary didn't want to ask, but the words came grudgingly to his lips anyway. "Did what?"

"Joined the army. Sally's father told me if I wanted to marry her, I had to prove that I could support her. I married her in my regimentals."

"Romantic."

"I took what he said to heart, though. Her father. It wasn't long before I was home just long enough to get her with child again, and then off I went to some other battle. The pay is better on active duty."

Zachary clenched his jaw and didn't say anything. At this point he didn't think he was supposed to do anything but absorb some wise words or other from someone who'd supposedly trodden all his paths before him. As if Mr. Edmund Witfeld had any idea what his life was like.

"Then, after daughter number five, I took a ball in the leg. It was enough to get me sent back home. I couldn't afford to support my family on half pay, so I had to sell my commission. I kept thinking if I'd been unmarried I could have lasted until my damned leg healed and gone out again."

"I'm sorry for your—"

"I'm not finished," Witfeld returned, with surprising force. "I hated being here, sitting among a clucking clutch of chicks and hens while my former mates were still out there having their adventures. So I closed myself up in the conservatory to hide, and started inventing things. I thought if I could devise the right thing, it would pay my way out of Wiltshire. I built Greek ruins to imagine myself in another life. If I kept myself distracted enough, maybe I'd forget that I'd been denied the opportunity for greater glory and fame."

"And has it worked?"

Edmund looked at the ground. "Well, what I finally began to realize was that I enjoyed what I was doing. The inventions, I mean. And when Caroline started coming up to the conservatory to paint, I also realized that I had a family. You should have seen her when she was twelve or thirteen. Even then, she would put some brush strokes on a canvas, and it became a flower. A damned flower, where when I did it, I had nothing but a mess. And I made her, as a distraction to keep me occupied while I was stuck in Wiltshire between deployments."

He cleared his throat. "My point being, I suppose, that I could have stayed a soldier and been dead now with some grand monument to my bravery. Or I could have seven daughters I adore despite their excessive silliness, and a chance to perhaps invent something that might be useful to them or their children." Witfeld looked directly at Zachary. "So before you decide to run to some fleeting and deadly glory on the battlefield, do you really want to do what I did and waste twenty-two years before you realize what's truly important?"

It was clear now why Witfeld didn't allow soldiers into his house. And it wasn't for any reason his daughters would have imagined. "You're a good father," Zachary finally said.

"I'm trying to be one now. For a very long time I was an abysmal father. And that is why I have five silly daughters, and two who have sense in spite of me. If I'd done right by them, I might have no silly daughters, and seven I would be proud to set against any educated, privileged young lady in Mayfair."

Damnation, Zachary knew what the next step was supposed to be. He was supposed to do his part in aiding the Witfeld daughters, one of the two who had sense, at any rate, and return to the manor to pose for Caroline. There was more to this conversation than that, however. More for him to think about. Because thanks to Edmund's supplement to Caroline's speech, Zachary had just realized that he more closely resembled a waiting bag of fertilizer than he cared to admit. While on some level he'd known already, now he had to face it. She was right, and Melbourne had been right. He had no real goals, just a desire to be someone other than the spare's spare, the third Griffin brother.

At least the eldest Miss Witfeld knew what it was she wanted in life—and he'd apparently put himself in the position to deny it to her. Or to help her gain her dream. In a way, that felt more significant than any silliness he might be contemplating for himself. And he had some serious contemplating to do, though he preferred to do that at length and in private, and bloody well not while galloping along the road literally headed in the wrong direction.

"Do you think the trout are ready?" he asked slowly.

Witfeld made a poor effort to conceal his smile of relief. "I'm sure they will be by the time we return."

"Good. I'm hungry."

Caroline sat in the morning room and covered her ears with her hands. Even that, though, didn't much help to lessen the cacophony around her. Her mother and at least three sisters were in hysterics, while Susan stood by the window sobbing. Anne yelled at Joanna and Julia to stop shrieking about losing their one hope for a happy future, while Grace kept repeating, "You called him fertilizer?" at the top of her lungs.

As loud as it all was, the screeching was still quieter than what her mind shouted at herself. And covering her ears couldn't block out any of that. Yes, perhaps she'd become overly focused on his parts rather than his person, but for goodness' sake, what did he care? He'd already made it perfectly clear that he wanted to avoid any entanglements in Wiltshire. Oh, she probably could have flattered him more, made more of a fuss over the perfection of his features and his manly form. And no, she shouldn't have called him fertilizer.

How much of his careless, haphazard presence was she supposed to have tolerated, though? After he'd sworn he would help her, he'd gone fishing, of all things, and left his stupid dog behind to make matters even worse. And then he'd left altogether when she'd protested.

Caroline shuddered. None of her plans or even her opinions of Zachary mattered now, because he was gone, and she had to convince Lord Eades to sit for her and to sign a letter of approval. She had more than a sneaking suspicion that he would hand over no such thing—encouraging the artistic ability of his son Theodore would be more important to him than aiding her. All he had to do was string her along for a week and then deny his approval, and for all intents and purposes she would belong to the Eades family.

She was so *stupid*. Zachary should have been a learning experience; undoubtedly a great many nobles were as aimless as he was. If she couldn't tolerate it in an otherwise charming, kind gentleman, she had no reason to think she could make her living among his kind.

A tear ran down her cheek. Of course no one else noticed, because they were all too occupied with their own miseries. She felt like yelling herself, pointing out that none of them had had so much as a pin-point's chance of netting Lord Zachary, but they wouldn't listen. They didn't want to hear it, and so they wouldn't. She, however, had a stronger sense of reality. And what she'd begun to realize was that the moment she'd opened her mouth to yell at Zachary for his inconsideration, she'd irretrievably ruined her own life.

"I said, *enough*!"

Caroline didn't know how many times her father had called for quiet, but she heard that one. So did the rest of the family. For a heartbeat the silence seemed louder than the yowling.

"Mr. Witfeld," her mother said tearfully, "I insist that Caroline be punished. Such an ungrateful girl! You can't—"

"Everyone go change for dinner. Be back down here in twenty minutes," her father snapped, his usual easy manner vanished. "I do not want to hear another word spoken until then. Is that clear? Nod, don't speak."

One by one everyone nodded.

"And Caroline, join me in my office. Now."

He turned on his heel and vanished. Caroline followed, pretending to ignore the glares boring into her back. Nothing they could say or do could make her feel more hopeless than she already did.

Her father stood beside his office door and gestured her to precede him. She stepped through the door, and he closed it behind her. Before she could wonder why he'd closed her in alone, Harold trotted up to lick her fingers. Startled, she lifted her head and spied the figure standing by the desk.

"Lord . . . I . . . Zachary, I . . ."

"If you sketch tonight and begin your painting in the morning," he said, unmoving, "will you complete it in time to meet your deadline?"

Caroline couldn't breathe. He was giving her another chance. She felt the blood leaving her face, and she still couldn't move, couldn't speak, couldn't do anything but keep repeating to herself that he'd come back.

"Jesus," he muttered, moving abruptly forward to help her into a chair. "Breathe, Caroline." He patted her none too gently on the back, and air rattled into her lungs again. "Better?" he asked after a moment.

"Yes, thank you," she managed. "But I thought you were going to Bath."

"I don't think I've ever been quite that angry before," he said in a low monotone.

"Then why . . . why—" She broke off. A tear plopped onto the back of her hand.

Zachary shrugged. "I deserved a little of what you said." He cleared his throat. "More than a little. And I don't think I quite understood exactly how important my cooperation was to you. If I had, I wouldn't have abused the privilege."

Despite his kind words, his voice didn't have the relaxed drawl she'd become accustomed to hearing. He was probably still angry; she would be. She tried to tell herself that she had a reason to be angry, as well, but she was too busy feeling grateful and trying to remember to breathe. "I apologize for what I said. It was thoughtless and mean, and I should never—"

"It was true, and you've given me some things to think about," he said gruffly. "Leave it at that." Stirring again, he made his way to the door. "I'll see you at dinner."

"Yes. I . . . thank you, Zachary. Thank you so much."

His hand touched her shoulder as he passed by, and then he and Harold were gone.

Caroline sat there for several minutes. Her thoughts refused to settle into anything cohesive, and mostly she just thanked God and her lucky stars for convincing Zachary Griffin to return. She'd certainly learned her lesson. From this moment on, she was going to remain polite, or remain silent. There wasn't going to be a third chance.

The door opened. "Everything settled?" her father asked, moving into her line of vision.

"He said he would sit for the portrait," she returned, still dazed. In the background the cacophony began again. Her sisters had discovered that Zachary had returned. And with that, another problem occurred to her. "I don't have much time, Papa. With the sketch pad ruined, I have to do at least one more preliminary drawing before I put paint to canvas." That was how it usually went, anyway. She would begin her painting based on a sketch. With Zachary, she'd felt she could draw him with her eyes closed, but the application was too important to risk by employing that questionable method.

"If I'd known what you'd scheduled for today, I never would have invited Zachary fishing." He sighed. "I tend to think, though, that your argument was bound to happen, regardless."

"I should have thought before I spoke. It was unpardonable, and I hope I didn't embarrass you."

"You spoke your mind. I've never found fault with your wits."

"What did you say to him, to convince him to return?"

"That's between him and me. Now. Which of your sisters made up that damned schedule for Zachary's time?"

"Anne."

"I'm revising it."

She looked over at him. "But—"

"You get that portrait painted, Caro. If you fail, it won't be because you didn't have the opportunity to try."

"Thank you, Papa."

"Mm hm. Go and change."

The second conversation gave her time to recover her feet and her balance, and she hurried upstairs to do as he bid. She didn't think there was an emotion she hadn't run through in the course of the day. Anticipation, anger, resignation, dread, frustration, fury, despondence, and suddenly hope.

When she returned downstairs to the dining room, everyone else had already seated themselves. For a moment she thought she might have to face more accusations and recriminations, but she might as well have been a tree stump for all the attention anyone paid her. Every pair of eyes was focused on Zachary, who'd apparently become even more handsome and gallant than he'd been a few scant hours before. Grateful as she was, the fawning and twittering began to make her head ache.

Zachary, however, smiled through it all. If she hadn't become so accustomed to reading and deciphering his expression, she would have thought him completely at ease, entirely the old Zachary. But she saw the coolness behind his eyes, the slight delay before he smiled or laughed. And if her sisters kept pushing their nonsense at him, she didn't know how long he would sit for it without pushing back.

Halfway through dinner, her father tapped his wineglass. "I have an announcement," he said. "Beginning in the morning and for however long it takes for Caroline to complete her portrait, the rest of you girls will leave her and Lord Zachary alone."

"But Papa, we have a sched—"

"Alone," he repeated with the same rare force in his voice

she'd heard earlier. She and Zachary weren't the only two who took what had happened very seriously. "You may pester him as much as he can stand during luncheons and dinners and in the evenings, but while there's light to paint by, you will make yourselves scarce."

"Yes, Papa," Anne said, nudging Grace. After a ripple of nudges around the table, all of her sisters agreed.

"Actually," Zachary said, "tonight I promised to sit again for Caroline so she can replace some of her ruined drawings, and then I will be training Harold. And I need a word in private with my aunt."

Caroline heard the unaccustomed seriousness in his voice, but she wasn't certain whether anyone else did. They were all still so wrapped up in the misery of being Zachary-deprived and the joy of his return that she doubted they would notice the roof caving in. "Is there something I might do to help?" she asked.

Cool gray eyes looked at her. "Will you give me twenty minutes?"

"Of course."

"Very well." Setting his napkin on the table, he pushed his chair back. "If you'll excuse me? And my compliments to the cook on the trout. The most excellent I've ever tasted."

After a second's hesitation, Lady Gladys followed suit. "I'll see you in the morning, girls, Mr. Witfeld."

"Good evening, Gladys," Sally Witfeld returned.

"Good evening," Caroline echoed more quietly. It was going to be a very long night.

"We're not planning a midnight escape, are we?" Aunt Tremaine said, taking a seat in her usual chair beneath the window and propping her swollen foot up on a pillowed footstool. She'd summoned tea, and she had the feeling she would be requesting something stronger by the time she and Zachary were finished with whatever was on his mind.

"Did you hear anything of the argument between myself and

Caroline?" he asked, beginning a slow pacing across the wooden floor.

"I mostly heard hysterics and something about fertilizer," she returned. "I retreated after that."

She expected his usual smile, but his expression remained quiet and very serious. "Do you believe that I'll join the army?"

"Not if Melbourne has anything to say about it."

He slowed, glancing at her before he continued pacing. "As I see things, the lot of you figured Melbourne wouldn't have to do a damned thing. You'd keep me out of London for a month or two, provide me a different setting, and eventually I'd forget my plans or find something else to occupy me." He paused. "Am I wrong?"

A few weeks ago she would have said something witty and distracting and changed the subject. This was a different Zachary than she was accustomed to, however. And she sensed that this one seriously wanted to hear the truth. And even more, that he was prepared to hear the truth. "No, you're not wrong. My gout is real, but it provided an opportunity which your brother and I discussed."

Zachary nodded, his thoughtful expression unchanged. "I'd like to stay here through the end of the month."

She tried not to let her surprise show. After all, three hours ago he'd been so eager to leave that he'd been willing to leave her behind. "Zachary, whatever Caro said, you have nothing to be ashamed of, and nothing to regret. You are a fine young man. You're well-liked, kind, charm—"

"I know I am," he interrupted, briefly grimacing. "That's my role in the family."

"Beg pardon?"

"You know. Sebastian's the humorless, unsmiling one, Charlemagne's the stubborn, ambitious one, Nell's the rebellious, clever one, and I'm the easygoing, charming one."

"And what's wrong with that?"

"It's not very challenging as far as life's ambitions go," he said, a touch of his usual humor entering his voice. "I want to be interested in and passionate about something, Aunt. And I have no idea what that might be."

"You're four-and-twenty, Zachary. You're not required to have all the answers yet."

"But you didn't argue about my assessment of myself either, did you?"

"I thought your statement was rhetorical."

A footman knocked with the tea, and Zachary retrieved the tray and placed it at her elbow. "Rhetorical or not, I'm as tired as anyone else of the way I find a project and then abandon it. I thought the army . . ." Trailing off, he sank onto the edge of her bed. "And I was wrong. So now I'm abandoning another one."

"At least you realized before you did any damage." She carefully kept her voice level, despite the abrupt desire to shout with joy, *Thank God.*

"Do me a favor and don't tell Melbourne. When I'm ready, I'll inform His Holiness myself."

"Zachary, this is nothing to feel badly about. You have a great many interests, and if you haven't yet decided which one intrigues you the most, there's nothing wrong with that. At least you have the luxury of time to discover what moves you, my dear."

He shook his head, obviously not happy with her answer. "That remains to be seen."

"Zach—"

"I do know one thing," he cut in. "I'm going to do whatever I can to see that Caroline gets that portrait finished and sent to Vienna before her deadline."

"That's very admirable."

"Yes, well, I have a dog to train, too." He tilted his head at her. "You're certain you don't mind staying in Wiltshire?"

Even if she did, she wasn't about to tell him so. Her gout, never as serious as she'd let on, was beginning to subside, but it still sufficed as an excuse. "Not a bit. It's a nice change, being in a household full of females."

"Very well." Zachary leaned down and kissed her on the cheek. "I'm going to go pose for some replacement drawings."

As he left, Gladys sat back and poured her tea. Well. She was glad she'd made an early evening of it. This new, more contemplative Zachary wasn't the only one who had some thinking to do.

Chapter 13

*Caroline paced the conservatory floor for nearly an hour be-*fore Zachary arrived. Despite their usual tendency to chat while she worked, they'd barely spoken a word while she'd sketched him the night before. Part of that had probably been because her sisters—though they'd been mostly silent as they'd promised—had refused to let Zachary out of their sight. She supposed she couldn't blame them, and actually she'd been almost relieved not to have another moment in private with her subject. And that was the other reason for their mutual silence—what in the world was she supposed to say to him? This morning, though, conversation could no longer be avoided.

The idea still made her nervous. She hadn't slept much at all the previous night, but she had dreamed just long enough to wake up with the solution to the problem with Zachary's portrait, which had troubled her from the beginning. Or she hoped she'd found the solution; she would have to see him first.

"I didn't know what you wanted me to wear," Zachary said, entering the room five minutes before their appointed time and half closing the door behind him. Her maid, Molly, waited just outside, close enough to lend propriety—though she hadn't yet helped much in that area—and far enough away that her mumbling and snoring wouldn't disturb the creative process. "I brought three coats and waistcoats. Which do you prefer?" He hefted them in his arms.

She drew a slow breath, very aware both that the air between them still wasn't easy and that the full, lifting sensation in her chest she always seemed to feel in his presence was stronger than ever. *My goodness.* "The dark gray," she said after a moment, willing herself to concentrate.

With a nod he shed the striped brown waistcoat he had on and dumped it onto the window seat. Again she wished she had the chance to paint him shirtless or even naked—especially after what she'd seen of him in the bathtub yesterday—but that would do her as little good at the Tannberg studio as a portrait of Lord and Lady Eades in powdered wigs, dressed as Romeo and Juliet. And when she next did a personal sketch of him, it would have to be completely from memory.

"How's that?" he asked, buttoning the dark gray waistcoat and shrugging into his lighter gray coat.

"Actually, would you mind leaving off your coat?"

He hesitated so briefly that she might have imagined it—but she didn't think she had. The air between them felt so . . . turbulent that she doubted he could avoid sensing it, as well. "Certainly," he replied. "Where do you want me?"

"I've been thinking," she said, hoping he wouldn't laugh—or, worse yet, refuse. "I'd like you to pose out by the ruins."

"The ruins?"

"Thanks to my father's pronouncement, my sisters won't be able to interfere, and you . . . suit out there. An adventurer in his natural habitat."

Zachary smiled briefly. "It's been several years since I went adventuring." Gazing out the window, he pulled his coat off again and slung it over one arm. "But I like the idea. What should I carry?"

"Oh. You . . . you don't need to help. I'll manage."

"Mm hm. Caroline, I did you a disservice yesterday. I won't be repeating my error. And if I could accept what you said yesterday, I doubt anything else you might say would injure me. Relax, my dear."

Caroline drew a deep breath. "I was too harsh."

"No, you weren't. A friend once told my brother that if you feel strongly enough about something to take action, for God's sake have the . . . strength of character not to apologize for it later."

She swallowed. "Very well."

Stopping very close to her, he slowly reached forward past her shoulder and picked up the canvas and tripod. She had the distinct sensation that he was smelling her hair, and goose bumps raised on her arms as he backed away again, tucking the monstrosity under his arm. "Lead the way," he said.

Whatever they'd said to one another yesterday, something had changed between them. It made her uneasy—because she liked the version of him that had appeared last night and again this morning. Very much.

"Like this?" Zachary asked, standing one foot up on the overturned faux Greek pillar.

"Perfect. Just turn your head a little more toward the pond . . . Yes. Like that."

"You're certain I don't look like some conqueror or something? Alexander the Great of Wiltshire?"

She gave her delicate, amused snort. He'd been waiting for the sound, and he smiled. According to his pride and his lineage, he should never have forgiven her for yesterday, should never have given leaving a second thought, should have been in Bath playing cards and drinking in a club right now.

And the Zachary that Melbourne knew would have fobbed Harold off on the first passerby he met. Instead, he'd spent three late hours demonstrating a patience he hadn't realized he owned, teaching Harold to sit on command. In the grand scheme of things it was undoubtedly trivial, but it meant something significant to him.

He'd thrice now deliberately gone out of his way to make clear to Caroline that he carried no grudge against her. And he knew precisely why. She'd not only said some rather sharp and insightful things but she'd also been right. Not just a little right—exactly, precisely, absolutely right.

His brothers called him a blockhead and joked about his aversion to responsibility, but they'd never called him useless. They wouldn't, he supposed; as far as family went, he wasn't useless to them. Melbourne kept his family close around him like so many precious gems, and he was part of the set. But for the rest of the world, and to himself, the outlook was considerably more grim. And he didn't like that one damned bit.

"You're frowning," she said, eyeing him critically. "Could you relax your face a little?"

"Apologies." He pasted the half-smile back on his face. "Are you sketching with pencil first?"

"I go back and forth. Even though I only have one complete drawing, thankfully I've sketched you enough now to be familiar with your features. Now I'm using pencil mostly for starting guidelines, since the light will be changing through the morning, and since I imagine you'll want to shift a little after a while."

"I shall remain a rock for as long as you require."

Her lips curved. "Yes, but this may take two days."

Which meant that if he hadn't been an idiot yesterday, she could be finishing up with his part of the posing today. "You'll still have enough time?"

"Yes."

He understood her expression, especially after her father's speech about how tight finances were in the Witfeld household. "I'll pay to help expedite delivery."

"That's not—"

"You're wasting daylight, Miss Witfeld. Paint me."

She worked in silence for a few moments, while he felt his mouth tightening again and worked to ease the expression. It wouldn't do her any good if she painted him looking like a madman, whether he actually resembled one or not.

"So you've seen the *Mona Lisa* and never been to Vienna," Caroline said as she glanced up at him in between pencil strokes. "Tell me more of your travels."

It was one thing for him to feel ill at ease, he decided. It was quite another for him to appear that way. Zachary took a breath. "Food or art?" he returned. "According to my family I'm an expert in one and have no eye for the other."

"I find that difficult to believe of anyone who could appreciate the *Mona Lisa* enough to stand gazing at her for an hour. You journeyed to Greece, did you not?"

"I did. Saw both the Parthenon and the Erechtheion. The sense of age there is both uplifting and almost . . . oppressive."

She paused for a bare moment. "Why oppressive?"

"Perhaps that's the wrong word. Heavy." He began to shake his head, then stilled again. She was so easy to talk to. "I can't really explain it," he continued. "I know they're symbols of knowledge and culture, and yet for me, anyway, they left me feeling . . . small. Insignificant."

"A small bump on the road of mankind?"

This time he did turn his head to face her. "Are you insulting me again?"

Caroline blushed. "Heavens, no. It's just that when reading Aristotle and Plato and even Shakespeare, that's occasionally how I feel. I greatly appreciate their knowledge and their skill, but it forces me to look inward. I sometimes wonder what's inside me that could possibly equal any of that greatness."

He gazed at her for a long moment, until she motioned at him to move his head again. "That's it. Precisely. I tried to explain Greece to Shay, and he said I must have eaten some spoiled cheese."

"How hard did you try to explain it to him? Really?"

"Not very. Shay doesn't appreciate my affinity for art. He appreciates that I know where in London to find the best roast pheasant."

"There's no reason you can't demonstrate both, is there?"

Christ, she sounded like Melbourne during one of the duke's attempts to convince him to choose a goal and pursue it. Obviously she'd taken his admonishment about standing behind one's beliefs to mean that she should feel free to continue criticizing him. "I don't know," he answered. "I've never actually tried that."

Her mouth quirked. "I think you have. After all, *I* know about your opinion of the Parthenon *and* your knowledge of pheasant dinners."

And now a compliment. "Thank you for that, but it's not necessary."

During the conversation she set down the pencil and picked up a paintbrush. Zachary badly wanted to see what she was doing, but he had no intention of causing more delays. His leg, the one bearing most of his weight, began to ache from being held so rigidly, but he ignored it.

"You may take a turn about the clearing if you want to stretch," she finally said. "I can place you back in position."

Thank Lucifer. He rolled his shoulders and lowered his left foot to the ground. "May I take a look?"

She nodded. "There's not much to see yet, but if you'd like."

Caroline hadn't blushed at the idea of someone else looking over her shoulder, but he didn't expect her to; she was a professional, and rightly proud of her skills. Stretching, he strolled over behind her.

And there he stood, a pale outline of himself, one leg bent and resting on a pencil line, right hand on his thigh and the left in his pocket. He didn't have much of a head, though the general shape was there, and rough ovals where his eyes would be. His hair was painted, though, black with a gold tint of sunlight above his temple, and a swath of color marked the line of his shoulder and his straight leg.

Ruins stretched around him, with the edge of the pond in the background to his left, and a herd of pencil cattle over his right shoulder. "It looks like I'm the master of my domain," he commented. "Or your father's domain, rather."

"That's what I wanted. You have that air about you, of confidence and ease. Aristocracy."

Now he hoped *he* wasn't blushing. Interesting that Caroline saw his faults probably more clearly than he did, and yet the compliments she gave: They rather stunned him, as did the fact that she'd found something she admired about him at all, and the fact that she'd said it aloud. Zachary cleared his throat, turning his gaze on the pond and cattle background. One cow in particular caught his attention. "That's your father's special cow, isn't it? The one you named Dimidius."

"Yes. I thought Papa would appreciate me putting her in the portrait."

"Does she really give twice the milk a standard breed does?"

Caroline shrugged. "She seems to. A good quality, too. Fine cream and butter. I've never measured the exact quantity. She's good-natured, and likes apples." She turned to look at him, then set down her brush, reached up, and tugged a little at his cravat.

He looked down at her fingers curled against his chest. "I can summon my valet if you'd prefer a different knot."

"No. It's fine. I just want the ruffle to show a little more." She continued to smooth at his chest.

"Caroline?"

She looked up, meeting his gaze. "Hm?"

"There's something else about yesterday."

"What?"

"You caught my attention."

Zachary cupped her face in his hands and kissed her. Her lips tasted like sweet strawberries. Across the clearing the maid napped, and with a sigh he deepened the kiss. Caroline leaned into him, sliding her hands up his shoulders and tousling his hair. Desire and arousal ran hot just under his skin—and for probably the first time in his life, he didn't give in to the sensation.

Instead he slowly and regretfully broke the embrace. "That was very sweet," he whispered.

"I'd like another anatomy lesson, Zachary," she breathed back.

Christ. He kissed her again, harder. "And I'd like to give you one. After."

"After?"

"After you've finished the portrait and you don't have a reason to be kind or grateful to me."

Her cheeks colored. "That's very gentlemanly of you, Zachary," she said shakily, lowering her hand from his hair.

"No, it's not. But it is fair warning." He caught her hand before she could back away. "Don't get me wrong, Caroline. Unless you change your mind, I fully intend to take advantage of you. But I won't be blamed for more delays." Zachary smiled grimly, meaning it. "Besides, isn't there some saying about anticipation sweetening the taste of something or other?"

Caroline chuckled a little breathlessly. "I have no idea. It sounds logical." She stood on her tiptoes and kissed him again, her hunger as tangible as his own. "Would you please go back to the column again?"

He hoped the portrait wouldn't show the ruined line of his trousers. As he returned to his position he concentrated on images of ugly chits and rotten vegetables. Standing still for the next session was going to be difficult enough without making her aware of just how much she aroused him.

Amazing, that twenty-four hours earlier he'd been ready to strangle her, and now he wanted nothing more than to hear her moan with pleasure. She might have a focus, but now he did as well—she drew him both literally and figuratively. No one had spoken to him as she had, and he was either going to prove her wrong or possess her. Or both.

Stop thinking about it, he ordered himself. He just needed to turn his attention to something else. He'd been thinking about something else right before she'd touched him and begun requesting anatomy lessons. What the devil had it been?

"Cows," he muttered.

"Beg pardon?"

Zachary cleared his throat. "Dimidius. How organized is your father's breeding program?"

Her fine cheek twitched. "It's actually quite . . . limited. We were only able to acquire two Guernsey cows and one mixed-blood South Devon bull. That's why it took so long to produce a cow. And then we could only breed one offspring, and that was with a South Devon bull belonging to an old army comrade of his. Papa didn't want any inbreeding."

Finances again. "So Dimidius's offspring might not possess the same milk-giving productivity as her dam."

"Correct. We won't know that for another year."

"What about the other local farmers? The sale of high-quality butter and cream alone could make the animals indispensable to the aristocracy. Aren't some of your neighbors willing to invest in cattle that might end up being so profitable? And their participation would certainly give a boost to the breeding population."

She shrugged as she dipped her brush in gray paint and swirled it into a touch of brown. "To be honest, Papa is known about Trowbridge as something of an . . . eccentric. Especially after he blew off the top of that windmill."

"The wind—" Intriguing, but beside the point. Zachary had probably fixated on the cow to distract himself from Caroline, but at the same time this was genuinely interesting. He'd bred horses, or at least advised on it, on and off for some time, and one of his progeny had won the Derby last year. Everyone, though, bred horses.

"May I ask you a question?" Caroline added some yellow to her mix and began applying it to the canvas.

"Certainly."

She glanced over her shoulder at the dozing maid. "A moment ago we were discussing your taking advantage of me, and then you began talking about cows. Am I supposed to interpret something from this?"

Zachary laughed. Thank God for honest, witty chits. And for this one in particular. "Good God, no."

"Oh, thank heavens. Because I would very much like to be taken advantage of."

Ugly chits, ugly chits. "I just happened to think that Dimidius could be a wasted opportunity."

"It takes a great deal of patience to breed cattle, Zachary. And Papa has a great many interests."

He understood. Edmund would undoubtedly do the best he

could, but without finances and the then inevitable diluting of the new bloodline, Dimidius would be the best and possibly only representative of her kind. Melbourne would never let such an opportunity fall by the wayside—not if he thought it could be turned profitable. And twice the milk—rich, high-quality milk, at that—produced from each cow in a herd could be turned extremely profitable.

The epiphany struck him like a bolt of lightning. Profitability, which would please Melbourne, and breeding, which interested him, and a fair share of patience and responsibility if he could manage to start up a successful breeding program. And an increased income for Witfeld, which would certainly help the family and its plethora of females.

He wanted to stride back to the house and find Edmund. Every muscle itched to set him into motion. Who would have thought that he would find his salvation in a damned cow?

Caroline stood twenty feet from him, painting and absorbed once again in her project. His own plans would mean spending even more time with her and her family, and he found that the idea—despite the chaos—appealed to him. Her auburn hair showed glints of red in the mottled sunlight, her green eyes lit to polished emerald by the excitement of what she was doing. He wanted her. Badly.

"What would you think, Caroline," he said slowly, "if I offered to assist your father with the Dimidius project?"

She lifted her head again. "I thought you were joining the army."

He shrugged. "Plans change."

Her eyes lowered from his, and with a slight nod she returned to her work.

He understood that look, though; he'd seen it before, mostly from his siblings. "What?" he demanded.

"Nothing. I don't want to make you angry again."

Zachary scowled. At her impatient breath, he wiped the expression from his face. "I told you that I'm not going anywhere until your painting is finished. So what were you thinking?"

"Fine. I was thinking that your plans change a great deal. I'd hate for you to get Papa's hopes up about something and then dash them again when something else more interesting catches your attention."

She did know him frighteningly well, considering their short acquaintance. Or rather, she knew the man he *had* been. A day—short in minutes, but long on time to think and see and understand—had altered him in a way he never would have expected, and it had made him aware of a Zachary Howard Griffin he never wanted to be again.

And just as clearly as he remembered his conversation with Caroline, he remembered the one with her father. In some ways, that had troubled him even more than her harsh words. No more mistakes—not ones born of boredom or impatience, anyway. It was time for him to choose a future and shape it into what he wanted and needed. "I won't change my plans this time." He meant it, and the clarity with which he felt that surprised—and pleased—him to his bones.

"Zachary, I hope that you're not changing your plans because of something I said."

"Of course I am." He faced her directly, ignoring her responding frown as he moved out of position. "For years my family's teased me about my aversion to responsibility. Right before I came here I think Melbourne tried to tell me what you succeeded in saying yesterday, but he was either too generous, or I just wasn't ready to hear it. Some things are going to change. And I thank you for pointing my faults out to me."

She set down the brush with a distinct thud. "Zachary, please do not put all of this on my head. For heaven's s—"

Zachary grinned. At least he wasn't the only troubled one. "I'm putting it all on your head, my dear. Now paint."

Chapter 14

At luncheon, the Witfeld girls sprang from the shrubbery like garden faeries. From their single-minded attention to Zachary and their enthusiasm about informing him what they'd done all morning while pining for his presence, Caroline decided they'd kept their word to their father and none of them had arrived early to spy.

And thank goodness for that. However increased the attraction she felt for Zachary, nothing could explain what had happened earlier. He'd approached her, complimented her work, and she'd simply . . . melted. Not touching him would have caused physical pain.

Luckily she'd kept enough of her wits about her not to end up immediately naked and ruined, but it hadn't helped her concentration. And then he'd begun talking about cows, of all things. *Cows.*

Perhaps it served her right, since she'd completely ignored yesterday's resolution to be quiet and polite. The way he continued to bait her, though, he could hardly expect anything else. But it wasn't just that; not even with Anne had she ever been able to speak so candidly about . . . everything.

She kept an eye on him as everyone trooped back to the mansion. He might think she'd suddenly decided she wanted him to ravish her, but she'd been contemplating it in theory since he'd removed his shirt. As of last night, though, the idea of an actual lesson had begun to seem less foolish.

Since she meant never to marry, and since after she reached Vienna she had no intention of doing anything to ruin her reputation and thereby her career, he was the best, most discreet chance she would have to experience being with a man. For heaven's sake, after the portrait left Wiltshire, so would he—and then so would she.

Or that had been the plan when they'd kissed. Since the cow discussion, she wasn't quite so certain what *he* meant to do. But that wouldn't matter, anyway, because *her* goals were not changing for anything. Yes, her plan for Zachary was perfect. Absolutely perfect. Emotion free, complication free, and wickedly enticing.

One thing did bother her, though, as they sat down to a luncheon of cucumber sandwiches, ham, and lemonade. Or two things did, rather. First, if he hadn't backed away, she would have simply fallen on him, even at the risk of not turning the portrait in on time. That made no sense at all. In fact it was so unlike her that it was almost frightening. And secondly, *he* had deferred their rendezvous in favor of her work.

She'd made an error. A stupid, inexplicable error, as far as she was concerned. And from this moment until the portrait was finished, nothing further could be allowed to distract her again. Especially not Lord Zachary Griffin. Afterwards, though . . . Her abdomen tightened deliciously.

Caroline frowned. So much for not allowing herself to be distracted. That had lasted for less than a minute. Still, she did have a considerable amount of willpower. She wouldn't have gotten this far if she didn't. Now she just needed to use it.

"Mama, even with Caroline taking all of Lord Zachary's time, we're not cancelling the ball, are we?" Grace asked.

"Of course not, dear. Your father gave the rest of you Lord Zachary's evenings, anyway."

Caroline started to point out that Zachary's evenings belonged to him, and that if he felt charitable he might choose to spend them in her sisters' company rather than his dog's, but he was chuckling. "I actually have a new game in mind for all of us to play tonight, if everyone is willing."

"Oh, yes!" the chorus of responses came.

"What sort of game is it," Susan asked, placing her hand over Zachary's, "that involves all of us?"

"You'll just have to wait and find out."

"Caro, you can't use Lord Zachary much after luncheon, can you?" Julia questioned, glaring at Susan. "The light will be wrong."

They would take him away from her if they could. And he was so notoriously easygoing, there was no telling what he would do if given the opportunity. "I have most of the light angles marked. I can't do as much, but enough to last another two hours or so." She looked at Zachary, to find him gazing at her. "If that's acceptable."

"I promised to stand out there all night, if necessary," he returned with an easy smile, "and once we finish for the day, I have an appointment with Harold."

"Your dog?" Violet protested.

Zachary nodded. "When I acquired him, I accepted a responsibility to train him to be a proper dog. I've been shirking that duty for far too long. So my apologies, ladies, but I'm spoken for until dinner."

Even his smile wasn't that same carefree one he'd worn a few days ago. It was more thoughtful, and as far as she was concerned, much more . . . intriguing. And he hadn't given in to their pleas. He'd kept his word to her—and to Harold.

"You know," Joanna said, slicing her ham, "I think art is wonderful. In fact, I've been working on my own painting."

"You?" Caroline blurted before she could stop herself.

"Yes. It's Apollo and Psyche." She sniffed. "I'm Psyche, and I'd like Lord Zachary to pose for Apollo." Joanna gazed at him from beneath her lashes. "If you would, of course."

"I, um—"

"I'm doing a painting, too!" Grace's fork clattered onto her plate as she sat forward.

"So am I," Violet put in, at even higher volume.

Wonderful. Caroline closed her eyes for a moment. She supposed it would have been amusing if it hadn't been so obviously pitiful. Out of all of her sisters, not even Anne had professed the least interest in art, except for that book showing sketches of naughty sculptures that Mrs. Williams had accidently shelved in her store. After seeing Zachary in the bath yesterday, Caroline was wishing she'd spent more time studying that particular book, herself.

"I'd like to see your work," Zachary said, his eyes dancing despite his solemn expression, "as soon as I've finished helping Miss Witfeld and Harold. After dinner, perhaps."

At least his sense of humor had survived. Thank goodness for that.

"How much longer are you going to keep Zachary to yourself, Caro?" Susan demanded.

"Yes, Caroline," her mother said. "I have to agree. I know finishing your portrait is important, but we have to be fair to your sisters."

"I—"

"You know, girls," Lady Gladys interrupted, "it occurred to me that even better than my sending you gifts at Christmas, we might go into Trowbridge and select them together. Mrs. Williams's shop has catalogs, I believe."

Thank heavens for Lady Gladys. Caroline sent her a grateful look amid the chorus of happy cheers, and the baroness winked at her. At least someone understood how important it was that she finish the portrait in a timely manner. Someone aside from Zachary, that was, since they had clearly come to an understanding about that.

As they stood from the table, though, obviously her sisters hadn't forgotten about their abrupt new love of the arts. "Caro," Joanna said in a whisper, grabbing her arm, "do you have any spare canvases?"

Caroline sighed. "In the wardrobe behind the conservatory door."

"I need a sketch pad," Violet said, tugging her other hand.

"They're stacked against the far wall."

"Thank you, Caro!" They all dashed off in a herd of flying skirts.

"Don't touch anything but the new ones!" she shouted after them. If they tried drawing on the backs of sketches she'd already done, heads were going to roll. Harold had already done enough damage.

"Shall we return to the ruins?" Zachary murmured, drawing her hand around his arm.

A shiver ran down her spine. Stating to herself that she was going to remain undistracted was one thing; not reacting when his skin touched hers was another, entirely. Waiting two or even three days with this . . . tension running through her veins and muscles, this awareness of his presence—it was worse than the wait for a new canvas. "Yes, of course. I've left poor Molly sitting out there by the ruins."

"She's probably still asleep," he returned in the same low voice. "Make certain you keep her with us for the next few days."

Goodness, he sounded so sure of himself. He probably knew exactly the effect he was having on her. "Please try not to distract me," she said half seriously. "I'd hate to have to spend all of the third day fixing my mistakes."

She felt his chuckle. "But I want to tell you all about what will happen the moment you set down your paintbrush and palette for the last time. The way I will strip you out of your gown, and pull the pins from your hair, and cover your bare skin with kisses."

Well, now she was going to faint. "I hope some of it is going to involve the part of your anatomy I glimpsed in the bath," she managed in a fairly level tone, knowing her face must be scarlet.

"It certainly will. That's a vital part, as a matter of fact." They reached the path that circled the pond and led directly to the ruins on the far side. As they moved between a high stand of elms and the willows that lined the bank, he put a hand over hers and stopped. "Speaking of vital," he whispered and drew her up against him.

Slowly he lowered his mouth over hers. Yes, their relationship had definitely altered in the past twenty-four hours. That thought occurred to her only fleetingly, though, because her mind refused to function any further. Instead she felt flooded with sensation— the ply of his mouth against hers, the heat, the pressure, the yearning that seemed to flow back and forth between them, his hands sliding from her shoulders and down her back to her hips, and the way he pulled her close against his body.

Caroline wrapped her arms around the back of his neck, hold- ing herself tightly against his lean, hard-muscled body. The kiss deepened, open-mouthed and plundering. She heard herself moan. Passion. The sensation was remarkable—and remarkably close to how she felt when a painting swept her away out of all reason. She wanted to climb inside him, to keep the feeling forever.

"Caro," he murmured, his voice muffled against her mouth.

She subsided, closing her eyes and trying to focus her mind. The painting. She needed to finish the painting.

With what she considered remarkable composure, she released him. His own arms loosened more slowly, his mouth still brush- ing hers. "There," he finally said huskily, "that should do me for another day or so."

Caroline smoothed his ruffled hair. "Are you certain about that?"

"No. You probably shouldn't ask me again."

She would keep that advice in mind. Because things were be- coming very confusing, and now that he was being nice and touching her and kissing her, she'd developed the alarming ten- dency to be distracted, despite every oath she'd made to herself. "I won't, then. Come on. I want to work on your face before we get the full afternoon sun."

As they reached the ruins in the clearing he shed his coat again, dumping it beside her paints. Her sisters were probably ransacking the conservatory right now, taking every blank canvas she had, ruining her brushes and making a mess of her organized sketch filing system.

Normally the idea would have had her pulling out her hair. After all, she used every spare penny she earned from painting to pay for her supplies. If they would leave her alone for the next two days, though, just long enough for her to finish one portrait and to . . . experience Zachary Griffin, she would forgive every bit of it. After all, they would be remaining in Wiltshire, left to the Martin Williamses and Peter Redfords, and she would be in Vienna, living her dream.

"Here?" he asked, placing a foot on the fallen pillar.

She compared the sketch to his position. "About eight inches back with your right foot, and about four with your left," she decided, narrowing her eyes.

Zachary complied, shifting and twisting slightly. "Better?"

"Perfect. Now tilt your head and gaze toward the horizon over my shoulder so I can do your eyes."

"The horizon over your shoulder isn't very exciting. Why can't I be looking at the artist?"

Because if he stood staring at her all afternoon his face would end up looking like a bowl of pudding. "Because I'm not your domain. Survey in that direction."

"All I survey is a tree stump and a bird eating a beetle."

"Good. Concentrate on the beetle. And relax your mouth." She picked up her narrow-tipped brush, touching it to her cheek to make certain it was clean and dry.

"I thought you were painting my face, not your own."

Her cheeks heated. "Obviously you're not looking at the beetle."

"The beetle's been consumed, and you're more interesting."

Finally she lifted her gaze to him to find him still studying her face, and with an intensity that sent her blood stirring again. No wonder his name in the society pages always seemed to be associated with some eligible young lady or other—at least according to Anne. "Zachary, tree stump. Please."

His broad shoulders lifted and lowered. "Fine. Tree stump."

"And don't scowl."

"But the bird is leaving a gift."

Her lips twitched, despite her determination to eliminate all nonsense from her thoughts. "Then you have the beetle to concentrate on again."

"I'm not spending the next hour staring at bird droppings."

This time she couldn't help chuckling. "It's for the sake of art."

"No, it's for the sake of Caroline Witfeld."

A sudden shiver made her hand tremble, and she had to take a step back and shake out her wrist. "Stop that, or you *will* be there all night."

"Very well. Just please don't name the painting *Lord Zachary Griffin Surveying Bird Droppings*."

"I promise."

He finally settled into his stance, and she could concentrate on his face. She liked his expression; confident and a little amused, with just a hint of wicked. If she could capture that as well as he wore it, Monsieur Tannberg would have to offer her the apprenticeship. The fact that the wickedness was for her—well, no one else would ever have to know that. After all, it was the very enigmatic quality of the *Mona Lisa* that made her so admired.

After forty minutes or so of banter about everything from ball gowns to da Vinci, Molly snorted and, from the sound of it, fell off the stone bench. "Molly?" Caroline called, pausing her brush stroke.

"Oh. Yes, Miss Witfeld. I must have dozed off for a moment. I beg your pardon."

"No harm," Caroline returned, keeping in mind that if she chastised the maid for her slumber, Molly likely wouldn't repeat it, or Barling would replace the maid with a more alert chaperone. "Would you please fetch Lord Zachary and myself a glass of lemonade? And get yourself something to eat."

"Yes, Miss Witfeld."

Touching her brush to the skin tone she'd mixed, Caroline made a light curve to indicate the lobe of Zachary's ear as it showed through his dark, breeze-blown hair. When she looked up at him again, though, she nearly dropped the brush. "What are you doing? Get back over there."

He didn't slow his approach. "I'm taking advantage of the absence of your attentive servant to deliver a kiss to the artist," he drawled.

"I told you that I need to finish your face today," she retorted, deciding to ignore him. She couldn't do the shadowing until tomorrow morning, but she could finish the skin-tone matting.

"Fine." He circled around behind her. "I look splendid," he said after a moment. "What's that, though?" He reached an arm over her shoulder to point.

"That's a mouth."

"My mouth does not look like that."

"Well, I can't see it at the moment, so fixing it will have to wait." His criticism didn't concern her; she hadn't gotten to his mouth, anyway, except to mark its placement with pencil and a line of peach-brown paint.

Light fingers brushed a wisp of hair from the back of her neck, and she froze as another tremble ran down her spine. Warm lips replaced his fingers, and she dropped the brush.

"Zach—"

"Shh. I'm demonstrating lips, to give you a better sense of mouth," he murmured, continuing his assault.

If she had a better sense of his mouth, she would be naked right now. Deft fingers peeled the neck of her gown down her shoulder, his lips following.

Caroline was beginning to understand why poets equated sexual ecstasy with death, because if he could make her feel this much with just his mouth on her bare shoulder, being naked, skin against skin, was going to kill her. She drew a shuddering breath. "Please stop."

His forehead lowered to rest on her shoulder. "Apologies. I was beginning to have fantasies about the tree stump."

She snorted, taking the moment to recover a little of her equilibrium. A very little. "Hopefully, then, you find me an improvement over dead wood and bark."

Laughter rumbled from his chest. "Good God, Caroline. Virgins aren't supposed to say such things."

"Aren't we? And why not?"

"Because you'll frighten we worldly men." With a last, much more chaste, kiss planted on her shoulder, he replaced her gown. "Might I at least please sit on my pillar for a moment and drink my lemonade?"

Molly bustled up the path. So that was why he'd given in to reason so readily. She would remember that he had very keen hearing. "Of course. I'll join you there."

"Good. I prefer a sweet with my sour."

She would have retorted, but Molly reached the clearing, curtsying as she offered Zachary a glass from the tray she carried. Caroline accepted one as well and sat beside him on her father's faux ruin.

"You are staying on schedule, despite my disruptions?" he asked, his expression growing more serious.

She realized she was learning to read his moods by the subtle changes in his face. That made sense, considering how long she'd been studying him. "Yes. Barring an act of God or nature, the painting will arrive in Vienna on time."

"Good. I should tell you that last evening I sent a note to my brother Shay to have his yacht waiting in Dover to take an urgent package across the Channel."

For a moment she couldn't speak. He'd offered to help expedite the portrait's delivery, of course, but she'd had no idea that he'd already taken steps. And he'd done so before she'd—before they'd—begun this new flirtation. "Thank you."

Zachary nodded. "My pleasure."

Goodness, she wanted to kiss him on that warm, sensuous mouth. Molly was noisily eating across the clearing, however, so any physical contact was obviously out of the question. To do so would mean ruin, a forced marriage, and no portrait painting in Vienna. She saw in his eyes that he immediately came to the same conclusion, though the swift emotion that crossed his face wasn't anything she could decipher.

"Did I say something wrong?" she asked quietly, so the maid couldn't hear.

"Not in the least. My bird flew away."

Chuckling, she sipped at her lemonade. "If you can last for another hour, I can do most of the gray tones of your trousers and waistcoat this evening by candlelight. I'm afraid I'll have to ask you to wear the same clothes tomorrow, though, so I can fill in the shadow tones."

Zachary nodded. "My valet may suffer an apoplexy, but I'll manage it."

She smiled. At his return grin, though, and the soft light in his eyes, she cleared her throat and concentrated on her lemonade. If she'd had any idea that speaking her mind to the point of insulting him would arouse both his attention and his interest, she would have kept her mouth shut. Caroline glanced sideways at Zachary as he drank. Who was she fooling? A kiss from him was as intoxicating as finding the perfect rose color to re-create the first blush of dawn.

He finished off his lemonade, a droplet running deliciously down his chin before he swiped it away with the back of one hand. For a fleeting second she'd wanted to lick it off. Caroline took a breath. *Steady.* One thing at a time. First the portrait, then an intimate moment with Zachary, and then Vienna.

The problem with that equation, though, was that Vienna seemed half the world away, and Zachary Griffin couldn't seem to stop kissing her any more than she wanted him to desist. *Two days.* She could wait two days.

Chapter 15

Zachary felt like Troy being overwhelmed by the legions of Greece. The moment he swallowed his last bite of baked ham, the assault began.

"Lord Zachary, will you pose for me?"

"Zachary, I want to paint you as Adonis."

"Play charades with us, Lord Zachary."

With a smile he didn't feel, Zachary pushed back from the dinner table. "Actually, I'd like a quick word with Mr. Witfeld, and then I'll join you in the drawing room for our game, if that's acceptable."

Susan shot to her feet. "I'll get my sketch pad."

Immediately the rest of the horde scampered, with the exception of his aunt, who only shook her head and looked amused; Mrs. Witfeld, who was so engrossed in counting acceptances to her party invitations that she'd missed half the meal conversation; and Caroline, who looked happier than he'd ever seen her.

Her dream was coming to fruition. And it pleased him immensely to have been the one to make that possible. If he'd stormed off and left, he never would have forgiven himself.

"Join me in my office, lad," Edmund said, gesturing for Zachary to precede him.

Once the two of them were alone, Zachary sat forward in his chair. "I've been thinking," he began.

"About what?"

"About Dimidius."

"My cow?"

"I spoke with Caroline, and she said it's been difficult to acquire enough animals of the correct lineage to begin a breeding program."

Edmund's expression hardened. "I only told you what I did the other day to convince you to return and assist Caroline. I was not asking for charity, my lord."

"I'm not offering any," Zachary returned briskly. "I'm offering a partnership."

If Mr. Witfeld looked less affronted, he looked doubly confused. "Please explain."

"Certainly. You have a cow that gives double the milk of a standard breed. I have money and resources to enable you to expand your breeding program and develop an entire herd."

"And what do you get out of it?"

That was the sticky part. "Since Melbourne is the head of the family, I'll have to write him about the details and ask for final approval, but I think a share in the profits would be fair."

"For the sale of the milk?"

"For the sale of the milk, the resulting quality cream and butter, and the cattle." Zachary sat forward. "If you're successful at repeating what you've done with Dimidius, there won't be a farmer in England who won't be interested in beginning his own herd. We could provide cows or stud bulls and save them years in crossbreeding, since we will have already done it."

"This is not a short-term project you're discussing, lad."

"I'm aware of that."

Edmund looked at him for a long moment. "You've given up on joining the army, then?"

Zachary grimaced. "To be honest, someone made me seriously reconsider throwing my life away for death and glory. And I've dabbled in horse breeding. It's fascinating, but I think that's every nobleman's hobby. This, though, has much greater potential than breeding a Derby winner or two." He took a slow breath. "And honestly, I'm tired of dabbling."

"What if the duke doesn't agree?"

He'd damned well better. "I have funds at my discretion. It would be a slower process without his resources and backing, but I do have some well-connected acquaintances. Just because Melbourne refused to see a good thing doesn't mean everyone would."

"You'd go around your brother?"

"I'd give him first chance. After that, as far as I'm concerned it's 'may the best cow win.' "

Slowly Edmund nodded. "I've been wanting to do something like this for years. It's why I bred Dimidius in the first place. But as you said, on the scale I've been working, at most I'd get half a dozen cattle and be able to sell my excess milk at the local market." He stuck out his hand. "By God, lad, if you can manage it, you've got a deal. And a partner."

Grinning, Zachary shook Witfeld's hand. "I'll write my brother tonight. You won't regret it, sir."

"Papa, please don't keep Lord Zachary in there all night," Joanna's voice came as she rapped at the closed door. "We get a share of him, too."

Witfeld smiled back at him. "I won't regret it, but you might."

Zachary had one more thing to do, one more thing to make right, before he could settle into the cattle breeding business. He left Edmund making some notes about their new venture and accompanied Joanna and Julia back upstairs to the drawing room.

All the girls were there, including Caroline. That surprised him, since she'd said she needed to paint this evening, but he had no doubt that come hell or high water, she would not miss her deadline.

Aunt Tremaine and Mrs. Witfeld were having a coze in the corner, but he didn't expect they'd interfere overly much. At the cacophony of pleas and demands aimed in his direction, he raised one hand. "May I have your attention for a moment?"

Everyone subsided to look at him expectantly.

"My thanks. First of all, I apologize for any miscues I may have caused at the assembly ball."

"Oh, no, Lord Zachary," Mrs. Witfeld broke in, putting a hand to her heart. "You were so gracious, dancing with all my dears."

He wished the family matriarch would make herself scarce or go back to counting invitation acceptances, but that wasn't likely to happen now. "Thank you, Mrs. Witfeld. However, I gave your daughters some imperfect, or at least incomplete, advice. I would like to rectify that."

"Yes, you did send us all after Martin Williams," Anne agreed.

"I hadn't realized—I didn't pay enough attention to realize— that you had all decided to choose the same man."

"I still choose you, Lord Zachary," Grace declared, blushing.

"And that is something else I'd like to make clear. I'm not here to marry, or to lead any of you astray."

"But—"

"Hush, Violet," Anne chastised. "Let him finish a blasted sentence."

He sent Anne an appreciative look. Caroline had yet to say a word, but he didn't really think she would. This wasn't her area of interest or concern. And as for being led astray, she'd done as he required, which was to invite him.

"What I *would* like to do, however," he continued, "is to give you a little insight into men, and to perhaps help you learn how to approach a man who interests you."

Mrs. Witfeld made another noise.

"You know, Sally," Aunt Tremaine said, lurching to her feet, "you promised to show me some embroidery you were working on. Perhaps we should leave the young ones to their entertainment."

"I—"

"Do come," his aunt cajoled. "I feel in need of a bit of exercise, anyway."

"Oh, very well. If you think they'll be all right without us."

"My nephew is a perfect gentleman." As she passed by, Aunt

Tremaine swatted him across the backside with her cane. "Behave," she whispered.

He planted a kiss on her cheek. "Of course."

Once the ladies departed, Zachary resumed his instruction. "Firstly, you can't all have the same man."

"But how do we decide who gets which man?" Julia demanded. "And don't say it should be by age, because that isn't fair."

"Actually, according to tradition, it *is* fair," he returned. "But that's not my decision. It's yours."

"Shouldn't the gentleman have some say in the matter?" Caroline put in unexpectedly.

"Another good point. Perhaps a one-at-a-time approach might serve. At any rate, I will tell you the three things any gentleman would love to hear."

"There are three?" Caroline asked again, lifting an eyebrow.

Despite the fact that every inch of him seemed attuned to her presence, he was beginning to wish that she would go away and work on the portrait. "There are more than three. These are the simplest, and the most likely to get a man's attention. After that, it's up to you."

"What are they?" Violet asked.

"First, ask if he would care to join you for a refreshment. Either food or drink will do, but in my experience, gentlemen love to eat."

"What if we're not at a soiree?" Grace asked. "What if we're in a store when we meet?"

At least one of them was still focused on Martin Williams, then. "Then use the second item. Tell him he's wearing a thoughtful expression, and you would very much like to know what he might be thinking." He glanced at Caroline, seeing her open her mouth to interject a question. "It implies that you believe the gentleman to be an intelligent and deep thinker, and that you value his opinion," he went on, forestalling her commentary. "It's very flattering. Trust me."

Even Anne was beginning to look impressed. Good. They all seemed to be perfectly pleasant girls, if several of them were a little feather-headed, and it wasn't their fault each one was disadvantaged by being constantly in competition with six—five—other sisters. And given their mother's grasp of subtle social niceties and the fact that none of them had ever been to London or to finishing school, someone needed to tell them.

"What's the third item?" Susan asked.

He looked at all the eager, upturned faces for a moment. All the men of England—or at least of Wiltshire—would hopefully forgive him for what he was about to unleash upon them. "It also has to do with food."

"Why am I not surprised?" Caroline muttered.

"Hush, Caro. You may not care to know this, but we do."

"Apologies, Joanna. Pray continue, Lord Zachary."

"Tell him that seeing him puts you in mind of a peach pie or a pudding or a butter biscuit you're particularly fond of. Then ask if he might wish to partake of it the next time he goes fishing."

"Fishing? We're to go fishing?"

"No, you're to offer to provide a treat for him the next time he goes. Then, whether he accepts or not, when he's fishing or thinking of fishing, he'll also be thinking of you and sweets. If your chosen gentleman has another hobby—shooting or driving or something—substitute that for fishing."

"That's brilliant," Susan breathed.

"But I would suggest that you make a lottery of the gentlemen you find acceptable, and each take a name. You might of course trade if you find your tastes run elsewhere or that you're more compatible with a different gentleman, but since you're sisters, I again remind you that if you all pursue the same man, he will either refuse all of you, or one of you will end up hurting the rest."

"Grace, go fetch some paper. We'll write down possibilities right now," Anne instructed.

Caroline stood. "Which seems to be my signal to depart. I have some work to do."

"And I have some correspondence," Zachary seconded, rising after her. "Ladies? I'll see you in the morning."

"Good night, Zachary," came the return chorus.

Caroline preceded him out the drawing room door. "That was interesting," she said over her shoulder as she headed for the stairs.

"I'm trying to be helpful."

"I think it was helpful. More so than the advice you gave them to ambush poor Martin Williams at the assembly, anyway."

"That wasn't my advice. I merely told them not to pin their hopes on me, and to find someone who would more appreciate their sweet dispositions." He followed her up the stairs, staying far enough below that he could admire the sway of her hips as she ascended. *Two days.* He could wait two days to bury himself in her.

"You were trying to rid yourself of them."

"No, I was trying to avoid setting your sisters against one another. In all honesty, though, I should have taken more care about what I said. I thought I could do a good deed without being put out."

She turned around, looking down at him. "Am I putting you out?"

"If you were, it would be no more than I deserved." He climbed a step, reaching out to take her hand in his. "But you're not."

"I keep wondering," she said quietly, "if you've become so thoughtful because you are, or because you're trying to gain something."

He knew what she meant. It would have been easy, he supposed, to charm his way beneath her skirt and then ridicule her for it afterwards. "I admire you, Caroline," he returned. "I envy you. I'm not angry at you."

"Why in the world do you envy me?"

"Because you've known forever what you want in life, and you've taken the steps to achieve it." He smiled. "You're teaching me some important lessons, and in return, I have a few to teach you."

She ran her gaze down the length of him and back again, with a leisurely intensity that made his mouth dry. "Then I look forward to it," she murmured.

Sebastian, Duke of Melbourne, sat finishing his morning coffee as the butler reappeared with a salver full of letters. "Thank you, Stanton," he said, motioning for the stack to be placed at his elbow.

"Very good, Your Grace."

He sifted through them absently, most of his thoughts on his meeting with the prime minister before luncheon. The new damned tariffs were strangling his business with America. The former Colonies wouldn't stand for much more of it, either.

"Any letters for me, Papa?" Peep asked from her seat at his right elbow.

"There's an invitation from Lady Jeffers for you to join her and her daughter in Hyde Park tomorrow," he said, handing it to her.

"I like Alice," his daughter commented, looking at the invitation, "but I think Lady Jeffers wants to marry you."

Sebastian glanced at her. He'd long since ceased to wonder at the insights of infants, but she still surprised him more than he would let on. "And that's not a good thing?"

Peep shook her head. "She laughs too much, when I don't think she means it."

That fairly well agreed with his own assessment of Lady Jeffers. "Do you want to attend, then?"

"Oh, yes. There are supposed to be acrobats."

"I'll accept on your behalf, then."

The messy scrawl of the Griffin House address across one of the missives caught his attention, and he freed it from the pile. Zachary. He broke the wax seal and unfolded it. " 'Melbourne,' " he read to himself, " 'I've been talking with Edmund Witfeld here in Wiltshire. He has a new breed of cow that gives rich milk in twice the quantity as a standard Guernsey. Would you be interested in investing? We need to increase breeding stock to be sure Dimidius isn't a fluke. Zachary.' "

Sebastian assumed Dimidius was the cow in question. For the first letter he'd received from Zachary since his brother had left London, this one was a bit surprising. A fortnight ago his youngest brother had been angry and resentful and set on joining the army and getting himself killed. Now it was cattle—which wasn't as odd as the fact that there was no chitchat, none of the amusing commentary that usually came from Zachary, and no mention that one of the Witfeld daughters was painting his portrait for some sort of business proposition.

He frowned a little, wishing Aunt Tremaine's long-winded letters contained a few more useful details. Between Zachary and his aunt he was lucky to have been informed that the pair of them were residing outside of Bath.

"That's Uncle Zachary's writing, isn't it?" Penelope said, bouncing up in her chair. "When is he coming home?"

"He doesn't say."

"Is Aunt Tremaine feeling better?"

"He doesn't say that, either."

She blew out her breath. "Well, what does he say, then?"

"He says he found a cow."

"A cow?"

"Yes. Her name is . . ." He checked again. "Dimidius."

Peep thought about that for a moment. "What's he going to do with her? I thought Aunt Tremaine said he got a dog."

"I haven't the faintest idea what's going on." And for once that was the truth, damn it all. Sebastian perused the letter again, then folded it to place the thing in his pocket. Breeding cattle could be an expensive and extremely long-term proposition, and he had no intention of sinking any of his funds into the project on a whim. And where Zachary's interests were concerned, nearly everything was a whim.

He would wait a day or two before he answered; by then, Zachary would likely be involved in a completely different project, so the refusal wouldn't anger him. As Sebastian sipped his coffee, he did feel a little gratitude toward Dimidius the cow. At least Zachary seemed to have forgotten the army. He could only pray that would continue.

"I've never seen them so concerned about talking to a man," Caroline said, grinning as she and Zachary left the house after luncheon. "One might almost think they've realized their efforts tomorrow at the soiree might not be in vain."

"I hope it all goes well for them. I'll certainly do my part." Zachary glanced at her, gauging her mood against the question he wanted to ask. "Did you ever wish to be married? When you were six or seven, perhaps?"

Caroline shrugged, her hand brushing his as they headed down the pond path toward the ruins. "I suppose the thought entered my mind. But back then it would have been all about riding on grand horses and living in huge castles with liveried servants and grand ballrooms, and rose petals carpeting all the floors."

Except for the rose petals, she might have been describing Melbourne Park. He wasn't about to say that aloud, though. Not when he could think of little but her bare skin against his and her moans of pleasure. *Tomorrow.* "You're still on schedule with the portrait, yes?"

"Yes. Barring disaster, it will be finished tomorrow and ready for me to post the day after."

"Good," he murmured, reaching over to feather her hair behind her ear. At her responding shiver, he went hard. Come hell or high water, she was going to finish that damned painting tomorrow.

As Caroline looked at the finished portrait, she knew she'd captured the essence of Zachary Griffin. The problems she'd initially encountered had vanished the moment she'd decided to paint him at the ruins. His adventurous, hopeful spirit had responded to the rather exotic location and appeared in his expression, on his face. The meld had been perfection.

Now that she'd painted the last stroke, though, she hesitated to say anything. In the warm summer air, the paint would dry enough that she could package the portrait in its waiting wooden box by tomorrow afternoon. She'd signed her name in one corner, but still she kept him standing over there amid the ruins.

Of course one step did remain—she needed his letter of approval. And to get that, she needed to tell him she'd completed the work. Caroline took a deep breath. "Would you like to take a look?"

He lowered his leg from its stance, bending to stretch his back. "You're finished?"

"I'm finished." A thrill ran down her spine; one that had nothing to do with the portrait, and everything to do with the promise he'd made her for afterward.

Zachary glanced at Molly, who was snoring quietly on the bench behind the roses, then approached to look at the portrait as she stepped aside. He gazed at it in silence for so long that she began to worry she'd made some error, invisible to her, but blatant to anyone and everyone else who would ever look at it. Oh, she was going to have to be the stupid Eades's stupid governess, after all.

"Caroline, it's stunning," he finally said. "If I didn't know who'd painted it, I would attribute it to Joshua Reynolds."

"Zach—"

"I'm serious," he interrupted. "If Monsieur Tannberg knows anything about talent, he'll take you on in a heartbeat."

She wanted to sing, to dance, and mostly to kiss him. "Thank you."

He shook his head. "Don't thank me. I only stood there. You did the work." With a smile he reached for his coat and dug into the inside pocket. "And because I did sneak a few looks at it yesterday and the day before, I had a feeling I could save us—you— a bit of time." Pulling a folded paper free, he handed it to her.

Caroline unfolded it. Addressed to Monsieur Tannberg, in simple terms it expressed not only Zachary's satisfaction with the portrait but also his pleasure and delight in working with such a skilled, professional artist. "You mean all of this," she whispered, moved beyond words.

"Now that I see the finished portrait, I'm glad I didn't say more. It speaks for itself."

"I mean, you didn't write it just because you want . . . you know."

Zachary smiled. "No," he said, shaking his head. "That letter says what it does because you deserve it."

Carefully she refolded the letter and set it on the easel. She so wanted to throw herself on him. He would think it was gratitude, though, and he wouldn't be wrong—but there was more to it than that. It would be a celebration, a symbol of completion, an exclamation mark that her life as she'd known it no longer existed.

"How long do you want to wait before you box the painting?" he asked, squatting down to pick up the blanket she'd brought to cover her legs against the chill earlier in the morning.

"Tomorrow afternoon, to be safe. It'll start drying nicely out here."

Zachary sent another look at Molly. Then he hooked a finger through the open buttonhole of Caroline's maroon pelisse and drew her toward him. As she stumbled against his chest, he tilted her chin up with his free hand and kissed her.

He'd been teasing, flirting with her when they'd kissed before. That became immediately evident as his mouth molded against hers, sending heat spearing down her spine. Caroline wrapped her fingers into his dark hair, moaning as she drank him in.

Abruptly he broke the kiss. "Shh," he breathed before she could protest, and shooting a glance toward their supposed chaperone. "This way."

Taking her hand, he helped her over the fallen pillar and into the small clearing behind it. Before she could say anything, thank him again for all that he'd done, his mouth found hers again. This could be enough, she decided, the heat and the floating. How could just a touching of lips and mouths feel so electric and arousing?

Then his hands brushed the outsides of her breasts, and he slowly slid his palms toward one another across her chest until they covered her nipples. She jumped as he pressed against her.

Good heavens. A warm, breathless tightness began between her legs. Abruptly kissing wasn't enough. She wanted more.

"Caroline," he murmured, moving his mouth to the base of her jaw, "I'm going to ask you once if you still want this. Answer me truthfully."

She lifted her eyes to his. "It's not fair that a man may do this whenever he wishes, as long as he is discreet, and a woman, even though she has decided to live a single life of propriety and quiet, may not. I am choosing my own path."

He grinned, eyes dancing. "Is that a 'yes'?"

Releasing his hair, she placed her hands over his, which still covered her breasts. Shifting, she undid one of the buttons of her pelisse, then moved his fingers to undo the next one. "That is a definite 'yes.' "

"Good."

In a second he had her pelisse open and had pushed it down her arms. This time when he kissed her, her knees felt wobbly. Lips, mouths, tongues—heavens, how could any woman be expected to forgo this simply because she'd decided to remain unmarried?

Pressed hard against him, her hands twined around his neck, his close around her waist, she could feel his arousal against her abdomen. Her breath came faster, her heart pounding. "Zachary, I don't know how much time we have."

"Twenty minutes before luncheon," he whispered back, reaching around her to undo the back of her gown with a skill that left her breathless. "Not enough time, but we'll just have to make due."

As he slid her dress and shift off her shoulders, the summer breeze against her bare skin made her shiver—not from cold but from anticipation. With stumbling fingers she undid the buttons of his waistcoat, then pulled the shirt from his trousers. He kept saying the right things, the sensitive ones, the concerned ones she wanted to hear. If it was part of a seduction, though, it was wasted energy. She wanted him, and this was the best opportunity she would have to indulge her passions.

He knelt on the blanket he'd tossed to the ground and drew her down beside him. "I want you to show me everything," Caroline murmured, sliding her hands beneath his shirt and up his bare chest.

"It's not so much a matter of showing, as of feeling," he returned, leaning forward to kiss her bare shoulder. He nudged her dress and shift down further, his mouth following. As his lips brushed the top of her breast, her breath caught.

"I see what you mean," she managed.

Zachary chuckled. "No, you don't. Not yet." He sat back a little and tugged her gown down to her waist. For a long moment he gazed at her bare breasts, then slowly lifted his hands to cup and caress them.

With a harsh breath, Caroline leaned into the caress. *Dear heaven.* She'd always considered herself led by thought and logic in everything but art, but this sensation was . . . extraordinary, and so deeply arousing that she wasn't certain she could stand much more. And then he took her left breast into his mouth and rolled his tongue across her nipple.

"Oh, God," she gasped.

He put an arm around behind her and guided her flat down on the blanket. Caroline arched her back as he switched his attention to her right breast, and she tangled her hands into his hair to hold him against her chest. When he chuckled again in response, she felt it all the way down to between her legs.

Shifting a little, he raised up only far enough to yank his shirt off over his head, then returned to his torment. She loved the feel of his bare skin, smooth and velvet, with muscles of steel beneath. Running her hands down his back, she stopped at his waist and trailed forward to fumble at the fastening of his trousers.

"Not yet," he said, pulling back away from her reach. His trousers half undone and an obvious bulge at the apex of his thighs, he took the top of her gown and pulled downward. She lifted her hips and the dress and shift came free, followed by her shoes as he removed them and tossed them one by one over his shoulder.

Caroline lay there, naked beneath the elm trees and climbing roses, as he took her left ankle and placed feather-light, glancing kisses along her skin and up the inside of her leg. She couldn't hold still, clasping her fingers and running her palms along her own hips and breasts as he moved slowly and agonizingly upward.

Sinking onto his stomach, Zachary parted her thighs a little further and leaned in. As his tongue darted inside her, she gasped again, bucking. "Please, Zachary," she quavered, trying to keep her voice down and barely remembering why, "I can't stand any more. I can't go any farther."

"Yes, you can," he returned, his own voice unsteady at the edges.

He worked his way down her other leg with the same maddening patience. How could he stand to take his time, when every inch of her body felt such an incredible urgency to be with him?

Finally he knelt upright again and finished unfastening his trousers. He lifted up a little and shucked the dark gray material down past his thighs. "You're the reason artists create sculptures," she breathed, sitting up to look at him.

"I was going to say the same thing about you, love, but thank you." With a warm smile, the expression in his eyes telling her exactly what he intended to do next, he moved over her. Taking her mouth in an open, hungry kiss, he followed her back down to the blanket, trailing his lips down her throat to her breasts again.

"Zachary, we're running out of time," she complained, grasping his hair to tug his face up to hers again.

"The next time, we are not going to rush."

The next time? She wasn't certain she would survive this encounter. "Please."

"Hold on," he whispered, lowering his hips until his manhood pressed against her. Very slowly, with a care she noted even though she wanted him to hurry, he pushed forward.

She felt a sharp pain when he entered her. She closed her eyes in surprise. Every ounce of her was centered deep inside her as his slow slide continued until he was buried completely.

"Jesus," he muttered, his arms shaking a little. "Open your eyes."

Caroline did so, gazing up at him just a few inches from her face. And then he began to move his hips. Bucking again, she grasped her hands around his shoulders, digging in her fingers at the deep, tight pull inside her. His mouth found hers again, and she drank him in, pulling his hard body as close to hers as she could. Even being joined as they were wasn't enough. She wanted more. She wanted everything.

His rhythm increased, and she couldn't help her small whimpering moans which matched his thrusts. The clenching inside her grew tighter and tighter, until with a gasp she shattered, clinging to him helplessly as her mind shut down completely.

He sped his motions, in out, in out, and then with a groan from deep in his chest, he withdrew and lowered his head to her shoulder. Breathing hard, she kissed his ear and tried to remember where they were, and why it was they needed to stop doing this and put their clothes back on. Not yet. She wasn't ready for the moment to end.

Chapter 16

Zachary shifted his weight onto one elbow, resting his head on his hand to look down at Caroline. Sweet Lucifer. Virgins weren't supposed to be that eager or that responsive, and they weren't supposed to arouse him to the point that he still wore his damned boots, with his trousers jammed around his knees. Virgins were supposed to be nervous and shy, and by this time they were supposed to be crying and lamenting their ruin.

Caroline, though, ran her fingers across his chest, probably memorizing his musculature or something. And then her hand roved further down, her inquisitive touch making him jump. It had taken every bit of self-control and resolve he'd possessed to withdraw at the last moment. If there was one thing she didn't want to be, it was with child.

"You'd have to give me a short while before we could repeat the process," he said, leaning forward to kiss her lightly, "though I don't think we have time today, under the circumstances."

She kissed him back. "That was extraordinary," she commented, still sounding ragged and out of breath. "What would you do differently if you had more time?"

He lowered an eyebrow. "You weren't pleased?"

"I was very pleased. You just said you'd wished we had more time. So what would you have done if we did?"

Zachary ran the tip of a finger around her nipple, watching the bud contract again in response. "Well, there are other positions, for one thing."

"Goodness," she breathed, arching her back again.

Twenty damned minutes wasn't enough time. "And—"

"I've seen art books with naughty pictures," she interrupted, clearly trying to regain her strong sense of logic.

"Oh." He stifled a grin at her serious tone. "And there's mutual pleasuring, of course."

She lifted her head. "You didn't feel pleasure?"

"I felt pleasure. A great deal of pleasure. That's not what—"

"I thought you did." Turning her gaze toward his nether regions again, her eyes abruptly widened. "You mean—"

"Caro, Zachary, it's time for luncheon!"

Almost as an echo to Susan's yell, Molly snorted and mumbled something startled. *Bloody hell.* Kneeling again, Zachary grabbed a cloth, then yanked up his trousers and fastened them. At the sound of multiple feet prancing up the path, he grabbed his shirt and waistcoat and cravat. Caroline was struggling into her gown, and he helped her on with her pelisse and pulled it over the open, gaping back of her sprig muslin.

"Tell them I went for a walk," he hissed, and dove into the underbrush.

He found a good spot behind a half-collapsed faux stone wall and crouched down to pull on his shirt. From a few yards away he could hear Caroline calmly saying that they'd finished the portrait and he had felt the need to stretch his legs. Thank God she had sense—and thank goodness she wasn't one of her sisters, mad for marriage. Otherwise Edmund would probably be on his way from the house with a musket in his arms and a parson in tow.

Once he'd fastened the buttons on his waistcoat and tied his cravat as well as he could, he circled past the edge of the ruins to the path that led around the pond. Then, with a deep breath and a last check to make sure everything that should be fastened was, he headed back for the clearing.

"I thought I heard someone say luncheon," he said as the gaggle of females came into view.

"You should see the ballroom," Joanna said, prancing forward to take his arm. "I think Mama's bought all the yellow ribbon in Wiltshire. It's everywhere."

"It looks like a spider's web," Anne commented.

"No, it doesn't. It's lovely. And the yellow irises and lilies are being delivered right now." Julia took his other arm.

What he wanted to do was take Caroline's arm. Angling their retreat, he headed the twins toward the portrait. "Did you see the finished result?" he asked, freeing his arms to indicate the painting.

"It's lovely, Caro," Anne said, taking her eldest sister's hand. "Monsieur Tannberg will love it."

"Thank you," Caroline returned. "You go ahead. I need to bring it up to the house so it can finish drying."

"I'll help you, Miss Witfeld," Zachary said quickly. "We'll be along in a moment."

Zachary thought Anne threw him a suspicious look, but it might very well have been his own nerves. That had been a very close call. As the girls, complaining loudly about Caroline's monopoly of his time, vanished back down the path, he moved up beside her.

"I couldn't find my shoes," she whispered, picking up the painting and carefully settling it into its crate so she could transport the piece without smudging it.

He glanced down, catching a glimpse of bare toes as she leaned over the crate. Unexpected lust rolled down his spine again, heavy and hot. "I'll get them."

Climbing back over the fallen pillar, he rummaged through the undergrowth until he found the pair of pale green slippers. The rumpled blanket still lay there as well, and for a moment he stood gazing at it. Something had happened there; something other than the obvious. But he couldn't figure out what it was, exactly, that had transpired. Shaking himself, he folded the blanket and placed it on the far side of the pillar, so it would look as though he or Caroline had brought it outside and then simply forgotten it.

"Here you go," he said, surreptitiously dropping the shoes at her feet, then moving between her and the maid so she could step into them.

"Thank you."

Zachary cleared his throat. "And thank you, for not . . . panicking when your sisters arrived. That would have been awkward, to say the least." It wasn't precisely what he wanted to say, but one of them needed to speak.

She adjusted the portrait in its box. "I should thank *you,*" she said as she straightened. "You've given me a valuable anatomical insight. Would you mind carrying that into the house?"

When she went over to gather up her paints and her easel, he spent a few seconds looking at her backside. It was a very nice bottom, and one he wished he'd had more time to explore. Apparently, though, she'd been perfectly satisfied, both physically and in terms of higher education. Either that, or she was angry that he'd escaped and left her to tell the lies.

"Caroline, you know we couldn't be seen together," he said in a low voice.

"Of course we couldn't. I told you that I don't want to marry. And I certainly don't want to mislead you into thinking I'm going to become your mistress or some such thing. We had a bargain, and you fulfilled it admirably." She started off down the path, gesturing Molly to precede her. "Come along, my lord."

Grabbing up the box, he caught up to her. "Now just a damned minute," he grunted, catching her arm to slow her down and put more distance between them and the maid. "I had no intention of asking you to be my mistress. And I certainly don't need your reassurance over my performance. You knew as well as I did that we only had twenty minutes."

Her mouth twitched. "Perhaps I misspoke, Zachary. I only wanted to assure you that I wasn't going to make a scene or become clinging and missish. I have no designs on you." She reached over and patted the side of the box. "Or rather I do have designs, but only on your portrait."

So that was that. Damnation. Not only was she not missish and no longer virginal but she had also recovered her wits more quickly and more thoroughly than he had. Foremost in his mind was the thought that he wanted to taste her sweet lips again and lay her down somewhere secluded where he could take more than twenty minutes to run his hands along her soft skin and make her cry out with pleasure.

He understood her rationale very well. She had better things to do than spend time making love with him. Fine. *Fine.* "I suppose this means you'll have time to spare this evening," he ventured.

Unless he was mistaken, her step faltered a little. She'd probably forgotten what it was to have free moments. "Yes, I suppose I will."

"Good. Then you'll waltz with me. According to your sisters, the orchestra will be playing at least a dozen of them."

"I doubt that. Even Mama would notice the scandal of that many waltzes."

"But however many there are, one of them is mine."

Her shoulders squared. "You might ask instead of issuing a command."

A command? That was usually Melbourne's forte. Besides, if he asked, she might say no. "Will you waltz with me?" he asked anyway.

"We've done so before. I don't see why we shouldn't tonight."

"Good." Hopefully by this evening she would have had enough time to at least consider how pleasurable it would be to roll around naked with him again. If not, the waltz would remind her. He'd make bloody certain of that.

Once back at the house he sat and had luncheon, then borrowed one of Edmund's almanacs and went upstairs to do some research on local cattle breeds. He had the feeling that Dimidius hadn't been the result of a simple crossbreeding—otherwise someone else would have deciphered the secret already. Luckily Witfeld had taken copious notes on Dimidius's lineage; now

Zachary needed to figure out where the cow's ancestors, both direct and more distant, had come from, and which ones had contributed to her particular attributes.

Harold jumped up, barking, when someone rapped on his door. Hoping it was Caroline, Zachary straightened from the table beneath the window. "Come in."

Aunt Tremaine swung the door open. "Hiding?"

"No. I'm doing research."

She closed the door behind her, leaning down to give Harold a scratch between the ears. At least the dog hadn't leapt up on her this time. Patience—and training—did seem to have some merits. *Good dog.* "Research on what?" she asked.

"Cattle."

"Ah."

He returned to comparing Edmund's notes with the almanac, but he could feel her gaze boring into the top of his skull. With a sigh he looked up again. "Is there something I can do for you?"

"You're sending our coach away with Caro's portrait tomorrow."

"Just to meet the mail stage in Trowbridge. I'm making certain it gets to Vienna before her deadline."

"That's a gentlemanly thing to do."

As opposed to bedding Caroline, which had been exceedingly ungentlemanly. Aunt Tremaine, though, didn't possess the ability to read minds any more than Melbourne did, and Zachary wasn't about to confess to anything. "I delayed her by at least a day. It seemed a fair exchange."

His aunt trundled over to the bed and sat on the near edge. "I've been thinking of continuing on to Bath," she finally said.

Zachary fought the urge to lurch to his feet and shout a protest. "I am at your disposal, of course," he made himself say, "but if you're asking for my opinion, as I said before, I would like to stay for another week or two."

"And why is that again?"

"The cows," he returned, daring her to read something more

into it. "I wrote Melbourne about beginning a breeding program. I don't suppose you've been introduced to Dimidius?"

"The milk cow? Sally mentioned her as one of Edmund's silly little projects."

"If I'm correct, it's not so silly, and I wouldn't call it anything close to little. It could be monumental."

Aunt Tremaine idly twirled her cane from one hand to the other. Over the years she'd become so adept with the thing that she'd likely be lethal with a sword. "Well," she said after a moment, "I certainly have no objection to staying on. It's rather refreshing to be so far from Society's politics."

He smiled. "The curse of being part of the extended Griffin family."

"Not so much a curse as a responsibility." She winked as she climbed to her feet. "Though after the ball tonight, I may be agreeing with you." Halfway to the door she paused to look back at him. "You do know that half of Wiltshire is expected to attend."

"Oh, joyful day," he muttered, and went back to his notes.

As Caroline made her way downstairs she could hear the musicians tuning their instruments and the loud buzz of early arrivals. Apparently word of their blue-blooded guest had spread even farther since the assembly rooms, and no one wanted to miss viewing him.

None of the eager guests tonight had seen him naked, though. None of them had been in his arms or felt his passion. None of them—

"Caro," Anne said, reaching the landing behind her. "You look lovely. I don't think I've ever seen you in violet before."

She shrugged, pretending that she hadn't spent two hours trying on gowns. "I ordered it for the spring and never wore it." She glanced down at the low-cut bodice. "It's not too much, is it?"

"Heavens, no. You finished your portrait; you deserve to enjoy yourself a little tonight."

"Thank you. I shall do my utmost."

Anne laughed, wrapping her hand around Caroline's arm. "I

like that you can tease again. You've been so serious over the past few weeks."

Caroline did feel lighter. After all, the portrait would drive off to London tomorrow afternoon; she'd done all she could to impress Monsieur Tannberg. It wasn't just that, however; she felt more . . . confident, more relaxed . . . more adult, she supposed, as though her world had widened. And that, she suspected, had a great deal more to do with what she and Zachary had done this afternoon than with finishing a painting.

It had been tempting to sneak off and kiss him again, because she could get very used to being with him. Thank goodness he'd insulted her with his worry over being discovered with her; she thought she'd made it perfectly clear that she didn't want a long-term companion. And she certainly didn't want to be his mistress. It was a perfect non-relationship, as long as they both remembered that that was exactly what it was.

He was easy to find as she entered the large ballroom. All she had to do was seek out the largest concentration of marriageable females and there he was in the middle of them.

"Oh, look at that Lydia Reynolds," Anne muttered, stopping beside her, "fluttering her eyes at Zachary. She looks like a barn owl."

"Anne, be charitable," Caroline returned. "It's not as though we aren't guilty of the same behavior."

" 'We'?" her sister repeated. "*Me,* perhaps, but not you." Anne tugged her closer. "May I tell you a secret?"

"Of course."

"We all drew names two nights ago to decide which gentleman we would approach. Mine was George Bennett."

"I like Mr. Bennett." The magistrate's son at least had a sense of humor, and he was quite pleasant on the eyes.

"Yes, but I'm turning my aim elsewhere."

Caroline frowned a little. "You aren't going to poach Martin Williams."

"Heavens, no. Susan can have him." Anne leaned closer still.

"Since everyone's attention is going to be elsewhere, I'm going to approach Lord Zachary."

The muscles in Caroline's abdomen clenched. "I thought he'd made it clear that he is not going to marry a Witfeld girl," she said, surprised at the ugly, tight feeling.

Anne shrugged. "I don't want to spend the rest of my life in Wiltshire any more than you do."

"What does that mean?"

Pulling her arm free, Anne sketched a curtsy. "I don't know yet. We'll have to wait and see."

Oh, dear. Caroline gazed after her sister as Anne strolled across the room to join the gaggle around Zachary. Caroline's first thought was that she needed to warn him: Anne only needed to compromise herself in his presence and propriety would demand a marriage. Caroline had come within a hair's breadth of having that very thing happen to her that afternoon herself.

"Caroline," her mother crowed, grabbing her daughter's arm, "isn't it wonderful? I've outdone myself. Everyone will be talking about the Witfeld soiree for the rest of the Season."

"I don't doubt it, Mama. You've done wonders."

"Mr. Henneker tried to give me orange lilies at the last moment, but I told him that would never do. It turned out he was trying to save the yellow ones for a soiree at Granston. *They* will be having the orange ones now, I imagine."

Caroline made herself smile, though most of her attention remained on Anne as her sister took Zachary's arm and said something that had him laughing. Blast it all, she didn't like it. And not simply because Anne's plan, whatever it was, seemed terribly underhanded.

Zachary meant not to marry, for one thing, and they all knew it. For another, he had just begun a new project, and though he'd apparently done this same thing before, Caroline very much wanted him to succeed this time. If Anne trapped him into marriage, he would probably run off to the army just to escape the dismay of his powerful family. Even worse, he might fall in love with Anne and stay in Wiltshire, so that whenever Caroline came to visit, she would have to see them together.

"Caroline? You look pale. Poor dear, you've been working so hard." Her mother patted her cheek.

"Yes, I'm a bit tired," Caroline improvised, "but I'll manage. So tell me, Mama, are you going to dance tonight?"

Sally Witfeld giggled. "Heavens, no. I won't stand up with a single gentleman when all of my daughters are seeking husbands."

"I'm not seeking a husband."

"Of course you aren't, dear. But if one should come along . . ."

Her mother left the sentence hanging as she minced over to welcome Lord and Lady Eades to the soiree. Caroline backed up against the wall so she could watch the guests enter. Martin Williams arrived with his mother on his arm, and Susan immediately approached, said something, then led them toward the refreshment table. So her greeting was either Zachary's number one or number three suggestion for conversation, since both of those had concerned food. And it apparently worked—or at least it didn't send Martin screaming into the night this time.

One by one her sisters found a single gentleman—undoubtedly the bachelor each had drawn by lot—and engaged him in conversation. Even Anne at least had a punch with George Bennett. It was so nice seeing them behaving like young ladies rather than a crazed mob of banshees. Zachary had performed a genuine miracle.

Despite her stated lack of interest in continuing her intimate contact with Zachary, Caroline couldn't keep her gaze from straying to him again. He wore dark gray with a gray-and-green-striped waistcoat, and a single onyx pin through his cravat. Warm desire twined its leisurely way down her spine. He'd promised her more than what they could do in twenty minutes, though she'd never felt as excited and aroused and fulfilled in her life. To think that that had only been a taste—the idea left her mouth dry and her heart pounding.

Thank goodness he would be leaving soon. His aunt still

needed to travel to Bath, and he'd posed for her portrait as he'd promised. If he was serious about Dimidius and a cattle-breeding project, he and her father could correspond to their hearts' content. But staying in Wiltshire—she couldn't imagine him doing so for two minutes longer than he had to. And neither, of course, would she.

"Miss Witfeld."

She curtsied at the nasal drawl. "Lady Eades. Lord Eades."

"Your mother says you finished your portrait project," the countess continued. "I presume you decided to use Lord Zachary for your submission?"

"I did. Thank you for your interest."

"Yes, well, I hope you don't think we are willing to wait indefinitely for you to accept the generous position we've offered you," the earl put in. "When will you receive an answer?"

"It may be a fortnight or more. They will inform me of the schedule once they receive my application." She also wanted to inform them that she had no intention of accepting their offer, but even if she left Wiltshire her family would remain behind. There was no sense in angering the local aristocracy just because the thought of being a governess horrified her. "I do appreciate your patience," she continued, curtsying. "If you'll excuse me?"

As she turned around, she slammed into a broad gray-and-green-clothed chest. Reflexively she grabbed Zachary's lapels, while his arms slid easily around her hips.

"Beg pardon," he said, grinning.

Flushing, she pulled out of his grip. "I should have been looking."

"I *was* looking," he returned more quietly. "You take my breath away."

"That's because I ran into you," she said, giving in to a grin. "You'll recover."

Zachary chuckled. "Very clever. I don't suppose you left me a spot on your dance card?"

Her dance card was completely blank. "Don't you think you should dance with our guests?"

"I'm a guest. And I want to dance with you. You already agreed, remember? Give over your card." He held out his hand.

With a sigh she gave it to him, a shiver running down her spine as their fingers brushed. Heavens, was it going to be like this with him from now on? Half of her hoped so. *Delicious.*

Gazing down at the card, he glanced up at her from beneath his dark lashes. "I want them all," he whispered.

Warm heat started between her legs, and her bodice began to feel too tight. "You would cause a riot."

With a slow breath he scribbled his name on one of the lines. "It occurs to me that tonight should be in your honor," he said. "You've accomplished so much."

"I haven't accomplished anything yet."

Zachary handed the card back. "You've done everything you can. We'll send the portrait off tomorrow, and then the next step is up to Monsieur Tannberg. And you should be proud of yourself, Caroline. Aside from the fact that the portrait is stunning, you found a dream and have taken the road to realizing it."

Because she didn't quite think she could meet his dark gaze any longer, she looked down at her card. "The last waltz?"

A slow, sensuous smile curved his mouth. "Anticipation," he murmured and, with a slight bow, vanished back into the crowd.

Chapter 17

Caroline couldn't remember a happier evening. She'd done it. She'd gotten an invitation to a studio, had accepted the entrance criteria, had fulfilled them, and was about to send in the best work she'd ever done. The rest was up to the hopefully professional eye of Monsieur Tannberg.

"Another dance that long, and I shall be dead," Frank Anderton said breathlessly, leading her back to her busy mother.

"The musicians likely feel the same way," Caroline answered the solicitor, grinning.

The next dance after the orchestra rested would be the evening's last waltz, and her smile had been appearing with increasing frequency for the last hour. Very well, she could admit it. She was excited. She did anticipate being in Zachary's arms again, even if it was fully clothed and in front of a hundred guests.

At the moment, though, he didn't seem to be feeling any of the same yearning she did. Rather, he stood talking with Anne and George Bennett. From their expressions, she couldn't tell which gentleman found her sister more charming. She knew quite well which man Anne favored.

"I'm going for a breath of air," she said abruptly, tugging on her mother's sleeve.

"Don't be long, dear," Sally said absently, barely pausing in her chat with Mrs. Williams and Harriet Caldwell.

Although guests wandered about everywhere, the hallway and

music room were at least a little cooler than the ballroom. Caroline paced to the library and back. She was not jealous of Anne. It was only that Zachary seemed to be making a genuine effort to change his life, and it wasn't fair for Anne to even contemplate ruining that for him. Of course Anne probably wasn't thinking about Zachary or his future as much as she was planning her own.

"I have no idea," she heard a female voice say from around the corner in front of her. "Perhaps it was a family pet."

A nasal male chuckle followed. "Or perhaps they wanted to honor the creature before making him into a rooster stew."

"Look over here," a third voice drawled, "she's painted the family dog."

Caroline froze. She recognized two of the voices—Lord and Lady Eades. The third voice sounded like Vincent Powell, another of the local gentry.

"Are those her sisters? They look like six daughters of King Lear."

They'd asked her to make them look Shakespearean. Letting them dress up in their great-grandmother's old clothes had been the only way she'd been able to convince them to pose together for her.

"Did you hear that she's applied to a portrait studio?"

More laughter. "Hopefully they'll have dogs and roosters as clients."

Oh, that wasn't fair. She sketched and painted everything that she could. It was her father who'd decided to hang some of her work in the hallway.

"Poor girl. She's not a great talent, though she does try hard. We offered her a position teaching Theodore and our other children, but she seems to think she'll actually be going to Vienna."

"Pardon me," another low voice came, and Caroline's breath caught. *Zachary.*

"My lord. We were just admiring some of Miss Witfeld's artwork. Very quaint, don't you think?"

"Not so much quaint," he returned without pause, "as showing incredible talent." She heard him step forward. "Do you realize she painted that rooster when she was fourteen?"

"But it's a rooster."

"Charles Collins once painted a lobster, and John Wootton frequently painted dogs. And not nearly as well as Miss Witfeld does."

"You're an expert in art, then?"

"I spent six months in Paris, studying under a master. I don't have the natural talent, though, that Miss Witfeld obviously does."

"She painted a portrait of my wife and me as Egyptian pharaohs," Lord Eades said begrudgingly in his nasal voice.

"She did a portrait of me with my prize bull," Mr. Powell seconded in a more courteous tone of his own.

"I'd keep them safe," Zachary said coolly. "They may be worth a small fortune some day. But speaking of prize bulls, Mr. Powell, what do you know about Edmund Witfeld's cattle breeding program?"

She could feel the hesitation in the air. They wanted to make fun of her father but didn't dare do so in Zachary's presence. *Good.*

"Ah, not a great deal. He has a cow he's always bragging about."

"A cow that could be the beginning of something very large. Would you and Lord Eades care to meet with us tomorrow morning? If money's to be made, I would prefer that Wiltshire benefit from it before I go farther afield."

She listened while they practically fell over one another to agree to the meeting. Then, realizing they might round the corner at any moment, she abruptly turned around and hurried back down the hall. So that was what the local gentry thought of her—she was as eccentric as her father, someone to be humored to her face and ridiculed when her back was turned.

A hand touched her shoulder. "Caroline."

Flinching, she nearly ran into the wall. "Oh, Zachary. I was just taking a breath of—"

Zachary put a hand over her mouth. "You heard those idiots, didn't you?" he whispered.

She pulled his hand down. "I don't know what you're—"

"No, *they* didn't know what they were talking about. I doubt any of them have ever been to a museum or gallery, much less studied art. Don't let their ignorance upset you."

"I'm not upset," she lied.

He continued gazing at her, their hands still entwined.

"It's just that I know how they make fun of my father sometimes," she blurted, not certain why she felt the need to confide in him, or the trust to do so. "It . . . hurt, a little, to realize that they say the same things about me."

"Hm. As far as I'm concerned, they can keep saying them, because you'll be in Vienna laughing at their sorry little lives."

A smile touched Caroline's mouth. "You're nicer than I gave you credit for."

"Me?" Both eyebrows lifting, he put his free hand to his chest. "I'm a hardened rake or some such thing."

"I've been thinking about that, too. You aren't a rake at all."

His brows lowered. "I'm not?"

"No. I don't think you set out to seduce women. I think you're just so pleasant and charming and considerate that they all fall at your feet without your even realizing it."

He drew her a little closer. "Have you fallen at my feet, then, Caroline?"

Oh, dear. "I was referring to my sisters."

"I thought so." Zachary leaned down and kissed her, slow and soft and warm.

For a moment she closed her eyes, drinking in the sensation. The orchestra began playing again, though, and reality and logic returned with a bump. "Stop that," she hissed, shoving at his chest. "You wouldn't want someone to catch us."

"Neither would you. Come dance with me." He caught her hand again, this time placing it over his dark gray sleeve.

"How did you come to be in the hallway, anyway?" she asked as they returned to the ballroom.

"I was looking for you."

Accompanied by the same lifting sensation she felt when they kissed, Caroline was swept into the waltz. For a horrifying moment she wondered whether everyone could see in her expression how much she liked dancing with him, and whether they would realize that the waltz wasn't the only thing she'd done in his arms. As she glanced about the room, though, it swiftly became clear that no one was even looking at her. No, all eyes—especially the female ones—were trained on her dance partner.

"You never said you studied art for six months in Paris," she ventured after a moment.

"I didn't study at all in Paris. Not formally. Lying about my background seemed the least combative way to make them see my point."

"Did you know I was listening?"

"No."

His gaze held hers, warm and sincere. He'd become so much more than she'd realized; or rather, she'd discovered so much more about him than she had expected. "So you weren't trying to gain my gratitude."

Zachary chuckled. "My love," he whispered, tilting his forehead against hers as they danced, "I've already been inside you. I don't need your gratitude."

She swallowed, her mouth dry.

"What I want is your respect, Caroline. Because I have a great deal of respect for you."

Unexpectedly she had to stifle the sudden desire to kiss him again. She bit her lower lip, trying to shake herself out of that very troubling thought. "I do respect you," she finally said.

"Not if everything I do still surprises you."

Zachary Griffin was definitely more astute than she'd originally given him credit for. Perhaps he was right; she did feel grateful, since after all she wouldn't have a very good chance at a position in Vienna if not for him. But respect? A few days ago she'd told him he was a waste of air. If he'd wanted to punish her for that, though, there were myriad ways he could have done so before this moment.

"It surprises me less and less," she conceded.

"That's something, I suppose." He didn't sound offended— though he didn't sound overjoyed, either.

"Now that you've fulfilled your promise to me, I suppose you'll be leaving for Bath," she said, mostly to change the subject. The sooner he left, the better for her equilibrium. She'd wanted to be with him, but she certainly hadn't expected to continue to desire him afterwards. It was a complication she didn't need.

"Actually, Aunt Tremaine and I are going to stay for another week or two," he returned smoothly. She had a suspicion that he knew exactly what she was thinking, and that troubled her immensely.

"You are? Why?"

"Are you in a hurry to be rid of us?"

"No. Of course not. It's just . . . why would you want to stay in Wiltshire if you're not obligated to do so?"

"Several reasons," he said. "One of which is Dimidius."

"Yes, I heard you recruiting Lord Eades and Mr. Powell. You were serious, then?"

"Extremely serious. And the more I read of your father's notes about how he came to breed Dimidius, the more interested I am. I think that by luck he may have stumbled onto something that farmers and breeders have been attempting to do for decades."

"But he just bred a Guernsey cow with a South Devon bull."

"The cow wasn't pure Guernsey. It's more complicated than that. And so, unless you ask me to leave, I would like to stay and figure this out, and maybe begin an expanded breeding program to see if I can reproduce your father's results." Zachary gazed at her for a long moment. "Unless you ask me to leave," he repeated.

He was leaving it up to her. And with every ounce of her being she wanted to ask him to go away and allow her to simplify what was becoming a very complicated life. "If you're serious about your interest in the cattle, then I think you should stay," she heard herself say.

"I'm serious about my interest," he returned, that slow smile of his appearing again and making her heart flip-flop. "Very serious."

"Twice the milk, Witfeld? You can't be serious." Vincent Powell kicked the toe of his boot against the paddock fencing.

"I measured the average amount of milk given by six of my milk cows against that of Dimidius. Twice is a solid figure." The Witfeld patriarch spoke calmly enough, but after what Zachary had overheard last night he had a fairly good idea how the neighbors viewed Edmund's inventions, and how aware Witfeld was of that fact. That made this morning's conversation very interesting for more than one reason. "And it's a rich quality, too. Ideal for butter and cream on the best tables in Bath and London."

"I hardly—"

Zachary stepped forward. "I've seen his research," he interrupted. "It looks valid. I'm willing to risk my pocketbook on it, in fact. I'm not asking you to do that. All I need is your cooperation and some of your time."

"For what, pray tell?" Lord Eades asked, reluctance written in the stiff line of his back and the arms folded across his chest.

"I propose to supply you with animals, to be fed and bred as per my and Edmund's instructions. Before I do so, I need your word that these animals won't be sold to market, or slaughtered, or used for anything but the stated purpose of perfecting a new breed of dairy cows."

"And how long are we supposed to go along with this?"

Zachary took a breath. He'd only had time for some very preliminary calculations and figures, but of course the local farmers expected him to have answers. If he didn't, or if he said something blatantly wrong, the entire plan would fold before it ever began. "It can't be a short-term program," he said slowly, making every effort to demonstrate the famous Griffin confidence. "In order to maintain control over the progress of the breeding, I am willing to provide one hundred percent monetary support for the next five years. At that time we should have enough of a breeding population to assess whether it will be profitable to continue or not."

"Five years," Powell repeated, glancing at Eades.

"I mean to bring in at least four more local farmers to supplement the program and to prevent inbreeding," Zachary continued. "But I spoke with Edmund, and he wanted your support first, because the community will follow as the two of you lead." He had no idea if that was true or not, but it sounded good.

"You're talking about a great deal of money, my lord."

Zachary smiled. "I have a great deal of money."

Both men turned to view Dimidius again as she happily nuzzled into a large bucket of oats, her calf beside her. She was fairly attractive as cows went, large and healthy looking, a mottled white and red with a complacent temperament.

"All right, Lord Zachary," Eades said, offering his hand. "You have a deal. But we expect to reap a percentage of any profits that result from our participation."

Zachary shook it. "You will. I promise you that. And Zachary is fine."

He shook Powell's hand, as well, and stepped back to encourage the two men to include Witfeld. Once everyone had agreed and shaken hands, Zachary pulled a bottle of whiskey and some glasses from inside a wagon bed where he'd hidden them. "To seal our partnership," he said with a grin.

"You are a good lad, Zachary," Powell said, smiling. "When do we begin?"

Now came the hard part. "I have a few area farms to visit, to check on their stock, so I would say the animals will begin arriving within the next fortnight, and quite possibly sooner."

"Excellent."

Witfeld poured a generous amount of whiskey into each glass, then raised his. "To Dimidius."

Zachary and his new partners lifted their glasses, as well. He, at least, felt like he needed a drink. "To Dimidius."

"All right, you may look now."

Zachary blinked, looking up from the legal manual he'd borrowed from Frank Anderton. After all, if he was going to go through all of this, he wanted some assurance that one of his farmer assistants couldn't take a cow and sell all of their research without repercussion. "Beg pardon?"

Joanna put down her paintbrush and smoothed at her blue sprig muslin gown. "I said I've finished, and you may look at the portrait."

With a quickly hidden grimace, he stood. He'd forgotten that he was being painted yet again. "By the way, I neglected to ask how your evening with Mr. Thomas went."

"Oh, very well." She bounced on her toes. "He's taking me on a picnic tomorrow."

"Excellent. Then why are you painting *me?*"

"I'm not painting you. Not any longer."

Curious now, Zachary circled the makeshift easel to look at the painting. He blinked again, trying to clear his eyes. "That's a toga, is it not?"

"Yes. It began as you portraying the Greek god Apollo, but then when I drew John Thomas's name out of the basket I thought I should make him the subject."

"Of course. Good thinking." In truth, the head perched on the neckless toga-wearing figure with the horse-shaped legs could have been anyone from Prinny to the mad Emperor Nero, but from the size of the nose he was rather glad it wasn't supposed to be him. "Has Mr. Thomas seen it yet?"

"No. I thought I would present it to him at the picnic."

Wonderful. "I think he will be very pleasantly surprised," Zachary said diplomatically. "I wager no one's ever troubled to paint him before."

"That was my thinking."

From Joanna's excited smile, he'd said the right thing. And at least she'd set her sights on someone aside from him.

"Ah, there you are," Caroline's sweet voice came, and his heart thudded.

"Good afternoon, Miss Witfeld," he said, facing the doorway.

"Good afternoon. I was just in Trowbridge, and ran into Mr. Anderton. He sent this along." She hefted a large, leather-bound legal volume. "He said it has more to do with racing carriages, but you might find some of it useful."

"In case we accidently breed racing cows?" he suggested, taking the book from her.

She snorted, covering her face with one hand. God, he adored when she did that.

"I think it had more to do with proprietary research and development. Would you like me to take a look?"

"Are you volunteering to assist me?" he asked, his fingers itching to brush a straying auburn hair from her face, to touch her soft skin.

"I have nearly a fortnight before I can expect to hear from Vienna," she returned. "I may as well attempt to repay you for your help by offering mine."

"I accept."

"If you two are finished trying to polite one another to death," Joanna said sarcastically, "come and look at my painting, Caro. It's John Thomas."

Caroline complied, the expression on her face absolutely still. "My goodness," she said after a moment, her voice, a little ragged at the edges, the only indication that Joanna's artwork amused her. "You've made a wonderful use of color. And your brush strokes are so delicate."

Joanna puffed up like a songbird. "You see? I could have been an artist too, if I'd chosen to do so."

"I don't doubt it."

"I'm going to go show Julia. She'll be terribly jealous, because she spilled punch on her gentleman, and I don't think he likes her."

Zachary watched Joanna and her painting out the door, then turned to Caroline. Mindful of the maid darning socks in the corner, Zachary surreptitiously reached over to run his finger across the back of Caroline's hand. "Thank you again for volunteering."

"I need to do something to keep from going mad while I wait to hear from Vienna."

He grinned. "Glad to be of service."

"Speaking of service," she returned, "how many more portraits are you posing for?"

He thought she'd been about to suggest they find somewhere private and resume their acquaintance. Trying to focus his thoughts again while ignoring the sudden discomfort to his nether regions was supremely difficult. "It began as four, but since the ball, most of them seem to have lost interest."

"That's good, isn't it?"

She spoke smoothly enough, but a thrill ran down his spine nevertheless. *She wasn't jealous, was she?* He didn't dare ask her aloud. Not when the best he could hope for was that she would want another anatomy lesson. "Not to show favoritism," he said, "but I have to say your work did most resemble me."

Caroline chuckled. "Thank you, I think. Have you heard yet from your brother about whether he means to support the breeding program?"

"Not yet. He occasionally takes his time to make up his mind, but he'd be foolish not to be interested in this. And Melbourne is not a fool."

Flipping open the book on racing carriages, Caroline sank back in her chair. "What am I looking for?"

"Any precedents you can find on protecting research, I would think."

"Or on racing cows, of course."

Zachary smiled at her, gazing into her twinkling green eyes. He could become very used to this, he realized, just sitting at a table across from her and chatting. The thought made him uneasy, and he looked down again. "Definitely look into that, if you find it."

Chapter 18

Charlemagne dropped into the chair opposite Sebastian's desk, flinging a stack of correspondence onto the mahogany surface as he sat. "You've one from Aunt Tremaine," he said, leaning forward for the letter opener and slicing the wax on a letter of his own.

The Duke of Melbourne glanced from the disheveled stack of bills and letters to his younger brother. "I'm in the middle of something," he said, shoving the mess off his ledger book.

Shay continued reading his own letter. "I just wanted to know if Aunt mentioned cows, or if that was just Zach being . . . well, Zach."

With an annoyed frown, Sebastian found the missive in question and slit open the wax seal. "Far be it from me to stifle your curiosity," he returned and tossed it at his brother's head. "Read it to me."

Setting aside his own letter, Charlemagne unfolded their aunt's. He cleared his throat. " 'Dear Melbourne,' " he read, doing a fair imitation of Aunt Tremaine's honeyed voice, " 'I'm pleased to tell you that the weather here in Wiltshire has been a delight. Caroline—the eldest Miss Witfeld, as I mentioned before—finished Zachary's portrait and has posted it to Charlemagne. Hopefully that rapscallion has sent it on to Vienna.' Well, that's very nice, isn't it? Of course I sent it on to Vienna."

"Continue," Sebastian ordered, not bothering to hide his amusement.

"Fine. 'I believe Zachary has informed you of his new obsession—cows.'" Shay looked up at his brother. "There are so many things I'd like to say in response to that, Seb."

"Don't."

"You're an old stick, Melbourne."

Sebastian held out his hand. "Give me the damned letter."

"I'm reading, I'm reading. 'He's convinced six of the local farmers to participate, and tomorrow he's going north to Heddington to purchase two dozen or so cows in an attempt to repeat Edmund's initial results.'"

Shay continued reading a litany of which farmers Zachary had talked into assisting, but Sebastian missed most of it. Rather, he was absorbed with the idea that Zach might actually be serious. His youngest brother was famously persuasive, but he generally limited that skill to wagering or to convincing pretty young ladies to join him in his bed. When it came to projects—and lovers— Zachary preferred them short-term and simple.

This was different. He'd apparently gone out of his way to recruit assistance, and he'd done so without approval from his own bloody family.

". . . burne? Sebastian?"

He shook himself. "What?"

"I think I'm getting to the good part. I didn't want you to miss it." Shay folded the letter against the crease to straighten it.

"I'm glad to hear there is a good part," Sebastian returned. He cared for his aunt, but for God's sake she could ramble. "Go on."

"'I have decided to forgo Bath altogether and will remain here in Wiltshire indefinitely. Zachary has agreed to stay as well, at least until Caroline hears from the art studio in Vienna. You should commission a portrait from her, Melbourne. She is stunningly talented, and quite intelligent. Your brother has pressed her into service, as well, and she seems quite useful as an assistant.

"'Please thank Shay for the book of poetry he sent along with Zachary, and inquire whether he minds if I pass it along to dear

Caroline. I'm certain she, more than the rest of her sisters, will appreciate its merits. It's in fair condition except for the cover, which Harold ripped off. All my love to Peep, GT.' " Charlemagne handed the letter back. "Let her know she can do whatever she pleases with the book. Eloisa Harding presented me with another copy of it, anyway." He grinned. "And under some very romantic circumstances, I might add."

"Spare me the tales of your exploits, Shay," Melbourne said shortly, perusing the letter again. "Damnation."

"What's wrong? It's only a book. I'm just surprised he hasn't lost the dog yet."

Charlemagne might have a remarkable head for business, but he could be amazingly obtuse in other areas. "See what you can do to clear your calendar for the next fortnight or so," Sebastian returned, standing. "I want us to be in Wiltshire by the end of the week."

"Wiltshire? Why the devil are we going to Wiltshire? You don't think Zachary's serious about the blasted cows, do you?"

"It's not the cows I'm worried about. It's . . ." He flipped the letter over again. "It's 'stunningly talented, and quite intelligent' Caroline Witfeld. Damned Aunt Tremaine is matchmaking."

"But I thought you told Zachary to show some responsibility. It seems as though—"

Sebastian stopped halfway to the door. "I told him to get a dog," he snapped, and headed for the stairs.

From his aunt's frequent letters he knew quite well that the Witfelds had seven daughters with reputations for man-hungry silliness. In the face of that, combined with Aunt Tremaine's meddling, it made sense that Zachary's sudden and uncharacteristic interest in cattle breeding had been prompted by a female. Whether Zach was aware of the Witfeld chit's machinations or not, it had suddenly become very likely that in the process of meandering around the countryside looking at cows, he would find himself trapped into a disadvantageous marriage, and that romantically minded Aunt Tremaine might be hoping for that very thing.

Obviously she had counted on the distance between London and Wiltshire to provide her a safe cushion in which she could work her mischief between his brother and a gentleman farmer's daughter. Well, she'd miscalculated.

"You don't need me to go with you," Caroline said over her shoulder as she ascended the staircase toward the conservatory.

"I could certainly use a second opinion," Zachary returned, following close on her heels.

It was supposed to have been easy, she reflected. An afternoon of intimacy to gain a knowledge of male anatomy and to indulge a private fantasy she meant never to give in to again. Why, then, did her breathing constrict every time she was in the same room with Zachary Griffin, and why did her heart pound when he spoke to her in his low, quiet drawl? And why had she dreamed for four nights in a row that he'd shared her bed again, and that she had not only enjoyed it but also encouraged it?

"My father is your second opinion."

He caught her arm as she headed into the room. "Very well. I want your company," he murmured, turning her to face him. "I would like to spend a day with you where I'm not frozen with one foot on a pillar."

"We spent two hours together in the library yesterday."

"Yes, we did. With a table and a stack of books and papers between us." Zachary let her go, but he walked to the bow windows rather than leaving again. *Damnation.* She made a show of going through some of her sketches. She would need to organize them next week to decide which ones she wanted to take with her to Vienna.

"I need to know something," he said after a moment.

Her muscles froze for the briefest of moments. "What is it you need to know?"

"First, look at me."

Caroline faced him, nonchalantly sweeping her arms behind her back so he wouldn't see that his intimate tone made her hands tremble. "Yes?"

His dark gray eyes were serious, and rather than approach her, he sank down on the padded window seat. "I'm going to be here for another few weeks," he said after a moment. "Are we going to spend that entire time across the room from one another?"

Her heart thudded. "Across the room? I hardly think—"

"You know what I mean, Caroline." Glancing toward the door, he lowered his voice still further. "I want you again. Do you want me?"

"Heavens," she said, grateful she could attribute the shake in her voice to shock rather than lust. Perhaps she could fool him, anyway. She certainly wasn't fooling herself. "I only asked you for an anatomy lesson."

With a low growl he pushed to his feet. Before she could move, he'd reached her. Taking her shoulders in his hands, he pulled her forward and kissed her. It wasn't a tender or a flirtatious kiss this time. Rough, hard, and deep, it told her very clearly what he wanted, and how much he wanted it.

Her legs felt boneless, and she leaned into his hard body. Self-control, good intentions, logic—none of it mattered. She couldn't even remember why she'd decided that being with him only once was the wisest decision she could make. "Zachary," she breathed, sliding her arms around his neck.

"Zachary, are you ready?"

At the sound of her father's voice on the landing, she pushed away from Zachary, nearly sending him through the window, and her stumbling into a stack of paintings. Swiftly she turned around, putting her back to the door. If her father saw her face now, he would know everything. And if he knew, she'd never make it to Vienna. She would be forced to become Lady Caroline Griffin, and she'd have to hold tea parties and embroider her husband's initials in his handkerchiefs. With all his important Society acquaintances, she'd probably never have time to pick up a brush again even for her own amusement. As if it were amusement rather than sanity.

"I'll be right down," Zachary returned in a carrying voice. "Come, Caroline."

"I don't think so."

Zachary moved up behind her again. "Come spend the day with your father and me. The fresh air will do both of us good."

"The fresh air might be beneficial, but spending time with you couldn't possibly lead to anything good."

His hands slid along her shoulders. "I promise to be as discreet as you. And aside from that, you have some insight into the local gentry that I don't."

"My father—"

"Your father wants this project to succeed as much as I do. Help me."

She had no idea how he could so easily turn from a passionate kiss to his theories on cattle breeding. As for her, she still couldn't breathe. *Men.* "Oh, very well. But keep your distance."

He grinned as she moved past him to the doorway. "No promises."

Edmund Witfeld was waiting outside by the four-seater curricle as they left the house. Caroline hurried forward, intending to have her father rather than Zachary hand her into the carriage. Obviously the less physical contact she had with Zachary, the better for her peace of mind. It was only for another few days, she reminded herself. After that, he could wander about Wiltshire flirting to his heart's content, because she would be on the Continent.

Halfway across the drive she slowed. Anne strolled around the far side of the carriage. She'd worn a pretty green bonnet and her green-and-yellow sprig muslin and obviously planned on going somewhere. As her sister smiled and curtsied at Zachary, Caroline abruptly realized just where it was Anne intended to venture this morning.

"Anne?" she said anyway, furrowing her brow in a frown that felt very real.

"Lord Zachary mentioned that you were going on a trip to visit some of our neighbors," Anne commented, holding out a hand for Zachary to help her into the open carriage, "and I invited myself. He was too polite to refuse."

"Nonsense," Zachary said warmly. "The more the merrier, I always say."

Oh, really? A moment ago he had been practically tearing off her clothes, and now he was happily adding members to their party. His feelings toward and about her didn't matter, though, as long as he remained steadfast about the cattle. And over the past days her doubts about his resolve had grown smaller and smaller.

"Miss Witfeld?" he asked, offering his hand.

She shook herself, taking his hand before she remembered that she'd decided not to. He followed her into the curricle, taking the seat beside Anne and leaving Papa to sit beside her.

Zachary had said over and over that he wasn't in Wiltshire to find a wife. If Anne had something nefarious in mind, then, that was awful. If he'd been lying and he *did* want a bride, why hadn't he asked *her?* She would have said no, of course, but he'd never even intimated that he would consider her for marriage. There was one worse scenario: Zachary had fooled all of them, her most of all, and Anne was the next sister on his list to seduce.

Caroline studied his face as he and Anne chatted and laughed. She noticed the thoughtful expression in his eyes before he answered a question, the easy laugh, and the way he deferred to her father for questions about Dimidius and her calf.

No. He wasn't some Lothario out to have his wicked way with every Witfeld female in the county. If he had been, six of them would have been no challenge at all, and the seventh had already succumbed to . . . something that had compelled her to trust him.

That put any blame for any new seductions squarely on Anne's shoulders. Caroline turned her attention to her sister as they reached the first property just south of Heddington and left the carriage to follow the suddenly eager landowner out to his pasture.

Anne had always been the most decisive of the Witfeld girls, with the possible exception of herself, but whereas Caroline had her painting to distract her from the isolation of Wiltshire and to guide her to a more vibrant life, Anne had only her wits.

"Oh, dear," Caroline muttered as her sister made a show of petting some cow or other. That sudden bovine affection was no doubt planned to demonstrate Anne's interest in the project and thereby warm Zachary's heart toward her.

"Oh, dear, what?" Zachary murmured from directly behind her.

Heavens. She hadn't even been aware he was that close. "Nothing," she said, turning around.

"I hadn't realized Anne knew anything about your father's inventions. She seems quite interested in cattle breeding, though."

Caroline barely refrained from rolling her eyes at him. "Yes, she does, doesn't she?"

"What's that supposed to mean?"

"I'm not going to say anything about my sister's character or interests," Caroline shot back in the same low voice. "All I *am* going to say is that if you aren't completely serious about this project of yours, you need to tell my father immediately. This family cannot afford to be the victim of your frivolity."

He grabbed her hand, pulling her away from the group chatting about cattle. " 'Frivolity'? Anne asked to join us, and I didn't see any reason why she shouldn't. So other than being polite, what have I done to make you angry?"

Caroline opened her mouth, then closed it again. "I apologize," she said finally. "My perceptions are my own and are not necessarily reality."

Zachary released her, his angry expression easing a little. "Anne is happily in pursuit of George Bennett. If she wants to use my presence to increase Mr. Bennett's interest, I have no objection."

"Did she say that? That she's trying to make Mr. Bennett jealous?"

He shrugged. "She mentioned that Mr. Bennett seems to pay her more mind when she's talking with me." A slow grin touched his mouth. "Just like you pay me more mind when I'm talking with Anne."

"Oh! That is not true." Her face heated.

In response, his smile deepened. "Whatever pleases you, Caroline."

Oh, for heaven's sake, what was she doing? Zachary Griffin's championing of any of her father's projects in itself was enough to raise the entire household's standing in the eyes of the community. His monetary support and informed guidance could change the lives of their family and of anyone else involved.

And so she needed to stop blurting out insults simply because she was frustrated and confused. Because of two words from her sister she'd decided that Anne must be trying to seduce Zachary, and that he was powerless to resist her. She was acting like an infant, jealous that someone else was playing with her new, favorite toy. The fact that firstly the toy wasn't hers and that secondly she wasn't going to be about much longer to play with him only made her more pitiful.

Pitiful, and being stared at by the toy in question. "I'm sorry," she said again. "I think that I'm just unused to having nothing to do. I'm certain I'll recover."

"Ah." He offered her his arm, covering her hand with his for a moment when she took his sleeve. "I can think of something to occupy you," he murmured.

She looked up at his face. "And what might that be?" she asked more boldly than she felt. After all, though, he might very well be talking about cow research again. It wouldn't be the first time he'd teased her like that.

"More sex with me."

"Shh."

Zachary glanced up at the rest of their party, almost as though he'd forgotten their presence. "Very well. If it's easier for you to pretend that nothing happened but an anatomy lesson, I'll let you get away with it."

"I'm not trying to 'get away' with anything."

Nodding, he led the way back to the group. "Keep telling yourself that, darling. But keep in mind that in some rare circles I'm considered rather bright, and exceptionally desirable. And I have eyes that see the same things you do. Even more, perhaps."

Her heart had begun pounding again. "I have no idea what you're talking about, Zachary. So please—"

"Shh," he repeated in a soft drawl. "Convince yourself; not me."

He released her before she could conjure a response and went to talk for a moment with her father. Caroline scowled after him. Oh, he might think he was intelligent and perceptive, but he had no idea what she was thinking. On the other hand, she knew exactly what *he* wanted, because he kept telling her.

Would it be so terrible to indulge herself one more time with Zachary Griffin before she left for her new life? As she took in Anne grasping his sleeve and audibly admiring his skill at negotiating herd prices, she knew the answer. It would be a very, very, *very* bad idea.

Chapter 19

At four and twenty, with numerous female admirers and more than a handful of satisfied former lovers in his past, Zachary believed he didn't have much—if anything—to learn from a chit. Caroline Witfeld, however, seemed determined to prove him wrong.

When he'd decided on joining the army, it had seemed ridiculous even to contemplate a marriage. He knew war widows, and he didn't intend to leave one of his own behind. And in truth, it hadn't been that difficult a choice. Most females seemed so intent on being pleasant and proper and whatever else they could think of in an attempt to impress a Griffin male that he found most of them dull.

"What do you think it is, Lord Zachary?" Violet asked from beside him.

He shook himself, focusing his gaze again on Aunt Tremaine as she blew out her cheeks and stretched out her arms. "I think I'm glad that I'm not on my aunt's team," he returned, chuckling.

"Wait until *you* have to enact a charade," Aunt Tremaine said, eating a pretend leg of something and tossing it over her shoulder. "I've seen some of your attempts, if you'll recall."

Seated opposite him, Caroline was falling over her sister Joanna's shoulder with the force of her laughter. She didn't laugh often; more frequently she gave that infectious, absurdly delicate snort, a short laugh, or a chuckle, before she sobered again, as though she was afraid that if she was anything but serious, she would lose sight of, and grip on, her goals.

She was unlike anyone he'd ever met, and she was certainly the first female to think herself better than he. As far as finding her passion and pursuing it, she'd definitely seen the light well before he had. And even when he'd thought he had finally made his choice, it had been her passion and insight that had prompted him to look beyond the obvious and beyond himself. With the army he might have found his glory and death on the battlefield, but in cattle breeding, though slower paced and infinitely less glorious, he could improve more lives than his own.

Hm. In return he'd taught Caroline one lesson, but she did have more to learn. And considering the favor she'd done in aiming him in a better direction, he looked forward to delivering a little more instruction.

And he didn't consider her dull. Not in the slightest. When he looked at her, it dawned on him that more than his choice of career had changed. She had changed *him*. Just how much, he was still discovering, but it wasn't something he would recover from. It wasn't anything he *wanted* to recover from.

He liked the way Edmund listened to his plans, weighed them, and found them sound. He liked the way the local landowners he'd roped into participating came to him with questions and that he had answers for them. The excitement of his new path had begun to deepen into a quiet satisfaction he'd never felt before. He didn't intend to give it up. But he did know whom to thank for opening his eyes.

Caroline met his gaze for a heartbeat, then looked away again. No, he could never see her as dull. Not as a woman, an artist, or a . . . wife.

Christ. Where had that come from? It seemed a huge leap, to move from not seeking death and glory to the idea of marriage. He stood.

"Zachary?" Edmund asked, shifting in his own chair.

"Apologies," he said abruptly, panic and exhilaration jolting into his chest. "I've a headache. I'll be back in a few minutes. Just need a breath of air."

He dodged Barling the butler and made it out the front door without incident. With a full moon, the path toward the pond and the near cattle pasture shone violet and gray, and he headed in that direction.

As he walked, he tried to quiet the bashing-about of his thoughts. Just because he could consider marriage didn't mean he'd actually decided to marry. And simply because he liked and admired Caroline didn't mean he wanted to marry her. Even if he did, *she* didn't want to marry *him*. No, she was going to Vienna, likely within the week.

He leaned against the wood railing that marked the edge of the pasture. Ridiculous. Of course he didn't want to get married. It was only that thanks to Caroline and her father he'd abruptly seen his future and his life more clearly than ever before. That had led to changes—changes that he thus far found amazingly interesting and challenging. Changes led to thoughts about more changes, and aside from changing careers the largest change he could make would be to move from bachelor to married man. So of course the thought had occurred to him. That didn't mean he had to do anything about it.

Dimidius wandered up, undoubtedly looking for a carrot or an apple. Absently Zachary scratched behind her ear. How odd, that he'd found his future in a cow. A pretty cow, but a cow nonetheless.

"Am I interrupting?" Caroline said from behind him.

Just barely managing not to jump, Zachary continued scratching Dimidius. "The conversation was a little one-sided," he conceded. "How did you escape charades?"

"I guessed that your aunt was Henry the Eighth and then went to fetch a shawl," she returned.

"Ah, old Henry. I thought she was enacting my brother Charlemagne."

"I've been thinking."

She wasn't the only one. "About what?" he asked.

"About how I should be hearing from Monsieur Tannberg in five days."

And then she'd be gone, without a backward glance. "That's right. Do you need my help packing?"

"No."

"Then—"

Her hands slid up his shoulder blades. "You've made some statements over the past few days," she said, her palms shifting to his chest as he turned around, "and I was wondering if they were just talk."

This was much better than petting a cow. "No, Miss Witfeld. They weren't just talk."

"Prove it."

He went hard. The tales about the full moon causing insanity were apparently true, but he wasn't going to waste any damned time trying to find a cure for this particular madness.

They kissed, hard and heated and leaving no doubt that she wasn't flirting or teasing. "We can't do this here," he muttered, casting his gaze about the property.

"The stable?" she suggested, tugging his coat down his shoulders.

"Not very romantic."

She slowed, meeting his gaze. "We can't go back to the house. Someone would see us. And I'm certainly not walking three miles to the inn outside of Trowbridge. They know my family there, anyway."

He grinned at her annoyance. "You've convinced me. The stable it is."

Zachary took her hand. Her fingers curled around his as they made their way around the drive and to the back door of the stable. Only one stable hand slept inside, and he was in the tack room at the front of the building. Up in the loft, they would be undisturbed.

Caroline climbed the ladder first, giving Zachary an enticing sight of her bare legs as she ascended. He'd been teasing at her for days, but in truth he was surprised she'd succumbed. If Caroline was one thing, it was focused. Something had talked her into straying tonight, though, and he intended to enjoy it. Of course in his imagination this second time would have been on a soft bed with silk sheets and surrounded by flickering candlelight, but opportunity and intention didn't always coincide.

His coat landed on a pile of hay, followed by his waistcoat and his boots. There would be no settling for shoving his trousers down to his thighs and humping tonight. "Come here," he whispered, kissing her again.

She turned her back to him, and he undid the fastenings down the back of her gown. Despite wanting to hurry, to lay her on her back and take her before her better sense returned, he made himself go slowly, alternating open buttons with kisses to the nape of her neck until he could feel her trembling beneath his hands.

"Zachary."

As she faced him again he slowly pulled down the front of her gown and slipped the straps of her shift off her shoulders to her waist. He would have preferred daylight or at least the damned romantic candlelight, but the white-blue glow of the moon through the open loft doors gave her skin an unearthly shimmer that intoxicated him.

Her gown pooled around her feet, and she stepped out of it, into the circle of his arms. With her help he pulled his shirt off over his head and dumped it onto the growing pile of discarded clothes. His cock strained at his trousers, and when her fingers brushed along the material, he flinched.

Before he could unfasten his pants, she pushed his hands away and did it herself. Whatever shyness or tentativeness she'd felt before, she'd obviously overcome. Zachary stepped out of his trousers and stood there for a moment, naked, just gazing at the ivory-skinned goddess before him.

Her own gaze lowered to his cock. Reaching out one hand, she wrapped her fingers around him. "More anatomy lessons?" he asked shakily, when he could speak.

"I didn't get a very good look at you before," she said absently, as she gently stroked the length of him.

His half-closed eyes flew open. "Sweet . . . explore to your heart's content, then. By all means."

She took him at his word, running her hands along his cock and beneath his scrotum, while he clenched his jaw and took it. If she was gaining information for a painting or a sculpture, it was going to be an interesting one.

"Zachary, how does it feel?" she murmured.

"If it feels this good for much longer, I won't be able to hold up my part of this exchange."

A slow smile curved her lips, and she sank onto her knees. Her gaze lifting to his, she kissed the tip of his manhood.

"Christ, Caro. That's enough of that."

Settling onto his own knees in front of her, he took her mouth in a hard, open-mouthed kiss. Their tongues tangled, their mutual need pulling them closer. Gently he slid his arms around her back and tilted her backward until she lay flat on the hay and piled clothes.

Moving over her, he took her right breast into his mouth, sucking as he caressed and teased the other one. Turnabout was fair play, and since she'd nearly sent him over the edge with just her hand and her fingers, he felt free to do the same to her. His gaze lifting to hers and his mouth still occupied with her breasts, he dipped a finger between her thighs.

Caroline gasped, her fingers digging into his shoulders and then relaxing as her head tipped back. He didn't need to ask how she felt; her damp heat made him shake. Raising up to kiss her again, he parted her thighs further and slid his finger deeper inside her.

She moaned, bucking beneath his ministrations. Despite the ache in his own groin, he trailed his mouth from her breast down her belly and then lifted her knees in his hands. He leaned in, flicking his tongue inside her.

"Oh, my God," she gasped, flinging her arms out, her hands grasping at his hair. "Stop, please. Please, please stop."

Her hands, though, pulled him in closer against her rather than pushing him away. He lifted his head. "Say what you mean, Caroline. If you want me to stop, I will." It would kill him, but he would.

"No, no. It's . . . it's just too much. I can't hold on."

He knew what she meant. He was very close to the edge himself. "Then let go, love," he murmured, lowering his face again.

He shifted his kisses to the inside of her thighs, trailing his mouth along her legs and back up again to lick her breasts. He wanted her on her back, helpless and moaning while he found his release inside her. But he'd made her a promise—several of them, in fact—and if she was going to Vienna at the end of a week, she was going to remember tonight.

Stretching out along her body, he took her mouth again. Sliding his arms around her, he rolled them so that she was on top, with him looking up at her. "Sit up," he said roughly.

He sat with her, lifting her hips and then guiding her down slowly onto his turgid member. Christ, she felt so tight, and so hot. Moaning, impaled, she sank along his chest, kissing his nipples as he'd done hers.

Unable to hold still, he angled his hips up against her again and again, as slowly and deeply as he could stand. He felt her growing tighter, clenching around him, and then the bucking, shattering pulsation as she came. Zachary held her down on him, muffling her cry with his mouth.

She collapsed, gasping and limp, across his chest. Zachary pulled the pins from her hair, tangling the auburn mass through his fingers while they tried to regain their breath. With every wiggle and sigh and breath she made he came closer to losing control, and he fought for every second.

As she sat up again, he shifted his hands to her breasts, warm and slick with sweat. "You feel very nice," he murmured.

"Does this feel nice, too?" she asked breathlessly, lifting up onto her knees and sinking back again.

Damnation, she caught on quickly. Finally giving in to need, he lowered his hands to her thighs, rocking her against him as he thrust upward. Harder, deeper, faster, again and again, until he felt her moving along with him once more, straight to oblivion. Twisting his waist, he flipped both of them over again, her thighs spread on either side of his hips and ankles wrapped around his thighs, their bodies rocking as he pinned her to the hay-covered floor. As she shattered, he sped his pace, growling as he left her at the last possible moment.

Caroline kept a hand on the back of his head, the other around his shoulder, as their breathing slowed to something close to normal. For perhaps the first time in her life, she didn't want to move—didn't want to go anywhere or do anything, or think about anything.

That, though, was both foolish and dangerous. She made herself stir a little. "We should go back inside before they miss us."

"No." Zachary grabbed a discarded cloth, then sank down again beside her, still touching skin to skin. He leaned over and kissed her, more quiet and gathered this time.

"We can't stay here."

"Maybe not, but we don't have to go back yet."

Reaching up, she ran a finger along his lower lip. He'd said he meant to pleasure her, and she felt completely shattered. But there was still the nagging thought that this could all just have been about him. Considering how good she felt, that shouldn't have mattered. But it did. "Zachary, are you a rake?"

His chest rumbled with his deep, responding laughter. "You said I wasn't."

"But was I correct?"

He looked down for a moment, that thoughtful expression touching his face again. "I don't consider myself one. I suppose there are those who would disagree."

"What makes a rake?"

"This isn't a conversation about art."

She supposed she deserved that, considering the way she'd dismissed their last encounter. "I'm going to Vienna. Whatever information you could give me would be useful."

"Vienna. Yes, that's right." He drew a breath, his fingers slowly and lightly, almost absently, tracing a trail across her breasts. "A rake. A rake is only interested in himself, in his own pleasure, and he doesn't care about the feelings or reputations of his conquests except insofar as there's no scandal that could trap him or force him to alter his ways."

She didn't want to move or breathe, or do anything that would make him stop touching her. "Then I agree; you aren't a rake."

"Thank you."

"And I'm not a mistress."

He looked at her, his gray eyes as black and deep as wells in the moonlight. "I never asked you to be one. I wouldn't mind if you stayed, and if your business took you to London instead of Vienna I wouldn't object, but I'm not trying to govern your life, Caroline."

"I know that. I know. It's just . . . I did want to be with you again, but I am still going to Vienna. I am going to be a painter."

Zachary smiled. "You *are* a painter."

She sat up. "Yes, well, now I'm going to get paid for it. And I'll get respect for it."

Rolling onto his back, Zachary put a hand behind his head and watched as she pulled on her shift. Just his eyes on her left a warmth radiating beneath her skin, but she did her best to ignore it. Men might very well look at her that way in the future, after all, but she had no intention of erring with anyone she didn't trust.

Caroline paused as she slipped her muslin gown back over her shoulders. Trust. She did trust him—more than she would have believed from their first meeting.

"Here, let me," he said, standing to hand over her hair clips and fasten the back of her gown.

The tug and pull of the material, together with knowing that a very handsome and very naked man stood inches from her, made her heart pound all over again. And beneath the heat and the renewed lust, that annoyed her. For heaven's sake, she'd become some sort of wanton harlot. She'd been with him twice, and she was not going to give in to that weakness again. Tuesday couldn't come soon enough, obviously, because the more swiftly she left Wiltshire, the more swiftly she would be able to put him out of her mind.

"Thank you," she said as he finished.

He turned her around. Hands on her shoulders, he bent his head to kiss her. At the soft, possessive touch, she swore that her toes curled in her slippers. Fine, he could be possessive of her until they reached the house. After that, their interlude was over with.

She pinned up her hair and waited while he dressed, pretending that he didn't fascinate her and that her fingers didn't itch with the desire to touch him again, to undo every button he fastened. When they both looked relatively composed, they descended the ladder, and he took her hand as they made their way back around the stable and up the curving drive. Then, before she could pull her fingers away, he released her.

"Back to charades, I suppose," he said in a low voice, brushing a strand of her hair back behind her ear.

Caroline mentally shook herself. This pleasant haze that had enveloped her needed to go away. Otherwise everyone in her family would know what she and Zachary had been up to. "And back to cows."

"Yes. Speaking of which, the dozen head I purchased should be at Powell's in the morning. Care to accompany me while I explain how I want the project to go?"

"I believe I can fit that into my schedule."

He smiled. "Good." Gently he kissed her again.

Oh, she should have refused. What was wrong with her? While he lurked in the shadows on the portico, she hurried into the house, up the stairs to her bedchamber for her shawl, and back down into the drawing room. As she'd anticipated, no one had missed her.

Rather, they were wondering whether someone should go and find Lord Zachary, or whether they should send for a physician to tend his headache. Anne shifted off her chair to sit on the couch beside Caroline.

"Did you have trouble finding your shawl?" she asked.

"I got distracted looking out the window," Caroline improvised. "The moon is full, and the shadows along the creek and pond are exquisite."

Anne nodded. "Did you see anything else exquisite out there?"

Caroline hoped she wasn't blushing. "The dew is sparkling in the field."

"Goose. I meant Lord Zachary. He's wandering out there somewhere." Anne sighed. "Probably looking at cows. I liked it better when he was set on being a soldier."

"I didn't. For heaven's sake, did you want him to go out and get killed, simply because he would look well in a crimson uniform?"

"Of course not. But you have to admit that the army is more glamorous than herds of cows and their milk."

Caroline didn't agree; it was the light in his eyes that she found attractive, not the task he pursued. Saying that, though, was out of the question. "Papa was a soldier, and now he's a farmer. I prefer him here," was all she said.

Zachary strolled back into the room. The instantaneous cacophony drowned out whatever Anne had been about to say. Everyone wanted to know whether he felt better, or if he needed a whiskey or warm milk or some tea with honey.

"I feel much better, thank you," he said loudly, quieting the mob. "All I needed was some fresh air."

"You have hay on your coat," Susan said, brushing at the fine, dark material.

"Dimidius nearly knocked me down," he returned easily, grinning.

Realizing she was staring, Caroline cleared her throat and turned her gaze away, only to see Lady Gladys looking at her. *Wonderful. Four more blasted days, Caroline.* If she could control herself for four more days, all of her dreams would come true.

Even so, she had the suspicion that tonight she would be dreaming of a dark-haired lord in a hayloft, and how very wicked and alive and free he made her feel.

Chapter 20

Zachary looked at Caroline sideways. "You actually want to know my opinion of the Parthenon?"

"If I didn't want to know, I wouldn't have asked."

"But your father re-created it."

They headed up the rutted road leading to Vincent Powell's small estate. Sagramore had obviously been cooped up for too long, because the gelding was galloping circles around Caroline's more sedate mare, Heather. Zachary would have enjoyed a good run, too, but he had no intention of rushing through the outing. Even with a groomsman trotting along behind them, he relished another few hours with Caroline. There were far too few of them left, as far as he was concerned.

"He worked from sketches and, I'm afraid, a fair share of imagination," she returned. "I want to know what the actual ruins are like."

She didn't mean merely a physical description. It drew him to her, the way she sought out his opinions and impressions. "I remember white," he said slowly. "White pillars surrounded by downward slopes of white rock and earth. It was hot and dry, except for a slow breeze coming off the sea." He closed his eyes for a moment. "And quiet. Visitors chatted, and there were birds about, but even with the low noise it felt . . . still. Waiting." Shaking himself, he grinned. "Not that I expected Apollo or Athena to make an appearance."

She gazed at him for several hard beats of his heart. "I could feel myself there," Caroline finally said. "It must have been wondrous." A moment later she cleared her throat and looked away again.

Stealing a look at her profile, her slender body in her hunter green riding habit and the matching hat tilted over her auburn hair, he wanted to take her there, to let her see it with her own eyes. That, though, was far beyond the bounds of any agreement they'd made together. "I have a question for you now."

"Yes?"

Think, Zachary. You know what you can't ask. "What accommodations does Monsieur Tannberg have for his apprentices and artisans at his studio?" he ventured. "You're not going to have to sleep on a bench, are you?"

She snorted. "He owns a small building and rents the apartments out to his employees at a reasonable rate."

"And will you be happy, living in an apartment in Vienna?"

"I'll be doing what I've always dreamed of doing, so yes, I'll be happy."

"You are accustomed to living with eight other people. That's a large change." Zachary wasn't quite certain what he was trying to say or to discover, but he did know it was important to find out whether her goal was to be a painter or to escape from Wiltshire.

"Half the time my family doesn't know I'm here. And no, I'm not complaining—it's merely a statement of fact. They all have their own lives, and their own goals and dreams. Mine are different."

"Anne seems to understand."

A slight frown crossed her face, then vanished again. "Anne is very bright. But her aim is the same as the rest of my sisters."

"To find a husband."

"In her case, to find a husband and escape Wiltshire."

He took a breath, wondering whether he was simply insane to keep asking these questions. "Would you consider marrying, if your husband was a patron of the arts or another painter or something?"

"What would be the point?"

"Love, companionsh—"

"When my parents married," she interrupted, her voice harder, "my mother, who had gone to finishing school along with your aunt, found that her most useful accomplishments were embroidery, hosting soirees, and the occasional playing of the pianoforte, and all of that was secondary to her ability to have children. I am not going to live that life."

Despite the bite of her words, he sensed that she blamed not her father for expecting those qualities from Sally Witfeld but rather her mother for living up—or rather, down—to those expectations. "She seems happy enough," he offered.

Caroline glared at him. "Yes, she's turned twittering and helplessness into an art. I've simply chosen to pursue another kind of art."

"So if I, for example, were to ask you to marry me, you wouldn't be interested?" he asked, hoping to God that she couldn't hear the serious edge in his voice. If she hadn't been so ready to leave, and if their remaining time together hadn't been so short, he could probably have found a way to cure himself of this odd . . . happiness and pleasure he felt whenever he spoke with her or touched her or even set eyes on her.

"Of course not. Marrying a Griffin would be even worse than being exiled to Wiltshire."

"And why is that?" he returned, doing his best to sound amused rather than deeply offended at the insult to his highly aristocratic lineage. Her answer hadn't surprised him, and in a sense he was relieved, but damnation, he'd practically proposed. She didn't have to sound like she'd just swallowed a beetle.

"You're a duke's brother. State events, dining with simpering politicians, mimicking Society's latest bon mots, expressing no opinion of my own—I would rather paint houses than live like that."

"There are several ladies who could prove you wrong," he returned, unsuccessfully attempting to keep his light tone. "Authors, activists, adventurers. My sister, as well. I respect her opinion over just about anyone's."

"I see. And other than your sister, how many of these ladies are married?"

His jaw clenched. "Several of them."

"Mm hm. Look, your cows have arrived," she said, and he turned his gaze from her to the pasture ahead of them.

Vincent Powell stood on the lowest rung of the pasture railing as they arrived. "Good morning, Zachary, Miss Witfeld. I seem to have twelve Guernsey heifers."

Zachary swung down from Sagramore and stepped over to help Caroline to the ground. "Yes, you do. Two South Devon bulls will be arriving tomorrow. We'll need to split up the cows for them—I want to know which bull is producing which calves, since the offspring will be the next step in the process."

"They're a healthy-looking herd," Powell commented, grudging approval in his voice.

Apparently Zachary had managed to convert him to the cause. Of course the venture wasn't costing the farmer a damned pence, so that probably helped, as well. "Seven of them are pure-bred Guernseys," he said, joining Powell on the railing, "and five have some Hereford blood, since Herefords fatten well on plain grass. I want to see which produces more milk to start with, and at a lower cost."

"How many head are you giving over to Eades?"

"The same. I've had to purchase another two dozen from farther north, and three bulls from South Devonshire. Then your other neighbors—Samms, Donnelly, Hallett, and Prentiss—will have eight head each, and Witfeld's adding another twenty to his herd as the control group since he's farther along in the program."

"You've put some work into this, haven't you, lad?" Powell said. "And some blunt, as well."

Zachary shrugged, though the older man's comments pleased him. "I want to give us a solid foundation."

"And what about the Duke of Melbourne's involvement?"

"I'm expecting his answer any day now. If he agrees to invest, we'll probably double the breeding population to start with. If not, well, you're looking at all your Guernseys for the next six months."

"What about pasture size? If I double this herd, then—"

"I'm doing the figures right now. By the end of the week I'll know how much land I need to purchase for you, and how much grain I'll need to supplement."

Powell stuck out his hand. "Thank you, Zachary."

Zachary shook it. "We haven't accomplished anything yet."

"Aye, but I'm beginning to feel optimistic. And you didn't have to include me, especially after . . ." The farmer trailed off, glancing in Caroline's direction.

"We all make mistakes." Zachary hopped down from the fence to take Caroline's arm. Even annoyed with her, he couldn't shake the desire, the need, to touch her on some pretext or other. "Will you give us a tour, Powell?"

"It would be my pleasure."

By the time they finished touring Mr. Powell's pastures and pens, Caroline began to wonder whether the Witfelds were Zachary's greatest admirers, after all. She told her companion that as they cantered back toward Witfeld Manor while the farmer waved at them until they rounded a hedge out of sight.

"He's enthusiastic. There's nothing wrong with that," Zachary returned. "In fact, I'm thankful for it. One naysayer is all we would need to have the whole lot of them refusing to give over pasture land."

"Pasture land that you're compensating them for losing, you mean."

He slowed Sagramore to a walk, and she reined Heather in beside them. Since their silly conversation about marriage this morning he'd seemed a little out-of-sorts, and she'd begun to think that he'd been serious. The idea horrified her: not that she would mind more intimacy with him, but the rest of the marriage trappings, even with someone as amiable as he was—and despite his protest that there were married ladies who lived productive, independent lives—would kill her. She knew it.

"If you think I'm making a poor decision, I wish you'd tell me," he said after a moment, his gaze on the wheat field that bordered Witfeld land.

"I don't think you're making a poor decision," she returned. "But would it matter if I did?"

"Not particularly."

She hesitated, surprised that he'd so easily dismissed her participation. "Oh."

He chuckled, glancing at her. "You have a great deal of intelligence and common sense, Caroline. Of course I would prefer that you think I'm being brilliant and progressive."

And abruptly the world felt right again. "You *are* being brilliant and progressive. I just hope the cows cooperate."

"From your mouth to God's ear, love."

When they arrived at the foot of the drive, both Anne and Joanna stood waving at them. Caroline glanced at Zachary as they neared, but she couldn't see anything in his expression but his typical easygoing politeness. She didn't know why she was so worried, anyway; even if Anne did have some plan in mind to snare Zachary, it couldn't possibly be the first time a lady had tried to trick or cajole him into marriage.

Even so, she wanted to warn him—but what kind of sister would that make her? Especially when Anne had been the most understanding and supportive of all her siblings? If he hadn't asked her about marriage, the decision whether to warn him or not would have been easier, but now she had no idea what to say to him. And yet saying nothing at all seemed cowardly.

"Good morning," he said to the young ladies as they reached them.

"Good morning, Zachary," Joanna returned, grabbing the toe of his boot. "I need to speak with you."

"I was here first," Anne argued.

"Perhaps you might let Lord Zachary down from his horse before you assault him," Caroline suggested, urging Heather between Sagramore and Anne.

"You don't have any say over his time any longer, Caro," Joanna said, following as they returned to the stable. "The portrait is gone to Vienna, so we should be entitled to as much time with him as you. Even more, since you hogged him for days."

"I didn't hog him. I—"

"Perhaps we might go for a walk by the pond, Miss Joanna," Zachary suggested, dismounting. "Miss Anne, will an afternoon stroll suffice?"

Anne smiled. "Yes, of course. Thank you."

Joanna seemed in a large hurry to go, and she practically dragged him out of the stable yard toward the path. Zachary went along with her, mostly because he needed to think about his future and Caroline's future and how they seemed determined not to become intertwined. She was so damned stubborn. Of course he hadn't made much of an effort to declare his intentions, either—mostly because he wasn't precisely certain what he was doing, and partly because he had enough pride that he didn't want to be rejected.

No, he didn't want her to leave for Vienna, where he'd probably never see her again, and no, he didn't want last night to be the last time he ever held her in his arms. Damnation, he liked talking with her, and he liked that she listened and didn't dismiss his interest in art or even in cattle breeding. Hell, she shared the same interests. And she was intelligent—probably more than he was. At least she'd applied herself more diligently to her passion, while he'd wallowed about for four-and-twenty years looking for his.

"I gave John Thomas the portrait I painted," Joanna said, still practically towing him toward the tree-lined path.

"You did? That's splendid. What did he say?"

"He said it looked like a potato with a turnip stuck on top. And then he ate all of the baked chicken and apple pie I'd brought for our picnic luncheon, all the while telling me how Mary Gorman has a thousand-pound dowry and how skilled her pianoforte playing is."

"That wasn't very polite. Do you think he means to wed Mary Gorman, then?"

"I'm sure he does. And now everyone but me will have a beau and a husband, and all my stupid sisters will laugh at me."

"No, they won't, Joanna. We'll find someone else for you. Someone who appreciates your painting, and your apple pie."

Maybe he didn't need to propose to Caroline to keep her, he mused. The Griffins were wealthy enough; he could travel to Vienna for a visit at least twice a year. Zachary frowned. Twice a year? And what would he do the rest of the time? There were always chits willing to spend the night with him, but for some damned reason the idea of endless liaisons with innumerable ladies just didn't appeal to him any longer. They were just to pass the time, and now he'd found someone worth spending his time with.

And thanks to that someone, he'd also finally found the right path for himself, unlikely as it seemed. Cattle breeding. The idea of finding the right combination of breed, sex, and temperament to create an entirely new dairy cow interested and intrigued him mightily. He'd always had more of an academic bent than he'd felt comfortable admitting, especially in the face of his family's teasing. According to them, food and ladies took up what space there was in his brain.

And he'd gone along with that because he hadn't had a suitable retort. Now, though, thanks to a portraitist, a gentleman farmer, and a cow, he did. Life was very odd, at times.

"Oh, you're not even listening," Joanna wailed.

He started. "Of course I'm listening. I've been going through the list of local gentlemen. What do—"

"There aren't that many men here. And my sisters already have five of them. And stupid Mary Gorman has one, and I don't."

"Joanna, you're only twenty years old. There's no reason for you to lose hope. I'm certain—"

Joanna screamed at the top of her lungs, then collapsed. So startled he nearly let her fall to the ground, Zachary grabbed her around the waist and went down with her. Holding her across his bent knees, he leaned over her face to tap her cheek.

"Joanna?"

Her eyes remained closed, her body limp in his arms. *Bloody hell.* He hadn't said anything alarming, he didn't think, and she'd been fine a moment ago.

"Over here!" a groom's voice came from down the path. "I think it was Miss Joanna, Mr. Witfeld!"

Before Zachary could lift his head to look toward the voices, Joanna's arms raised and wrapped around his neck, pulling his face down for a wet, solid kiss.

His heart stopped. He should have seen it. He should have realized that Joanna had no intention of being shown up by her sisters.

He tried to pull away, but the only way he could manage it would be to throw her into the dirt. "Joanna, let go," he growled, pulling against her arms.

The underbrush crashed sideways, and Anne stumbled, panting, onto the path. With one glance at his face she half-fell onto her knees on the other side of Joanna. "Papa!" she yelled. "We're down here! Joanna's fainted!"

Joanna lifted her head and glared at her sister. "Go away!" she hissed.

"If you're unconscious, you should probably let him go," Anne returned smoothly. "Because otherwise your story and my story aren't going to match." She looked at Zachary again. "And I believe Zachary's story will follow mine."

"You witch!"

Mr. Witfeld and two grooms rounded the bend at a run. "What's happened?"

"I have no idea," Anne said, standing and fanning one hand over her sister's face. "We were walking, and then she screamed and collapsed. I think she was stung by a bee."

"Wendell, go fetch Dr. Ingley," Witfeld ordered, sinking down in Anne's place. "I'm glad you were here, Zachary."

Personally Zachary thought that at the moment he would have

been happier in Bedlam with the other lunatics. "All I could do was catch her," he returned, lurching to his feet with the limp Joanna in his arms and handing her over to her father. Left to his own devices, he probably would have been tempted to stumble and dump her into the pond.

"We'll follow you, Papa," Anne said, taking Zachary's arm.

While Witfeld hurried back to the house, Zachary followed more slowly with Anne. "Thank you," he said after a moment, his heart still pounding. Jesus Christ, that had been close. "How did you come to follow us?"

She shrugged. "I had a suspicion."

Zachary took a deep breath. "Forgive me for saying this, but from your mother's statements I thought she would be happy if one of you were to marry me, whatever the circumstances."

"She probably would. Perhaps I'm too firm a believer in fair play." With a slight smile she looked up at him again. "And perhaps I see things that some of the others don't."

He lowered his brow. "What things?"

"The stalk of hay in Caro's hair last night, her bare feet the day she finished your portrait. Things like that."

Shit. "But you didn't say anything."

"I love Caro. I know what she wants to do with her life. Ruining that for her wouldn't serve anything." She shot him a look he couldn't decipher. "I think you're staying here in Wiltshire for more reasons than cows. And I think you would make Joanna a terrible husband."

"Really. Why is that?"

She chuckled. "So now you're offended?"

"Not at all," he returned quickly. "Your statements seem a bit contradictory, though."

"Joanna's not Caroline." She leaned closer. "And Caro's leaving in a very few days."

"I'm aware of that."

Anne grinned, releasing him to skip ahead and join her father. "Quite the conundrum, isn't it?"

That was the understatement of the decade. Caroline wanted

nothing more than to go, he wanted her to stay, and he wasn't certain that any kind of declaration from him would cause her to change her mind. And ultimately, his pride was the least of his concerns. He'd lived a fairly sunny life, or so he'd thought. Caroline had shown him that he'd been waiting about in the shadows for something extraordinary to find him. Thanks to her, he'd found something—or rather *someone*—extraordinary. He liked living in that bright sunlight, and he couldn't do it if she went to Vienna. If she went anywhere where he couldn't join her.

At the sound of the commotion coming from the morning room, Caroline closed the farmer's almanac and emerged from the library. "What's happened?" she asked Grace as her sister charged by.

"Joanna fainted, and Zachary caught her. Isn't that heroic of him?"

"Yes, heroic," she returned, heading down the hall. For goodness' sake, her family *was* insane. Her sister could faint, and they still only thought of Zachary. Of course he would catch Joanna—he was a gentleman, and an observant and considerate one.

Anne intercepted her in the morning room doorway and dragged her back to the library. "I have to talk to you," she whispered, closing the door once they were inside.

"Is Joanna well? Grace said she—"

"She screamed and fell on Zachary, then grabbed him and kissed him when she heard Papa coming."

Caroline gasped. Her heart stopped, then began thudding like a hammer. Shaking, she felt behind her for a chair and sat heavily. "She didn't."

"She did. If she hadn't mentioned something this morning about being able to laugh at all of us, I would never have suspected. It was quite clever, really."

"It was shameful. What did Zachary do? What did Papa say? Are they—"

She couldn't finish her own sentence. *Zachary to be married to Joanna?* Didn't Joanna realize they would never suit? She was far too silly and flighty for him. He might be easygoing, but for God's sake, he wasn't silly. If Papa forced them to marry, she wouldn't be surprised if Zachary threw away the breeding project out of spite and then went to join the army after all, just to escape Joanna and the rest of them.

"It's all right, Caro," Anne said after a moment, putting a hand on her shoulder. "I followed them. By the time Papa arrived, I was there to play escort and tell him that she'd fainted."

Caroline closed her eyes. There had been no compromise, then, so there would be no marriage. "Thank goodness. What must Zachary think? I wouldn't be surprised if he packed his bags and left today."

"I don't think he's going anywhere as long as you're still in Wiltshire. You're not that blind to everything not on canvas, are you?"

"What are you talking about?"

Anne sighed and returned to the door. "Apparently nothing. But I wanted you to know, since Zachary may want to discuss it— and he seems to like talking with you."

"I thought you had designs on him." Caroline could scarcely say the words without growling.

"He's a very nice man. So perhaps I do, and perhaps I don't. After you leave for Vienna, what would you care, anyway?"

"I don't—that is—oh, go away, Anne."

Her sister sketched a curtsy and left the room. For several minutes Caroline sat where she was. It would have been a disaster. Everyone knew that a Griffin wouldn't marry a poor country aristocrat like a Witfeld unless there had been some kind of scandal.

As for the rest, the idea of Zachary setting up a household with Joanna, and sharing a bed with Joanna, and kissing and holding Joanna—or Anne, once Caroline left, since Zachary was undoubtedly now exceedingly grateful: She refused to think about it at all. It wasn't any of her affair, or her concern, what he did with his private life after she left. Except that she was still there, and she didn't want him touching anyone but her.

Chapter 21

Caroline found Zachary up in the conservatory, pacing. "Are you well?" she asked, swallowing.

He stopped, facing her. "Yes. Joanna faint—"

"Anne told me. I'm so sorry."

His shoulders lowered. "It's not your fault. Though the faint and kiss technique—and sneakiness in general—wasn't part of my instruction, I did inform her of several ways to net a man."

"And she very nearly netted you."

"Very nearly. I owe Anne a great deal."

That was what she'd been afraid of. "Well, Anne may have her own agenda as well, I'm afraid," she said, telling herself that she was only reluctantly giving him the information. She could wrestle with her conscience later.

"That settles it, then. I'm not going walking with anyone but you."

"Why am I exempt?"

"Because you don't want to get married." Zachary took a slow step closer. "Or do you, Caroline? Are you certain you would never wish to marry, even under the most ideal of circumstances?"

For a moment she couldn't breathe. *Stop it,* she ordered herself. "I hope that no one whom I consider a friend would ever ask me that question," she said slowly, unable to keep her voice from shaking, "because my friend would know what I want to do with my life, and how marriage would prevent it."

"I want to breed cattle," he said in a tight, hard voice, approaching her. "That doesn't preclude me from adding another dimension to my life. You can have more than one happiness, you know."

"*You* can, perhaps. You're a man, and a lord, and a Griffin. I am Miss Witfeld of Wiltshire, a viscount's great-granddaughter. And it . . . horrifies me to think of a life where what I want to do would be considered a hobby to be smirked at and barely tolerated—or worse, discouraged or forbidden for fear of harming the reputation of my husband and his family."

"But Caroline—"

She put a hand over his mouth, then replaced it with her lips. They kissed for a long moment, the heat and desire of it sending her blood pounding through her veins. "Don't ask me, Zachary," she whispered against his mouth. "Please."

He released her a little abruptly, striding to the window and back. "Very well. I won't ask you. I will ask, though, what you intend to do if Monsieur Tannberg says no."

"He won't."

"But if he does? Would you rather be a governess to the Eades than be married to someone who would encourage you to continue painting?"

"A hobby again?" she snapped, not certain whether she was shaken more by the thought of not being accepted by Monsieur Tannberg or by the near proposal. "At least if I were a governess I could continue to send out applications. Once I was married, all hope would be lost."

"Christ," he snarled. "You encourage me to find my passion in life, but I don't think you understand what life is."

"I do understand. And I intend to make the most of it."

"You're wrong."

"No, *you're* wr—"

"Bloody hell," he interrupted, stopping dead in his tracks as he looked down at the drive.

She started at the vehemence of his tone. "What's wrong?" she asked, alarmed.

"That."

She moved up beside him, following the point of his finger. A large black carriage stood in her front drive, a red crest emblazoned on the door. One of the symbols on the shield was a griffin. As they watched, a second, smaller coach pulled up behind it.

"Your family?"

"At least one of them. With luggage."

His family? "The . . . the duke?"

"I don't know yet. But since I only asked Melbourne for a note approving my plan, I don't think either he or Charlemagne driving out to Wiltshire during the Season can be good."

He strode downstairs. As she caught up to him, she could hear her mother trilling in the drawing room, and they headed in that direction.

"Oh, no, it's been no bother at all," Sally Witfeld was saying amid a clustering of nervous giggles. "Gladys is such a dear friend, and Lord Zachary has been a perfect gentleman."

Well, perhaps not a gentleman, Caroline reflected as they walked through the half-open doors, but being with him had been lively, warm perfection. And it absolutely, positively had to end. "Mama?" she said, stopping inside the doorway.

Not one, but two well-dressed men stood at the sound of her voice. Mrs. Witfeld lurched to her feet as well, while Zachary stopped in the doorway behind her, close enough that she could feel his large, warm presence.

"Caro, my dear! Look! The Duke of Melbourne and his brother Lord Charlemagne have come to visit us, all the way in Wiltshire!"

They'd come to see their brother and their aunt, but Caroline didn't correct her mother. Rather, she took a moment to look at the two men. She could see that they were Zachary's brothers; they had the same dark brown hair, compelling gray eyes, and lean, athletic build. The taller of the two, the one her mother had gestured at first, seemed to be looking at her rather intently, and she sketched a belated curtsy.

"Your Grace, my lord."

"Miss Witfeld. So you're the artist."

"Yes, Your Grace."

"What the devil are you two doing here?" Zachary broke in, moving past her.

"And hello to you, Zach." The middle brother, Charlemagne, pulled Zachary into a hug.

Zachary broke the embrace, facing his other brother. "Well?"

"You sent me a letter," the Duke of Melbourne said in a quiet, controlled drawl. "I came to see what you were talking about."

"You came all the way to Wiltshire to look at cows," Zachary said, making the sentence a statement rather than a question.

"You have been here for longer than we expected." The duke made his way around the admiring, giggling flock of Caroline's younger sisters. "Why don't you show me this Dimidius I've read so much about?"

The other one, Charlemagne, stepped forward. "Yes. And someone offered to show me their needlework?"

Caroline hung back as Zachary and the duke left the room, and the rest of the girls mobbed the remaining brother. Whatever lessons Zachary had taught them about how to approach a man and win his approval apparently didn't apply when a Griffin male was present. Even Joanna waded in, her fainting spell apparently forgotten.

Well, she didn't need to show off any of her work—Monsieur Tannberg's opinion was the only one she cared for at the moment. What she did need to do, though, was begin packing. Packing, and not thinking about what Zachary had said, and why he would want to marry her.

"Aunt Tremaine looks as though she's feeling better," Melbourne commented as they walked down the curving drive.

"She seems to be," Zachary agreed. Every bone in his body was suspicious over his brothers' presence, but he had no idea what, precisely, had prompted their journey. For both of them to appear—especially in the middle of both the social and business Season—meant that it was serious. He'd played the game of deciphering the rather enigmatic Sebastian before, but he hadn't been in the midst of trying to propose to a damned obstinate female or evading other chits fainting on him at the same time, plus beginning the most complex breeding program he'd ever heard of. Sebastian could have picked a worse time to arrive, but it would have been difficult to find one. "I don't think her gout was very serious to begin with, though."

"Are we back to that again? My inventing errands to get you out of London?"

Whatever the circumstances had been, Zachary had several weeks ago become more amenable to being in Wiltshire, so he shrugged. "I suppose not. How's Peep?"

"Angry that we left her in London with Mrs. Beacham. She does say hello, though, and would like to meet your cow."

"Dimidius isn't *my* cow. She belongs to Witfeld."

"Then how is any of this beneficial to me? You were rather light on the details."

Trying to pull his thoughts away from Caroline, Zachary outlined his program, including all the pertinent details about herd size, breeding schedule, and estimated cost over the first year. He had the feeling that Sebastian was only half listening, but knowing his brother, the duke might very well have questioned Eades and Witfeld and half the other farmers involved before he'd arrived at Witfeld Manor.

They stopped outside the cow pasture, and Zachary pointed out Dimidius and her calf. Melbourne watched the animals for several minutes, his expression unreadable.

"Most of my business is in trade and shipping," the duke said finally.

"Yes, I know. All the things that give me an aching head."

"All the things that make a great deal of money for the family."

"Does this mean you're not interested?"

"I'm not interested yet. I'd like more information."

Zachary nodded, his jaw clenching. "What if I said it would keep me from joining the army?" Moving away from the fence, he waited until Sebastian joined him, then started back toward the house.

"*I'm* keeping you from joining the army. Jumping from one hobby to another isn't any kind of solution, Zach. I would like to know how in God's name you came up with cows."

Zachary supposed he should have expected that no one in his family would believe this new project was any different from the two dozen others he'd pursued and discarded. They couldn't see into his heart or his mind. "If you want more information, then read over my notes. I haven't finished my outline or all my research yet, and even with the assistance of Witfeld and Miss Witfeld there are still some factors I won't be able to determine for the next year or so, but I intend to pursue this."

"Speaking of Miss Witfeld, you finished posing for the portrait?"

"You know I did. Shay shipped it off to Vienna for me."

"For her, you mean."

Zachary frowned. This was starting to feel like an interrogation. "I asked him to do me a favor. Are we debating semantics, now? Perhaps you should decide what you're going to be angry or disappointed with me for, and we'll concentrate on that."

"I haven't spoken with you in a month. I'm catching up."

"Yes, well, I have some work to do, so I'd rather you got to the point."

Melbourne stopped. "What are you so angry about?"

Zachary kept walking. "I'm angry because both you and Shay are here, without bothering to send word first so I could prepare a decent plan for you to see, and I'm angry because you decided to reject whatever it was I was proposing without even seeing it first."

"I've seen it before, Zachary. A hundred times. What kind of conclusion am I supposed to come to?"

"People bloody change, Melbourne. Why don't you take a minute to look around before you hand down your damned proclamations?" Zachary turned around, clenching his fists to keep from going after his brother. He couldn't remember ever being this frustrated and angry with Sebastian before, and they'd had similar disagreements twenty times. Maybe it was because this time he meant his side of the argument. "And by the way, I only asked if you wanted to participate. The project goes on with or without you, Your Grace."

"Zachary—"

"Bugger off, Sebastian. You're uninvited from being involved."

Apparently word spread on the wind in Wiltshire County, Sebastian noted. He and Shay hadn't been there for two hours before nine additional visitors from the town of Trowbridge and the surrounding area came calling at Witfeld Manor.

Some grocer's son named Williams sat in the morning room sending moon-eyed looks at one of the girls while Sally Witfeld chattered in Sebastian's ear. Across from him two more of the daughters, twins, obviously, whispered and giggled to one another while batting their lashes at him and Shay.

Charlemagne sat forward to pick up his cup of tea. "What the devil are we doing here again, Melbourne?" he murmured. "And where in damnation is Zachary?"

Considering the reception he'd received from Zachary, Sebastian wasn't entirely certain of the answer to either question. But he *was* certain that something other than plans for cattle breeding was going on, and with Witfeld's seven unmarried daughters all apparently pursuing every single male in the county, he wasn't leaving until he was satisfied that Zachary was out of danger. "We're looking into things," he returned under his breath. "And he's about somewhere." He wasn't about to admit aloud that he had no idea where Zachary had stalked off to.

The most obvious source of information would be Aunt Tremaine, but he hadn't yet managed a moment alone with her. Nor did that seem likely to happen until sometime this evening. Very well, then. He'd turned patience into an art form.

In the meantime, he didn't think Mrs. Witfeld would object if he asked to speak with one of her daughters. Motioning Charlemagne to stay where he was, he stood. "Where might I find Miss Witfeld?" he asked. "I would be interested in seeing some of her paintings."

"She's probably in her conservatory," Mrs. Witfeld answered, flipping her hand. "But you don't want to speak with her; she's going to Vienna in a few days, and doesn't want to marry. You should chat with Joanna, here. She's very pleasant, and fainted this morning. Your brother saved her."

"Did he, then?" Melbourne eyed the girl. She looked healthy enough. "I shan't overset her delicate constitution," he continued. "Will someone show me to the conservatory?"

One of the other girls rose. "I will, Your Grace."

"Which one are you?" he asked, falling in behind her.

"I'm Anne. I don't paint, and I don't faint."

He reassessed his opinion of Anne upward a little. "Neither do I."

"Do you raise cattle?"

"I have cattle on several of my estates."

"I'll wager none of them give as much milk as Dimidius."

Sebastian clenched his jaw. He would hear an opinion from Zachary, but he had no intention of listening to them from little girls of inferior breeding. "I don't wish to discuss cattle," he said, keeping his tone mild.

"Then you came to Wiltshire for a different reason," she returned promptly.

Obviously not all of the Witfelds were as dim as he'd originally thought. Interesting. "If I did, it would be my own reason," he said. People didn't question him or his motives; especially not chits half his age.

"We're actually in sheep country, you know," she continued, apparently unaffected by his tone.

"Yes, I know."

"And bricks. Trowbridge is also known for fine textiles."

"So I've heard." He was beginning to think she was intentionally baiting him, which made for a select choice of scenarios. Either she was insane, which he didn't believe, or she was angry at his presence. That made more sense, especially if the Witfelds were set on Zachary marrying one of the daughters. Logic didn't always win out, however, and he preferred to know things for certain before he acted. "Given your county's fame for sheep and bricks and textiles, why did your father decide to breed cattle?"

"So you wish to discuss cattle again, now?"

Sebastian took a slow, controlled breath. "Yes, I do."

"Very well. He didn't, really—decide to breed cattle, I mean. He had a theory about combining breeds, but Zachary is the one who realized how significant Dimidius could be. He has five or six local farmers and landowners using part of their land to help increase breeding stock."

So the Witfelds genuinely liked Zach. He wasn't surprised; his youngest brother was notoriously charming and good-natured.

"I'd wager all of you enjoyed having Zachary and Aunt Tremaine here in Wiltshire."

"Yes. If Zachary hadn't agreed to pose for Caro's portrait, she would have had to use Lord and Lady Eades." Anne slowed halfway up the stairs, looking under her arm at him. "They like to dress as historical figures, and I'm not certain how the art studio would have received a work like that."

"Indeed."

They stopped at a door just off the stairs, and Anne knocked. "Caro? The Duke of Melbourne wants to see your paintings."

After a moment the door opened. "Certainly," the slender, auburn-haired female said, stepping back so they could enter.

The conservatory had a solid oak floor, and half the room was taken up by a curving bow window with a low, padded seat running beneath it. On the far wall shelves and organized stacks of books and sketch pads and paintings filled every inch of space, while to his right he could barely make out the back wall for all the paintings covering it.

He walked closer, taking in family portraits, landscapes, paintings of dogs and cats and chickens, people he recognized from their visits this morning and more he didn't recognize who must be neighbors he hadn't yet met. As he put a thoughtful expression on his face he heard Miss Witfeld move up behind him, and he waited for her to make excuses for some of the less polished works or the rather odd subjects.

"Is this the sum total of your work?" he asked after a moment, when she didn't venture a comment.

"No. Some of it is in the hallway behind the drawing room, and a great many of the local families have the portraits I did of them."

"So these are the paintings you are the least proud of?"

"The paintings I'm the least proud of are in the fireplace," she returned smoothly. "My father wanted one of each of us in the hallway, and he chose a few of his other favorites to accompany them."

Still no simpering, no polite effacing of her talent that he would have expected to hear from most ladies with whom he was acquainted. Sebastian studied the paintings more closely. Most of the better-acclaimed artists of the generation had taken pains to become acquainted with him; they invariably seemed in need of a patron or a client. And he collected some artworks, painted by the finest British artists, as his contribution to the artistic community.

"You have talent," he said after a moment, moving slowly along the wall.

"Thank you."

Sebastian faced her, ignoring the other chit, Anne, still standing beside the door. "I'm not a large fan of paintings of animals, I'm afraid."

She tilted her head a little, her gaze meeting his with a fearlessness he noted. "I didn't paint them for you, Your Grace. Is there anything else you would like to survey?"

"I hear that you are going to Vienna in the next few days."

"I've applied for an apprenticeship there," she returned.

"How do your mother and father feel about your traveling to the Continent?"

"You would have to ask them, Your Grace."

"But it is your intention to be a portraitist in Vienna, whichever . . . offers or obstacles might land in your path?"

She hesitated, her color deepening a little. To Sebastian that alone spoke as loudly as an alarm bell, but he waited, unmoving, for her to respond. Cows, portraits, the army; he could deal with all of that. His concern was Zachary. And Zachary had a very open heart, despite his polished veneer of experience. Something had happened here in Wiltshire, something that hadn't happened in a dozen or so liaisons and short-lived affairs in which his brother had engaged previously.

"My sisters, my father, and even my mother will tell you, Your Grace, that my one aim in life is to be a successful portraitist. I'm not likely to be swayed by any conflicting obstacles or offers."

"And what—"

"Melbourne." Zachary stood in the doorway, an annoyed expression on his face. "That's enough."

"I'm inquiring about Miss Witfeld's plans," Sebastian returned, assessing his brother's expression. "You've been here for longer than I have; I'm catching up."

"You sound like the Spanish Inquisition." Zachary turned his attention to Miss Witfeld. "I'm going into Trowbridge to borrow that new book from Anderton and to order another shipment of feed grain. Care to join me?"

"Certainly," she said, sketching a curtsy in Sebastian's direction. "I have a few items to purchase for Vienna."

Nodding, Zachary gestured her out the door and followed behind her, slowing to send Sebastian another glare over his shoulder. *Hm.* Interesting.

"Would you like to visit anyone else, Your Grace?" the young one, Anne, asked. "You might enjoy seeing some of my father's other inventions. He has an egg roller that Zachary assisted him with."

"By all means," Sebastian said, beginning to find this all a little amusing. Apparently he'd stumbled on the infant Greek goddess of Chaos to be his guide. And he'd learned that whatever Miss Witfeld's intentions, Zachary's were much clearer. "Lead on."

Shay managed to wrangle an invitation to accompany the two of them into town, which of course meant that half the female population of Witfeld Manor then had to join them, as well. Zachary sent his brother an annoyed glance as the fully loaded barouche passed between them. He wheeled Sagramore back around, deciding he could at least ride beside Caroline even if he couldn't ride with her.

On his borrowed gelding, Charlemagne moved up beside him. "What's that sour look for?" his brother asked.

"What do you think?"

"None of this is my fault. Melbourne said to pack, so I packed. Had to pass on a very nice offer for shares in a porcelain manufacturer to do it. And if you think I was going to spend another second being mobbed in that house, you're mad."

"So now you can be mobbed out-of-doors."

"At least out here I have more avenues of escape."

"I wish you'd escape back to London. You didn't even bring me any cigars, I'll wager."

Charlemagne looked at him. "You can hardly blame him for being concerned, Zach. From joining the army to breeding cows in the space of one month is a bit much even for you."

"It's not like that," Zachary shot back, trying to keep a rein on his temper. Yelling at Shay wouldn't do any good; as his brother had said, journeying to Wiltshire had been Melbourne's idea. And from the way the duke had been questioning Caroline, it seemed that Sebastian suspected he'd embarked on yet another frivolous venture for no better reason than to net a female's favors. For once his brother had no idea what was going on.

"Then explain what it is, Zach. I don't have a gypsy with me to tell your fortune."

Zachary glanced over at the barouche to see Caroline sending him a look of her own. Only three damned days until she would have her answer from Vienna, and she could be gone within a day after that. Only three days, and now his brothers were here to further complicate what was already an indecipherable mess. And with them present, his odds of arranging another private rendezvous had decreased considerably as well, damn it all.

"I figured some things out," he said quietly, dropping back while Shay slowed beside him. "I thought about the army, and I thought about *why* I wanted to join the army, and I realized what I wanted from life."

"And you can get that thing from cows."

"I can get that thing from developing a plan and following through with it, and working to see that not only this part of Wiltshire but perhaps even all of England will eventually be able to benefit from it."

"So you're a philanthropist now."

"If you're only going to make fun, I'm finished. You're not the one I need to convince of anything, anyway."

"Ouch," Shay returned, scowling. "And to think, I might have been purchasing table crockery right now."

Zachary snorted. "And you think *my* plans are idiotic? At least if the milk production part fails, I can still eat the cows."

"Fair enough. If it makes any difference, I don't think Seb's opposed to your project. He just wants to know more about it."

"And about whether I'll follow through with it. I will. And I don't particularly care whether he approves of what I'm doing or not." How could he explain it without sounding like a Bedlamite, anyway? How could he tell his cynical brothers that he'd never been as excited or as enthusiastic about anything before, and that if he could only convince Caroline to stay, he would consider that he'd found a perfect moment and a perfect life?

"I'll pass that along. But I do have another question."

"And what might that be?"

"You've been here for four weeks," his older brother said, pitching his voice even lower. "Which of the Witfeld chits are you plowing? I don't want to step on your toes."

It was too direct to be a question from Sebastian, but the suggestion of it might have been the duke's. "Become acquainted with them and you might decide not to be so insulting," he commented, evading the question with every ounce of skill he possessed. "Parents of limited means have managed to raise seven charming girls. I admire them for that. It can't always have been a pleasant prospect."

Shay grimaced. "Consider me chastised. Aunt Tremaine wouldn't allow you to get away with anything, anyway, I suppose."

Charlemagne could suppose all he liked; Zachary wasn't about to tell him how important Caroline was becoming to his life. Not when letting her go seemed to be the best thing he could do for her.

Chapter 22

"But Mr. Witfeld!"

"However much you think it will elevate our status with our neighbors, Mrs. Witfeld, we cannot afford another party simply because a duke has arrived—uninvited, by the way—on our doorstep!"

Caroline stopped halfway through her father's office door and turned around again. *Don't notice me,* she prayed fervently as she edged the door closed. If there was one thing she didn't want, it was to be caught in the middle of an argument between her parents. Especially now, when she was already arguing with herself.

"Caroline!"

"Damnation," she muttered, swinging the door open again. "Yes, Papa?"

"Your mother thinks we need to hold another soiree to welcome the Duke of Melbourne to our household. What is your opinion?"

"I don't think the duke or Lord Charlemagne means to stay in Wiltshire long enough to attend a party," she said. "They can hardly be comfortable staying in Grace and Violet's rooms. And I know Anne and Susan aren't happy to be sharing with Grace and Violet."

"But if we hold a party, they will have to stay!" her mother broke in, twisting a handkerchief in her hands and ignoring the rest of her daughter's commentary. "No one else has ever had three such gentlemen under their roof all at one time."

Her father, though, was looking at Caroline. "How long do you think they mean to stay, then?"

"I think the duke is only here to look at Zachary's plans and to be certain he's not being coerced into remaining in Wiltshire."

" 'Coerced'? How?"

This was going to be the difficult part. She might not have had much experience with powerful patriarchs of powerful families, but she knew precisely what the Duke of Melbourne suspected, and she knew that he suspected her of being the cause of Zachary's interest in cattle and in Wiltshire. And apparently he wouldn't be entirely wrong. "We are a family of seven attractive daughters, Papa," she said with a smile she didn't feel.

"Yes, we are," her mother broke in. "And you and your sisters have had a month to make Lord Zachary fall in love with one of you, and what do we hear? He's more interested in a cow!"

"Mama, this program of his could be so beneficial to our family that I can't even begin to state it. And its success will raise our status in Wiltshire."

"With whom—farmers?"

"Don't bother, Caro," her father commented, flipping open his ledger book. "I've been trying to explain it to your mother for days. She wants a son-in-law, not a plump purse."

"No, I want both!" Harumphing, her mother stalked out of the room.

"I'm sorry you had to witness that, Caro," her father said, obviously unconcerned. "What can I do for you? And I've set aside twenty pounds for any miscellaneous traveling expenses you might have—and in case you'd like to purchase a new gown to impress your new employer."

"I don't have the position yet, Papa," she said, sinking into the chair opposite him. "Thank you so much for the offer, but I can't ask you to do that."

"You don't have to ask."

She blinked back unexpected tears. She knew precisely how

dear even twenty pounds could be to the family. And it made what she needed to tell him even more difficult. But it also made it more important. "Papa, I think I know why Melbourne is here."

"It's not because of Dimidius?"

"I think it's because of me."

He closed the ledger again. "Do you know that Melbourne's yearly income is rumored to be somewhere over a hundred thousand pounds?"

Caroline blinked at the figure. "Wh— No, I didn't. But what—"

"However valuable Dimidius and her kind might turn out to be for us and for the finer tables of England, a yearly investment of a few thousand quid is not enough to ruffle that man's feathers."

"I don't—"

He leaned forward, putting his hand over hers as she fiddled with his letter opener. "I may have been a bit preoccupied lately, but I'm not blind, my dear. I know His Grace isn't here because of the cows." Her father gave her fingers a squeeze and released her. "Now. Tell me whatever you will; I promise to listen quietly and be reasonable."

Oh, dear. She'd tried to think of her conversation with Zachary in academic, logical terms: He'd offered her an alternative to the path she'd chosen for herself, and she'd declined. Logic, though, couldn't explain the ache in her chest at the thought of never seeing him, never chatting with him again. It didn't explain much of anything so much as it seemed to provide an excuse. "Zachary asked . . . well, not precisely *asked,* but suggested . . ." she stumbled, her voice shaking, "he intimated that he would perhaps like to marry me."

For a moment the entire house seemed so quiet that she swore she could hear the grandfather clock ticking up in the library. "Good God," her father finally said, his face paling. He cleared his throat. "I see. And your reply was?"

Oh, was he disappointed? Even a tiny portion of a hundred thousand pounds would make life in Wiltshire so much easier. She reached for the level, logical part of herself she'd been leaning on so heavily today. "I told him that I wanted to be a portraitist, and that I couldn't do that as any man's wife, and I asked him not to ask me."

After a long moment her father nodded. "And he complied, I assume?"

"Yes. But I wanted you to know that . . . that His Grace probably suspects something, and that he wants to make certain one of the precious Griffins isn't going to wed someone of inferior standing."

"Caroline, I would set you up against any noblewoman in England, and you would come out the better," he returned. "But I wouldn't have you miserable in even the most advantageous marriage."

That was the thing. She hadn't merely been speculating about her future if she married into the Griffin family, and the appearance of the Duke of Melbourne made that even more certain. He wouldn't allow a female painter who insisted on having a studio and clients and her own income into the family, and she had no intention of giving up her dream.

The problem, though, was that her waking dreams and her sleeping dreams were drifting further and further apart. And the idea that one day Zachary would marry someone else—someone *not her*—hurt almost more than she could stand. "You're not angry, Papa?"

"You have a dream, Caroline. I wouldn't have you turn your back on it for anything in the world." He leaned across the desk and squeezed her fingers. "But I want you to be certain. Marrying Zachary could open a great many doors for you."

"But it would close one very important door, wouldn't it?" she returned, at the edge of begging him to agree with her—or to disagree with her. Oh, she didn't know.

He smiled. "The frustrating thing about doors, my dear, is that it's difficult to know precisely what you'll find on the other side until you've stepped through."

She stood. "I was afraid you were going to say that."

"It's an interesting problem, to have too many choices. And I don't think I can advise you to do anything but discover which path makes you happiest, and follow it."

Goodness. "Thank you, Papa. You've given me more to think about." Her heart and her mind both full, Caroline mumbled something and escaped. She felt very much in need of a long, long walk. On her way down the hall, however, she spied Zachary lurking in the morning room next to the window. She stopped, debating whether she could face talking with him again. It would have been so much easier if she didn't like him, admire him, trust him so much. But maybe he had the answer—no one else had ever caused her to ask herself such questions.

"You're looking very thoughtful," she said, quoting his earlier lessons on how to impress a man and trying very hard to make her heart stop beating so hard before he heard it banging about. "Is something troubling you? I'd very much like to know what it is. Or I could fetch you some pie."

"Very amusing." He gestured at her. "Come here and look at this."

Frowning, she joined him at the window. For a moment, she couldn't move beyond the sensation of his solid warmth behind her, close enough to touch, to lean into, to lose herself inside. *Steady, Caro.* This wasn't about losing herself; it was about finding a logical solution to her dilemma. Then, following the point of his finger, she spied her sister Susan leaning against an oak tree while Martin Williams stood speaking to her adamantly.

"Are they fighting?"

"She's smiling. I think he may be declaring himself."

"You mean he's proposing?"

Zachary glanced at her before returning his gaze to the scene outside. "It does happen in the world. Men and women marry fairly frequently in fact, from what I've observed."

"Zachary—"

"One sister out of six isn't wonderful odds, but it's early yet. I have high hopes that at least one or two other of your siblings might receive proposals in the next few weeks."

From Caroline's expression she wasn't sure whether to nod,

flee, or yell at him. At the moment, though, Zachary didn't have a great deal of sympathy for her. He was the one who'd been rejected, after all. And despite that, he couldn't seem to stay away from her. He wasn't even angry as much as he was frustrated. True, if they married he couldn't see her going to Vienna, especially since his new business would obviously keep him in England, but neither would he expect her to stop painting once she put on his ring. How could she not feel the pull between them? And how could she ignore that, put it aside?

"I hope you're right," was all she said, still gazing outside.

He found himself wishing that he could paint her. He would have her posed just like she was now, still and thoughtful, her gaze out the window, to somewhere other than where she was. Would she be happy, he wondered, when she reached her destination? Thanks to her he'd reached his, and yet without her there, he found it lacking. "I love you," he said quietly.

Her face whipped up toward his, tears in her eyes. Then without a word she turned and left the room. For a long time he stood there, looking after her and wondering how his heart could continue beating with a gaping hole in his chest. He'd been rejected by chits before, but mostly because they'd found someone willing or eager to marry them, while he'd only been interested in some amusement. He'd never lost a woman to a bundle of paints and canvases before.

"That went well," he muttered, and headed for the liquor tray and the bottle of whiskey. It was definitely time for a drink.

"Good morning, Miss Witfeld."

Caroline looked down at the foot of the stairs, grateful that it wasn't Zachary who stood in the foyer looking up at her. The day before yesterday had very nearly been enough to kill her. "Lord Charlemagne."

"Zachary tells me there's some fine fishing hereabouts."

She nodded. "The Wylye River is a few miles away. Izaak Walton wrote his *Compleat Angler* about it. Every river and stream in the area is well stocked."

"Well, that sounds too splendid to pass by. Have you seen either of my brothers?"

"I believe His Grace is in the library. I haven't seen Lord Zachary yet today." She'd barely seen him over the past three days, though she could hardly blame him for that, since she'd been the one doing the avoiding. The last three words he'd said to her in private had kept her awake every night since then, tossing and turning in fits that swung from absolute euphoria to deepest despair. If only he'd been a penniless painter like herself. If only he lived in Vienna. If only he weren't a Griffin.

The front door slammed open, nearly sending Lord Charlemagne into the side table. "Caro!" Anne shrieked, doing a spin about the foyer before she bothered to look up the stairs.

"What in heaven's name is wrong?" Caroline asked, hurrying down to her sister as, with a graceful step, the middle Griffin brother moved backward, out of the way.

"It's here! It's here!"

"What's h—"

Her father came through the door, a box in his arms. "It's from Vienna," he said, his voice choked and his smile beaming.

Oh. Oh dear, oh dear, oh dear. Her hands shook so hard that she could only clench them together as she stared at the box. What could it be? The portrait? That made sense. They'd returned the original works she'd sent, the ones that had won her an application. Zachary's portrait should go to Zachary, and the Tannberg studio wouldn't have space to keep the work of every applicant. They were a business, not a gallery. Except that she wanted to take the painting with her to put in her room in Vienna. If she couldn't have him, at least she could have his likeness. He hadn't paid her for it, after all, and—

"Shall we all go to the morning room?" her father prompted.

She shook herself. For heaven's sake, the most important moment of her life and she was lost in thoughts of someone else. "Yes, yes. We should fetch Mama."

"I'll do it," Anne said and bolted up the stairs, yelling.

Dazed, Caroline followed her father into the morning room.

She'd been expecting an answer since she'd sent an application, and the fact that the response had come a day early shouldn't have thrown her so far out of her own skin. But it had, and now she was fighting her way back to reality so she wouldn't begin sobbing like a simpering fool when she read the letter from Monsieur Tannberg.

She took a seat, and her father set the box in her lap, bending to kiss her on the forehead before he sat in one of the chairs close by. Whether they'd all supported her dream or not, she felt deeply that her family should be present when she opened the box, and she waited as singly and in pairs they hurried into the room. The wait gave her the few moments she needed to compose herself, anyway.

That composure faltered a little as Zachary slipped into the room, Charlemagne on his heels. Her sisters made more of a fuss when the Duke of Melbourne arrived, but though her gaze was on the box, half her attention remained on Zachary. He looked like he hadn't done much sleeping, either.

"Oh, goodness," her mother tittered, sweeping into the room like a grande dame entering a ballroom, "I'm positively shaking with anticipation. Open it, Caro my dear, at once!"

Caroline took a deep breath and let it out again. "Very well."

She pried open the box with the crow her father had provided. Beneath the layer of padded cloth she'd originally provided lay Zachary's portrait, a folded letter on top of it. As she removed the painting and set it to lean against the chair beside her feet, she heard a murmured comment pass between Melbourne and the middle brother. It sounded like a compliment, but she was too nervous to pay any attention.

Setting the box aside, she slid her finger beneath the wax seal of the letter and unfolded the stiff paper.

"Read it out loud, Caro," Anne urged, bouncing on her toes.

Caroline cleared her throat. " 'Dear Miss Witfeld. When you submitted your application we were under the impression that you were a man. This studio is not in the . . . habit of hiring females.' " Her voice faltered, but the slow, dark feeling of nightmare sank into her, making her feel as though something, some-one else entirely was forcing her to continue.

" 'Your style is admirably clean and skillful, but with a typical female's lack of sensibility you have idealized your subject be-yond what is generally tolerated. We have returned said work. In our estimation you have a fair amount of skill, and we suggest you seek employment teaching painting to children as more befits an artist of your sex. With regards, Monsieur Raoul Tannberg, Tannberg Studios, Vienna.' "

And so it was over. No fanfare, no drama, no hope for a future acceptance. The only studio that had asked for her application, and they'd thought she was a man. In truth, she had applied as M. Witfeld after twenty-six rejections. Perhaps in the back of her mind she'd done it on purpose, thinking, hoping that they would be so impressed with her work that her sex wouldn't matter. Ob-viously it did.

"Oh, Mr. Witfeld!" her mother cried, and fainted.

In the ensuing chaos, Caroline sat where she was, reading the letter over and over again. She felt numb. After the first stab, noth-ing seemed able to touch her. In a sense she understood why the studio wouldn't wish to hire a female; their success rested on hav-ing clients, and if clients disapproved of her, they would go else-where. But they'd asked to see her work, and she hadn't actually lied about her identity. If they'd looked for clues, they would have found them.

But as for saying that her portrait of Zachary was idealized, that was simply ridiculous. She'd drawn and painted him pre-cisely as he was. It wasn't her fault if he was exceptionally hand-some, and it wasn't her fault if his expression inspired admiration and confidence.

A hand touched her shoulder. "Caroline?"

She jumped at the low voice. *Zachary.* What was she supposed to say? That faced with the reality of having to work for Lord and Lady Eades, she *would* rather be married to him? The wording, the timing, sounded in her mind as awful as it felt in her heart.

Zachary sat beside her, taking her clenched fist between his warm hands. So now he wasn't even trying to hide that he favored her. Did he think she'd been backed into a corner? Did he want her to be forced into marrying him? Her thoughts flew so quickly that she couldn't slow them long enough to compose a sentence. She wanted him to go away, and she wanted him to stay right there.

"I'm so sorry," he said quietly.

"Are you?"

"I know how much you wanted this. Of course I'm sorry. I could write to Tannberg again, and see if the Griffin name could influence him to change his m—"

"No," she said, standing. She still had too much to think about, but she did know that getting a position because Zachary threatened someone wasn't anything she wanted.

"You still have an alternative to taking a governess position at Eades's manor, Caroline. I haven't changed m—"

"If I may," the Duke of Melbourne broke in, "after seeing Miss Witfeld's work in the conservatory the other day I took the liberty of writing a friend of mine about her considerable skills." He pulled a letter from his pocket and walked forward, handing it to her. "That is his answer."

Wonderful. He probably had a more prestigious governess position lined up for her in northernmost Yorkshire. Anything to keep a Witfeld from marrying a Griffin. She unfolded the missive. And froze as her eyes caught the signature line.

"This is from Thomas Lawrence," she breathed, numbness turning to a shaking buzz beneath her skin.

"He is willing to offer you an apprentice position with his studio in London," the duke said, his gaze on Zachary rather than her, "with the proviso that you begin by the end of the month."

The end of the month. That would give her three days to pack and make her way to London. "I sent Sir Thomas a letter before," she said, fighting to keep a grasp on reality, "and his secretary's reply was only that Sir Thomas did not take on apprentices, and certainly not females."

"I'm more persuasive than you are," Melbourne said succinctly.

"But—"

"Miss Witfeld, didn't you tell me several days ago that your quest to be a professional artist wouldn't be swayed by any obstacles or conflicts? I've recommended you to Lawrence; it is still up to you to impress him. But you have three days to journey to London if you wish to prove your conviction."

"Melbourne, that's very generous of you," Zachary said, anger deep in his voice, "but I would like to know why you've decided to use your influence to aid Miss Witfeld."

"You're the one who's been so supportive of her efforts," his brother returned smoothly. "I'm doing my part as well."

"Like hell you are. I won't—"

"Enough!" Caroline snapped.

Melbourne was practically daring her to decline the offer, to admit that all of her talk about marriage as a last resort for females when they had nothing else available to them was just that—talk. And then there was Zachary himself, ready with his consolation prize of marriage with someone who would at least tolerate her if she continued to dabble with painting. Except it wouldn't be merely consolation: She could imagine that for a while she would be very happy. Until she wanted to pick up a paintbrush again, that was.

So she had three choices now—two more than she'd expected. Governess to the earl's son, marriage to Zachary, or an apprenticeship with Thomas Lawrence. And either of the first two meant admitting that her dream was finished, unattainable, and never to be realized.

She looked at her parents' expectant faces. Her mother didn't know for certain what Zachary offered, but she would prefer a good marriage for one of her daughters over anything. Her father would want her to take the apprenticeship, to succeed at realizing a dream when he'd never had the chance to do so.

"Caroline," Zachary whispered from her shoulder, "please take time to think about th—"

"I'd best pack," she broke in, clenching Lawrence's note to her chest. "I need to be in London in three days."

Her sisters began cheering, but her gaze was on Zachary. With a stiff nod, his jaw clenched, he turned and left the room.

Chapter 23

"You had no bloody right!"

"Lower your voice, Zachary," Melbourne returned from his seat in front of the library fire.

He certainly hadn't lost any time in making himself at home in Witfeld Manor, Zachary noted, but then his brother always found himself lavishly welcomed wherever he went. "So you want me to be gentlemanly about this?" he growled. "To maintain a calm demeanor and sit down for a nice chat? Perhaps we could discuss our differences over a game of chess and a brandy."

The only thing that enabled Zachary to speak in a half-reasonable voice at all was the fact that Melbourne had banished Shay from the room. If nothing else it told him that the duke took the situation seriously. And he'd damn well better.

"Pardon me if I'm wrong," his oldest brother said in the same even tone he'd used previously, "but I thought you were encouraging Miss Witfeld's artistic endeavors."

"It's not about that."

"Then enlighten me. What is this about?"

Hell, Melbourne knew anyway, or he wouldn't have taken the steps that he had to remove Caroline from Wiltshire in general and from Zachary's grasp in particular. "You don't even know her," Zachary growled. "You might have made an attempt to do so before you stepped into the middle of my affairs."

"Your affairs? I assisted Miss Witfeld. Your present affair is cows, is it not?"

"Play your little games all you want, Sebastian, but eventually one of them is going to bite you in the ass. I want to marry that woman. I love her."

Sebastian looked at him for a long moment, something undecipherable touching his eyes and then sliding away again. "Does she know that?"

Zachary sputtered. "Of course she does."

"Then I don't see why you're blaming me for anything. *She* accepted that position with Lawrence. I didn't force her into it."

No, his brother hadn't. And that was the reason Zachary didn't feel calm enough to talk with Caroline just yet. Taking it out on Sebastian was easier. If he became any angrier, he was simply going to boil. No doubt, though, bloody Melbourne did own a share of the blame. He'd swept in with his usual insight and razor-sharp timing and overturned the turnip cart. *His* turnip cart. "You might have given her time to think before you surprised her like that and then practically dared her to refuse the offer."

"I'm not apologizing for anything, Zachary. I've spoken with Aunt Tremaine, and under the circumstances she would like to travel on to Bath. You'll accompany her."

"I will not. I have an obligation to these people. I've begun a breeding program, and I'm going to see it through. I told you that."

The duke paused again, eyeing him. "I'll contribute five thousand pounds if you can write up a proposal and prove to me how much this program could be worth."

"Five thousand pounds? That's more of an insult than if you refused to participate at all." Zachary stalked to the window and back, for a brief moment glad he was too angry to feel hurt by the growing pile of insults. "I already told you not to participate. Stay out of it. This is my project, and I don't want you involved."

"My offer is five thousand pounds for the purchase of cattle this year," Melbourne said more forcefully, his calm veneer slipping for the first time in the conversation. "And I suggest you take it. In addition, if I approve your proposal, I'll contribute one hundred percent of expenses."

"Are you bribing me to leave Wiltshire, then?"

"There are six other daughters here. Your staying isn't worth the risk."

Zachary's fists clenched. "If you continue in this vein, Melbourne, I'm going to break some fences so badly they'll never be mended."

"If you're sincere about your breeding program, it will take up most of your free time. Caroline Witfeld wants to be a painter, Zachary. She doesn't want you."

"I didn't ask your opinion, and I bloody well didn't ask for your interference."

Melbourne shrugged. "I'm doing what I think is necessary for the sake of my brother and the family. Decide now, Zachary. Agree to *my* proposal, and I'll arrange for Miss Witfeld to have private transportation to London, and for her to find suitable accommodations there."

"And if I don't agree, she's on her own?"

"*You* can't find her a place to live without ruining her. The Griffin family, however, can."

"I want to talk to Caroline."

"Then talk to her. But it seems to me that she's already made up her mind."

"You're an arrogant bastard, Sebastian, and I hope that one day you'll get yours as squarely as you hand it out."

"I already have, I think," his brother said quietly, and picked up a book.

Sebastian meant losing his wife, of course. Under other circumstances Zachary would have apologized for the remark, but not today. Today he wanted to put his fist through something. Caroline had chosen, and it hadn't been him. It would have been one thing if she'd been accepted in Vienna—he'd known from the beginning that that had been her dream. It would have been hard, but he would have understood.

No, he'd lost to a last-minute ambush. And her unwavering dream wasn't something he could fight—if it had been another man, he would have called for pistols at daybreak. But this was all her. Melbourne was right about that; he'd merely seen it and used it to his advantage.

Zachary could see so clearly that what she was searching for wouldn't give her a complete life. Perhaps he could still make *her* see that—though the one weak point to her general common sense and logic seemed to be her art. And in truth it wasn't all for her sake; he wasn't certain how much longer he could stand the pain in his heart.

Sending Melbourne another glare, he slammed out of the library and went looking for Caroline. Her bedchamber door was half open, and he pushed through it without knocking.

Her maid, arms full of clothing, squeaked. "Miss Witfeld! It's Lord Zachary, ma'am."

Caroline turned to face him. "I'm a bit busy at the moment, Lord Zachary. Perhaps we'll have time to chat at dinner."

"Don't you dare," he snapped. "You, Molly. Out."

"But—"

"Out!"

Muttering something apologetic, the maid scurried out the door. Zachary shut it behind her.

"Don't order my maid about," Caroline said belatedly, her skin paling. "I need her assistance."

Zachary picked up another pile of clothes and threw it into a waiting portmanteau. "There. How's that?"

"Stop it, Zachary!"

He ignored her. "Here, how about some books?" He dumped a handful on top of the clothes. "Oh, wait, you don't need to read. You'll be painting." He pulled the tomes out and threw them on the floor.

She put her hands on her hips, her expression furious. "Zach—"

"What about a portrait of your family? Yes, that'll do. Then you can see their faces flat there on the canvas. What more do you need? That's how you see everything, isn't it? Flat on a canvas."

"Leave this room at once. I do not have to tolerate th—"

Zachary spied his portrait leaning against her reading chair and picked it up. "You can't have this."

"Put that down!"

"No. If you want to see me, you'll have to look up the real thing. You don't get to pretend to have a life, look at my painting and remember that we made love, and remember how alive you felt." He looked hard at her, willing her to understand. "On second thought, keep it." Setting it down again, he stalked up to her. "I want you to remember. I want you to discover that having one thing you want doesn't mean your life is complete. That when you seek something to the exclusion of everything else, you haven't found life at all. All you'll have is a portr—"

She slapped him. Hard. He curled his fingers against the sudden flash of fury and frustration, holding his muscles rigid.

"How dare you?" she bit out. "Until a few weeks ago you were going to join the army. What was it before that? The navy? Becoming a priest? Raising horses? Becoming a professional wagerer? Buying chickens? What makes you think you are the least bit qualified to tell me what a goal is, or what a life is?"

She'd actually hit on a few of his earlier schemes. Despite his anger it shook him to realize how well she'd come to know him. But she didn't know everything. "At least I kept an open mind. And I learned my lessons. I've seen my future, and I want you in it."

"After what you just said to me? I wouldn't marry you if my alternative was making bricks. Go away. Now."

For a moment he stood there, shaking. "Fine." He turned his back on her, yanking open the door and nearly sending the startled maid stumbling back into the room. "Enjoy your damned life, Caroline. I hope it's all you've dreamed of."

He headed for Sally Witfeld's room, where his aunt was commiserating with her misery-turned-to-joy over Caroline's rapidly evolving future. "Aunt Tremaine," he said, when a servant admitted him, "I want to leave before dark."

Obviously Melbourne had informed her of her part in the play, because she nodded. "I'll be ready."

He had one last person to inform, though he was loathe to give Melbourne the satisfaction. By way of compromise he found Shay, playing whist with Joanna, Julia, and Grace. Apparently the girls had given up trying to mob every male in sight, but then he had been coaching them for a month on their tactics.

"Zachary," his brother greeted him. "I'm thinking we should teach these young ladies how to play faro."

"Oh, yes, please!" Julia urged, giggling.

Zachary shook his head. "Tell Melbourne that Aunt Tremaine and I will be on the road to Bath by sunset. And that I expect him to keep his word."

Joanna lurched to her feet. "But you can't leave!"

"My business takes me to Bath." He sketched a bow. "Excuse me. I need to finish packing."

He needed to begin packing, actually, but his valet would do the majority of that. Leaving instructions for Reed, he attached Harold to his leash and headed out for a long walk around the pond. It was more of an angry stalk around the pond, but even with his heart pounding and his breath harsh in his ears, nothing changed. He didn't feel better, didn't see that Caroline would be happier as a painter with her eyes on nothing but canvas and paint and people frozen in time than she would be with him.

If she didn't see it either, though, then perhaps he was expecting too much of her. If she never realized, if it never occurred to her, that more existed outside her little room with its pretty windows, then his pointing it out to her wouldn't make the least bit of difference. Obviously, it hadn't.

"Zachary," Edmund Witfeld's voice came, and Zachary looked around with a start. He spied Caroline's father seated on a boulder at the pond's edge. With a fishing pole in his hands and a bucket of fish beside him, he looked the very image of country serenity. Zachary envied him for it.

"I was walking," he said unnecessarily, giving Harold a short whistle when the dog started toward the fish. Immediately the pup dropped into a sit.

"So I see. Considering the ruckus in the house, I decided I needed a bit of air, myself."

"Aunt Tremaine and I are leaving for Bath," Zachary said stiffly. "My brother has professed an interest in the breeding program, and I'll be putting together a more detailed proposal for him." He hesitated. "It would be useful if I could correspond with you."

Witfeld turned around on the rock, facing him. "If you're continuing with this just to prove to Caroline or your brother that she wasn't the reason you decided to invest in Wiltshire cattle, Zachary, I wish you'd tell me now. I'm used to my neighbors thinking me peculiar, but I'd hate for them to think I led them into nonsense."

Zachary blew out his breath. "What do they call it when chance, fate, and common sense all have a moment of intersection? Serendipity? Whatever played into it, Edmund, I've found my serendipity, and I won't abandon it. I'll set up a ledger for keeping track of which cows are bred with which bulls, when calves are expected, and the rest, and I'll send it to you by the end of the week."

"Very well." Witfeld turned back to his fishing. "If it matters, lad," he said after a moment, "I think she wavered a bit. More than a bit."

"No. It doesn't matter."

With a last look at the pretty setting, Zachary headed back for the house. He didn't intend to be at Witfeld when Caroline left. It would tear his heart out to watch her ride away from him. The only thing he could do to survive was ride away first.

Two coaches stood in the drive, both large and black, and both bearing the red griffin coat of arms emblazoned on the door panels. One would be headed for Bath, and the other back to London.

Caroline watched through the conservatory window as her

family swarmed out of the house, surrounding the three tall men in their fashionable clothes and their beaver hats and their compelling, commanding gazes. She didn't care if they were leaving. She especially didn't care if Zachary was leaving.

"Good riddance," she muttered as he handed Aunt Tremaine into the lead coach and then followed her inside.

For a moment she thought Joanna and Grace were going to try to climb in after them, but the servants managed to get the door closed and back her family out of the way. After a few seconds the coach rattled off.

He had to know she would be watching, and from where, but he'd never even looked in her direction. Well, that was fine. It was all fine. She didn't care a lick. The only Griffin family member she owed anything to was the Duke of Melbourne, and he'd only acted as he had to keep her and Zachary apart. And though his actions had been extremely fortuitous for her, they hadn't been necessary. For a brief second she might have thought about what it would be like to be married to Zachary, but she wouldn't have done it. And now she was glad she hadn't, the arrogant, insufferable man.

She looked on as Melbourne and Charlemagne entered the remaining carriage, the duke having to extricate his hand from her mother's clutches. Oh, yes, the Witfelds were all so grateful. Their silly eldest daughter would have continued with her silly eccentricities for who knew how long if he hadn't stepped in and handed her such a wonderful opportunity.

Caroline turned away from the window as the second coach left the drive. She had brushes and canvases to pack. Sir Thomas Lawrence would want to see her work, whatever fine things Melbourne had said about her.

She would just put him—all of the Griffins—out of her thoughts. Zachary didn't know what he was talking about, anyway, to say that living her dream wasn't enough. As if she needed a man in her life to feel complete and happy. She was going to be a portraitist at the finest studio in England. There wasn't anything she wanted more than that. Nothing. No one.

That sentiment, though, didn't explain why she packed Zachary's portrait in with the other half dozen she meant to show her new employer. Tannberg had accused it of being too idealized, but she didn't actually need to show it to Lawrence. She just needed to have it with her.

Caroline looked at the painting for a long moment. That keen ache in her heart, in her lungs, and behind her eyes would go away. She only felt so . . . awful because she'd counted on Zachary to be happy for her, and instead he hadn't understood at all. That was why she was crying now—because he'd said those terrible, stupid things instead of simply wishing her well and telling her that he would look for her when he returned to London.

"Caro?"

Wiping at her face, Caroline set the portrait down before she faced Anne in her bedchamber doorway. "What is it?"

"They've gone."

"I know. I watched them leave."

Anne tilted her head. "I liked the duke. He was very sure of himself."

"Yes, he was."

"And Lord Charlemagne said when he's next in Wiltshire he will come by and see all of us."

Ha. She doubted that. "How nice of him."

Her sister's shoulders rose and fell. "And Zachary will of course be back. He told me three months, but I don't think it will be that long. And now that he has his business concerns becoming organized, his mind will of course turn to organizing his private life."

Caroline's hand shook, and she grabbed up a pelisse to fold. "I shouldn't be surprised."

"If I'm clever, I should be able to assist with having at least two more sisters betrothed before then. That should make things much easier for me."

"Anne, if you're trying to make me jealous, stop it. I don't even care. I'm going to London, and I daresay my days will be so full I won't even give him a second thought."

"If you don't care, my love, then why are you sitting here crying?"

Caroline wiped at her stupid, uncooperative tears again. "Only because when I leave Wiltshire, I have to leave you and Papa."

Anne came forward and hugged her from behind. "Perhaps not for long. If Papa and Zachary's plans work as they expect, we'll be able to afford to come visit you in London. Maybe even for Christmas. And we'll write every day."

"Yes. I want to know how the project is going."

"Will you want to know anything else?"

About whether Zachary was heartbroken, or whether he waltzed off with some other female the moment he left her presence? With Anne, even? "The family, of course. And whether Lord and Lady Eades found someone else to tutor that awful Theodore and the other little monsters."

Anne chuckled. "I faithfully swear to tell you all the good gossip. Now come down for dinner. I'm certain Mama will want to tell you again how you are her favorite."

"That will be new."

"Yes, but it's bound to last for at least the next three days."

Caroline conjured a smile. "You are a very good sister, Anne."

"And so are you. When you are happy, I will be very prepared to be happy for you. Perhaps working with Lawrence will give you everything you want. I hope that it will."

"I know that it will," Caroline said firmly, fervently hoping she would turn out to be right.

Chapter 24

Two months later:

Zachary looked up from his desk at the rain outside the window. It had rained for the past week, and before that at least every other day for two months. Everyone in Bath went on and on about how the entire town would be washed away down the River Avon if the rain didn't stop, and how soirees and parties could mean the death of anyone who dared to attend. He didn't mind, though. He liked the rain. It fit his mood as no soiree or card party had a snowflake's chance in Hades of doing. Lifting his glass, he took another generous swallow of whiskey.

As he returned to reading the latest report from Edmund, his office door opened. "Set the tea on the table if you please, Andrews," he said, gesturing, while in front of the fire Harold lifted his head, wagged his tail, and went back to sleep again. Zachary didn't know why his aunt insisted on sending up hot tea for him every afternoon, anyway. He never drank it.

"Rain's choked out the stove again," Aunt Tremaine said, entering the room in place of the butler. "Your tea will be late."

"That's fine. I've enough whiskey to keep me." He gestured at the decanter, which was three-quarters empty.

"So I see. Are you going to the assembly rooms tonight?"

"No, I don't think so. Lady Haldridge will escort you, won't she?"

"Of course she will. Is that from Edmund?"

He nodded absently. "We're up to our first year's goal of thirty-five cows. Nine of them have a lineage comparable to that of Dimidius's dam, and he's fairly certain that at least two dozen of them are with calf."

"You should have a busy spring, then."

"Yes. The offspring are what I'm interested in."

She sighed audibly. "Sorry to say, I'm not. How is Sally?"

"Ecstatic. Susan's to be married on Saturday, and Julia and Grace are both betrothed."

"Three so far out of seven. She must be happy. I'll write to congratulate her."

He didn't correct her arithmetic, remind her that only six Witfeld girls wanted to marry, because that would mean admitting that he still thought about, obsessed over, Caroline. Zachary took another drink. "Yes. I'm thinking of hiring myself out to tutor chits in how to trap a husband."

"I may hire you for myself."

"Spare me, Aunt. You could have married a hundred times since Uncle Tremaine passed. You simply enjoy tormenting my sex."

"Speaking of torment, Zachary, how much longer are we going to stay here?"

Zachary glanced over the top of the letter. "You're the one with the gout."

"Not any longer. My gout's gone, and it's my head I'm beginning to worry about. Yours, too. This place is so dull and wet that I think I'm beginning to rot."

"The idea of being in Bath is to take the waters. The rain simply makes that more convenient."

"You are an evil boy. Take me back to London."

A tremor ran through him. *She* was in London. "It's easier to work uninterrupted here."

"The Season's over. There are more parties here now than in London. If you're going to come up with an excuse for remaining in Bath, at least make it a plausible one."

He set down the letter to refill his empty glass. "It's not an excuse."

"Zachary, if it continues to rain like this for another week, we may all be washed out to the Atlantic Ocean to drift about on chair cushions. We'll only be in London a short time, anyway. You know your brother likes to be at Melbourne Park for winter."

"Then we'll go straight from here to Devonshire."

His aunt stalked up to the desk. "*You* remain here until Michaelmas, then. *I'm* leaving for London in the morning. And I'm taking the carriage, so you'll have to ride Sagramore. Don't catch pneumonia."

"And you claim that *I'm* evil. Very well. Please inform Andrews that we'll be leaving on Thursday morning. I have a few appointments between now and then that I'm obligated to honor. I made them, after all." He made his voice sound as calm as he could, and hopefully she wouldn't detect that he was anything more than annoyed. "That's my compromise."

"Very well, then. Three days. And thank goodness. My next stratagem was going to be drugging and kidnaping you. I'm so pleased I didn't have to resort to that."

She might still have to. "I'll have Harold test my food tonight, just to be safe, then," he returned dryly. "Go dress for your ball. I have paperwork to finish. I'll have to inform Witfeld of my change of residence, and let Melbourne know we'll be arriving on Saturday."

Hopefully Witfeld wouldn't inform anyone else. Especially the daughter who currently resided in London, or any of the Witfeld family members who might be corresponding with her.

He'd managed to go for several weeks without hearing anything of her. All he knew was that Lawrence had taken her on, and that she'd been commissioned for several portraits. He didn't know precisely where in London she was residing, though it was safe to say it wouldn't be in Mayfair. If he stayed close to Griffin House once they returned, then he could be relatively certain of not running into her until the family left London for the winter.

It was vital that he never see her again. If he did . . . He could scoff at his aunt's threats of drugging and kidnaping, but when considered in conjunction with Caroline and measured against the deep, numb hole that remained in his heart, the plan made sense. Sense for a madman, but sense nonetheless.

"They're coming home?" Her night dress billowing around her knees, Peep did a dance around her father as he stood in the foyer. "Hurray!"

"About bloody time," Charlemagne muttered, handing his greatcoat over to Stanton.

"Papa, Uncle Shay said 'bloody.' "

"Yes, he did." Sebastian eyed his brother. "Go wash your mouth out with soap."

"I'll wash it out with a glass of claret. Care for one?" Shay headed upstairs for the billiards room.

"Make mine brandy." As his brother vanished, Sebastian swept his daughter into his arms. "And you, my darling, are up well past your bedtime."

"You and Uncle Shay shouldn't have gone out tonight," Penelope replied sternly. "Mrs. Beacham said it looked like it might snow."

"It didn't snow. It didn't even rain. In fact, it's barely the middle of September. Are you certain Mrs. Beacham said it might snow?"

"Well, *I* thought it might snow," his daughter amended, unrepentant.

"Ah. Perhaps a cup of hot chocolate will calm your shattered nerves, then."

"I think it might help."

"Stanton?" Sebastian glanced over his shoulder at the butler, then headed upstairs, his daughter in his arms.

"Right away, Your Grace."

"What else did Uncle Zachary say in his letter?" Peep asked.

"Just that he and Aunt Tremaine will be home on Saturday."

"And Harold?"

They were going to change the dog's name, whatever else happened. He had no intention of allowing the ill-mannered mutt to go about carrying his middle name. "I imagine so."

"On Saturday. Splendid. Does he know that Aunt Nell and Uncle Valentine are back from Venice?"

"I wrote to tell him several weeks ago."

"I think Uncle Valentine will be glad Uncle Zachary's coming home, too. I heard him tell Aunt Nell that if they have to spend Christmas at damned Melbourne Park, he could at least get some blasted pheasant and grouse hunting done at home at Deverill before they have to leave again." She looked him in the eye. "I don't think he likes being still in London."

"Probably not, or he wouldn't have cursed so much." He would have liked to have been back at Melbourne by now, himself, but business seemed to keep him later in London every year.

In addition to a general longing to be back in the country, he did have another reason for wishing they all could have been gone from London by the time Zachary left Bath. Caroline Witfeld was taking the city by storm. Thank God she'd arrived at the tail end of the Season, or she would have been feted and celebrated at every event. Mayfair liked an eccentric, and they loved one who actually had the skill to back up his or her reputation. Miss Witfeld had the skill in spades.

"Papa?"

"Yes, my dear?"

"I'll be glad when Uncle Zachary is home. I like everything better the way it used to be."

"So do I, Peep." Hopefully Zachary would, as well. Once they'd all settled back into their routines, they would all be happier. And Zachary would see other women, and find someone more acceptable, and eventually his youngest brother would thank him for putting Caroline Witfeld out of his reach.

Caroline sat in the corner of her small parlor, which doubled as a dining room, and ate roast mutton. With only her and Molly there, the apartment was stunningly quiet. While there were times when the bliss of that made her smile like a halfwit, this wasn't one of them.

Outside a late vendor's cart bell rang as he pulled his wares home, while farther away she could just make out the sounds of a raucous gathering, probably at The Kettle, the closest inn to her home.

Cheapside certainly wasn't Witfeld Manor, but, she reminded herself, she'd only been in London for two months. Already she was saving her pennies, and if things continued as they'd begun, before long she'd be able to move to a larger, nicer apartment in Islington or Brompton.

Mr. Francis Henning, the subject of the portrait she'd just completed, had been suitably impressed, and he'd assured her that by spring all of his acquaintances would be hammering at the studio doors for an appointment. Of course he'd also proposed marriage, but from what she'd heard he did that on a regular basis, and he'd seemed relieved when she'd declined.

Sir Thomas, while a bit aloof, was proving to be a fair master. He didn't offer friendship, but that wasn't what she wanted. What he did offer was a chance for experience and a level of professional acceptance she'd never experienced before.

As she finished her dinner and sipped at the small glass of wine she allowed herself, she unfolded the letter she'd received that day from Anne. " 'Dearest Caro,' " she read to herself, " 'You'll never believe it, but Peter Redford has proposed to Julia, and she has accepted. Mama is so heartened by the circumstances that she has already begun trying to convince Papa to give the rest of us a few weeks in London next Season. Can you imagine?' "

"Very well," Caroline answered, smiling a little. It wasn't only the smaller number of unmarried daughters that would persuade her father to take the remaining family to London; it was the supplement to his income, money the Griffins provided to him in return for his overseeing the breeding project. The amount was probably too generous, but if anyone deserved to not have to worry about money for once, it was her father.

She looked down at the paper again and resumed reading.

" 'The only unhappy family member is Joanna. I still think she blames herself more for not trapping ~~Za~~ a husband than for her greed and lack of patience. I do hope she finds someone before we arrive in London, or who knows what may happen.' "

"Indeed."

"Miss Witfeld," Molly said, coming into the room to clear the dishes, "would you like some tea?"

"Yes, that would be lovely. And then please turn down my bed; I'm quite tired."

"You've been working so hard, miss, that I'm not surprised to see you tired."

"I'm thankful to be busy," she returned, looking down at the missive again.

" 'You'll be happy to know that Grace is insanely jealous,' " the letter continued, " 'that you will see the new Paris fashions weeks before she will. If you're able, please send me a new catalog so I may tease her with it.

" 'That's all the news for today; it's raining, and I promised Papa I would help him complete the weekly report to go to Zachary—and I promise you, that's the last mention I will make of him. With loving regards, Anne.' "

The two mentions were enough. As far as Caroline knew, he was still in Bath. She looked up at her small mantel. Above it, in a pretty mahogany frame, rested his portrait. For the first few weeks in London she'd alternated between putting it up where she could see it and locking it in the linen closet with the bedsheets. Finally, though, she'd stopped taking it down, and now an evening didn't go by when she didn't spend at least ten minutes gazing at him.

Idealized or not, in the month she'd known him he'd become not only her lover but also her friend. And she missed both aspects of him. Some of the things he'd said to her that last day . . . She looked around her small parlor. It wasn't the size of it that troubled her; no, it was the fact that she was sitting there alone.

She'd found her dream, yet every night she sat by her bed-chamber window, looking out at the night, too restless to sleep and uncertain what she could do to smother and kill that deep feeling of longing and incompleteness. She should have been completely happy, completely content.

During the day, when she was painting, she felt that way—or she had at first. If she'd never met a Griffin, she was certain she would still feel that way. Now, though, more and more her mind wandered to faux Greek ruins and Zachary posing with the wind tousling his hair, and how she'd known exactly what he'd meant when he'd described seeing the *Mona Lisa* for the first time.

A tear ran down her cheek, and she brushed it away impatiently. It wasn't being alone that bothered her, and it wasn't that she needed a man in her life in order for her to be happy. For heaven's sake, she'd never had a man in her life until three months ago.

No, it was *the* man she missed, Zachary whom she wished she could talk with and listen to and touch. The last time she'd put her hands on him, though, it had been to slap him. If nothing else could have ended it, that would. He was a Griffin. He could have anyone he wanted, and she couldn't think of a reason why he would still want her.

"You're a fool, Caroline," she muttered to herself, folding her sister's letter again. She'd thought he was the one who'd needed to be taught a lesson, and he'd ended up teaching her one. Only now it was too late to learn from it.

Melbourne turned a page of Zachary's latest project update. "How conservative is this estimate of yours?" he asked, looking over his shoulder at his youngest brother.

"Extremely. I looked at both beef and milk prices over the last six years and took the low-side average, then factored in processing costs for cream and butter against bovine transport and butchering."

"I want to expand your breeding program."

"I don't." Zachary sat in the deep windowsill of Melbourne's office and absently kicked his boot heel against the wall. "There are too many conjectures in all of this. Once the new calves mature enough to be bred and they begin giving milk, we'll know if I found the correct combination of lineages. *Then* we can expand the breeding program."

"But if you're correct, doubling the herd size will give us a considerable head start on—"

"I'm not in that much of a hurry," Zachary interrupted. "I want it done correctly. Witfeld's the authority at the moment, and he agrees with me."

"Very well." His brother set the report aside again. "Has Peep bribed you into going riding yet? It's all she talked about once we knew you were returning to London."

"I'm going with her in the morning."

"Good. With luck I'll have the Primton property deeds in the next few days, and we can leave London for Melbourne Park."

Zachary realized he was supposed to give some sort of reply. He turned his gaze from his hands to look at his brother. "That's fine."

"Did Shay tell you the Huntleys are still in town? They've invited us to a small soiree tomorrow night."

Standing, Zachary made for the door. At his movement Harold silently rose and padded over beside him. Absently he scratched the dog's ear.

Nothing much seemed to affect him any longer. Instead he seemed to go through his days in a kind of slow blur, with only news from Edmund or one of the other farmers rousing him momentarily. "Please give my excuses," he said, opening the door. "I have some work to do."

"Major General Picton will be there."

Zachary slowed. "That would make my appearance there a bit embarrassing then, don't you think? The man did practically offer me a position with his regiment and then I vanished from London without a word to him, after all."

"Damnation, Zachary, sit down."

"Why?"

"This sulking is not going to change anything."

Zachary sighed, facing the empty hallway in front of him

rather than his brother behind him. "I'm not sulking, Sebastian. I'm keeping myself occupied, and I'm enjoying the work. I'm sorry if you expect me to explode at you or something, but frankly I don't feel much except the need for some sleep."

"You understand why I separated you from Miss Witfeld, don't you?"

"I understand perfectly. You didn't think the Griffin name could withstand one of us marrying a well-bred female who intended to earn her own way in the world."

"That's a bit simplistic."

"Yes, well, I hate to wound your feelings, but you weren't what separated us, Seb. Caroline did that. She views being married to me with the same horror that you view me marrying her. According to her, a married woman is expected to do nothing more and nothing less than give tea parties, embroider, dress well, bear children, and be otherwise useless." He faced his brother again. "It's amusing, isn't it, that her views equate so closely with yours?"

"Zach—"

"Excuse me. I need to send a letter off to Witfeld today."

As Zachary headed upstairs, Harold on his heels, he reflected that he'd hit on the crux of the problem. It wasn't so much that Sebastian didn't want the match; that wouldn't have stopped him for more than a moment, and certainly not any longer. The problem was that Caroline didn't want the match—or so she thought. At the time she hadn't had any actual experience to contradict her dream of an ideal life. Now, though, she'd had a chance to live that dream for several months. He wondered whether it still tasted as sweet.

He stopped in his bedchamber doorway. She was in London, and at least for the moment, he was in London. And maybe he couldn't convince her to marry him. But he could damned well try. And if he was lucky, he would kiss her and talk with her and hold her in his arms again. If he was *very* lucky . . .

A wave of heated energy ran through him. Grabbing his hat and gloves and snapping for Harold, he turned down the stairs again. "Stanton, I have an errand," he said as the butler pulled open the front door. "Please let Melbourne know I won't be back for . . . some time."

"Very good, Lord Zachary."

Oh, he hoped so. He damned well hoped so.

Chapter 25

Caroline dipped her paintbrush into a jar of alcohol. *Carefully* rubbing the bristles into a cotton cloth, she set aside the cleaned brush and reached for another.

Paint. She loved paint, the smell of it, the texture, the magnificent rainbow of colors. But over the past few weeks she'd begun to understand what Zachary had been trying to tell her that day. In the end, the people she met, the art she created, the life she'd made for herself were just . . . paint. And in learning that lesson she'd come to realize that she'd lost the most vibrant, most alive man she'd ever known. God, she missed him—the sound of his voice, his laugh, his unique, optimistic view of the world. Life felt . . . incomplete without him, no matter how well her career was going.

"Miss Witfeld?"

She started. "Yes, Bradley?"

Lawrence's assistant walked into the well-lit studio and handed her a folded paper. "Sir Thomas asked if you would meet a client for him. He has a luncheon appointment he can't break."

" 'Meet a client'?" she repeated. As far as she knew, all clients appeared at the studio for sittings.

"He's some eccentric old earl or something," Bradley said dismissively. "Doesn't like to leave his apartments. Sir Thomas has painted him before."

"He won't be angry if a substitute appears?"

"It's your task to convince him of your skill. Don't be late."

She looked down at the paper as Bradley left the studio. John, Lord Hogarty. The name didn't sound familiar, but at least it would break the routine she'd fallen into. And the address was in Mayfair, so it wasn't likely to be anything nefarious. It wouldn't be, anyway; if nothing else, her employer had immediately inspired her trust and confidence. Gathering her box of paints and newly cleaned brushes, she went to the office and knocked. "Sir Thomas?"

The painter looked up from his desk. "Caroline. Did Bradley give you that address?"

"Yes. Is there anything I should know?"

"Hogarty could be a good contact for you. He's a bit gimpy, but he knows his art. I've already sent over a note explaining your presence." He smiled. "Just do your usual fine work, and you'll have a client for life. Lord knows I could use some assistance."

"Thank you, Sir Thomas."

It wasn't the first time he'd sent one of his less-high-profile clients in her direction. And it wasn't the first time she had imagined opening a studio of her own. Sir Thomas was correct that he could use some help; once a painter became as well known as he was, there simply weren't enough hours in the day to paint every client who wanted his skills.

Outside she hailed a hack and gave the directions written on the note. As they crossed into Mayfair she couldn't help gazing out the coach's window, as she always did when, on rare occasion, she ventured into this part of town. She had no idea whether Zachary was even in London, but she had to look. It would hurt not to. Almost as much as it hurt not seeing him every day except as a painting on her wall.

Twenty minutes later the hack pulled to the side of the street and the driver banged on the roof. "Here you are, miss. Five shillings."

That was steep, but she wasn't about to stand in the street and haggle with him. She handed up the change and turned to face the house as he pulled back into the afternoon traffic.

"Goodness." She stood in front of a block of closely spaced town houses, each one containing two or three private apartments. It was a grand version of where she herself had been living, but far more elegant, even from the outside.

She found the address and ascended the steps to the front door. As soon as she swung the knocker, the door opened. "Yes, miss?" a large man in black livery asked.

"I'm here to see Lord Hogarty," she said. "Sir Thomas Lawrence sent me."

The butler nodded, stepping back from the entrance. "You are expected. This way, miss."

In a sense, what she had told Zachary about life as a married woman had been correct. As a Society lady she would never have been allowed to walk, unescorted by a maid, into a stranger's home. Those circles were for the most part unavailable to her socially, but individually the *ton*'s desire to be painted and kept in perpetuity outweighed their group snobbery. But being right didn't make her feel any better. Not any longer.

"In here, miss," the butler said, opening the door to what looked like the morning room. It was still quite well lit, even this late in the afternoon. "You may set out your canvas and paints. Lord Hogarty will be along shortly."

"Thank you," she said, noting that someone had already provided a tripod for her canvas.

She liked the room. It seemed a bit underdecorated, but from Bradley and Sir Thomas's description of Lord Hogarty, she wasn't all that surprised. He did have a few tasteful Greek vases sitting on the mantel. Setting down and arranging her things, she went closer to examine them.

Thanks to her father's interest in Greek ruins, faux and actual, she'd done a great deal of research on Greek art. Unless she was very much mistaken, the three vases were all black-ink genuine works, well preserved and priceless. Zachary would know. He had a keen insight into art—probably even more than he realized.

The door opened behind her. Moving away from the mantel, she turned to face her new client. And froze.

Zachary Griffin stood in the doorway gazing at her. Her heart stopped. Everything stopped. "What— What are you doing here?" she squeaked.

"I'm John Hogarty," he said, his low drawl making her tremble.

"No, you're not. What's going on?"

"This is my apartment."

She shook her head, backing toward her box of paints. "No. Sir Thomas said he'd painted Lord Hogarty, and that he could be a good client. None of this—"

"I asked him to say that."

"So my employer thinks I've gone on some sordid . . . rendezvous with a single man? How could you?"

"He thinks no such thing. I told him your family was here in London and that they wanted to surprise you."

"Well, thank goodness you haven't completely ruined me." Bending down, she picked up her paints and tucked them under her arm. Oh, she needed to get out before her heart caught up to her mind. "Please stand aside. I am leaving."

He stood aside. "I apologize. I wanted to see you again, and I didn't think you would agree to it."

"No, I wouldn't have," she lied. *He was here. And he wanted to see her.* Her heart pounded.

Zachary nodded. "Your father wrote me and said you were doing well."

"Yes. He said the same thing about you."

As he stood there by the door, willing her not to leave, willing himself not to move to stop her, all Zachary could do was watch her pick up her blank canvas and march toward him. Damnation. Two minutes wasn't enough with her. A lifetime wasn't enough, but if she didn't want to be there, he wasn't going to stop her from leaving. He needed to make her want to stay.

"My family's leaving for Devonshire in a week or so," he said, his voice a little unsteady.

"Good."

All right. So logic and gentle persuasion and gentlemanly conversation weren't going to work. With a hard breath Zachary slammed the door just as she reached it. "I'm trying to be proper about this," he growled, "to respect your wishes."

"Then let me g—"

"And then it occurred to me that you haven't done much to respect mine."

"Your wishes? And what, pray tell, are those?"

"These are my wishes."

Striding forward, he grabbed her by the shoulders, pulled her up against his chest, and lowered his mouth over hers. He could feel the surprise in her soft mouth, and then the greedy lust that matched his own. Her box of paints hit the floor and broke open, reds and yellows and greens going everywhere.

"Oh!"

"Shh," he urged, taking the canvas from her and dropping it to the floor amid the paints. He teased her mouth open with his lips, running his tongue along her teeth, running his hands along her body and keeping her hard against him.

He kissed her until neither of them could breathe, and then backed away an inch. "Now tell me you want to leave," he dared her.

"L-logically, this simply won't—"

"Hang bloody logic. You've studied art all your life, Caroline. What does art have to do with logic? What does logic have to do with finding the right color or the right pose or the right expression? Art moves, it changes, it grows, it lives. Just like love."

"Zachary, p—"

"Do you want to leave?"

She looked into his eyes for a long moment. "No."

He sank to the floor with her as she tugged the coat from his shoulders. His cravat followed as he unbuttoned what seemed like a thousand fastenings along the front of her pelisse. He needed to touch her, he needed to be inside her, or none of this would be real.

"I missed you," he breathed, kissing her again as he pulled the pelisse off her shoulders and went to work on the back of her gown.

"I missed you," she returned, tugging his shirt loose from his trousers and running her hands along his bare chest.

Once he had her dress off, he yanked off his boots, opened his trousers, and shoved them down to his feet so he could kick out of them. As he shifted, Zachary put one hand flat into the spattered red paint. "Damn."

"That'll never come off," she said shakily.

"Really?" He lay his palm on her thigh, curling his fingers around as he pulled her toward him, branding her with his red palm print. "Good."

Slowly he dragged her legs around his hips, watching her expression as his cock entered her. Putting his other hand in yellow paint, he closed his palm over her right breast, and the red over her left, marking her fair skin with perfect man-sized handprints.

"Zach— Oh," she moaned as he leaned forward, shifting to rise over her. Planting his hands on either side of her shoulders, he began pumping his hips, closing his eyes at the exquisite, tight slide of his body inside hers.

"Zachary," she panted, and he opened his eyes to look down at her again as she put a shaking hand into the blue paint, then planted it squarely on his chest.

He pressed closer against her in response, mixing his blue with her red and yellow as he thrust into her. She gripped his body against hers, planting more colors onto his back and buttocks. After that it seemed only fair to scoot her forward, still encasing him, until they were both smeared with mingled colors, front and back.

As she drew tighter and then shattered, pulsating, around him, he sped his own release and with a grunt collapsed on top of her. Before he could crush her with his weight he turned them so that he lay beneath, more paint smearing along his back.

If he looked anything close to what she did, they were both a glorious, multicolored mess. "You're more lovely than the *Mona*

Lisa," he said, when he could speak in a fairly normal voice again.

"I think we've used more colors than da Vinci, at any rate." She sat up, straddling his hips. "I was serious, Zachary. This will be the devil to take off."

"You certainly can't go home looking like this," he agreed, drawing light green circles around her breasts with his fingertips.

"I will certainly have to," she countered, gathering herself to rise.

He held onto her thighs, keeping her impaled across his hips. "I don't want you to stop painting, you know. I never intended to ask you to give that up."

She looked down at him with something in her eyes that he wanted to describe as regret and longing. "You wouldn't have had to ask. The wife of a Griffin—"

"—could do as she damn well pleased," he finished. "Who do you think would have the nerve to cut you in public?"

"But—"

"Work for Lawrence, or open your own studio. Open it here. I picked this room for today because of the light." He sat up so they were at the same eye level. "Just think about it, Caroline. If you want to be with me, we will make it work. I won't ask you to embroider my damned handkerchiefs, and you won't—"

She put a hand over his mouth. "I missed you," she whispered, leaning in to kiss him. When she straightened, she had blue across her mouth, as he likely did. "I understand now what you were talking about, about not being able to find a complete life in a flat painting."

"You do?" His heart, already hammering, began drumming like a regimental corps. "So if . . . if I asked you again to marry me, you might say yes?"

She nodded, a tear running down her painted cheek.

"Then will you marry me, Caroline? Will you be my wife?"

"Yes," she breathed. "I would very much like to marry you."

He pulled her into his arms, holding her tightly against him. *Thank God. Thank God.* "I've had so many things I've wanted to say, and not one damned person I know thinks I'm as amusing and clever as you seem to."

She snorted. "I've missed having a friend, as well."

"The—"

The hard banging on his front door made him jump. "Hogarty will get it," he said after a moment, kissing her softly again.

"Hogarty?"

"My servant. John Hogarty. I had to get a name from somewhere."

Hogarty scratched at the door. "My lord? The Duke of Melbourne is here to see—"

"Christ. Tell him to wait in the foyer. I'll be out in a moment."

"Very good, my lord."

Caroline scrambled to her feet beside him. As he looked down at himself, he knew there was no way he could possibly be rendered presentable in the next five minutes—probably not in the next hour. "Oh, well," he grumbled and pulled on his trousers.

Sebastian had to know sooner or later. It might as well be now.

For once in his life, Sebastian wasn't entirely certain what he wanted to say or what he wanted to accomplish. But the fact that Zachary had spent most of two days back at his old residence didn't bode well for any of them.

With the drinking and aloof sadness Sebastian sensed in his brother, intervening was worth another fight, as far as he was concerned. This . . . sorrow would not continue. Restless and concerned, he stood rock still in his brother's foyer and refused to pace.

"What is it, Melbourne?" Zachary's voice came from the morning room doorway.

Relaxing an inch that his brother hadn't refused to see him, Sebastian turned from perusing one of the framed paintings in the hallway. Zachary had a more refined taste than he'd expected. "I wanted to talk to . . . What the devil is wrong with you?"

Zachary grinned, a dark blue stain running from his chin up to one ear. "Not a thing. Why?"

"But the . . ." Sebastian trailed off, taking in the red and blue and green smears across his brother's bare chest and arms and hands. "You're very . . . colorful."

"And your point is?"

Sebastian gazed at his brother for a long moment. Something was definitely going on, and it was an odd and uncomfortable feeling not to know what it might be. He was used to being in control of not only himself but also everything around him. "I'm not entirely certain what my point is," he said finally. "Are you planning on moving away from Griffin House again?"

"I think it may be time."

It took a great deal of Sebastian's famous self-control to keep from reacting to that, and to smother the sudden memory of the days after Charlotte had died, when he'd been alone in a large, empty house except for a small, crying, three-year-old girl. But this wasn't about him. It was about Zachary. "You'll still winter at Melbourne Park, I hope."

"That would be up to you, Seb."

"Up to—"

The morning room door opened again, and Caroline Witfeld emerged. The puzzle pieces fell into place. Her mouth was the same blue, her hands and arms a myriad of blue and yellow streaks. She dipped a curtsy, her blue mouth quirked in what looked very much like amusement.

"Miss Witfeld," he said, automatically sketching a return bow.

Zachary took her hand. "Caroline and I are marrying," he said, his voice cool and confident and defiant.

"Yesterday you weren't speaking," Sebastian noted.

"We've resolved our differences."

"Colorfully, apparently."

Caroline blushed. Today hadn't gone remotely as she'd expected, but she wasn't about to complain about it. My goodness. When she'd set eyes on Zachary, time had simply stopped. And then he'd said all the right things, and more importantly, she'd seen the sincerity and the loneliness in his face. The loneliness that had mirrored her own. And now she would be able to wake up to him in the morning, and to see him when she went to sleep, and to chat and banter with him about anything she wished to during the day. It was too much.

"You're giving up your painting, then?" the duke asked, his keen gaze no doubt taking in her every expression.

She squared her shoulders, secretly grateful for Zachary's hand in hers. Standing up to the Duke of Melbourne wasn't easy even for his own family members—one of which she was apparently about to become. *Good heavens.* "No, I'm not."

"She may set up a studio here. We haven't decided yet."

Melbourne nodded. "I came here to tell Zachary that I've decided to step back from this. Apparently I didn't need to make the effort."

"You could make the effort of apologizing for interfering in the first place," Zachary suggested.

"If I do so, will you spend the winter at Melbourne?"

Caroline remembered what Zachary had told her, about how badly the duke had taken his wife's death, and how important it had become to him to have his family close by. "You may be inviting my entire family, you realize," she said with a slight smile. "I think you should know all the details before you issue an invitation."

"Your entire family," the duke repeated, humor touching his voice. "Well, I suppose if the Griffins can withstand having a professional portraitist in the family, we can survive Christmas with the Witfelds." He offered his hand to Zachary. "I apologize. I shouldn't have meddled. I didn't want to see you unhappy, and being without Miss Witfeld obviously made you so."

Zachary shook his oldest brother's hand. "I accept."

"And bring Miss Witfeld along for dinner. I've met her family, and now she needs to meet the rest of yours."

With a nod, the duke left. Still holding Caroline's hand, Zachary led the way toward the stairs. "Hogarty, have a bath brought up to my bedchamber," he said over his shoulder.

"Right away, my lord."

Caroline blushed, though with all the colors on her, Zachary probably couldn't tell. "Zachary, everyone will know . . . you know . . . what we've been doing."

"And they won't if you leave the house covered in paint?"

She sighed, leaning into his shoulder. "Which rest of your family is here?"

"My sister Eleanor and her husband Valentine, and Peep. Sebastian's daughter. She's six. And don't worry, she'll be ecstatic that your joining the family will help balance the ratio of females to males." He looked at her as they topped the stairs, then leaned down to kiss her, slow and deep. "I've been thinking," he murmured, brushing a stray hair behind her ear, "that I'd like to take you to Paris for our honeymoon."

"Paris," she repeated shakily. The Louvre was in Paris. The *Mona Lisa* was in Paris.

"And then Greece. And anywhere else you'd care to see. Then maybe my family will finally realize that my interest in art is very," and he kissed her again, "very," another kiss, "serious."

"Art and cows, you mean."

He laughed. "The cows are staying in Wiltshire. And you, my living work of art, are coming with me to take a bath." Zachary lifted her in his arms and carried her, laughing, into his bedchamber.

And coming January 2006

DON'T LOOK DOWN

The heat is on in Palm Beach as
Rick Addison and Samantha Jellicoe
get caught up in another
exciting romantic adventure.